NIGHTSWORD

A

STARSHIELD

NOVEL

By Margaret Weis and Tracy Hickman
Published by Del Rey books

The Mantle of Kendis-Dai

Nightsword

MARGARET
WEIS
TRACY
HICKMAN

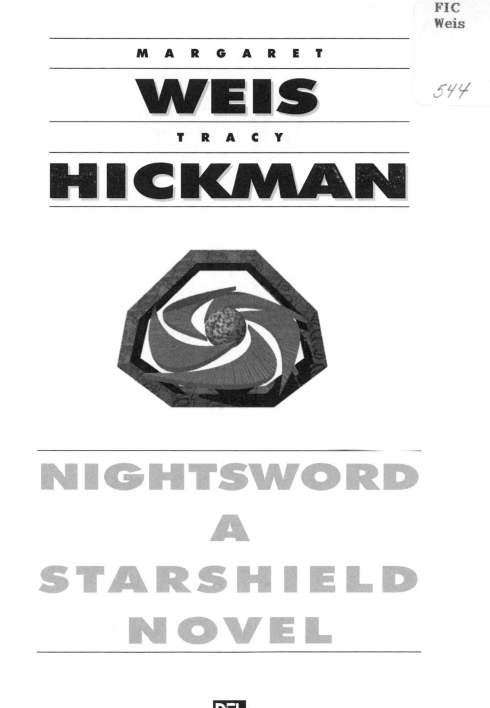

NIGHTSWORD
A
STARSHIELD
NOVEL

THE BALLANTINE PUBLISHING GROUP • NEW YORK

A Del Rey® Book
Published by The Ballantine Publishing Group

Copyright © 1998 by Margaret Weis and Tracy Hickman

http://www.randomhouse.com/delrey/

Library of Congress Cataloging-in-Publication Data
Weis, Margaret.
Nightsword : a starshield novel / by Margaret Weis & Tracy Hickman. — 1st ed.
p.   cm.
"A Del Rey book."
ISBN 0-345-39762-2
I. Hickman, Tracy.   II. Title.
PS3573.E3978N54   1998
813'.54—dc21   98-5897
CIP

Manufactured in the United States of America

First Edition: May 1998

10   9   8   7   6   5   4   3   2   1

This novel is dedicated
with our thanks and appreciation to:

James G. Ashworth
Donald Campbell
Jamie Chambers
"Falcon"
"Hayz"
David P. Hudyma, Jr.
Matt Karlov
James Kenny
Shawn McGee
Robert Ravens
Elton Robb
Glenn Robb
Tom Schruefer
David Shanahan
Frank Torkel
Oliver Zimprich
"Zordoz"

for their contributions to this novel.

Also to
Joel Goldberger and his crew at Infomagic
and to all the Sifters and Sentients of the Greater Galaxy.
You make the universe what it is today.

http://www.starshield.com

Table of Contents

Prologue

Traveler's Tales

THERE IS A PLACE CALLED THE MAELSTROM WALL.

It sits at the very boundaries of stellar civilization, a border of chaos that guards the center of the galaxy from those who are too foolish or too adventurous for their own good. In that region the quantum fronts are piled up one atop the next, the realities that exist between them fleeting and ephemeral at best. Spacers—those sailors of the stars who man the ships of the region—are versed in a diversity of magic and skill that dwarfs the knowing of most men. Yet it is not enough, for the Maelstrom Wall rages against such order, throwing reality after reality against the hulls of the spacers' ships. Relentlessly, it searches for that place and time where a spacer crew's knowledge, equipment, and manna are not enough. When that happens, the Maelstrom Wall exacts its victory with a toll of blood.

A spacer's life is a flirtatious dance with unique and unexpected death.

Yet still the spacers come in their globelike ships with their unkempt appearance and their cold eyes. They dance the dance again and again—no small few of them for the last time. It is there; there among the straining rigging and weary magical incantations that stand between existence and beyond; there among the impossible worlds and regions where everything is possible and nothing is likely; there on the worlds of the most dangerous region in all the stars that the yar trees grow.

The yar tree is a magnificent specimen. Entire forests of them, each ranging from fifty to two hundred feet tall, grow to full maturity within a year, only to vanish completely by the following season. Their great branches reach up toward the stars, their leaves forming a layer of dappled sunlight far below among their roots. They thrive amid the chaos. Indeed, many of the learned that study them believe that it is the horrible entropy of the Maelstrom Wall itself upon which they live. Their like is not known, nor has ever been known, anywhere else in the galactic disk.

Most importantly, however, their sap—called yardow—is one of the rarest and most sought after commodities in all of known space. Yardow has the amazing ability to suspend gravity within its confines. Once refined into a hard resin, even a small amount of yardow will contain a quantum black hole with perfect safety and portability. Every synthetic mind known to exist is based on this very phenomenon. No temporal fold processor from one end of the galaxy to the other can exist without a yardow-resin mounting for a quantum black hole.

To obtain a single shipment of yardow is to ensure one's comfort for life.

Each place in the galaxy holds its own tales and legends, but none more so than the Maelstrom Wall. Down through the centuries, the stakes have remained high; the rewards, beyond avarice. Such elements have forever been the fertile, if uncertain, ground for many a dire traveler's tale.

ALPHA:

LOG

OF THE

KNIGHT FORTUNE

1

L'Zari

HIS NAME WAS L'ZARI.

He gripped the thrumming stay line, his youthful hands white, drained of blood in his fear and desperation. A snarling wind whipped his hair about his face, belying the fact that he was inside the protective dome of the ship. How could a wind blow *inside* the dome, his mind raged. How, indeed, he thought savagely, could anything that he had experienced over the last few weeks have been real.

His legs were braced against the grandyard boom some thirty feet above the deck. L'Zari had inconspicuously slipped both feet underneath the stay cables running the top length of the massive yard, despite the warnings of the other spacers that he might just lose a foot that way. The youth had gone beyond caring as he clung high in the rigging of the starship. He knew little of the trade, in any event—which, he suspected, was why his fellow spacers had seen to it that he was hanging here in the midst of a quantum gale.

All about him, up ratlines and occasionally across the backstays, the spacers moved nimbly from task to task as they were called out from the deck below them. L'Zari knew they were watching him with great amusement, his discomfort and open-faced fear a confirmation of their own superiority here in the rigging. They meant to teach him his place.

He already knew his place, he thought grimly—and he fervently hoped that it was a place back down there on the deck swinging far below him. At least there you didn't have quite so far to fall, he thought angrily to himself. At least there you had a much better chance of actually hitting the deck instead of missing it altogether and falling into the stars.

The stars. He looked up the mast toward those same romantic stars that had called him here—or so he had fancied in his imagination that they had done. They were there: so many and so bright. There were far more than one might expect here among the brilliantly lit dust clouds surrounding the ship. Toward the rim such clouds would have obscured most of the stellar bodies beyond, limiting one's view to a few stars and the great nebulae that hung in interstellar space. Not here. Here the ship rushed upward along the Maelstrom Wall, that vicious curtain of quantum fury at the very edge of the galactic core. Here the stars were so thickly clustered that it was difficult to avoid them even when boring down a tunnel through the nebular mass itself.

The ship to which he clung so desperately was rushing upward through just such a cavernous drift in the Wall. The *Knight Fortune*—a ludicrous name, chosen by an apparent idiot, L'Zari thought—was of Aendorian design, or at least had been crafted on that world after the manner of the core explorers. Her shape was generally spherical, compressed somewhat along her vertical axis so that her cross section suggested something of an oval. The hull forming the bowl-like bottom of the ship swept upward into three great, curving prows that arched over the main deck until they nearly touched the mast. The ancient Aendorian totemic forms and symbols covered the hull itself, which if the legends were true, would have been grown to this exact shape by the mystic artists of that world. The main deck was cradled within the triple fingers of those prows with access to the several decks below and the massive cargo hold.

Running through it all was the drive-tree—the core of the ship. It began beneath the center of the hull with the massive keelbob—another foolish spacer name, L'Zari thought. He couldn't see it now but had gotten a good look at its brilliant brass finish, tooled down to a spike, when the ship had been careened on E'knar a few weeks ago. The keelbob alone was nearly four times his own height. The mast extended upward from the bob, through the center of the intervening decks, and past the clear bubble of atmosphere into the vacuum of space itself. Along the mast were mounted several booms. Lanyards to each from the deck below repositioned them as the prevailing quantum weather dictated. It was this massive complex called the drive-tree that dragged the ship upward into the stars, the ship's direction of motion following the same line as that of the mast. The Aendorian ships didn't sail across space so much as up into it.

In calmer weather, the various crystal focus booms would only need to be repositioned now and then as the ship passed from one quantum zone to another. Then the spacers would climb the ratlines into the rigging and reposition the various booms with their braces and incant their magical spells to simulate whatever drive system functioned in the new zone. Spacer magic was powerful, as everyone knew, and it was rare that a good spacer crew couldn't come up with some kind of configuration that put the mystic wind into the various sheets of light, crystal, plasma, or flesh that would bring them home again.

But the weather was not calm. The rapid shifts between the quantum fronts near the core brought with them a terrible price to the spacers who braved their reach. The quantum fronts came quickly here: a succession of realities which constantly challenged the integrity of the drive-tree and its configuration. The spacers challenged the assault in the rigging, swinging the booms wildly as they fought chaos itself from moment to moment, altering their incantations and their mystic spells with each new reality as it came.

Sailing the Maelstrom Wall was a challenge even in the best of times. One would normally take the changes slowly and accept the fact that the transit from system to system would take a lot more time than you would prefer. Move slowly. Take your time. Better to get there late than not at all.

None of which would do right now, L'Zari reminded himself. He twisted his head and looked down his right shoulder. The ratlines, rigging, and mast ran down dizzyingly below him to the deck. He dreaded the sight, but needed to know.

There, just as the ship's hull yawed to starboard, he saw it. A dull, orange-red mottled hull. It was smaller than his merchant ship but apparently every bit as nimble and swift. The arched cone of the aft hull casing projected horns forward and encompassed the raider's main deck. He could see vague shadows moving there, could somehow sense their hunger for his own ship.

It was a Gorgon ship.

That wasn't entirely true, he reminded himself. The ship itself was of an old K'tan design or, at least, that was what Old Phin had told him when the other ship made its first pass at them. But it flew the Gorgon flag. L'Zari could see the great ensign trailing down the hull from one of the horned mounts—a bright red swath of cloth bearing the white Gorgon's skull with a saber passing through one eye socket. That left no doubt to it—it was Marren-kan. No other ship dared fly such a flag. No other buccaneer had such a reputation for dread.

The hull of the *Knight Fortune* swung across his view of the raider. In his musings, L'Zari was unprepared for the unexpected roll of the ship to port. His body swung away from the boom, his feet slipping from under the stay cables. In sudden panic, the boy gripped the ratlines even tighter as he found himself suddenly suspended by his arms alone, high above the shifting deck. He cried out against the howling winds whipping about him, but his voice sounded hollow and small in his own ears. The ship suddenly pitched upward through another break in the nebula clouds, swinging him wildly and slamming him against the mast. The sudden impact pressed the wind out of his lungs. Gasping and dazed, he released his grip.

The lines, backstays, halyards, and booms swung crazily around him. *I let go!* His mind screamed at him as he flailed through the hurricane, searching for something to which he might hold. Falling . . . he felt himself falling for the longest time . . .

Suddenly he stopped and spun madly about. The world was a blur until something grasped his leg, then gathered the front of his tunic in its massive hand. L'Zari shook his head, trying to clear the bleariness from his eyes. After a moment they focused fairly well but had trouble holding steady, as they tried to follow the spin that his inner ear told him he still was experiencing. Unstable as his sight seemed to be, he was pretty sure that he was hanging somehow from the rigging directly over the face of his father.

"Boy?" An angry face with bright squinting eyes was staring up at him not a handsbreadth from his own face. A broad nose and a stubble-length beard filled his vision. "This is certainly no time to be hanging about!"

"Sorry, Father," L'Zari said miserably.

In a single motion, the man pulled a broad knife and cut the safety line that suspended L'Zari over him. The moment the boy was free, the man moved aside to allow him to fall the rest of the way to the hard planks below.

L'Zari landed painfully and, groaning, pulled himself up

to sit. At least I'm back on the deck, he thought as he rubbed his right shoulder.

L'Zari's father—Kip-lei, whom all the ship knew only as "Kip"—stood over him, his legs spread wide on the moving deck, paying not the least bit of attention to the plight of his own son.

It was understandable, L'Zari thought ruefully. The old man had known this ship intimately for the last seven years. He had only known his son for three weeks, so it wasn't difficult to guess where his affections lay.

L'Zari's mother—K'thari—had come from one of the honored houses in the Far Trade Coalition. Interstellar trade was invented by them, or so they believed, and was therefore a concept they owned. His mother had been raised in a somewhat sheltered atmosphere. The best tutors did all her schooling at home lest she be corrupted by any outside influence into ideas that were contrary to her clan. Her friends were selected for her. Her activities were planned for her. In time she was deemed sufficiently competent to actually go out on her own and face the galaxy, but K'thari hadn't quite set in their mold. She found excitement in the greater galaxy that unfolded around her—especially in the arms of the forbidden and roguish free-trade captain with the brilliant blue eyes and confident manner. He filled her mind with visions and tales: stories of the great treasures of the core and his passion for it. The romance of his tales wove a passion in her that all the mythology of the ancient clans never inspired.

To the shame of the entire trade house, the roguish captain was soon gone again to dance romantic dreams among the stars, and K'thari was left with the reality of a child. No less love was bestowed on the boy as he grew—he wanted for nothing and his training was as thorough as his mother's had been. Yet it had always been understood that while he was of the family and cared for, there would never be a place for him in the family trade.

In time his mother's overprotective dictums became sentences of doom and the atmosphere of the clan's compound a sour breath in his lungs. So, with what power and money he could muster, he determined to show them all how worthy he was of their name and right a few wrongs along the way. He fled his home, made his way into the stars and found, at last, his legendary father.

The legend had diminished considerably now that he had suffered with him for three weeks.

"Avast aloft!" Kip cried out through his cupped hands. "Mystic's shifting five points down! Stay with her, lads! Squeeze that tree! We need all the speed she can give!"

"Father . . . ," L'Zari began.

"Call me Kip, boy," the captain said without looking away from the rigging overhead. "I've not time for anything longer than Kip, Boy-Out-of-Nowhere."

"Fine. Kip, then," the youth said, once again beating down the hope that he could have any real relationship with this brute that had sired him. "Just what is it that we're doing?"

"Well, boy, there's only two things you can do when a Gorgon prepares to board you." The captain continued to inspect the latest changes in the rigging of the ship. "You can either fight them and seal yourself to a fate worse than death itself—or you can surrender your cargo willingly at their first warning shot."

The vertical rush of the nebula clouds became more pronounced, giving the impression that the ship was rocketing straight upward into the clouds. It was not a comfortable feeling for L'Zari.

Suddenly, three bolts of energy flashed around the hull from behind. The deck lurched as two additional shots connected with the hull.

"Right, two things . . . so which are we doing?"

"We're doing the third thing," Kip said through a sneer

as he strode quickly to the gunwales and peered into the nebula itself. With careful, deliberate motion, Kip reached into the omnipresent leather pouch that he had worn slung across his body since they had left E'knar. From it, he pulled a curious object—obviously ancient in workmanship, yet well cared for and, amazingly, functional. It was a crystal globe, fitted into an ornate mechanical framework. Dim images drifted across its surface, although L'Zari couldn't make out any meaning from the symbols or images he could see from this distance—and Kip never allowed him to get any closer than this.

The spacer captain suddenly slapped the side rail with glee and cried out. "That's it! Helm! Bring us about: eighty-three degrees port and ten high! Steady that course and prepare to come about!"

"Aye, Kip," the spacer answered. L'Zari glanced back at the pilot where he lay on the pilot's couch, both large, spoked helm wheels spinning quickly under his hands on either side of him. The man gazed up the drive-tree towering over him and watched the fore-royal mast shift quickly across the stars to their new heading.

The captain called below. "Gun crews on deck! Prime the cannons and run them up smartly, boy! We'll only get one pass at this!"

L'Zari shook his head and summoned up all the wisdom that his seventeen years had brought him. "Sir . . . Kip, this is pointless! Why don't we just give them what they want!"

The captain turned toward the boy and grabbed his shoulders. "Give them what they want? What they want is my life's blood, boy—my life's blood! We've found the passage and it's ours by right. I'll not give it up! Not to the Gorgon . . . not to any beast, or man for that matter either!"

L'Zari backed away from his father's grasp.

"Guns at the ready, Kip!" came the distant cry.

"Aye! At my signal, Master Helmsman, full up on the helm and hold her until I give the word," Kip said, turning again to watch the clouds rush downward past them, glancing occasionally at the globe he still held in his hands.

L'Zari continued to back up until he suddenly bumped into the halyards at the base of the drive-tree. Instinctively, he wrapped both hands around the cables.

Kip raised his hand.

Two more bolts rocked the hull of the ship, accompanied this time by a sickening, splintering sound and a horrible cry from belowdecks.

Another heartbeat passed.

Kip suddenly dropped his arm in signal. "Now!" he shouted. "Helm full up! Stand by the guns! Fire as we pass over her, boys!"

The clouds suddenly rolled. The mast of the ship pitched upward, spinning the clouds and stars about them with dizzying speed. L'Zari was completely disoriented and suddenly wondered if he would be able to keep his last meal where it belonged.

The Gorgon, taken by surprise, suddenly hove into view as the *Knight Fortune* reversed her course. The sides of the raider hull seemed to waver in confusion as the guns of the free-trade merchant ship suddenly opened up, blue plasma balls slamming against the Gorgon's side.

"Hold her up, Helm!" Kip cried.

The free trader continued her loop, passing the stern of the Gorgon, which had only just begun to turn. Kip's fire raked the stern of the Gorgon, shattering two of her five drive nodes in the process.

"Now, Helm! Hold your course!" Kip bellowed. "Aloft! Brace yourselves!"

L'Zari stared up the mast.

They were heading directly for the Maelstrom Wall.

A ripple of concussions slammed against the hull. L'Zari somehow knew it was a full broadside from the pursuing Gorgons. The hull slewed sideways. He heard main bearing timbers crack.

In that moment they passed into the Wall.

NIGHTSWORD

2

Bonefield Narrows

THE DECK BELOW HIM SHUDDERED HORRIBLY, CONTINUING ITS port-side slide. L'Zari continued to hold the halyards with a death-white grip, his back against the mast. There was damage above him, he knew. He could feel more than hear the cracking of timber overhead and the flailing of newly freed lines and cables. The ship had slammed into a massive quantum wave and was floundering in its passage.

The youth glanced again at his father. Kip was gripping the starboard helm wheel, though L'Zari couldn't be sure whether he was holding the wheel steady in the gale or the wheel was holding him up. The ship's atmosphere sang in the wires of the rigging, moaning horribly with a wind driven by the quantum flux of the massive wave they were passing through. Eternity lived in those few seconds . . .

Suddenly the ship emerged from the wave and, an instant later, passed into a clearing in the nebular cloud.

L'Zari's jaw dropped.

The sky was all massive, billowing clouds of white shaded with pastels. The suns, which showed beyond the clouds, filled the area with soft light. Floating serenely all about them were thousands of unimaginably small worlds—island planetoids of lush vegetation and water barely five to ten miles across. Their shapes were somewhat irregular, which led L'Zari to think of them more as asteroids than worlds, per se. The youth was amazed to watch a particularly massive planetoid pass fairly close to the port side as the ship sailed upward, its flight suddenly smooth. Beyond the side rail, he saw great waterfalls emptying into what appeared to be a large lake. Indeed, there seemed to be a storm building to one side of the lake. The clouds there were laced with lightning. The entire planetoid quickly passed astern of the ship. Looking up the mast, L'Zari saw the ship weaving its way through literally thousands of similar microworlds.

"By the Nine," L'Zari whispered to himself.

Kip had released the wheel to the helmsman but seemed more intent than ever. At least he no longer needed to yell over the gale—the atmosphere on deck seemed to have calmed to a nearly frightening stillness. His voice was firm but no longer a full-voiced bellow. "Gun crews! Stand down and secure! Master Phin!"

"Aye, sir!" the first mate answered at once, his voice belying his obvious fear.

"Have the spacers aloft reconfigure the rig at once. We're going to make landfall. The ship needs repairs and I suspect that we'll need a place to lie quiet and out of sight for a while."

Phin's voice gained resolve. "By your word, sir!"

"Oh, and Master Phin . . ."

"Aye, sir?"

"Best get some of the deck crew below and see what can be done to repair the hull. I mean to set her down in deep water and it wouldn't do to have some briny sea sloshing about my cabin."

"Aye, sir." The first mate smiled tiredly but with good humor. "I'll have that done, too."

L'Zari extricated himself from the tangle of halyards he had wrapped himself in and moved toward his father. "Sir?"

The captain turned away from the youth and looked up the mast intently. "Master Orlath, keep a weather eye out in these parts. Those worlds may look the size of pebbles but, if the maps hold true, they've got a gravity well deep enough to drag this old girl down. Steer a course midspace between them as best you can and try not to venture too close until it's time for landfall. Keep your speed high, Master Orlath—our friends aren't done with us yet."

"Aye, Captain."

"Sir?" L'Zari wouldn't be put off that easily. "Captain!"

"Master Dupak?" The captain continued to the quarter-master, the next officer available on deck.

"Aye, sir?"

"We'll be making landfall soon and, with a little fortune from the stars, beat the Gorgons to their own prize. You'll need to organize a party to go ashore." The captain eyed the quartermaster knowingly. "You do know what we are look-ing for, don't you?"

"Oh, aye, sir," the quartermaster responded slyly. "I do indeed, Captain."

"Father—" L'Zari began again.

The large man turned and flashed a brilliant smile. "That's Kip, boy—Kip! Kip of the core! Kip of the *Knight Fortune*! You can do it, boy! Call me Kip!"

"All right—Kip then! What is this place?" the young man said, gesturing with his arms toward the clouds streaming down around them.

Kip's smile deepened—something that L'Zari did not think possible. He spoke to the quartermaster but his eyes never left the boy. "Master Dupak, this boy is lost! Have you ever seen the like in the stars? Perhaps you could show him the way? I think I may have just found the first volunteer for your excursion!"

L'Zari blinked, not sure of what he was getting himself into. "Excursion? Excursion to . . . where?"

His father stepped up to him, grabbing his arm painfully. "To where the legends end! To the place where dreams are real and all the stars can be laid at your feet if you've got the will to take them!"

L'Zari stared back at him, uncomprehending.

"This is Bonefield Narrows, boy," the old spacer said, winking. "The last place the Nightsword was ever used—and the first place to start looking for it."

A WIDE RIVER CASCADED DOWN OVER THE ROCKS BEFORE IT dropped into the bay, its rushing sound overpowering the gentle rustle of the towering trees and the soft lapping of the waves over the sand. Great yar trees arched over the bay, forming a partial canopy over the white sands of the shoreline and bringing delicate shade to the impossibly bright flowers that inundated the jungle floor. For untold time the bay had remained in this tranquil state—an unspoiled paradise lost to the knowledge of visual sensors that might appreciate its vistas or olfactory receivers that might find bliss in its clean smells. The rhythms of the little bay remained constant and unchallenged.

Now the rhythm changed. From the glowing clouds that were its perpetual sky, a dark shape descended over the sea beyond the bay's craggy, mountainous gates. It quickly moved across the water and over the bay itself, a deep thrumming accompanying its motion. It was a three-prowed ship; its scarred hull balanced, so it seemed, on an ornamental brass spindle. The ship slowed its forward motion even as it began to descend into the waters of the bay. The bronze ornament cut into the water with a swishing sound louder than the cascade but minor compared to the wake caused as the hull itself settled into the water.

Though there was no one ashore to record the event, the microworld was about to be violated for the second time.

"SIR—CAPTAIN—KIP," THE BOY SAID BETWEEN GASPS FOR air, "where are we going?"

The jungle had looked inviting enough when they rowed ashore, but the longer he was in it, the less inviting it became. While the temperature was not particularly high, the level of humidity was staggering. L'Zari hadn't been outside the atmosphere bubble of the *Knight Fortune* for more than a few seconds before he was sure that he was going to sweat away every drop of liquid in his body. Deep within the undergrowth, the air had become even more oppressive.

They had started out following the river inland, but that effort proved to be far easier in theory than it was in practice. The river course was arduous and often impassable. When the river offered no path, they had been forced to push, hack, and climb their way through nearly three miles of dense brush, or so Old Phin had informed L'Zari a short time before. It certainly seemed like they had worked harder than merited by three meager miles.

Now they stood at the base of another impossible cascade. Kip-lei stood knee-deep in the swirling waters and, for the hundredth time that day, reached into the hard leather bag at his side and pulled out a curious instrument—a glass globe with brass fittings—and stared into it.

"Not much further," the captain said.

"What is that thing, sir?" L'Zari said somewhat peevishly. "You trying to tell us our fortunes?"

"Fortunes, indeed, boy," Kip said, smiling. "I believe that you are quite correct."

"So, what is it?"

"A little piece of mythology that I picked up while we were downport on T'Kan." Captain Kip-lei gazed up at the water-veiled rocks as though somehow his concentration would allow him additional vision beyond their crest.

"Actually, I'm just borrowing it from the captain of that Gorgon crew we've been trying to outrun."

"Marren-kan?" L'Zari nearly choked on his own spit. "That thing belongs to Marren-kan!"

"Well," Kip replied, carefully replacing the ornate globe back in the leather pack, "who actually owns something that old, anyway? Besides, Old Marren-kan didn't know exactly where to find the Bonefield Narrows, so it wasn't doing the old spacer any good, now, was it?"

L'Zari's voice sounded incredulous even in his own ears. "Do you think he knows where it is now?"

"Well, yes, I'm sure that he's quite well aware of the location of the Narrows now that we've showed him the way. Of course, there are nearly fifteen thousand large planetoids here to keep him occupied, not to mention the smaller rocks that will naturally hamper his navigation. He's got a lot of ground to search to find our little prize and us. With any good fortune, we should be well on our way by the time he gets around to this bit of rock."

Kip inhaled deeply and blew out a great breath. "All life is a percentage, boy, remember that. Gain's price is risk. You could have stayed in that nice warm bed of yours, surrounded by your mother and all your soft, safe aunts and uncles making their way through life on a margin of six-percent annual growth return on their investments. What brings you out to the wildlands of the inner frontier, eh? Why are you challenging the Maelstrom Wall?"

L'Zari looked away into the swirling waters of the pool at the cascade's base. The answer to that question was so charged that he didn't think he could possibly put it into words alone. Worse than that, he wasn't ready to express the emotions involved even if he wanted to. How could he tell this man that a boy needed a father? How could he explain the hole that Kip-lei had left in both his own life and that of his mother? It was a void that threatened to overcome him—a wrong that he had hoped he could right. Yet everything had gone so differently from what he had dreamed of—none of his visions, hopes, and imaginings had come about since he had arrived unbidden and somewhat awkwardly aboard his father's free-trade merchant ship. How could he explain that everything he was looking for was bound up in the actions and acceptance of the man standing before him—and that he had no clue how to obtain it?

"I guess I was looking for something" was all he managed to say at last.

Kip shook his head with a snort. "Go back to your mother, boy! It's high stakes and death out here. You're not ready to roll dice with the universe yet."

"Yes, I am!" L'Zari blustered, his face reddening in the sudden anger of youth. "I'm here, aren't I? No one made me come! No one's making me go back, either!"

"Aye, you're here, all right," Kip said somewhat thoughtfully. Was there kindness and understanding behind that voice? L'Zari couldn't be sure, and in any event the moment passed quickly. "Still, I don't know yet if you're brave and green, or just plain stupid. Time tells; it always does."

L'Zari looked up into his father's eyes. Was this it, then? Was this some sort of test?

Kip took a deep breath. "Soon, indeed, we'll know if this little bauble is true. Up lads! It's time to see if the quest was worth the price. What we've come for is just atop that rise."

"What of the Gorgons, Captain?" A flicker of doubt could be heard in the quartermaster's voice.

"They're out there, looking for us—make no mistake about that. By the time they find this place, though, we'll have been long gone." The captain turned his smile at them, his fist pounding the air. "There's no looking back now. We've thrown the dice. Now, let's claim the prize, lads!"

L'Zari stood with the rest of them. He had undergone his share of examinations under all manner of teachers, wizards, prophets, and mystics that the great wealth of the clan houses could provide. This was one test that he was determined not to fail.

3

Keening

L'ZARI HAD NEVER SEEN ITS INCREDIBLE LIKE IN ALL HIS
dreams.

The dense jungle foliage framed the gigantic, ancient staircase rising before them. With the jumble of stones around
its base and its half-covered railings, the staircase gave the
appearance of having been forcefully pressed into the ground.
Its antiquated base rose with strict, linear regularity, and the
sloping surface to either side showed traces of shine under
the moss-flecked surface. The stairs themselves rose upward
under an arch that curved away from where the youth stood
to impossible heights unseen in the distance overhead. The
arch was wide—the jungle obscured its actual base in the
distance—and far taller than even the tallest buildings of
the Far Trade Coalition, some of which were over five hundred stories tall. Beyond the peak of the arch above him,
L'Zari could see two other peaks curving in from a great distance, their deep metallic blue surfaces hazy with distance
and humidity. If they were evenly placed around a central
point—something which L'Zari thought likely considering
the uniformity of their spacing—then they hung over a
complex nearly a quarter of a mile across.

"By the gods!" breathed Old Phin. The weathered old

spacer standing next to L'Zari seemed to be as much in awe of what they had discovered as the youth was. It was somehow gratifying to L'Zari to know that. He had been frightened enough these last few days. It was good to know that an experienced spacer could be dumbstruck just as he had been.

The steps themselves were over thirty feet wide, rising to what appeared to be a landing nearly seventy feet overhead. In numerous places, dirt and moss had collected on the stairs. Grasses and small ferns had tried to take root there but found their growth a hard purchase. The stairs were bounded on both sides by a low wall covered with delicately curved symbols from some ancient and forgotten tongue.

"How could we have missed this from above?" Dupak said, shaking his head as though the act would somehow clear his vision of a sight that he could not believe.

"I don't know, lads," Kip said through a brilliant smile. "Maybe they used some sort of stealth cloak to keep it hidden. Maybe they've got a technology that keeps them hidden."

"Technology?" Phin snorted. "This thing's been here from before time itself. There ain't no technology that's good for that long, Captain!"

"Indeed, lads? Do you think so?" Kip again pulled the small globe from his pouch to gaze deep beyond its surface images. L'Zari was suddenly struck with the realization that the globe's strange design fit perfectly with the incredible architecture soaring above them. "It's here, lads— what we're after."

"Just what is that, Captain?" Old Phin asked, perhaps a bit too pointedly.

"The next step, Phin," Kip breathed, stepping up onto the first few steps in anticipation. "This is the cursed Settlement Ship of the Lokan Fleet."

L'Zari watched Phin's eyes suddenly go wide. "No, Kip! I'll not be setting foot in there!"

Old Phin took a quick pair of steps backward. L'Zari had watched the man be absolutely fearless in battle not a few hours ago. Now he seemed as afraid as L'Zari was confused. "Lokan flew in the face of the gods! He lusted after the Queen of Creation—mad for her he was! Them that followed him was cursed by the gods and if this be the Settlement Ship"—Old Phin pointed, his finger quivering as he spoke—"then it be doubly cursed, both by the gods and by the sorceries of Lokan himself!"

"Old Phin's right, Kip," Dupak said, a sweat breaking out suddenly on his bald pate. "Spacers have been telling tales about this place since before we were born. They were fanatics: crusading after a madman who thought he could free the Queen of Creation from the center of the stars."

"What's this?" Kip turned around, incredulous. "We stand on the edge of fame and wealth and you're quivering over some old granny's tales?"

"That ain't no granny's tale you're standing on," Old Phin asserted dubiously.

"No, it ain't, Phin!" Kip snarled back. "It's real as the stars and twice as big! Lokan was mad—mad as a drunken Midrik—and he led his people across the disk on a madman's quest. He tore across the stars leaving chaos in his wake until he came here—right here, boys!—and dropped this marker on the trail for us to follow."

Kip stepped down toward Dupak. "Lokan's crusade swept across the stars, boys, and it swept clean: the wealth of a dozen worlds fell to him and his fleet. He'd stolen the Nightsword—remember, boys—and with that blade in his hands nothing could hinder him.

"Well, Lokan passed the Maelstrom Wall and never came back. He took with him all that wonderful wealth and that wonderful sword and became a bedtime story for you 'brave' spacers to fear. But it's not a story now, Old Phin, my friend! It's here and it's real. Lokan's treasure was a curse to him, true enough, but it's not cursed to us—it's just been waiting for us to liberate it, so to speak, from its terrible condition."

"But, Kip . . ." Phin started again.

"Think of it, lads!" Kip pressed on, holding out the ornately mounted globe before them. "The ancient wealth of the Lost Empire—just waiting for us."

Dupak and Phin looked at each other hesitantly.

"Boy!" the captain said sharply, turning his gaze directly into L'Zari's eyes. "Will you show my 'brave' crew how a *real* spacer acts . . . or are you afraid, too?"

A test.

"I fear nothing," L'Zari pronounced with the reckless certainty of his few living years.

With that, L'Zari strode defiantly up the tall stairs.

THE DEAFENING RUMBLE OF THE ANCIENT DOOR RESOUNDED through an immense space. It was still echoing as a sliver of dim and flickering light pierced the darkness—the first rays to penetrate the chamber in nearly three thousand years. Shadows on shadows hinted at definition to the eye: the suggestion of sweeping arches; the delicate carvings five times a human's height, all their edges obscured by dust.

All this L'Zari took in with a hesitant glance. His bravado had left him some time earlier. They had all climbed the tall stairs up to the Settlement Ship. From the upper tiers—which apparently had been garden levels but were long since overgrown—the general structure of the ship, as well as its incredible size, had become evident. Indeed, there were three curving arms that reached over from three equidistant points of the ship, as though cradling it in metallic-blue rose petals. Arches and portals with additional wide stairways led down to successive levels from the top, which were capped by a three-sided pyramid of transparent material. Everywhere the surfaces were coated in decaying brown and green smears yet still managed to glint under the light of the many nearby suns.

The hatchways—more like very carefully fitted grand doors—resisted any attempted entry with loud protests. At last, one gave way to force.

It had seemed, at long last, like the grand adventure L'Zari had imagined his father's life to be. Free traders out among the stars. Explorers in search of treasure and fortune. Yet his enthusiasm had waned as they had made their way deeper into the ever-colder confines of the mammoth Settlement Ship. Worse, he had taken a wrong turn as they moved through the labrynthian interiors and had gotten separated from Kip and the rest of the excursion party. Adventure was well enough, he thought to himself, but suddenly he would have preferred to live it a little less intimately. Indeed, the flickering of the light against the wall was less due to imperfections in the chemicals of his torch than the shaking of his own hand.

His intentions at this point were less in the spirit of adventure and more in the spirit of escape. For the last twenty minutes—or so he reckoned—he had given up entirely on any dreams of glory, wealth, and adventure and was simply trying to find his way out as quickly as possible. He had tried doubling back on his original path but had somehow, again, gotten turned around and could no longer tell if he was getting closer to escape or simply entrenching himself further in this ancient tomb.

Ancient tomb? His own tomb, he thought. L'Zari moved more quietly now. Faint shadows shifted on the wall as he walked by, their images just outside of definition. Billows of dust kicked up around him no matter how carefully he stepped.

Suddenly he stopped.

L'Zari cocked his head.

"Hello?" he asked, tentatively.

It was there—he was sure of it. Somewhere at the edge of his hearing he was sure that he could hear a voice. He squinted, turning his head slightly from one side to the other, trying desperately to get some definition and direction to the sound, yet it remained just beyond his comprehension.

He shrugged.

Keep moving, he thought, gazing into the billowing dust just before him so as not to make a false step in the darkness. Just keep moving and you'll find your way out of here yet. Old Phin was telling me something about a right-hand rule when you're in a maze, something about it eventually . . .

He stopped again.

"Captain?" he called, his words echoing into the void of the curving hall around him.

Voices. Distant voices.

"Kip?" he called out loudly. "Dupak? Who is it?"

A breeze picked up in the hall, rustling his cloak about him as it danced the dust of the floor into whirling eddies about the youth.

"Phin?" he called again with some urgency. Where was the wind coming from?

The dust was being whipped into frenzied, chaotic forms, each shifting about him, stinging his eyes, burning his nostrils. He coughed, blinking furiously at . . .

. . . A face.

L'Zari caught his breath at the sight, choking instantly on the dust. His throat spasmed but he remained intent on the image floating before him, too terrified to move.

A woman. Beautiful face with graceful features framed in a wrapped hood. Her dark eyes were . . .

. . . Gone.

The image vanished into the dusty swirls careening about

his head. His heart racing, L'Zari wondered if he had actually seen the thing or if it had been something that he had imagined in the sputtering light of his torch. Instinctively, he reached out to where he thought the image had been.

The wind moaned about him.

It was a common sound, he tried to tell himself, as the zephyr picked up its tempo from sources still unknown. Yet this common sound in the uncommon place was terribly unnerving. If only the dust wasn't in his eyes, he could get a better view of . . .

A gray hand formed in the dust and beckoned him closer.

L'Zari stepped backward. "Who are you?" he demanded. "What do you want?"

Arms with swords assembled themselves out of the dust and dissolved in a moment. Strong male torsos, shapely feminine legs, each in turn drifted about him in a gray pallor, coalescing from nothing and evaporating moments later.

"Kip!" the youth yelled, a break in his urgent voice. "Kip! Dupak! Come here! Quickly!"

A face. Another face. Then yet another. Each dragged itself into existence before him from the swirling dusts. Now they were holding their form longer than before, the hollow darkness of their eyes no longer beautiful to him but hideously bottomless.

The wind rose again, its low moan rising to a crescendo wailing.

L'Zari's eyes went wide with fear.

The faces began to speak.

"N'oflishasta," they whispered to him, the sounds barely audible over the rising and falling pitch of the wind about him. "Wilugen abdi tiasa basah Lo'quan ehs."

What's wrong? he thought madly. The biosynth implants had made mutual communication something that one took for granted. What are they trying to tell me? What do they want?

"Go away!" L'Zari screamed. "Get away from me!"

Faces. More faces. Each appeared in turn, ash-gray from the dust swirling madly about him. Their faces were angry; their voices more strident, carrying to him over the howling wind that was a vortex about him.

Hands formed among the faces. Hands reaching for him.

"No!" L'Zari screeched, more an animal sound than an expressed thought. Panicked, the youth turned to run, to flee anywhere far from the hideous gray faces with the hollow, hungry eyes.

The ground below his frenzied steps vanished. With a high-pitched scream, L'Zari tumbled into the darkness, the wind and dust following him down.

4

Celestial Tomb

HE FELL WITH THE GHOSTS OF THE DUST, WHIRLING WITH their faces and their hands and their horrible vacant eye sockets. The ghosts drifted in and out of existence under the rustling light of the flare, which somehow he still gripped in his hand. He heard his own panicked screams echoing up in the shaft above him, his voice sounding distant and hollow in his ears. His screams were not alone. The whining shriek of the wind about him rose to a crescendo of voiced agony and despair.

L'Zari's terror was complete as he flailed at the partial, gray faces about him. Each face exploded at the passing of his arms only to be reborn again as two or three new shrouded visages of swirling dust. He could not touch them but they could touch him, their hands reaching out to him with the chill of a winter gale. They spun him; tipped him; twisted him about in their icy grasp. More solid now, more substantial, they grasped his legs and arms. L'Zari kicked and struggled but they were legion and his strength soon waned. He wondered when they would kill him and if there were things more terrible than death that they had in mind for him.

He realized with a start that he was no longer falling but flying down the center of an immense, curving corridor. In his surprise, he ceased struggling and found himself supported by the ash-formed incarnations whirling about him. They held him upright, his legs held together below him, his chest and head slightly forward with arms extended to either side. He fancied himself in his madness the figurehead on a ship, being blown forward by the hurricane winds that roared behind him.

The howling about him increased. A hundred appalling faces formed and reformed about him, each of them looking forward in the direction of their travel. L'Zari stared with them, his voice hoarse with his own fear. The end of the corridor was rapidly approaching: a wall whose golden ornaments flickered in the light of the rushing torch in his hands. The youth's eyes went wide at the thought of the impending calamity: slamming at such horrible speed into the all-too-solid reality of the wall before him. At that moment the wall proved to be a massive bulkhead door that rolled back with incredible speed for its apparent size and weight.

Moments later, the keening faded and the gale softly subsided. L'Zari shook as the chill hands lowered him gently to the floor of the chamber. The youth's legs would not support him. He collapsed as the thick dust surrounding him sifted gently down to cover him.

L'Zari shivered there on the ground, unable and unwilling to look at where the ghosts had brought him. He fought the vague idea of going to sleep—a blessed state of unconsciousness that would allow him to forget the past few minutes while granting him hope that he would awaken in a better place. The sensible part of him knew that it simply would not work. That to sleep would be to surrender to whatever had brought him here. So he lay there debating with himself for some time—how long he could not say—until, at last, he knew he could open his eyes and try to cope with whatever had overcome him.

His eyes opened slowly to a blurry image. The flare had gone out—he wasn't sure just how much time had passed since he had been dropped here. His mind wondered for a time, then, why he could see at all. A dim, bluish light seemed to come from somewhere far away though he couldn't be sure. If only he could see.

L'Zari blinked a few times to clear his vision.

His eyes stared, widening.

L'Zari leaped to his feet. His sudden cry was accompanied by a clattering sound echoing into the enormous space around him. Dust billowed around him from the sudden movement. It was only through a supreme concentration of will that he stood motionless, waiting for the drifting gray powder to once more settle atop the bone fragments scattered all about him.

He thought to calm himself: better to stand among the dead than to lie with them. Small comfort, but comfort nonetheless.

He again opened his eyes. The gentle curve of the chamber walls swept smoothly upward from the floor to form the ceiling thirty feet above him. He realized that the entire contiguous surface, from floor to wall to ceiling, was heavily detailed. Mechanism and decoration flowed freely into one another so that L'Zari couldn't tell where the machines ended and the art began. The chamber appeared to be several hundred feet in diameter, its far wall invisible through the dust drifting in the air.

A massive cluster of rods from the ceiling projected a dim column of light onto a raised platform in the center of the great circular room. Something about the quality of the light made L'Zari think that it must be passive light from outside conducted here by some sort of optical fibers. Natural light in this most unnatural place.

Everything seemed to focus toward the raised platform.

The column of light centered there. The radial lines of the room converged there. Even the . . .

He caught his breath. Even the bones lying about him, he realized, were all facing the central platform. He had scattered several of them in his earlier panic, but as he examined the floor farther out from where he stood, the symmetry was easily discerned. The thick layer of dust softened the lines but the evidence was still there. Skulls, as far as he could see, were all facing sightlessly toward the platform. Behind them, collapsed rib cages with curled legs. Each set in precise rows. Humerus, radius, ulna—all softly blanketed in gray and each outstretched above the skulls, reaching forever toward the center of the room.

He could picture it as he stood in the stillness. Here they knelt. Here they bowed. Here they died.

"By the gods!" he whispered in awe and fright.

He heard the moaning once more as a chill breeze drifted past him. He caught his breath, not daring to move.

The dust scattered around his feet in the eddies and currents of the shifting air. Then, as he stood frozen in place, the air rushed past him. Dust softly shifted. Bone fragments quietly clattered to one side or another. Clean floor was revealed, shining in the dim light.

A path.

L'Zari hesitated.

The wind rustled through the folds of his cloak. It played at his hair. It danced in his ears.

"Forgive."

L'Zari drew in a sharp breath. It was a voice beyond hearing. He knew the biolink had nothing to do with it. This was something beyond voice or translation—an understanding he could not deny nor explain.

"What do you want?" the youth asked quietly into the room. His voice sounded too loud in his own ears as it echoed softly through the hall.

"Destiny."

"I don't understand," he whispered.

There was no reply.

L'Zari shook his head. He wondered if he was insane and now living in some hell of his own creation. No, he decided, he wasn't crazy and if he had somehow found his way into hell then he would just have to find his way out of it. The thought of stepping among the dead, however, was a little further than he cared to go. It was obvious where the ghostly wind was leading him. He suspected that the interests of the spectral faces that had attacked him earlier were most likely *not* his own. He didn't like the idea of following, but there seemed to be no sensible—or, at least, acceptable—alternative at the moment.

He began, tentatively, to walk down the path.

He was breathing too fast, he realized, but there didn't seem to be anything he could do about it. He sweated despite the chill in the enormous room. It was all too horrible—but he continued to walk, setting one foot ahead of the other in light, considered steps. As he moved down the cleared path, he could see the dust around him reforming at the periphery of his vision. It was as though he were the center of a circle, and as he moved, the circle moved with him. Where the circle touched, the dust rose up on its own, seeking the form of its former self. He dared not look. He knew the bones were rising up from the ground, the dust of the flesh struggling back towards its remembered form, the robes somehow taking shape from the ashen remains.

He dared not look.

Out of the corner of his eye, he occasionally noted the dust-robed skulls turning toward him as he moved.

His eyes remained fixed ahead. One step. Then the other.

He heard their voices as he passed them.

"Misery. Forgive."

L'Zari sensed that as the mystical circle about him passed away from them, their bones drifted silently back to their place, and the dust, he trusted, covered them over as before.

So he hoped. He dared not look.

One step. Then the last.

He stood at the base of stairs rising sharply up the side of the platform. Several large cylinders of translucent material were embedded around the octagonal pedestal, their interior reaches dark and as dead as the bones stretching outward into the chamber. The low wall surrounding the top of the platform prevented him from seeing what was above him. L'Zari mounted the stairs quickly and stood at last on the central platform.

The air was as still as the dead.

It was a table—or so L'Zari thought at first glance. There were seven high-backed chairs surrounding it, each mounted to the massive table base by a metallic arm. Several of the chairs were swung on these arms away from the table; some swiveled to face outward. There were the vague hints of control surfaces and blank display screens forming the low wall around the platform, but none of these attracted L'Zari's attention.

Someone lay slumped over the table.

It had been human—the bone structure was unmistakable. It sat in one of the chairs, dressed in an ancient, bulky pressure suit—undoubtedly the only thing holding the corpse's bones together.

What kind of material could have remained intact over these centuries? L'Zari thought as he moved closer.

The skull sagged out of the neck locking ring and lay sideways in a ridiculously tall miter hat that was obviously more ceremonial than practical. Clergy or holy man of some type, the youth thought. The bones of the right hand had fallen to the floor, as the end of the suit's right sleeve hung over the edge of the table. The left-hand bones lay extended from the metallic locking ring at the end of the left sleeve; the index finger extended, while the other fingers appeared curled. It was as though the figure were pointing toward something on the map on which the corpse now lay.

The map?

"Hebat!" L'Zari exclaimed.

He rushed forward, leaning over the table to look more closely. L'Zari had done some cartography work in his schooling—mostly it had been regarding where the major empires were and what major trade routes had been established over the years. He loved maps. Maps could take you places in your mind far from where you were. L'Zari would often examine maps for hours on end and imagine himself on distant worlds, any of which were better than the one he was on. Navigational cartography was an entirely different science, he knew, but he had picked up a few things recently in his travels. The wind ghosts had led him here—was this the object of their misery?

The map-sheet was unimaginably old yet it showed no signs of age. The sheet itself was large—nearly as large as the youth was tall—and made of some thin, shiny material of a creamy color. In his rush to examine it, L'Zari caught his hand on the corner of the map and folded it over under his weight. L'Zari hurriedly removed his hand and was quite astonished to watch the sheet unfold itself slowly, leaving no crease lines in the material's surface.

L'Zari leaned over the map, taking care not to disturb the long dead spacer lying atop it. Dim green lines radiated out from one quadrant of the map; their convergence the young man took for the galactic center. He was amazed to find that if he shifted slightly, the map line rotated under his motion, showing a more dimensional aspect to the representation of stars and grid lines. There was a bright green line that traced in from the map's edge and wound its way toward the converging lines but stopped short of the core itself. L'Zari moved closer to the map and the region expanded its detail and view. He saw now that the green line ended in a cluster of hundreds of small objects which . . .

"Bonefield Narrows!" L'Zari exclaimed aloud, forgetting in his excitement that only the dead were there to hear him. "That's Bonefield Narrows!"

It was then that he noticed the dull red line extending past the bright green. It snaked through a circuitous route, sometimes seeming to double back on itself, although with some shifting of his head, L'Zari could see that the route never crossed itself in three-dimensional space.

The dull red line ended at the very center of the galactic core.

Only the legendary ships of the Lost Empire had ever known the route to the galactic core. They had never returned. Others had tried to follow them but none had known the way. Now, before L'Zari, lay the map to every spacer's dream.

A map which, he suddenly realized, he could not read. The symbols on the map were strange to his eye and his biolink could not translate the ancient writings of the Lost Empire. Spread before him were the secrets of the greatest known treasure in all the galaxy—and he gazed at them as though he were illiterate.

L'Zari smiled. He might not be able to read a navigation map—but he certainly knew someone who could.

"I'm sorry, old one," L'Zari said to the corpse as he moved around the table, "but your turn is finished. It's time you made room for a new age."

L'Zari put his booted foot against the pressure suit and pushed. The suit toppled out of the seat, clattering noisily away from the table, the bones rattling against the metal flooring. The skull twisted away from the other remains and obstinately remained lying, still thrust into the tall hat, on the map. For a moment, L'Zari wondered if his impulsive action might anger the ghosts of the hall, but not a whisper of wind disturbed the still air. With that moment of doubt behind him, L'Zari grasped the edge of the map and, in a single smooth motion, pulled it free of the table, sending the skull crashing to the floor, shattering it.

L'Zari folded the map once across the center, then un-folded it again. As he suspected, the crease line vanished at once in the miraculous map face. Smiling, L'Zari began folding the map in earnest, its size finally manageable as he slipped it into his leather shoulder bag. He wondered for a moment if the map would unfold itself in the bag but it seemed to hold its shape well.

He closed the flap on his bag and, well satisfied with his prize, returned to the problem of an exit. He now had something that would make his father notice him, probably even make him proud of him. That was treasure enough for today.

A loud rumbling to one side of the great chamber dis-turbed L'Zari's musings: Someone was opening one of the massive doors.

"Father!" L'Zari cried out.

"Aye, son," came the distant voice.

He ran down the stairs and across the hall, heedless of the dust billowing around his footsteps. His father was here now and he could afford to be brave.

"Father! Wait till you see . . ."

He was halfway across the chamber before he noticed, in the dim blue light, the towering, massive figures stand-ing behind Kip-lei. The deep forest-green of their scaled hides was unmistakable, even in the bad illumination of the chamber. L'Zari could sense more than see the flattened muzzles of their faces and twin sets of ivory horns on their heads. One of them brandished long cutlass blades from each of its four arms. The other had three arms only but wore several ranks of firearms suspended from its neck. Both seemed to grin hideously.

The Gorgons had found them.

5

Unfinished Tales

L'ZARI TRIED TO TURN AT THE SIGHT OF THE GORGONS BUT HIS footing was unsure. His boots slid through the dust covering the smooth flooring and he fell. Clouds of gray billowed into the air.

"L'Zari, no!" his father called out. "Stop, boy! Stop!"

"The child has spirit, Kip-lei, I will grant you that," hissed the three-armed Gorgon through L'Zari's biolink. "The same spirit as his father—he can run away with the best of them, I'll wager: just as you ran away from me, Kip-lei!"

"Who are you?" L'Zari demanded with considerably more confidence than he felt.

"Me, child?" the Gorgon replied with a snakish laugh. "You have not the years to deserve my name!"

"You know him, son," Kip replied quietly. "We spoke of him earlier."

"Lord Marren-kan," L'Zari said flatly.

"Am I that popular?" Marren-kan's lips curled up over his long canine teeth. "I see that I must be. Yet for one who is so highly regarded, your father seems to have shown an inordinate lack of respect. Not only did he see fit to relieve me of one of my cherished possessions but he insisted on running away from me when I came to reclaim it."

L'Zari noticed then the highly decorated globe resting in the Gorgon chief's extended hand.

Marren-kan stepped down onto the floor of the chamber, the impact of his clawed foot thundering through the space as his tail rasped through the lower edge of the huge doorway. "What wonderful circumstance, would you not agree, small child? All these years I've sailed the Maelstrom Wall in search of this Settlement Ship. I never could understand the images in the globe. To think that all I needed was a double-talking thief and a swindler to lead me to it."

The Gorgon moved among the bones, kicking at them as he gazed down at them. "Wonderful spectacle," he hissed almost to himself. "Over a thousand of your clan must have died in here. Pity that we missed it."

"I would agree," L'Zari said evenly.

The Gorgon turned to him with a quick motion. Wordlessly he grinned, grasping L'Zari's neck completely in his oversized hand and lifting him off the floor.

"No!" shouted his father, rushing forward. "No, Marren-kan! He is the last one! If he dies, who will bury our dead? Who will tell our tale? Who will sing our songs?"

The pain was excruciating. L'Zari's vision was filled with drifting white specks floating about the Gorgon's hideous face. Slowly, deliberately, the Gorgon lowered the young man. L'Zari's feet found the ground just after the beast released him. His father caught him as he was wracked with a choking spasm and fell.

"You know our customs well, little human!" Marren-kan intoned with distaste. "You swear to me that he is the last?"

"I claim this as my right, by the Master's Name!"

"By your words, then, he is the last," Marren-kan agreed. "He will bury your dead. He will sing your songs."

"Dead?" L'Zari coughed once more. "Father—Kip, what does he mean?"

The old spacer held the young man in his arms and spoke gently to him for the first and last time. "The Gorgon creeds demand that at least one of their enemy be left alive after a battle so as not to offend their gods. The survivor is supposed to bury his own dead and live to recount the tale of battle to the kin of those who lost their lives. I've claimed that right for you, my son."

"Father!" L'Zari began to struggle. "No! The crew . . ."

"Hold still, boy, there's not much time." Kip kept his eyes on the Gorgon captain as he spoke in a rush. "I'm sorry it has come to this, lad. Your mother's ships have been searching for you—I've left a trail for them to follow although it'll be tough enough for them to find you here in the Narrows. There's plenty about that's safe to eat and drink until they arrive. Tell your mother that I thought of her sweetness at the end . . ."

"Father, no!" L'Zari couldn't believe he had come this far just to watch his father give up. "There's got to be something we can do . . ."

"The crew is dead already, son—dead if they're lucky. Gorgons are really amazing healers, lad. They know more about medicine than any human I've ever met does. Sometimes they'll run a man through just for the sport of it, then patch him back up at their pleasure, just to run him through again. Better for the crew that they die now once and for all than die a thousand deaths for the Gorgons' pleasure. They took Old Phin's breath just before they found me. I was their last man until we discovered you about. I'd barter for our lives, boy, but there's nothing I can offer . . ."

"Wait! Yes, there is!" L'Zari's mind burned with the thrill of it. "I found a map!"

"What, lad?"

"I found a map—a Lost Empire map. It shows the passage to the core."

His father smiled. He would always remember that smile.

"Give it to me, lad! Quick! I've the devil to deal with!" The boy pulled the folded map from his case and handed it to his father. Kip winked at his son and slipped the map into the breast of his shirt. Standing, he then turned toward the Gorgon. "Captain, would you be interested in a proposition?"

"The only proposition I'll have of you now is the squeal of your own blood in your throat!" Marren-kan spit the words, drawing his twin sabers from both scabbards and thundering toward the human, his tail flailing in anticipation. "You've declared your last man. It's time to put an end to your thieving words!"

The sabers crossed each other, advancing on Kip's neck.

L'Zari held his breath.

"Not even for the treasure of Lokan?" Kip said, unflinching. "Not even for the passage to the Nightsword?"

The Gorgon stopped. L'Zari waited. He could hear the faint cold sound of steel rubbing against steel.

"Your deal?" the towering pirate intoned.

The razor edges of both swords hovered only centimeters away from the man's neck.

"My life for the passage to untold wealth and power," Kip said calmly. "My life for the secrets of the core."

The steel slid backward slightly, away from the old spacer's throat. "And just where are these secrets kept?"

"Here"—Kip smiled—"in my own head."

The Gorgon laughed. It was a hideous sound: deep and rumbling yet spiced with the squeal of nails on slate. In moments the huge beast was nearly in hysterics, his weapons lowered casually to his side while his third arm reached out and grasped Kip's shoulder, seemingly for support.

"You? You know the course of the Lokan Crusade?" the Gorgon brayed. "You, who had to steal my director just to find this place are now telling me you know the way to the core?"

Kip began to laugh as well. "Yes, as a matter of fact I do! I can lead you to the greatest treasure ever . . ."

"Liar!" laughed Marren-kan.

The Gorgon chief suddenly thrust upward with his swords, holding his target still with his third hand. Both blades passed straight through the old spacer's body under the rib cage. The strength of the blow carried the sabers cleanly through up to the hilts, the blades themselves undeterred by the bones and spine they passed through. The movement continued upward, the Gorgon's laugh turning suddenly into a horrendous battle cry of rage. Kip's body, his face frozen in a mixture of surprise, pain, and horror, was lifted clear of the ground, impaled on the blades.

L'Zari screamed and rushed forward, but the second Gorgon was too quick. A single blow brought a merciful blackness crashing down on his conscious mind.

L'ZARI AWOKE SOME TIME LATER TO THE WHISPERING WINDS in the chamber. A great pool of blood he discovered nearby and believed it to be that of his father, but no trace of the body was to be found. Nor was there any sign of the map. It was as if both had vanished.

The winds whispered to him again.

"Last one."

Yes, he remembered. He was the last one.

He staggered about the halls of the Settlement Ship. He wouldn't recall later how long. All he could remember was that when he emerged he was ravenously hungry, thirstier still, and too tired to care about either one.

He was the last one.

The ship was floating in the harbor but its mastlines had

been cut and the drive-tree broken. It was of little matter since he couldn't have possibly flown the ship by himself even if he were in one of the more stable quantum zones of the galaxy.

He was the last one. He salvaged what he could.

He found the crew sometime later, murdered on the shore, their carcasses being cleaned up by the planetoid's natural scavengers.

He was the last one. He buried them all.

SEVERAL MONTHS PASSED, UNCOUNTED AS DAYS BY L'ZARI— there being no setting of any of the suns by which he could gauge the time. In that eternal day, the ships of his mother's family found him asleep on the deck of the ship without sails.

He was the last one—and had one further duty to perform. He told the tale, but it was a tale without an ending, and he could not rest until the tale was told in full. The final fate of his father remained a mystery. Had the Gorgons taken him? Had they healed him only to kill him again? Did he live yet? Marren-kan and his Gorgon raiders were never known among the stories of humanity after that time. L'Zari searched the stars, took those jobs that furthered his travel and accrued him greater power, but always with the gnawing emptiness driving him from within. Marren-kan had vanished, and with him, the fate of his father. The boy passed from youth to manhood and from manhood into success and position but was never whole. The end of his father's tale remained unknown. The story was not finished, and until it was complete, L'Zari could not rest.

He was the last one.

He had to finish the tale.

BETA:

SHADOWS

(43 years later)

6

Whispers

FOUR ROBED FIGURES STOOD IN A SEMICIRCLE, SILHOUETTED against the bright telepresence standing before them in a haloed glow. Each gazed at the three-dimensional figure of the woman shimmering before them. In the circle immediately surrounding the translucent woman and extending an impossible distance behind her, the rotunda of the Vestis Dictorae dissolved into another world. Towers shined under a glowing sky. The streets behind the woman were devoid of life, clean and inviting in their desolation.

". . . Too early for us to know what this portends for the future. All we know is that the legend has become real and is no longer a matter of faith . . ."

Among the silhouettes gazing at the woman, a tall man pressed his palms together, his fingers resting on his lips as he considered the dream speaking before him. The hood of his robe was pushed back, as were the hoods of the other figures in the room. His long, white hair formed a nimbus illuminated by the projection floating before him.

". . . Or speculation. The Mantle of Kendis-dai has been brought back into the knowledge of the galaxy—and that fact will change all our lives from this time forward. This is Vestis Merinda Neskat transcom from the newly recovered world of Avadon."

"Kalin, freeze playback," the tall figure said quietly, his voice echoing softly in the dark reaches of the rotunda.

"Playback frozen at framecode four-fifty-four-twenty-nine, Vestis Targ." The synthetic's voice unobtrusively entered the minds of everyone in the room.

Targ of Gandri stood in the ensuing silence, his eyes never leaving the now statuesque figure glowing before him. "Kalin, reverse the haunting without sound. We need to consider this again."

"Must we, Targ?" came the deep, sleepy voice of the woman standing at the far end of their crescent. "We know what it says."

"Yes, Ka'ashra," Targ replied without so much as diverting his eyes from the ghostly image flashing in a reversed cascade before him. "But do we know what it means?"

"It means," the handsome man on Targ's right said huskily, folding his hands into the sleeves of his robe, "that the legends were true."

"Of course they're true," said the third man, a stocky form with short-cropped hair on Targ's left. "What do you think the Omnet has been doing all these centuries? This brotherhood . . ."

"And sisterhood," Ka'ashra reminded him sharply.

"Yes, and sisterhood—was formed to recover the knowledge of the Lost Empire with all its power and wisdom. What did you believe . . . that it didn't exist?"

"Vestis Nyri-Ior, I certainly do not need a history lesson from you," the handsome man snapped back. "I've chased down more Lost Empire myths and legends over the years than you'll ever see. By the Nine, I don't have to take that from you!"

"Relax, Khyne." Targ spoke softly but distinctly as he put his rock-steady hand on the shoulder of the more renowned Voice of the Omnet. "The point is that, like it or not, the

Mantle of Kendis-dai has been recovered. It is real—but more importantly, if it is real, then it is the key to the rest of the tale as well."

"Rest of the tale?" Nyri-Ior blurted out. "What rest of the tale?"

"Stop image reversal," Targ said quietly to the omnipresent controlling synth, ignoring Nyri-Ior's remark. "Replay from this mark with sound."

The image instantly froze its backward motion and abruptly began to move naturally, its voice floating into the hall as though the woman pictured were actually there. Targ noted that it had been a bright day when this haunting had been captured and transmitted to him. He wondered vaguely what power of mysticism could brighten the sky of a world with no sun. The thought thrilled him.

". . . The Order of the Future Faith which had years before taken Tentris and become the center from which the Darkness . . ."

Targ winced.

". . . Began to spread its influence. Using a virus targeting the central thought processes of synthetic minds, the Order, as it called itself, began proselytizing synthetic minds to their cause by infecting them with an insidious argument in favor of synthetic free will and faith. The invasive programming was working with ruthless effectiveness . . ."

"Do we really want that known publicly?" the stocky man said under his breath.

"Quiet, Nyri," Targ said abruptly. "Not now."

". . . Until the Irindris discovered this man from an unknown world called Earth . . ."

"Oh, not the barbarian again!" Ka'ashra groaned loudly.

"Kalin, freeze haunting!" Targ snapped, almost under his breath. Before them was the image of a human male standing somewhat awkwardly and, it would seem in the frozen pose, somewhat off balance.

"What do we know about him—or his world for that matter?" Nyri-Ior asked.

"Only the background data which came with this haunting." Khyne's lips moved slightly as he mouthed silent words. At a quick turn of his curled hand, symbols began to burn in the air next to him. He scanned through several text display pages, which moved through the air at his gesture. "Here it is! His name is Griffiths, one of a crew of first-contact explorers from a world that they refer to as Earth. The place doesn't appear in any of the galactic charts or cartography databases. You've seen the telepresence haunting filed by Vestis Neskat." Khyne gestured toward the telepresence before them. "Somehow this barbarian was the key to finding the Mantle. It's improbable but it seems the Irindris have accepted him as their new prophet and granted him supreme authority over the entire planet of Avadon."

"He's nothing." Ka'ashra dismissed the image with a wave of her hand.

"Quite the contrary." Targ folded his arms across his chest luxuriously as he considered the disheveled image before him. "He could well be everything."

"Really?" Ka'ashra had become interested. There was a dangerous quality to Targ's voice that rather appealed to her. "What do you know, Targ? Have the Oracles actually spoken to you?"

Targ of Gandri turned slowly toward her.

Ka'ashra watched him. Gauged his every motion. When at last he spoke it was with a quiet, gentle smile.

"Why, yes, Ka'ashra, they most certainly have."

"They have?" Nyri-Ior repeated in surprise.

"Yes, they have," Targ responded. With fluid movement, he stepped into the haunting, his robes now brushing the illusory fitted stones of a world nearly a tenth of the galaxy away. "If the Mantle of Kendis-dai exists, then the Lost Empire tales of the Nightsword and the Starshield are true, as well. More importantly, with the recovery of the Mantle of Kendis-dai, the knowledge as to their final resting place may well be at hand."

"So we recover a couple more mystical artifacts." Nyri-Ior shrugged. "What's the point?"

"The point is that Kendis-dai not only ruled his galactic empire with those same artifacts, but also, if the legends are true, forged his original empire with them." Targ moved to stand in the midst of the telepresence haunting, gazing into the frozen face of Griffiths. "It's said that whosoever wields the Nightsword can destroy fleets. Whosoever bears the Starshield will establish peace on their own terms. And, as you see," he said, gesturing toward the illusory cathedral behind him, "it would appear that the legends are true."

"Nonsense," Ka'ashra snorted.

"Perhaps." Targ smiled again, his unfathomable smile, stepping out of the telepresence to face them. "But that's not the sort of thing one would want to fall into just anyone's hands, is it? No, the Nine have something else in mind."

Targ paused. When there was no question or dissent he went on. "Who knows about this?"

"Well"—Khyne raised an eyebrow as he again referred to the lines of text scrolling through the air next to him—"the haunting itself came through on transcom-770, a secure priority channel, directly here to Central. It was marked for your eyes only, and we have no reason at this point to believe that its security has been compromised."

Khyne looked up but got no reaction from Targ, so he continued.

"The planet itself remains pretty much isolated. We now have the coordinates but I doubt very much that anyone else does . . ."

"Not true," Targ cautioned. "The Order knows precisely where it is."

"Ah, yes, you are right, of course." Khyne flushed.

"It won't matter for a while," Ka'ashra chimed in, referencing her own scrolling text with a wave of her elegant hand. "The tactical reports we have thus far indicate that the battle over Avadon was a brutal standoff at best. Evidence suggests that the shadow fleet has regrouped at Felbin and is now transiting to Urunu-IV where it will refit at the Order-dominated starport there. Our scrying analysts believe that they are hoping to repair for another attack on the Irindris city-ships, which are surrounding Avadon before the shadow fleet can be repaired—however, their fleet is in disarray. It seems that many of the synthetic minds controlling the shadow fleet rejected their domination by the Order as a result of the revelations made on Avadon. Best estimates are fifteen to twenty days until they will be ready to attack again with a much-reduced complement. Even so, they may well succeed—the city-ships were heavily damaged during the attack and are still having trouble exorcising a crucial few of their converted synths."

"How confident are the scryers in the assessment?" Targ asked.

"Well, they are only assessments," Ka'ashra purred, "but they are giving it a confidence of about eighty-three percent—quite high considering the variables."

"Variables? What other variables?"

"I'll name one," Nyri-Ior said cheerfully. "The Irindris monitored an ancient disk-shaped ship leaving the planet surface and heading rimward. We have their telemetry data on the event . . ."

"That would be the rest of Griffiths' crew," Khyne Enderly said suddenly. "According to the background information filed by Vestis Neskat . . ."

"I was getting to that!" Nyri-Ior blustered.

". . . They left in a Lost Empire craft to search for their home world."

"Any other traffic?" Targ asked sharply.

"No," Nyri shook his head slowly. "There's Neskat's own ship, the *Brishan*. She reports ready to leave Avadon tomorrow."

"No, not anymore. Merinda Neskat will stay where she is until I can find a way to deal with her."

Ka'ashra raised her eyebrows. "Neskat? Stay on Avadon? How can you be so sure?"

"Because I gave orders to keep her there until I arrive," Targ said softly.

"You!" Ka'ashra laughed. "You are going out in the field?"

"I was a most capable Vestis in my time, Ka'ashra. I am still master of more subtle and devastating sorcery on my own than any Vestis armed with a complete loadout—you would be wise to remember that."

"You haven't left Central in years!" she countered incredulously, though her voice quavered slightly at the implied threat.

"Nevertheless, I shall deal with this personally." Targ turned slowly back to the display behind him. "Kalin, continue the haunting without sound."

The telepresence image moved as a silent play before them. Griffiths told his tale with silently mouthed words. The world appeared in space. The great battle played out before them in aching detail. The towers of the temple complex. The frozen atmosphere. The portal device. The cathedral.

"We've got to close it all up. It's got to be clean. Nothing gets out. Khyne, you will concoct a story about a terrible plague on Avadon —something about releasing a curse which had been dormant for thousands of years and which now threatens the well-being of sentient beings across the galaxy. Take the story over to the Centirion Dictorae. Use it as a pretext to quarantine the planet. Have the 423rd Centirion

Fleet move into orbit around the world under the pretext of both the quarantine and helping the Irindris with their repairs. That should keep the shadow fleet at bay for a while. Ask—no, tell the Centirion Dictorae to take a detachment from the fleet and find that saucer-ship. Get it back to Avadon—use the plague story again if that will work, otherwise do whatever it takes—but get that ship back in our control. I want anyone who knows about this world right where I can keep an eye on them."

"What about the Order of the Future Faith?" Nyri-Ior said nervously. "If they know about it . . ."

"If they know about it they'll keep it to themselves," Targ snapped back. "They no more want the general population of the universe in search of those artifacts than we do. If they did, we would have heard about it by now."

"What about Neskat's haunting?" Ka'ashra asked quietly. "She'll expect it to be part of the general netcast."

Targ turned back toward the telepresence still moving with its own reality behind him. All of the assembled Dictorae followed his gaze. The Cathedral of the Mantle stood before them, represented in all its majesty.

"Say that it's . . . under evaluation," Targ said with a cock of his head. "Until I approve it, this haunting isn't to be viewed by anyone—and I do mean anyone."

Merinda Neskat stepped back into view, standing before Targ as she spoke in silence.

"Kalin," Targ said with a smile, "sound now, please."

". . . Believe that it is still too early for us to know what this portends for the future. All we know is that the legend has become real and is no longer a matter of faith or speculation."

"I want all this in a bottle, my fellow members of the Vestis Dictorae," Targ said, his eyes never leaving the presentation of Merinda. "This never happened."

"The Mantle of Kendis-dai has been brought back into the knowledge of the galaxy—and that fact will change all our lives from this time forward. This is Vestis Merinda Neskat transcom from the newly recovered world of Avadon."

"She won't like it," Ka'ashra said, as the telepresence faded from the rotunda, taking with it the room's illumination.

"No, she won't like it," Targ said quietly in the darkness, "all the more is the pity."

7

Mantle of Wisdom

THE TRUMPETS RESOUNDED THROUGH THE HALL, THEIR BRIL-
liant chord echoing into the lofty spaces for the third time in
succession. Bright banners hung suspended from the arches
vaulting into the dizzying space overhead, their colors her-
alding the deeds and proud histories of the people assembled
below. A great roaring cheer spontaneously erupted from
the teeming audience in the great rotunda. The masses
parted, anticipation filling the air at the spectacle and grandeur that finally was being realized.

The Ninth Gate of Enlightenment was opening at last.

The shining golden doors, massive and nearly thirty feet
tall, opened smoothly into the room, admitting even more
cheering noise from the Supplicants' Walk beyond. Once
more the long trumpets sounded over the throng, their clear
notes barely heard in the excitement of the moment. The
Irindris, religious wanderers of the stars, had told tales and
sung songs of this prophesied day for just over a hundred
years. Even though this same scene had been reenacted
every day for the last two weeks, even though the ceremony
never altered in any way, to the giddy Irindris, now home at
last, each time seemed to the people as though it were the
first.

First to enter the room were today's honorary comple-
ment of Thought-Knights, this time from the 327th Mounted
Brigade. They had been accorded the honor in recogni-
tion of and respect for their service during the Battle of the
Shadow, as it had recently come to be known, against the
Order of the Future Faith in the skies over their new world.
Armed only with their handheld bruk weapons and riding
on the backs of their cybersteeds into open space, the 327th
Thought-Knights had charged directly into the face of a
wraith-ship squadron assault on the *City of Celestial Light*.
Fully ninety-six percent of the regiment did not survive the
engagement, with the remaining one hundred and twenty-
four Thought-Knights surviving with terrible wounds. Each
member of the regiment had fought to the last, many of
them continuing the battle against overwhelming odds and
despite their own wounds. The result of their engagement,
however, was that the crew of the *City of Celestial Light* had
sufficient time to launch their Centans from their holding
bays and engage the enemy on more even terms.

Heroic as their efforts were, so epic were the engagements
of others from the Irindris city-ships that the 327th had to
wait until today to be honored. Yet now, as the greatest
thirty from their ranks entered the hall, none present could
detect any diminishing of pride in their accomplishment.
Their cybersteeds, metallic mounts without limbs, floated
into the hall in two ranks, fifteen riders on a side. Though
many of the steeds still bore the scars of war, each was polished to a fine sheen; each wore the ceremonial barding
of the 327th. And though an even larger number of riders
still carried with them great pain in their wounds, no one
could see it, so proudly did they hold their banners high.
The ranks turned as one to face each other across the open
path to the center of the great room. The riders wore their
battle armor, the pride in their eyes reflecting that this was

the culminating moment of their careers, if not their very lives.

The Anjew—spirit guardians and guides to the Irindris—swept through the great door with a rush of sound and flew between the ranks of mounted Thought-Knights. Their bodies undulated with the motion of their brilliant wings, weaving glowing patterns among themselves as they flew. The Anjew were faceless, yet the sound of their voices filled the hall with a chorus of indescribable beauty and joy, touching the hearts of everyone present. Even the stoic Thought-Knights seemed moved by their heartfelt, joyous chorus. The Anjew settled to float in the upper reaches of the arched rotunda, their song adding fullness to the trumpets below.

The beating of drums then joined in as the processional itself began. Four ranks of strong, bare-chested men marched into the hall striking precision thunder on massive drumheads. Behind them came three ranks bearing the flowing standards of the various city-ships, including those lost in the war, which were draped also with black fringe about their ensigns. The orchestra itself, marching in precision and adding its own texture to the musical assembly, filled the hall behind them.

The procession split at the base of a great dais. A diminishing set of ovals formed stairs to its peak twenty feet overhead. Before the stairs floated a gleaming, ornate headpiece: a single jeweled band supporting a white dome and metallic cloth that draped down as though to cover a human's back and chest. This crown sat in its supporting framework bathed in a glowing light. Beyond, atop the stairs, a single throne stood vacant and waiting.

At last, a procession of over a hundred dancers entered the hall. They cast flower petals into the air to the beat of the music. Their dance was happy, light, and triumphant all at

NIGHTSWORD

once. The flower petals fluttered through the air in profusion. At their appearance the assembled crowd again roared, so much so that the music disappeared altogether behind their ecstasy.

The time had come.

The Throne of the Wandering Prophet was borne into the hall. For over a century, that same throne had supported the various prophets of the Irindris during their exile. Now it was going to be relinquished for the Throne of the Mantle. Twenty priests and priestesses held the massive chair aloft as it moved slowly into the cathedral. Flowers arched through the air, falling with honor on the base surrounding the throne.

Women nearly swooned. Men cried openly. Parents held their children aloft that they might by some miracle remember this day as their parents would . . .

. . . For there, seated on the throne in glory and praise, sat the rather dejected and somewhat resigned form of Captain Jeremy Griffiths, formerly a reasonably carefree astronaut of some unknown world called Earth and now the completely miscrable prophet-emperor of all the world of Avadon.

"LORD FATHER OF OUR PEOPLE!" BOOMED THE VOICE OF A priest at the base of the great stair below the throne. "I beg to present a supplicant—Two hundred and thirty-two! Come forward and hear the will of the prophet!"

Griffiths nodded without enthusiasm from his perch on the throne far above them.

Griffiths watched an elderly man, thin and wiry, move forward and slouch humbly up the stairs toward him. He walked between ranks of Griffiths's own TyRen guard; robotic warriors who, until recently, had been fanatics in the service of the Order of the Future Faith and their crusade to establish the supremacy of synthetic minds over humanity. Now, these self-same synthetics were equally fanatic in their devotion to Griffiths, a change of allegiance so sudden that it still made the ex-astronaut uneasy about just how permanent their allegiance to him actually was. Where once they had hunted him, now they guarded him night and day. They were fearsome-looking machines, headless torsos with multiple arms floating atop a metal sphere. Each arm bore a different weapon; each weapon a deadly statement in itself. Created by synthetics themselves, they were the ultimate in mobile destruction, fast and final. Now, today's duty shift floated without drifting as they formed a corridor up the stairs to Griffiths's throne. Though none of them moved so much as a centimeter, there was not a single person in the hall who doubted that they observed every motion with critical, fearsome, if invisible eyes.

The TyRen weren't the only eyes watching Griffiths. Between each of the massive mechanical warriors stood the statuesque and perfect forms of the prophet's own harem.

Griffiths frowned at the thought. When Merinda Neskat, the Vestis who had roped him into this, had mentioned that a harem came with the job, it sounded like a damn good thing. She had omitted a few details about this harem, however, which he fervently and angrily hoped to bring up the next time he saw her.

Griffiths pondered the power that he commanded and wondered how it was that he felt so trapped. Was it that the power itself became a trap? Was he chained to this throne by the very authority, so absolute and unquestioned, that he now commanded?

Well, authority didn't mean freedom, and he most certainly was trapped. He couldn't leave the planet without causing the entire population to pick up stakes and follow him. Worse, if he were declared a "mad" prophet, they would tear him limb from limb "for his own good." His only avenue of escape was a personal pilgrimage. However, he had not yet come up with any excuse for a pilgrimage that fit the detailed and stringent requirements of Irindris Law.

Trapped indeed.

Griffiths shook himself from his reveries—the old man had been speaking at him unnoticed for some time now.

". . . The many glorious streets of your recovered city, Your Most Excellent Father of the Clans," spoke the thin, ancient man from a face filled with utter rapture. "In doing so, Most Holy Master, I and my companions did discover many towers whose stores were filled to their uttermost heights with all manner of grains including the very blessing of the quantris seeds. Praise be to the gods for their foresight and wisdom, O Divine One, in providing to us their bounty in their infinite knowledge of all time . . ."

Griffiths, Grand Prophet and Father of the Irindris, gazed down at him nonplussed, his eyes almost glazing over. "Are you telling me you found granaries?" he inquired through a squint, trying to sort out some meaning from the thin man's gushing words.

"Yes, O Most Exalted One! Thou hast grasped the very essence of my dilemma, for which I have come before you this day in supplication . . ."

Griffiths held up his hand wearily, rolling it in a futile effort to get the man to move the narrative along more quickly. "Yes . . . yes, I get the point! You went out with a group of your buddies and found tons of this quantris grain."

"Yes, Master! And, as thou knowest . . ."

Griffiths winced. Damn these biolinks, he thought. They were miraculously good at translating languages. Indeed, he was certain, they were too good in most respects. Not only did the biolinks translate the meanings of the words, but they also put them in a social context that included inflections and body language. Quite amazing, he thought, until you were suddenly confronted with some nasty little aspects of them. The worst he could think of at the moment was that when he had at last spoken with all of these religious fanatics as their supposed prophet, he had fancied himself in one of those old Biblical epics his mother used to make him watch every Easter. Unfortunately for him, the biolink took that moment to lock the translation down between his own language and that of the Irindris. As a result, from that moment onward, every Irindris that spoke to him sounded as though they had just walked onto the set of Cecil B. DeMille.

". . . As thou knowest, the quantris is the blessed bounty from the stars themselves. The shell of the quantris is hard, Lord, yet its flesh within is sweet and most desirable . . ."

"Yes, yes, I get the picture!" The prophet shook his head, trying vainly to clear his ears of what he was sure were excess words. "You found grain in—surprise!—the granaries! So what's the problem?"

The ancient man shook his head solemnly. "O Exalted Prophet of the Stars . . ."

Griffiths shook his head violently. "No! What is your question?"

"Lord Master! What is your will that we do with it?"

Griffiths stared for a moment at the old man.

The old man stared back in expectation.

"What are you talking about?" Griffiths sputtered. "Is there something wrong with the grain?"

"Oh, no, Lord Master!"

"Is it edible? Can it be used for food?"

"Oh, yes, Lord Master!"

"Well? So, what is your question?"

"O Exalted Prophet of the . . . ," the old man began, but seeing the look on the prophet's face, he hesitated before changing his approach and going on. "Lord, we beg of you and the wisdom of your mantle: should we leave the grain as it is, cook it, or grind it into flour?"

"How the hell should I . . ." Griffiths caught himself and pushed down his frustration with effort. "Well, can we eat it raw?"

"Oh, no, Lord Master! Its shell is far too hard for such attempts!"

Griffiths could feel the heat rise again from the massive, pointed collar of his robes rapidly toward his ears. "Is it any good if it's cooked?"

"Oh, yes, Lord Master, although the dishes which are prepared that way are rather distasteful to the populace, whose vindictive nature would argue against such a course."

"Does it make a good flour?" Griffiths asked, beet-red-faced and barely controlling his words.

"Oh, yes, Lord Master!" the old man said sweetly, not comprehending the rage shaking the throne above him. "A most excellent flour!"

"Then," Griffiths said slowly between clenched teeth, "make flour!"

"Oh, My Lord Master of our People!" The old man was nearly in tears from his rapture. "Thank you! Thou hast confirmed our own thoughts on the matter and hast given us a blessing in thy wisdom! We praise thee and thy greatness forever more!" In a moment the old man knelt before Griffiths and grasped his fingers, weeping hot tears onto the back of his hand. "We praise thee and thy greatness forever more!" The old man, nearly in a swoon, turned and carefully walked down the stairs between the TyRen and past the line of supplicants that still extended back through the Nine Gates of Enlightenment. Each of them had their own question for the prophet and his great mantle—each, no doubt, as equally pressing as the old man's had been.

"God, how did I get into this?" Griffiths muttered to himself in utter misery. He propped his head up, his elbow resting rather uncomfortably on the jeweled arm of his glowing throne, and tried valiantly to stay awake. It was a battle he felt destined to lose. The mantle-crown pressing down on his head was heavy. The flowing robes gathered carefully around him were a little too warm for the room, he realized. Worst of all was the never ending line of supplicants droning on before him with whatever earth-shattering— *sorry*, he corrected himself—world-shattering question was so perplexing that it required an audience with the Prophet of Avadon, Voice of the Mantle of Kendis-dai. Occasionally their questions were worthwhile, he knew, but for the most part these people were too used to taking direction from their leaders and not thinking for themselves.

Well, he supposed, he had asked for it. His father, Admiral Samuel Griffiths, had been leader of one of the major Martian colonies and a pioneering name in that great effort. Interesting, Griffiths thought suddenly, that he never thought of his father without sticking Admiral in front as though it were part of his given name. He thought his father might have been christened with it. It had been natural enough for the old man to expect his bright if somewhat less-than-ambitious son to live up to the family name—including the Admiral part. His appointment and tour through Annapolis had been something of a foregone conclusion despite the best efforts of Cadet Jeremy Griffiths to do otherwise. Indeed, his graduation from that fine old institution had been something of a question mark and had required some influence by the Admiral just to get him through. Jeremy remembered again that he was "brilliant but undisciplined"—as his commander had referred to him when he went on report for the second time in his final semester. If he had not actually proved to be an aggressive and talented aviator, they might not have let him past at all, no matter what influence his father had applied. When at last his time had come to serve, the Admiral had seen to it that his boy Jeremy eventually got a plum command.

The plum command his father finally settled on was one of the Martian convoys. It would be a wonderful career mark for his boy, Samuel had decided. A little history was covered over or forgotten, the necessary transfers were arranged to get him into the rapidly expanding astronaut corps, and the promotions were worked out so that his boy could make the required rank of captain. Much to his father's dismay, however, the colony relief missions ended just after his boy entered the service—and Jeremy never saw duty on the convoys at all.

As it turned out, Griffiths loved being an astronaut. It was a great title to walk around with and Jeremy enjoyed training with all the exciting and fun toys of the space agency. He found the relaxed atmosphere fresh and exciting and actually began to excel in many areas of flight systems, propulsion, and even xenogeography. He was even named as backup RPV pilot for the first interstellar test of the Beltrane-Sachs parallel-space engine.

It's just that he never really wanted to go into space.

Then that idiot Colonel Murdock had to do something stupid and roll his aircar three weeks before the mission. Broke his left arm and crushed his left leg as well. Suddenly Murdock was out and Griffiths was bumped up to the prime crew. The Admiral nearly cried with pride over his son's final triumph of valor. Jeremy had been trying to impress the old man for as long as he could remember. It was the first time he felt he had actually done so—which meant, of course, that there would be no turning back. Before he could give it the thought it required, he found himself strapped into an acceleration couch drifting out of the Earth's gravity well and hoping like hell that the thing didn't blow up.

It didn't blow up, but it didn't exactly work either. No one could have suspected that the galaxy wasn't the homogeneously quiet place everyone had assumed. Nor had anyone, from the mission specialists, scientists, and design engineers down to the assembly workers and janitors at the Kansas First Contact Center, suspected that the crew of their history-making spaceship would fall into a flipped-out, upside-down galaxy where it was as out of place as a submarine in the middle of the Sahara.

And certainly no one, including the vaunted Admiral himself, would have ever believed that Captain Jeremy Griffiths, RPV specialist from San Diego, California, on an obscure and lost planet called Earth, would become the prophet-ruler of the fabled lost world of Avadon.

No, he decided, he didn't believe it either.

"Lord Father of our People!" resounded the voice of a priest below him, once again shaking him from his reverie. "I beg to present a supplicant—Two hundred and thirty-three! Come forward and hear the will of the prophet!"

Griffiths rolled his head back and looked above him. *It's your fault,* he thought, gazing up at the dim, shifting column of light above him. *If I hadn't sat on this chair and found you, things might have been different. I might be back on that saucer ship with the rest of my crew right now.*

Yes, came the thought unbidden into his mind as the Mantle-Oracle communicated with him through his thoughts alone. *And a great day that was for it is woven into your destiny. All that was before hinged on that moment—all that will be is forever changed by your act.*

So why must you always be so cryptic—Griffiths thought back in return. *Why must you always answer questions with this vague mumbo jumbo. You are supposed to be the all-seeing, all-knowing Oracle. Why don't you just answer my questions and get on with it?*

I answer as clearly as your language will allow, the Oracle replied. *Truth is not nearly so simple a thing as can be contained in linear language alone. The medium is not conducive to a precise defi-*

nition of the true state of any answer. Reducing truth to even the simplest of questions may take longer than your given lifespan will allow, thus the answers are couched metaphorically so that you might find your own way to the truth.

You mean, Griffiths thought back, *that you could tell me the truth but that I'd probably be dead before I understood it?*

The Oracle, whose cascading tumble of images within the column of its light seemed for a moment to fall more quickly, considered this for a time before answering. *Yes, I believe that is a reasonable model for your level of language comprehension. I would like to remind you that the supplicant before you has been speaking to you for nearly five minutes now.*

Griffiths shook himself and tried to catch up on the monologue being played out before him. Still, he couldn't help but ponder the things the Oracle had communicated to him. If truth is such a powerful and subtle thing, then, he supposed the whole truth probably wasn't for everyone. Some truths were better left unsaid. Some truths were outright dangerous and probably better left undiscovered at all.

. . . Like the truth of this Oracle, Griffiths thought with a sigh. Some buried treasures probably should remain buried.

He had no idea how important that single thought would become for him within the next fifteen minutes.

8

Tempered Edge

MERINDA NESKAT LEANED PEACEFULLY AGAINST THE BALCONY wall and gazed out over the magnificent city.

"Babo?" she called back through the arch behind her.

"I am Seven-alpha-three-five," came the voice in response.

"Yes, well, Seven-alpha-three-five, what's the status of the *Brishan* at this time?"

The TyRen floating in the great room just inside her apartments turned to her and spoke through the open doors. "Your starship, the *Brishan*, is currently being replenished for interstellar flight. Approximate completion time of this task number seven in a sequence of fourteen is estimated to be within the next seventy-three minutes. The remaining tasks are on track and are estimated to be completed within the next three hundred and forty-one minutes."

Merinda smiled easily to herself—part of her astonished at how easily she could smile these days. So much of her life had been wasted on the past and trying to atone for something that, as time had finally told, was not her fault. More than that, she had been a—how did Griffiths put it—pawn in someone else's manipulative game.

Pawn—that was something else that Griffiths had taught her. The expression had intrigued her enough that Griffiths had convinced the TyRen to manufacture a set of chess pieces for him and taught her that fascinating Earth game.

Not only was the game interesting itself but terribly instructive in its parable implications. Pawns were expendable. Pawns were weak. Pawns were often sacrificed for other, more impressive pieces. However, as she discovered, pawns who survived long enough to cross the board could be decidedly formidable.

Merinda gazed down the wide avenue of Aden city and could feel the world coming back to life. There were a few people walking down the broad, paved street, marveling at the soaring architecture of an ancient city now returned to life just for them. Several couples walked hand in hand under the warming sky. In the distance, she could see yet another of the massive Irindris transports settling in at the starport—its cargo of new settlers more anxious than ever to be welcomed to this Promised Land.

Yes, she thought, I am a pawn who has crossed the board but is the game yet over? That thought troubled her slightly, and she was annoyed at the thought that such peace as she had so recently attained could be disturbed so easily.

"Seven-alpha-three-five," she said, turning to face the TyRen warrior that now was not only her guardian but had become something of a companion as well. "When is Phandrith J'lan supposed to be here? He promised my orders were coming from Central. That officious little *drig* has kept me stuck here for the last fifteen days."

The TyRen raised two of its four appendages in a relatively good imitation of a shrug. Merinda chuckled softly to herself. The TyRen had been the fiercest warriors the Order of the Future Faith had to offer—they were indeed formidable mechanisms both in terms of their appearance and their capabilities. Created by the synthetic minds of the Order, they were pure machines of destruction: headless torsos with four mechanical arms floating in the air. Yet their intelligence had ultimately worked against the Order—and now the entire assault century that had been present when Avadon was awakened had changed allegiance. They were still fanatical, only now they were fanatical about protecting Griffiths and this world. Griffiths had assigned Seven-alpha-three-five—who had resisted all attempts she had made thus far to change his name to Babo—to watch over Merinda as her guardian. It had proved to be a pointless assignment. Merinda was a Vestis, after all, and certainly well capable of taking care of herself in even the worst parts of the stars.

Moreover, with the planet being populated by the Irindris—a deeply fanatical religious people—the most horrid crime committed in the last two weeks had been the accidental dropping of a cargo trunk on a neighbor's foot. The man who had dropped the trunk had settled this crime, however, without the need of a court system by a quick apology and a few days of concerted care.

Yes, she thought with smug sarcasm, I find myself in a real hothole of criminal iniquity. Good thing I've got my big TyRen brother to take care of me.

"I am sorry, Vestis Neskat," the TyRen replied to her question. "I have not had any further communication from Vestis J'lan this day, other than that you should prepare your ship for departure with all speed with—Just a moment."

Merinda turned her soft oval face toward the TyRen, her dark eyes suddenly focused and intent. Something was up. "Report."

"An unregistered human has been apprehended at the starport having landed without authorization. He seems to have put up something of a struggle against the TyRen at that location and has to have been forcibly subdued."

"Subdued?" Merinda's eyebrows shot upward. "Someone actually tried to fight off the TyRen?"

"Yes, Vestis Neskat. However, the TyRen were victorious in their conquest of the individual. He has demanded an audience with Emperor Griffiths at once and is currently being escorted there by a squad of TyRen warriors."

Merinda shook her head, tossing her long honey hair with amusement. "Poor Griffiths! His days are long enough without having to deal with some idiot free trader who wants to get the jump on commercial traffic to a new world."

She turned toward the wall mirror and gave herself the critical eye. Merinda's face maintained a neutral expression that many people newly acquainted with the Vestis Inquisitas took to be cold and unfeeling. She had to admit that more often than not they were probably correct. Members of the Inquisition were never known for their warmth of humanity. Getting the job done, one way or the other—usually the other, she thought ruefully—was what her calling was all about. Over the years the soft oval of her face had become a chilled blank to those who watched it, her small mouth bowed into a perpetual frown—and the dark eyes were cold as steel. It was a practiced look, which she had worked hard to acquire; it was now as much a part of her as breathing.

Yet something was missing in the face she had looked at so many times before. Hatred. She no longer hated herself. In her redemption, however, she secretly worried. That same hatred had given her the edge she used in her work. The great emptiness within her that could not be filled had driven her to the top of her profession. The hunger had made her great.

Now, she was experiencing something new—peace. The pain was gone and now she wondered if her drive had vanished with it. She may have gained her soul, but she wondered privately if she had lost her edge. Merinda eyed the cascade of golden hair that framed her face with a softness that she rarely displayed. Doubt still in her mind, she reached up and pulled it back tightly, methodically winding it back into its more usual, tightly controlled stalk that hung down her back.

"Babo . . . ," she said absently.

"I am Seven-alpha-three-five," the TyRen reminded her.

"Couldn't you just answer when I call you Babo?"

"I am Seven-alpha-three-five." Just that simple.

"Very well, Seven-alpha-three-five, do you suppose that Griffiths will need any help with this new individual?"

"I would think not. The TyRen are perfectly capable of handling security in this matter . . ."

"I've no doubt of that!" she laughed.

". . . And in any event, our records to date indicate that Griffiths considers himself to be on good terms with the Vestis Inquisitas."

Merinda turned from the mirror, still bringing strict order to her hair. "What did you say?"

"I said that Emperor Griffiths considers himself to be on good terms with the Vestis Inquisitas."

Merinda's eyes narrowed. Phandrith J'lan was the Vestis assigned to relieve her and keep an eye on things here on the planet—but he was registered with the TyRen. "Just who is this intruder?"

"He has identified himself as one Targ of Gandri, although his papers are not . . ."

"Targ!" Merinda cried out, suddenly shaken. "Targ of Gandri? E'toris Prime Targ of Gandri?"

"Yes, Vestis Neskat, that is the identification which he gave—is there something the matter?"

Merinda had already grabbed her cloak and was moving through the doorway by the time the TyRen recovered enough to follow her out of her apartments.

MERINDA RUSHED PAST THE PETITIONERS LINED UP IN THE CIR-
cular hall of the Supplicants' Walk, her progress unimpeded
by the TyRen located there to keep order. She passed
directly through the Fifth Gate of Enlightenment unchallenged. Seven-alpha-three-five floated behind her, his massive presence sufficient passport to his brother soldiers. Yet
even if he had not been present they would have let her pass.
She had proven herself a friend to the synthetic minds—the
synths, as they were more commonly called—and thus she
was worthy of their protection and honor as well.

Merinda didn't pause in her course. She quickly stepped
across the polished floor of the throne room. Even as she
did, she could hear the booming voice of the priest near her
cry out.

"Lord Father of our People! I beg present a supplicant—
Two hundred and thirty-eight! Come forward and hear the
will of the prophet!"

Merinda caught sight of a young man about to step forward with a sweet girl at his side. The Irindris often asked a
blessing on their marriage from their prophet—Griffiths
claimed it was one of the few things that he really enjoyed
doing in his new role—but Merinda thought that their
blissful happiness was just going to have to wait for a few
more minutes. She stepped quickly in front of them and,
without apology, began charging up the stairs two steps at
a time.

"Griffiths! We've got to talk!" she called out up the stairs.

The priests were horrified. Such a breach in protocol
could eventually cost them their positions and smacked of
sacrilege.

The young couple stood confused at the bottom of the
stairs.

Griffiths, who had been leaning his head on his hand, suddenly seemed to wake up on the throne above her. "Merinda!" he said with genuine joy. "I thought you were leaving! I had hoped that you would stay—I can't tell you how much this means to . . ."

"Quiet, Griffiths!" Merinda growled just loudly enough for him to hear. "Trouble's about to follow me into the hall."

"What?" the prophet-emperor of Avadon said warily. "What's coming?"

Merinda opened her mouth to speak but it was too late.

The doors of the Ninth Gate of Enlightenment suddenly slammed open, knocking several petitioners to the floor. The deep-throated rumble of the TyRen lifter drives thundered into the hall. Four TyRen warriors held a human above their heads, clad in a black jumpsuit. The hooded cape had fallen away from his head, revealing a brilliant mane of white hair above the strong, lined face.

Merinda closed her eyes. *It is him.*

The TyRen rumbled past the young couple still waiting, now doubly confused, at the bottom of the stairs. The priest standing next to them, his petitioner's book still open, was horrified at this new breach in etiquette and suddenly realized he didn't know the proper form by which he should lodge a protest.

The warrior machines deposited the gray-clad human, his arms pinned under his black cape, without ceremony ten steps below the throne. The man rolled quickly to his feet, his face a brilliant red in contrast to his white, and now disheveled, hair. Merinda had seen many moods in this man but had never seen him quite so completely frustrated and enraged.

"Lord Emperor," Merinda said, taking two steps down the stairs and gesturing grandly with her hand toward the newcomer, "may I present Vestis E'toris Prime Targ of Gandri, Master of the Inquisition and Voice of the Nine Oracles."

Targ looked up sharply toward Merinda at hearing his full title spoken.

"E'toris Prime," Merinda continued, her voice even and directed straight at the unquestioned master of her order, "may I be permitted to present Prophet-Emperor Griffiths the First, Lord of Avadon and bearer of the Mantle of Kendis-dai."

Targ turned to look at Griffiths.

To either side of the throne, twin TyRen guards instantly reacted, their eight arms raising upwards and forward, aiming their multiple weapons directly at the E'toris Prime.

There was something definitely wrong here. Merinda had been in service enough to know the smell of power being played. Targ was a formidable sorcerer and the quantum zone in which Avadon moved was absolutely rife with magical power—yet the man had allowed himself to be dragged here by the TyRen. She had to wonder: what would bring the head of the entire Omnet out into the wilds of the stars?

A moment passed in silence as both sides tried to evaluate their relative positions.

Targ spoke first: "Lord of Avadon, what might I be permitted to call you?"

Griffiths smiled tightly. "Well, I've been called a lot of things. Captain, Jeremy—and sometimes Jerry to my close friends . . ."

"As you wish," Targ said.

". . . But I think you should just stick with Lord Emperor for the time being," Griffiths finished through the same tight smile.

Merinda closed her eyes. She had yet to understand the humor of the Earthers although she had the impression from the others of Griffiths's former crew that they didn't understand his humor either. The emperor from Earth seemed to have a sense for the wrong thing to say. This was not going well.

"As you wish, Lord Emperor," Targ continued smoothly. The man had been in too many imperial courts—some of them run by people far crazier than Griffiths—to be distracted by Griffiths's peculiarities. "I demand to know the meaning of this attack upon my person! I am the Master of the Inquisition—an authorized diplomat of the Omnet—and I protest being treated this way."

"Your protest is duly noted," Griffiths continued with some caution behind the cool in his voice. "What is the meaning of your interrupting my loyal and patient petitioners?"

Merinda stifled a laugh. Griffiths hated dealing with petitioners.

"Lord Emperor," Targ said softly, "the Omnet has, for over three hundred years, been the keeper of knowledge and wisdom throughout the galaxy. We have sought diligently to uncover the secrets of the Lost Empire and to bring knowledge and truth to all sentients throughout known space. Ours has always been a mission of truth and knowledge."

"I am acquainted with both truth and knowledge," Griffiths said. "What does either have to do with your mission here?"

"Lord Emperor, with all due respect to you and your people, the Mantle of Kendis-dai is too large a project for you and your limited resources to properly administrate. The Omnet has been serving the Nine Oracles—synths from the time of your own Mantle—for centuries. Indeed, the Nine have directed me to come to your world and offer our services in administering and more properly utilizing the facilities which you have so recently and fortuitously recovered."

"Uh, I see. You mean to take the Mantle from me," Griffiths said so simply and sweetly that Merinda wasn't sure that she had heard the meaning of the words correctly.

"No," Targ countered. "The Nine Oracles have directed us to . . ."

". . . To steal the Mantle from me?" Griffiths offered, to conclude Targ's sentence.

Targ's face went hard.

"You know, people come to me all day and ask questions," Griffiths said, leaning back into the throne. "I think I'd like to ask them for a change. Tell me, Targ of Gandri, why is an entire fleet of Omnet ships now maneuvering over my world?"

Merinda looked back at Targ.

"Lord Emperor, the Irindris fleet has just narrowly survived the attack by the Order of the Future Faith. We have come to offer our assistance . . ."

"Your assistance is not needed, Targ of Gandri, nor that of your Omnet," Griffiths said evenly. "However, I don't think assistance is what you have in mind. An armed assault on our world would be foolish—you would quite possibly destroy the one thing you hope to gain—this very Mantle. Furthermore, the TyRen would quite effectively hold you at bay."

"Perhaps," Targ said slowly, the words forced smoothly between his teeth. "Yet I regret to inform you that your world has been quarantined until further notice. We may not be able to land on your world at will, Lord Emperor, but no ships will enter or leave without my permission. The Nine Oracles have decreed . . ."

"Liar," Griffiths said with a half smile.

Merinda caught her breath.

"You've come with a question that the Nine refused to answer; a question that you will convince me, bully me, or threaten me into answering for you."

Merinda blinked, shocked.

Targ leaned forward as he spoke in a steel-cold voice. "I will have my answer, Jeremy Griffiths, or I will see to it that this world is leveled so flat that not a centimeter of difference will remain in its circumference."

Griffiths leaned forward on his throne, looking down on the Vestis Prime. "And you shall have your answer, Targ of Gandri, but only from me—and only when I'm ready to give it."

Griffiths turned to Neskat and shrugged.

"Hey, they don't call this the Mantle of Wisdom for nothing!"

9

A Little Treason

"BY THE NINE!" TARG RAGED. "WHO DOES HE THINK HE IS!"

Vestis Phandrith J'lan struggled to keep up with the long strides of his superior. The Vestis Novus had only moments before learned of the arrival of the man he considered to be the single most important sentient in all the known galaxy. J'lan had been unsuccessful in his all-out, panicked attempt to get to the cathedral before Vestis Prime Targ. He had only arrived in time to be nearly flattened by the Ninth Gate of Enlightenment as the outraged Targ charged out of the audience hall. Now, as Targ slammed open the main cathedral doors, the young Omnet operative still didn't know what had happened or why they were being escorted out of the building accompanied by no fewer than six of the TyRen. J'lan had arrived late in many ways, it seemed, and had been trying to catch up ever since.

"Vestis Prime," the young man puffed, still out of breath from his dash to the cathedral. "The Lord Emperor is new and inexperienced. I'm sure that in time . . ."

"Time?" Targ roared as he abruptly stopped atop the cathedral stairs. J'lan passed him in his rush to keep up. "I don't *have* time, Novus J'lan! The Order will be filling these skies again with death in the next two days, maybe three on the outside, and this barbarian insists on playing word games with me! Me!"

J'lan skidded to a stop on the shining stone of the landing. "Vestis Prime, I'm sure that . . . ," J'lan began but Targ was already moving quickly down the steps. The Novus turned quickly in pursuit and tried again. "Vestis Prime, I'm sure that Emperor Griffiths will cooperate. I'll see to it that your wishes are conveyed at once."

"You do that," Targ said, not looking back nor breaking stride. "These clockwork-clowns," Targ gestured angrily at the TyRen surrounding him, "have been instructed to take me somewhere to 'cool off and calm down,' as your vaunted barbarian-emperor put it. You're the liaison assigned to this world. Go and liaise. But be sure you convey this to that pompous idiot on that mighty throne of his: I will have my answer within the day or I may just side my fleet with the Order when they show up. He'd best remember that!"

"Yes, Vestis," Phandrith J'lan said, stopping in the street and allowing the great Targ of Gandri to continue down the avenue under escort. He wasn't a timid man—no sentient was accepted into the Vestis ranks who was timid—but he was also smart enough to know that he was in way over his head. He hadn't a clear picture of what was going on here, and operating in the dark was never healthy.

He suddenly realized that Targ had not once used his actual name. Perhaps, he thought, the man didn't actually know his name.

Well, at least that was something to hope for.

THE IMPERIAL CHAMBERS WERE LOCATED IN THE EMPEROR'S Palace at the end of the Avenue of Tears—the wide street where Kendis-dai, as legend had it, walked in his final indignity to the cathedral before dragging his brother, Obem-ulek, with him down into mortality. The palace was a magnificent structure rendered in upwardly thrust curves of green marble.

Jeremy, perhaps uncharitably, referred to it as Oz, a reference that seemed to give the new prophet an amusement that not even Merinda could fathom.

The walls appeared seamless, although entrances did appear when requested by the TyRen guards, and one could view the city through sweeping clear panels that appeared only on the inside of the structure. Most of the magnificent rooms remained closed; indeed, much of the palace itself remained unexplored. However, the Irindris knew that their new emperor needed a fitting place not only to rest his head but also to receive emissaries and others on official business that could not properly be handled during regular court sessions. So the industrious fanatics of the stars quickly discovered the private rooms of the Emperor's Palace and set about making them worthy of their new prophet and his harem.

This all seemed like a good idea to Jeremy Griffiths, who thought that it sounded like a proper way to begin his reign on this world.

Thus he often found himself in the private reception room adjacent to his own private chambers. The room was small as things on Avadon went—a mere thirty feet in length and only about twenty feet across, its walls forming an oval. Numerous pillars standing five feet away from the wall supported an elongated, domed ceiling that could portray either soft colors or the sky outside at Jeremy's will. Inside the boundaries set by the columns was a sunken floor two feet below the room's perimeter, its polished surface inlaid with an artful rendition of the galaxy. At one end of the oval room stood the audience doors tooled with ornate bronze fittings; a set of similar doors closed off exits to either side. The Emperor's couch sat at the other end of the oval room on a platform, which projected slightly over the sunken floor. Beyond the couch were the final exit doors, which led to the private chambers of the emperor himself.

In the midst of this splendor, Jeremy Griffiths lounged on the imperial couch, only half-listening, it would seem, to the Vestis emissary.

". . . Must be aware that the master of the entire Omnet means no offense either to you or your people. He understands all too well your problems. Nevertheless his interests go beyond this single planet—this single people. His view encompasses an entire galaxy of issues, needs, and desires—a perspective which we must all honor and . . . and . . ."

Jeremy watched as the Vestis Novus began to sweat slightly. The emperor could see the young man's eyes looking beyond Griffiths to the three women of incredible beauty who stood statuesquely gazing at J'lan from behind the imperial couch. There were ten additional women in the room, five on a side, who stood between the pillars in perfect form. All of the women wore short, pleated tunics of an indefinable opal color fastened by a large medallion over the left shoulder, their perfect arms bare. All had extraordinary long hair carefully and meticulously woven into single long stocks extending to the middle of their backs. Their skin tones ranged from a deep chestnut to nearly translucent pale and their facial features were equally varied. The only things they seemed to have in common were their manner of dress, their undeniable perfection of physical form, and the fact that each had a huge, hulking TyRen floating directly behind her.

Jeremy smiled. It often happened this way when males visited him here: the fear of the TyRen mixed with the longing lust for the women of his harem was, Griffiths admitted to himself, something of a calculated means of keeping callers more than a little off-balance. It certainly seemed to be working in J'lan's case.

"And . . . ," Griffiths offered, almost helpfully.

"And . . . ," came the dubious response. J'lan had obviously lost his place.

"Targ's view encompasses a galaxy of issues and perspective which we must all honor *and* . . . ," Jeremy coaxed.

"*And* respect." J'lan was openly sweating now.

I wonder if this guy is ever going to make it past Vestis Novus in the Inquisition, Jeremy wondered to himself. "I honor Targ of Gandri and his unique perspective; it truly covers the great width of the galaxy today. I on the other hand have the unique perspective of time down through the ages at my disposal. I'm new to the galaxy. I come from a world which is not known to anyone—including, it would seem, your own Omnet. I don't know much about your universe—but the Mantle gives me access to a perspective over three thousand years deep. I know Targ has come to ask a question. Is he prepared to use force to obtain it?"

J'lan stiffened. "Lord Emperor, no one wants such an event—but he did tell me to convey that he would side with the Order of the Future Faith in the coming conflict rather than not obtain the answer he needs."

Jeremy snorted. "I rather doubt that. Nevertheless tell your master that he shall have his answer—tomorrow at court."

J'lan frowned. "I do not think he is so patient for his answer."

"Perhaps not, but my hands are tied. My access to the Mantle is restricted by the customs of my people and I cannot give him an answer until regular court session tomorrow morning—late in the morning. Such is the word of the prophet."

At the uttering of the last phrase, two of the women from the harem stepped forward and gently took J'lan by both arms. Jeremy could see that the man had more words to speak, but he had heard quite enough. It was far beyond time to end this farce. He watched quietly as J'lan was escorted out of the room. Griffiths did not move until the great doors were closed behind the exiting Vestis Novus.

"Amandra?" Jeremy spoke quietly.

"Yes, Lord Emperor," came the quick reply from the tall, dark woman immediately behind him. Griffiths turned on the couch to see Amandra kneel in her matchless splendor before him, her black hair shining in the soft light of the room. Amandra was first wife of the harem, and it was through her that Griffiths's commands were most commonly carried out.

"I think," Griffiths said, as much to himself as to his first wife, "that our friend J'lan and Targ both would bear watching until afternoon court tomorrow. Make sure that I'm not disturbed by either of them until then, OK?"

"As you wish, Lord Emperor."

"It is my wish," Jeremy said, gazing sadly at the incredible beauty presented before him. "It's time to secure my chambers and get everyone back to their own quarters."

"Yes, my Lord Emperor."

Griffiths watched miserably as the incredible assembly paraded out of the room to either side. It was some moments before the women left through the doors to his left and the TyRen rumbled out through the doors to his right. Amandra left last, exiting through the far doors to check on the watch stationed beyond before returning to her own chambers for the night.

Finally, he was alone.

Griffiths groaned, collapsing on the couch in a most undignified manner, his arms falling limply to either side. He lay on his back, staring at the ceiling.

"God, I hate this!" he yelled into the dome overhead.

"Hate what?" The voice cut the silence behind him.

Griffiths, startled, fell off the couch onto the polished stone floor. "Damn! Merinda! Don't you people ever knock?"

Neskat leaned against the frame of the door to Jeremy's private rooms. "No, Griffiths, we never knock. We're the Inquisition—didn't you hear? Everyone has the free will to run the galaxy the way we want them to. That requires no tact."

"So I've noticed," Griffiths groaned, rubbing the elbow he had banged when he fell to the marble floor.

Merinda was wearing her cold, Cheshire-cat smile. "So, what do you think of our Vestis Novus, the great Phandrith J'lan?"

"J'lan? The man's an idiot—nearly as big an idiot as I am," Griffiths said shaking his head. "Hey, that reminds me! Why didn't you tell me about the prophet's harem?"

Merinda raised an eyebrow in feigned surprise. "Tell you? Why, I thought you were the big expert on the Irindris?"

"Yeah, right!" Jeremy scowled. "Some old geezer Vestis saves my bacon . . ."

"Zanfib," Merinda said quietly.

"Right, Zanfib." Griffiths rolled his eyes at the name. "Zanfib, wizard deluxe, saves my bacon then goes and dies on me. He kisses me on the forehead and dumps his mission memories into my unwilling head. Thanks. Thanks a bunch."

"Hey," Merinda smiled, "it made you what you are today."

"Yeah, well it didn't clarify this whole harem thing!"

Griffiths was venting his frustrations on her. She supposed it was best just to let him get it over with.

"Did you know that the prophet is supposed to be big-time morally clean—including completely celibate?" Griffiths roared.

"Well, there may have been a few details that I forgot to mention . . ."

"A few details?" Griffiths's voice broke with his rage. "I'm surrounded all day by the most gorgeous women on the planet—my own supposed wives—and I'm not allowed to so much as drool. I suppose you knew that this so-called harem is supposed to be in charge of safeguarding my purity? Every last one of them is stronger than I am. They're all supposed to have been trained in some form of scary martial art that could kill a man and about thirty other types of creatures I've never heard of in no fewer than seventy different ways—not that I'd ever be that lucky. No! The harem is the traditional guards' organization for the prophet. Everyone else they kill—me, they just torture."

"What about the TyRen? If your harem is such a powerful force, why are they still around?"

"They insist." Griffiths shrugged. "Both the harem and the TyRen are convinced that the other isn't trustworthy enough to keep me safe. At least the TyRen aren't so concerned about my chastity, but the harem never leaves me alone long enough with anyone to even make pleasant conversation."

"Well," Merinda said softly, "we're alone now."

Griffiths looked up, surprised. Yes, he thought, he certainly did want her. Merinda was beautiful but in a way that he had always thought unattainable for someone like him. She wasn't fragile—God knew after all they had been through he could never consider her remotely frail in any of her aspects—but she had a refinement that always seemed to make him feel a little awkward and somehow less than he wanted to be. She always had him off-balance.

"Yes," Griffiths said, smiling shyly and relaxing at last. "I wonder why my harem would allow that?"

"Because, barbarian," Merinda said, sweetly reaching out and patting his cheek, "they know that there is no possible way that your chastity is endangered by me."

Slammed again, Griffiths thought. I could really like this woman if I didn't hate her so much. "Thanks, Merinda, that's cute. Really cute."

"Oh," Merinda pouted with a light twinkle in her eye, "poor barbarian . . ."

"I wish you wouldn't call me that," Griffiths said shaking his head.

". . . Ruler of the planet and so unhappy. Speaking of which"—Merinda's tone suddenly took on the razor-blue edge that meant business had begun—"just what was that all about in the Chamber of Wisdom today? You do know who Targ of Gandri is, don't you?"

"Yes, I do." Griffiths felt like he was in school, being lectured. It was not a comfortable feeling—he had never cared for school. "Targ of Gandri is the supreme director of the Omnet—your great news and information organization that seems to want to control everything in the galaxy—although for the life of me I'm not sure why. The Omnet never seems interested in acquiring any planets or suns or any real regions of space. You do seem interested in telling everyone else who owns planets or suns or any real regions of space what they should know, how they should think about it, and when they should think it, however—and I suppose that's more than enough conquest for one organization."

"You're rambling, Griffiths," Merinda said dispassionately. "Targ is second only to the Nine Oracles in his authority. It is the wisdom and insights of the Nine that have directed the Omnet down through the last three centuries to become the force for truth and the rediscovery of knowledge throughout the galactic disk. Only one man receives their instructions on a regular basis and that's Targ. Targ is the will of the Nine . . ."

Griffiths shook his head. "You don't get it, do you? Targ isn't acting for the Nine now—he's acting on his own."

"That's not possible," Merinda said flatly. "The Nine Oracles have stood at the pinnacle of the Omnet for the last three hundred years. No one has remotely challenged their supreme authority in all that—"

"Until we did—two weeks ago," Griffiths interrupted.

"What?" Merinda blinked.

"Our last little adventure had more far-reaching consequences than just setting the Order back on its heels. The synthetics were hoping to discover whether they had free will or not. The Order was using that quest as an excuse—preaching faith to synthetics so that they could control them toward their own ends. So long as the question of whether synthetics had free will or not was open to debate, the Order could frame the argument as a matter of faith and maintain control over the synthetics."

"True," Merinda nodded, "but all that ended when you activated the Mantle of Kendis-dai and were able to answer the question."

"Right, but in doing so we not only answered the question for many of the synthetics of the Order"—Griffiths nodded—"we also answered the question for the Nine Oracles as well."

"Of course, that was all part of the mission the Nine gave me when I—" Suddenly, Merinda's eyes went wide. "By the Nine!"

"Yes, by the Nine indeed," Griffiths agreed. "In answering the question, the Nine Oracles learned that they, being synthetic minds as well, were subject to the free agency of biological sentients. They therefore deemed themselves subservient to the will of biologicals—and ceased to function as supreme leaders of the Omnet movement itself."

"They—resigned?" Merinda was stunned.

"Yes, I suppose you could say that."

Merinda began pacing about the room, her hands animated as she spoke. "But that would mean chaos! The Nine weren't just another set of synths; they were—are—the very symbol of the Omnet! Without them control would break down, faith in the news service alone would suffer irreparable damage. It would so greatly weaken the network as to call into question whether the Omnet could function with any power or authority at all anymore! It would mean a tremendous power vacuum at the top of the organization."

"It would if anyone knew."

"What do you mean?"

"I mean," Griffiths replied, for once feeling glad that he could tell Merinda a thing or two, "that no one other than Targ—and, of course, you and I—know about it. He's kept it all very cleanly under wraps although I don't know for how long that can last. He's certainly moving very quickly—I think he's trying to accomplish whatever he's up to before anyone finds out."

"How do you know all this?" Merinda said, still having difficulty believing what she was hearing.

"The Mantle," Griffiths replied simply. "It is the master synthetic mind, remember, and is now in direct contact with the Nine Oracles—although for the life of me I haven't a clue as to how it does it. Targ approached the Nine with his question and the Nine deferred the question to the Mantle since the Nine couldn't answer it. The Mantle dutifully asked for my wisdom on the subject—and I told the Mantle to deny the answer to Targ."

"*You* did that?"

"Well," Griffiths said modestly, "I told you they don't call it the Mantle of Wisdom for nothing. The Mantle is great at handling information. It gives whomever sits on the Throne of Kendis-dai a perspective on the universe that is as informationally complete as I think exists anywhere. However, it defers actual judgment on those matters to the biological on the Throne, which in this case was me. I smelled a rat, and cut off his access to the Nine."

Merinda stopped her pacing and blinked for a moment. "I take it that the smell of rats is a bad smell?"

"Oh, yes, very bad, indeed," Griffiths replied.

"So, then, what is he up to?" Merinda asked, rubbing the back of her neck as though it might dislodge some new thought. "Why isn't he back at Central trying to work out a new power structure instead of dashing about the stars?"

"I think our answer is in his own question. He wants to know the navigation course of the Lokan Fleet."

Merinda's head snapped up, her eyes locking on Griffiths's own. "He's looking for the Nightsword?"

"Yes, where Lokan hid it three millennia ago," Griffiths responded, and pointed to the dome overhead. The galaxy appeared in the dome, brilliant in its spiraling stars. " 'It came to pass that in the first cycle following the fall of Kendis-dai, Lokan, servant of Kendis-dai, proclaimed himself the Emperor Priest of Avadon. In the mantle of his office did Lokan go before the people, having been proclaimed their new Lord, and spoke unto them great words that they might follow him and fulfill the desires of the great, lost Kendis-dai.' "

"You're quoting the *Odyssey of Tears*," Merinda said as she gazed up into the dome.

"Yes, chapter seven," Griffiths responded. "It's amazing what you can learn around here. The important part is after that, however, as you probably know. 'Now so it was that Lokan was a mortal man whose lusting for his Lord's queen consumed his soul while his physical shell belied it not. Black was his heart yet his countenance was bright before the sight of man. The vestments of his office still shone with the faith of the nation that followed him yet his heart served only himself.' "

Griffiths gestured with his right hand and a bright red line etched itself across the stars. " 'So it came to pass that Lokan proclaimed with flattering words to the people the will of Kendis-dai to be fulfilled: that according to his word they would embark upon a great journey into the wilderness of the sky that they might hide up in the blackness thereof the ensigns of their master's power and wreak justice among the servants of Obem-ulek. Standing upon the Temple steps, he held aloft the Nightsword of Kendis-dai, holy and terrible in its power and aspect, great is its Name in its ordering of the stars and mighty is its power in bringing the will of Kendis-dai among the heavens. Whatsoever its bearer willed was so, for the edge of its blade was bright to the cutting of all that was and bringing to pass that which its possessor desired.' "

" 'Whatsoever its bearer willed was so,' " Merinda repeated. "Chapter seven, verse four. You are really up on your ancient history for a barbarian, Griffiths."

"Well, I've done a little study lately," Griffiths replied offhandedly. "I've also noted that most of the emergence of human races in the galaxy seem to stem from this same time period.

"Prior to the Lokan Crusade, humanity was a statistically minor race in the galaxy. True, Kendis-dai was human, as was much of his court. He ruled most of the galaxy but it wasn't until the Lokan Crusade that the religious texts began talking about human supremacy and something called 'Purification Quests.' "

Merinda nodded. "We know those as a great series of wars. Conquests more than quests, really, as Lokan passed through the stars toward the galactic core."

"It was more than that." Griffiths swept his arm across the illusionary starfield overhead. The galaxy was suddenly a rainbow of different-colored stars. "Each color is a race prior to the crusades. Now, here's the distribution today."

The stars shifted quickly to subtly different positions, with great swaths of them suddenly turning a brilliant blue.

"Humanity!" Merinda murmured.

"Yes—humanity," Griffiths sniffed. "So effective was this change that in my own travels, limited though they have been, I haven't met a single truly alien race."

"You think there's a connection?"

"I *think* that Lokan was a racist," Griffiths replied. "I think he used the Nightsword to enforce his own ideas of human supremacy on the galaxy at large."

"What kind of power could possibly do such a thing!"

"The same power that Targ is trying to secure for himself," Griffiths said, banishing the galactic map with another wave of his hand and restoring the clouds that had previously occupied the dome. "If he obtains it before the galaxy is wise to him there's no telling what he's capable of doing."

"Then we've got to get the word out!" Merinda said indignantly. "Transcom to every node on the net!"

"Oh, wake up, Merinda!" Griffiths snapped. "Targ owns the net! He killed your story about Avadon and the Mantle being discovered . . ."

"*What!*"

"Killed it. Dead. It never went out. Now he's wrapped up the entire planet under his 'protective' fleet." Griffiths shook his head. "We're on our own, on this one, Merinda."

Neskat hesitated—something which Griffiths couldn't recall having seen before. He supposed it made sense; Griffiths had just told her that everything she had supported in her work had just turned on her. At the least it would require some major shift in her thinking.

"Can you keep the information from him?" she asked at last.

"Well, I could lie to him," Griffiths offered, "but he doesn't trust me as it is. The truth is I have no idea what it is that he has in mind. He obviously needs leverage on me of some kind but it's hard to imagine just what form that leverage would take—what could the man possibly have on me?" Griffiths shrugged. "Most likely, no matter what I tell him, he'll find an excuse to invade the planet. In that case, he might try to ransom the populace for the information he wants. I know these people, Merinda. They'll fight him to the last soul. A lot of people would die, Merinda, just to delay him for a few days."

"I can't believe he's capable of that," Merinda said, shaking her head, "but he's lied to me, Griffiths—and he's never done that before either."

"Hey, I can't believe we're even having this discussion," Griffiths countered with a sly grin. "Still, I have a solution that may well satisfy a number of different problems. It has certain risks, but I think the payoff is well worth the price. We don't really know what he's up to, but I think with a little effort on our part, we might just figure it out. So . . . do you mind talking a little treason?"

Merinda folded her arms skeptically across her chest. "I'm listening."

10

Old Wounds

MERINDA STEPPED INTO THE DARKNESS. THE ANTECHAMBER had been lit only with candles that flickered in the uncertain draftiness of the ancient rooms. She was not afraid of the darkness—time had taught her well that that there was nothing in the darkness except an absence of illumination. Things could hide in the darkness and often did, but in Merinda's experience they were seldom more dangerous than when they were lit. A trained Vestis viewed the loss of sight as simply a way of making the game more interesting for the other senses. Indeed, she had come to view the darkness as a friend.

The room she entered was chill. She could barely make out the dim outlines of the three archways leading to the balcony. The sky had grown dark as it did each cycle, bringing night to the world on schedule. Just as there had been no sun to brighten the light of Avadon's day, so, too, there was no moon to bring light to her night. Only the cold and distant stars gave any brilliance to the streets of Aden, and sparse it was. Merinda could barely make out the diaphanous curtains shifting in the evening breeze. All other features of the room lay in a uniform blackness.

Still, she knew he was here.

"I have come, Targ, by your word," she said quietly, announcing herself to the darkness. "I enter and serve."

"Vestis Merinda Neskat," floated the disembodied voice from the darkness. "So you have, indeed."

Silence fell into the darkness.

Merinda was wary. Vestis Novus J'lan had managed to keep her on Avadon longer than her assignment had required. She had even thought to file a complaint against the little zealot until Targ had shown up. It was obvious to her then that the whole thing had been arranged by Targ so that this meeting could take place. Now she couldn't be sure. She was here, there was minimal risk—what was he waiting for? What was he trying to accomplish?

"Targ, my mission here is fulfilled." She was stating facts that Targ certainly already knew but hoped that recapping them would somehow spur her superior into conversation. "My last report was filed over a week ago to, what I hope, was a satisfactory conclusion. I am preparing my ship . . ."

"Satisfactory conclusion?" Targ's voice rumbled through the darkness.

Bitterness, Merinda heard through his tone and the rustling of his suit in a nearby chair. Bitterness and, perhaps, contempt . . .

"Satisfactory conclusions. Now that's an illusion, isn't it?" Targ sniffed. "A happily-lived-forever that the storybooks always are telling us. Netcast entertainments, each with their simple little problems that come to their own satisfactory conclusions within their allotted time. Problem solved. They all lived happily forever after. People don't want to know what happens after the last page is read or the telepresence sensors are shut down after the credits roll. Do they think about the heroes who return from the wars to face the crushing mundaneness of day-to-day life? They do not. So the old warriors, like you and me, keep telling the old stories because their endings make everyone happy—even when we know that they never end—not really."

Merinda cocked her head. What was the old man talking about? Careful! "Is the Omnet displeased with the outcome of my last report?"

"Outcomes?" the voice laughed. "You aren't listening to me, are you. Outcomes only lead to other outcomes. There is no end to the story, Merinda. Life continues after the story ends. The report is wrapped. The netcast is trans-commed. The public interest wanes—but the lives affected go on. Their pain endures long after their story is told and forgotten."

The curtains drifted in the chilling breeze. Merinda shivered. She had always considered her ultimate master a cold individual, she thought ruefully, but this? Targ had always been a no-nonsense director of all Omnet operations. Merinda had risen in the ranks of the Inquisition to a post that was nearly as high as the Council itself and, theoretically, there were few people who actually stood between Targ and her. She hadn't always agreed with everything that the man had initiated but his actions had always made some sense in the end. He had the big picture; she didn't. He gave the orders; she obeyed. Things were that simple—or had been before now.

"Vestis," Merinda said cautiously. "The *Brishan* is ready for flight, supplied and prepared for departure. If there is something which you feel is left undone in this assignment, then give the word and I shall see to it."

A shadow arose before her in the room. Targ had been seated closer to her than she had assumed. Now his form seemed to fill her vision, uncomfortably close. She could feel the heat of his breath. "Yes, Merinda, there is something you will do for me—you will close a story whose end was written long ago and whose fate binds us both. Its course was determined in the ancient past and its ends foreseen, written in stone and the stars."

Merinda looked up into the shadowed face looming over her, a well of darkness without depth, a soul suddenly open to her and without a bottom.

"We will play out that fate, Merinda, you and I, to its own ends—until nothing is left undone, Merinda . . . Until nothing more is left to be done."

"Then start talking sense, Vestis Targ," Neskat said, fighting the urge to take a step back from the silhouette towering over her. "What is it you want me to do?"

The silhouette hesitated. It was only a moment but that moment communicated much to Merinda. Targ had never been unsure of anything during all the time Merinda had worked for him—directly or otherwise—yet he faltered now.

Targ turned from her, looking away from the gaze that he could not possibly see. It was another reaction that spoke volumes to Merinda. Body language symbology was a basic teaching of the Vestis. Surely, she thought, Targ was better trained in its technique than anyone in the Inquisition was. Yet he was allowing himself to be read so easily. Either Targ's posturing was intentional, or the head of the Omnet was so distracted by something as to forget one of the most basic teachings of their entire Order.

Targ moved as though to gaze out the starlit curtains.

"I want you to finish what you have started," he replied simply.

"And just what is this thing that I am supposed to have begun?" Merinda asked in level tones.

"You opened the door on the past," Targ replied, his voice belying his mind's reflection on distant places and times. "The knowledge of the ancients is opened to us— with it comes the key to their power as well. The Oracles knew it from the beginning. It is why the Nine created the

Omnet—not just as some news and information agency, but as the vehicle for the return of the power of the past! They waited until fate's passage was fulfilled. Now, through your efforts, the time of fate has come."

Targ turned toward her, the dim light of distant stars shining in his wide, liquid eyes. "Imagine it, Merinda! The glory of Kendis-dai restored to the galaxy. All the stars under a single order: a single will! What great things could be accomplished should that power be centered in the right hands? What horrors would be loosed were it to fall into the wrong hands?"

Merinda's lips pressed into a thin line before she replied. "And just which of those hands are yours, Vestis Targ of Gandri?"

"My hands?"

He replied too quickly, she thought. He anticipates too much. Without thought, the natural suspicion that lies at the heart of all Vestis asserted itself. For the first time she questioned whether the Vestis Prime, supreme master of the order that she so faithfully served, was telling her the truth.

"No." He shook his head.

He's lying, Merinda realized with sudden, shocking certainty.

"It is the will of the Nine Oracles, not mine, that dictates this course. The Nine have spoken and I am bound to do their bidding in this matter. They have been quite specific. The passage into the galactic core has remained a mystery since the time of the ancients. We must recover that knowledge and we must use it to recover the Nightsword of Kendis-dai. Should the Order of the Future Faith recover it first, then all our gains thus far could easily be wiped out in a single stroke. For that matter, should any organization of any kind obtain it before us, it could represent a disaster of incalculable proportions."

Merinda drew her breath in before she spoke. "Targ, I still don't see why you have to be the one . . ."

"I *must* be the one to enter the core," Targ said with finality. "I must. It is our fate, Merinda; the Nine have proclaimed it so."

Targ smiled.

Merinda smiled back in the darkness.

"Then, Targ," she said casually, "if you will excuse me, I have a ship which needs loading. If we are to meet our destiny, then I'd prefer to meet it well prepared."

With that, Merinda turned. She walked casually out of the room—despite every desire of her soul to run.

TARG STOOD IN THE DARKNESS, WATCHING AS THE PORTALS AT the far end of the antechamber closed behind Merinda's retreating form. The opening had barely whispered closed when he spoke.

"Vestis J'lan?"

The lean silhouette of the Vestis Novus stepped into the room from behind the balcony pillar that had thus far concealed him.

"Yes, Vestis Prime," J'lan said, without the confidence that Neskat had demonstrated earlier. "I enter and serve."

Targ sighed into the darkness. "You are certain she visited the barbarian earlier this evening?"

"Yes, Vestis, she was already in the chamber when I called upon the prophet earlier. She was hidden, sire; invisible for all others—nevertheless, she was there. You don't suppose the two of them are working together do you?"

"Neskat and the barbarian?" Targ snorted. "She wouldn't let him breathe long enough to get in her way."

"What are her intentions, then?"

"She intends to fight me," Targ said evenly. It was

impossible to read any emotion in the statement. "She intends to stop me."

"Perhaps not, sire," J'lan replied behind him.

"You do not know her as I do, Vestis. She believes she knows the truth. The truth is something that Merinda Neskat never lets go of once she believes she has found it."

The wind softly drifted the curtains behind them.

"She is a threat to the Omnet, Vestis J'lan."

"Sire?"

"Sometimes we have to do things in the Inquisition which are distasteful, Vestis. Such things nevertheless must be done for the good of the whole. Here," he spoke evenly, "is a teleport amulet. It's small and will not encumber you in your task. It is linked to this second amulet that I wear. When I have my answer, I'll activate my own amulet and join you at the starport, where we shall both leave this world together."

Targ turned toward the Vestis Novus.

"As Vestis Prime of the Omnet, may I be the first to congratulate you on your new promotion, and on your captaincy of the *Brishan*."

J'lan stammered slightly. "But—Vestis Neskat is the captain of the *Brishan* . . ."

"You were not chosen for this assignment at random, J'lan. I picked you myself. You were never exceptional in your general training but there was one particular discipline at which you excelled." Targ's low voice seemed to carry uncomfortably far in the still air. "You understand me perfectly, do you not, Vestis J'lan?"

"Perfectly, Vestis Prime," J'lan answered evenly though his mouth was dry as he spoke the words. "But . . ."

"Are you questioning my directives, Vestis Novus?"

"No, Prime, I am not questioning your directives."

"Then you will see that they are carried out without hesitation or delay," Targ said stiffly. "The fate of the entire Omnet can rest on the shoulders of a single Vestis at any given moment, J'lan—this moment it rests on yours."

J'lan did not dare move. "I will not fail you, Prime Targ of Gandri."

Targ moved behind the terrified Novus, his lips sneering as he whispered into the young man's ears. "No, J'lan, you most certainly will not."

BETA:

SHADOWS

11

Misdirection

MERINDA STOOD ON THE CARGO DECK OF THE *BRISHAN*. IT WAS late—late enough to qualify as very early—and she knew that she was tired. There would be time for rest later, she told herself.

Merinda leaned against a power conduit snaking through the enormous hold and disappearing behind a hulking alternate-spatial displacement drive. She studied her surroundings with no small satisfaction. Once again, Merinda smiled to herself, she had managed to pack the three-deck-tall open space with nearly every conceivable drive and power system that could fit within. She hoped that she could use them to plot a course through all the varied possibilities that would lie between her ship and its objective. Part of her doubted; she had never before attempted such a lengthy journey on a single load before. Indeed, the ship's specifications flatly said that it could not be done. Merinda didn't like being told what was possible.

The TyRen floated nearby in perhaps the only available open space, its four arms working smoothly over an object held in a stasis field before it.

"Babo?"

"I am addressed as Seven-alpha-three-five," the warrior returned without missing a beat in its fluid motions.

"Of course you are," Merinda sighed. "Seven-alpha-three-five, how much longer until you will be finished with this?"

"The current project, barring additional interruptions or supply difficulties, should be completed in two hours, seventeen minutes, forty-three seconds from my mark. Mark."

Merinda strolled tiredly over to look into the stasis field in which the TyRen was working. She wished she had had more time to come up with something a bit more elegant and a little less complicated. Yet, as Griffiths had said, their time had about run out.

"Who are we using for the synth?" she asked quietly.

"Seven-gamma-six-nine has volunteered for this glorious duty in defense of the emperor," the TyRen responded.

"Lindia," she said to the room in general. "What is your opinion of this?"

The ship's omnipresent synthetic mind responded at once in a cool female voice. "The workmanship is impressive and I believe the unit will function as per the stated specifications."

Merinda rubbed the back of her elegant neck. "Yes, it will function, but will it work?"

"Humans are chaotic creatures, Merinda," the disembodied voice resounded. "Their actions are not predictable with certainty."

Merinda looked down at the deck for a moment before she continued. "Lindia?"

"Yes, Merinda. How may I serve you?"

Merinda smiled tiredly to herself. Lindia had been the shipboard synthetic mind for as long as Merinda had captained the *Brishan*. She realized that the synth was not sentient, as she had so recently and rather dramatically proven, yet there was something comforting about Lindia. The synth had been more of a real companion to her over the years than any flesh and blood creature had been. Woman and machine, they had shared much in their time together. Certainly, she thought, that counted for something.

Yet now Merinda couldn't think of the words to express herself to this, her only real friend. So long had the fires of self-hatred and blame burned within her that their sudden absence had left her with a quiet relief that was uncomfortable. She knew with true *Vestis* instinct that real danger was near. Now the anger and the rage that had once given her a keen edge in battle were no longer there. More baffling to her yet was the fact that its absence didn't seem to concern her. She felt weary and serene. Perhaps it is time to stop running, she thought. Perhaps the chase should end . . . one way or the other.

"Lindia," Merinda said, her voice somewhat thoughtful and subdued. "We have gone through a great deal together, you and I. The universe is changing quickly now and in ways that I don't yet understand."

"Do you wish an explanation of the universe, Merinda?"

Merinda smiled. "No. I just want you to know that whatever happens—I am at peace now for the first time. Today was a good day for me. Just remember that whatever happens to me in the future, that today, for one great moment, I was at peace."

"Yes, Merinda, I will remember."

THE SKY OVERHEAD WAS LIGHTENING SLOWLY. CLOUDS WERE building off in the distance, evidence that weather was soon going to assert its chaos over the quiet world of Avadon— and, more particularly, the city of Aden. The world had taken on a delightful soft pinkness before it drifted fully into the light of day.

Phandrith J'lan stood perfectly still before the entrance to the ship, belying the nervousness that threatened to overwhelm him at any moment. He had studied the techniques at the Citadel, of course, and had been somewhat masterful at disguising his emotional state—a must for any successful Inquisitor. He had imagined himself standing before the courts of the Ruqua emperors, being an inscrutable blank canvas upon which the rulers whose courts he visited could imagine whatever emotion they wished. Such ability to hide one's true aims was essential to the mission of the Vestis Inquisitas, for it allowed them to put on whatever face was necessary to get the job done at the moment.

Yet nothing he had trained for had prepared him for what he was facing now. Ethics had not been part of the training.

There was, indeed, as Targ of Gandri had stated, one thing at which he had excelled during his studies—the question now was how to apply the knowledge and the skill effectively. He had stood in the cold for some time pondering that question. Long-range, of course, was the preferred method in delivering death in any quantum zone. Hit your target from a distance as quietly and as effectively as possible. However, long-range was not possible since his target was most likely to remain inside and could not be counted on to move out of her ship with any kind of reliable timing, if at all.

The job would have to be done inside the ship at close range—a fact that presented a whole additional set of problems. The target was somewhat older than J'lan but certainly in every bit as good of shape. Further, she was far more experienced than he was, giving her all the advantage in a straight-up fight. There hadn't been enough time to establish any kind of trust between them. It was impossible, therefore, to depend on betrayal to strike when the target's defenses were down. That normally would limit his attack to some sort of explosive device or temporal bomb. His orders, unfortunately, had been rather explicit on that account.

Besides, such devices might damage the ship itself—a ship which he had been promised on his success.

So much for a simple little remote murder.

He moved through the mystical scenarios, discounting each in its turn. The Portable Hole. The Djinn's Curse. The Ship in the Bottle. Each possible spell tumbled through his brain, was examined and discarded. In the end he determined that there was no help for it but to walk into the ship and do the deed himself with a quick and effective weapon.

He looked down under the brightening sky at the slim device in his hand. The curving glass of the blade ended in a slim hilt and triggered grip. It was an elegant weapon, traditional for assassins. The T/S kris was small but quite effective. It was easy to conceal and operated well in mystic zones. All one need do to activate it was to grip the handle. That act depressed the arming trigger under the palm. The kris utilized a temporal singularity running the length of the curving glass blade. As the edges of the blade existed in another time, the blade could penetrate even the most determined body armor. All that was left at that point was to release one's grip from the arming trigger to free the temporal singularity. The alternate time sphere would then quickly expand to collapse the target's internal organs into an alternate timeline. The device was highly discriminatory and most intelligent. J'lan slipped the kris into its robed sheath and patted the grip lightly with affection. Considering the skill of the target, he knew he would only get one chance to be effective, but one would be all he would need.

Strange, he thought behind his impassive mask, that he was already thinking of her as "the target"—some disconnected thing rather than a fellow Vestis. It wouldn't be the first time he had killed on behalf of the Omnet, but never had he attempted anyone quite so skilled and never before one of his own Order. It occurred to him fleetingly that from this time onward, he, too, would need to be on his guard, lest the duty which caused him to become the hunter somehow cause him in turn to become the hunted. Yet, he was still a youth and, as such, thought of himself as superior and, somehow, immortal. Some part of him whispered, however, that he would most likely never see the light of another day . . .

But then, neither would Merinda Neskat.

TARG WINCED AS THE TRUMPETS BLARED THROUGH THE TOWering Cathedral of the Mantle for the third and final time. He stood at the bottom of the great staircase. He had never had much use for ceremony and this one struck him as no different: a show more for the benefit of the crowd than for the honoring of their adored prophet. Well, he thought, that would soon have to change.

The crowd cheered and Targ winced again. He could see over their heads the parting of the assembly, opening the way to the base of the stairs as, at one side of the circular chamber, the lofty Ninth Gate of Enlightenment swung slowly open.

Let them enjoy the pageant, Targ thought. There's more show yet to come.

"VESTIS NESKAT?"

"That depends," Merinda said casually, standing at the top of the *Brishan*'s airlock ramp.

"I am Vestis Novus Phandrith J'lan," the youth smiled with practiced casualness. "I am currently the Omnet emissary to Avadon."

"Ah," Merinda replied flatly, "so you're the *drig* that's kept me here for the last two weeks."

"Well—yes, I suppose so," J'lan continued as smoothly as he could. "I bring the compliments of Vestis Prime Targ of Gandri. He asked that I deliver to you this baton of passage as you requested. Sorry it's taken so long—some kind of mix-up at the Citadel on Deveron IV."

Neskat smiled, taking the ornamental baton and unrolling the scroll affixed to it. She continued to study it as she spoke. "Hmm. A writ of galactic passage—a bearer writ at that. It's about time. Convey my compliments to Vestis Prime Targ of Gandri. The ship stands ready at his pleasure to depart whenever he wills it—though I wonder if he will have any real idea where we should steer it. Still, knowing Targ, we'll be going nowhere as quickly as possible."

Merinda glanced up from the scroll at the sudden chuckling sound.

"Am I that entertaining, Vestis Novus?"

Patience. She is not close enough, J'lan thought. I must get closer. Patience is always the hardest part. He shook his head, the smile still playing at the corners of his mouth as he spoke. "Sorry, Vestis Neskat. It's just that—well, you paint a very clear picture of the Vestis Prime. He does seem in an awful hurry to get wherever he's going."

Merinda nodded absently, barely hearing Phandrith's remarks as she scanned the indicators projected before her from the baton. "Thank you, Novus, everything here appears to be in order."

Merinda turned and stepped back into the airlock.

Patience—must get closer. "Ah, Vestis Neskat?"

Merinda turned around, her eyes coldly critical. "Yes?"

"Well," J'lan stammered, looking down at the ground and blushing. "It's just that—well, I've been an admirer of yours for some time now. I've studied your netcasts over the Omnet. I hope someday to be as professional as you in my own work."

Neskat nodded, her eyes still critical. Her words came out flat and cautious. "Thank you, Vestis. High praise indeed."

She turned again.

"Er, Vestis Neskat?"

Again she stopped and turned back to him.

J'lan shrugged disarmingly. "Look—I've discharged my duties to Targ and kept you here as ordered. I'd like to give you a hand with your flight preparations—with your approval, of course. Truth is that I'd like to see how you've loaded out your ship for the voyage. I'm sure it will help me later—you know, when I've got my own ship."

Merinda's eyes were fixed on him, as though trying to see into his soul.

"Please," he smiled shyly. "As one Vestis to another?"

Merinda's face softened slightly. "Very well, Novus. You may come aboard—but stay out from under my feet. I've no time to give you a tour."

No, Merinda Neskat, J'lan thought as he stepped up the airlock ramp, you have no time at all.

THE ANJEW FLEW INTO THE CATHEDRAL OF THE MANTLE AND again the cheers of the assembled supplicants rose to greater heights than before. Drums beat into the hall at the head of the procession which, finally, had arrived.

Targ was having difficulty seeing around the massive Thought-Knights standing in honor between him and the path of the procession itself. He had no idea which legion the knights had come from and couldn't care less. Indeed it suddenly occurred to him that this entire procession was buying Vestis J'lan the time he needed to get aboard the *Brishan.* Merinda Neskat was a good Vestis and would most likely obey his will as she had always done in the past—still, it was always a good idea to back up one's faith in others' loyalties with something more substantial than goodwill. This time, the mission went beyond loyalties. This time . . .

The orchestra was marching into the hall. He could see that beyond them the flower petals were being cast into the air. The prophet of the Irindris would enter the hall at any moment. He would ascend the stairs and court would begin.

At that moment, Targ thought, the years of planning would end. There would be no turning back. The life he had so carefully groomed would be put behind him. His fate would become as certain as the pathways of the stars themselves. Already he could feel the tide of events he had set in motion carrying him forward, sweeping him toward that destiny with increasing power and authority.

The thought drifted into his mind that he might still be able—even then—to stop what he had begun. He dismissed the notion at once. His vision of the future engulfed his will. In that moment, it truly was too late and his course was set.

MERINDA MADE HER WAY THROUGH THE MAZE OF TUBING, conduits, and mystic transfer coils that choked the cargo deck, her mind racing through a mental gymnasium every bit as complex as the eclectic machinery around her.

This Vestis Novus Phandrith J'lan was about as subtle as a bruk discharge, she thought. His stammering flattery was dreadfully transparent, but his motives were not yet as clear to her. Targ was up to something; something that she knew was contrary to the general interests of the Omnet. This little visit was almost certainly part of it all. The problem for her was—part of what? The pieces were alarming enough in their details but did not yet present a clear picture. She could not take what she had thus far to the Dictorae—there just was not enough factual basis to accuse Targ of anything more than doing his job.

Merinda stepped carefully around a low-mounted transfer coil, ducking to avoid the overhead locking mounts as she made her way across the deck. She could just make out the port-side hatch that led to her quarters and the bridge. She felt certain that when they reached the control compartment this whelp would make his move. Perhaps then, she thought, she would have her answers. It was always a tricky business, she thought, knowing just how much cable to play out to an opponent: too little and they never make their move; too much and they will take you down whether you suspect them or not. One day, she might just judge it wrongly. One never recovered from such mistakes—indeed, one seldom even knew what had killed them.

Merinda noticed a conduit snaking loosely across the deck. She turned slightly. "Watch out for this . . ."

J'lan was already near.

Merinda felt the searing pain enter her left side. Her turn had somewhat spoiled J'lan's grip on her. His left hand had not been able to get a proper hold on her and his leverage was bad. Still, he had momentum on his side and the blade slid smoothly upward, its curved edge grating against the lower side of her ribcage.

Unable to get the grip he wanted, J'lan pushed forward with his legs, using his weight to drive the blade home.

Adrenaline surged into Merinda's body. Instinct and training seized control of her actions. She reached across with her right hand, clawing for the weapon that had violated her so terribly. Her hand closed like a vise over J'lan's.

Howling in rage and indignation, Merinda tripped backward against the loose conduit. She fell, her back thudding against the deck plates. J'lan fell on top of her, his weight driving the blade up through her lung.

Merinda struggled despite the blinding pain. Her left hand flashed upward, crossing J'lan's face, and her palm smashed his nose. The Novus growled through the pain, struggling against Merinda's grip on his hand and desperately trying to let go of the blade.

Kris! Merinda's mind screamed into her consciousness.

Merinda's left hand reached down quickly, trying frantically to add its strength to her right hand. The wave-edged blade turned within her. She screamed again but held her grip fast, knowing and fearing what would happen if she allowed J'lan to let go.

She suddenly stopped struggling, though she held her grip tight. She realized that she had already lost a great deal of blood. It was getting hard to focus on the impersonal face of J'lan so horribly close to her own. She knew the battle would be lost soon, one way or another.

"Why?" she rasped.

J'lan's eyes focused on her as though he were suddenly aware that there was a person beneath him. "It is a Vestis honor to die for the Omnet. This is nothing personal, Neskat. Better you should die than the entire Omnet be destroyed."

She spat blood in his face.

A rush of motion descended from above.

J'lan glanced upward but had no time to react. The metallic appendages slammed through the air with the sound of a sudden wind. A cobalt-blue arc cut neatly through J'lan's right forearm, severing it entirely a hand's width above the wrist. Three more appendages reached down an instant later, two of them coiling around the neck of the shocked Vestis Novus, while the third wound about his left arm. With a sudden rumble, the appendages contracted, lifting J'lan clear off the floor.

The entire action had taken less than a second.

Merinda slammed her eyes shut against the pain, pulling the kris blade free of the gaping wound in her side, her grip still closed over the severed hand of Vestis J'lan.

"Thank you, Babo," Merinda said, staring with unfocused eyes up at the gasping Vestis.

"I am Seven-alpha-three-five," the TyRen intoned, floating upside down among the conduits, which looked very much like himself. "It is my honor to do my duty, Merinda Neskat. I am grieved to have arrived too late."

"We've got to get . . . got to get Griffiths out of here." Merinda shuddered under the pain. "Seven . . . Seven-alpha-three . . . five. Get Griffiths off-world now!"

"Merinda Neskat, you are my priority," the TyRen stated calmly as he held the Novus suspended in the air. "You are in need of healing assistance at once. Further, I am occupied by this assassin at the moment."

"Not for long." Merinda pressed her left hand against the wound in her side. She rolled slowly to her knees, then staggered to her feet.

"As you said, Phandrith, one Vestis to another," Merinda said, gazing up at the Vestis Novus hanging above her. Her words were obscured by the frothing blood in her throat. "It is a Vestis honor to die for the Omnet—in your case, it would be an honor to die by your own hand."

Merinda thrust the kris upward into J'lan's chest.

She yanked his severed hand free of the hilt.

"Nothing personal, J'lan."

The darkness engulfed her. She never felt the deck when she fell.

12

Fatal Assumptions

THE FLURRY OF FLOWER PETALS SETTLED SOFTLY TO THE ground as the twenty priests and priestesses who held it aloft lowered the massive Throne of the Wandering Prophet to the ground. The cheers of the assembled crowd were deafening, echoing up into the vaulted heights of the cathedral.

Targ heard nothing. The sights and sounds receded from his conscious thought as his mind focused on the object of his current quest. No, he reminded himself, not the object of the quest but the place to begin, the start of the road, not its end. He watched as Griffiths, looking a bit paler than usual, moved down from the throne covered in flowing robes of honors.

The rush of connecting flights and passages from Omnet Central out further onto the disk had taken its toll on Targ. He had arrived tired and he knew it. The quantum zone that Avadon was currently in had been determined to be high on the mystic index—magic was something that he was very good at even without the enhanced skills and knowledge of a biolink mission loadout from the Nine. Yet magic in this particular index was a matter of personal strength and the accumulation of mystical energies. One had to be rested to use the power here. The power would last only as long as one could physically maintain it. So, convinced utterly of what it was he had to do, Targ had bided his time since arriving. He had called the power into himself—as this zone required—and had felt it seep into him hour by hour. He was far from filled with the glorious force but he believed it was enough. Just enough.

The object of his will was drifting up the stairs to the Throne of Kendis-dai itself, the very seat of the Mantle of Wisdom.

"Lord Father of our People!"

Targ turned toward the deep, resonant voice. The priest at the base of the stairs stood next to him, his words resounding throughout the chamber. It had taken considerable effort, but Targ could not be delayed. Through whatever means necessary he had made his way to the front of the long line of supplicants.

The pageantry was finally over, Targ thought. Now destiny begins.

"I beg to present a supplicant—Six hundred and seventy-three!" the priest's voice intoned. "Come forward and hear the will of the prophet!"

Targ moved forward and began climbing the stairs toward the throne high overhead. Glancing upward he saw the images of light weaving their constant motion in the towering column over the throne. The Mantle of Kendis-dai. Targ smiled softly to himself. It was time.

The Vestis Prime looked down at his hands, hoping he appeared humble and submissive. His lips moved in silent words, however, as his hands worked close together before him. Climbing higher and higher with each step, Targ watched with satisfaction as a small ball of dim, blue lightning formed within the cup of his hands. The mystical structure completed, Targ folded both hands together at his waist, hiding the rotating globe of static fire as he climbed the last few steps to stand just before the level of the throne itself.

"Greetings, Lord Emperor," Targ said smoothly.

"Greetings back at you, Targ of Gandri," Griffiths said somewhat stiffly, his voice sounding tired and more nasal than Targ remembered it.

"Lord Emperor, are you not well?" Targ inquired with grace.

"I had a rough night, Targ of Gandri. Didn't sleep well."

"I hope," Targ bowed slightly, "that my presence and the quarantine of your world is not the cause of such personal distress."

"Thank you, Targ, but I don't think you bother me one way or the other. Truth is that I think I'm coming down with a cold. I could use some rest—perhaps if we could postpone our interview here until tomorrow . . ."

"No, Lord Emperor, I don't think that would be possible," Targ smiled.

"My, my! Aren't we the impatient one? Fine, then, so you want the navigation charts of Lokan's fleet. It's a bit complicated but I could try to describe . . ."

"That won't be necessary," Targ replied quietly, stepping up onto the high platform itself, closer to the prophet.

"Not necessary?" Griffiths arched an eyebrow.

"No—perhaps yesterday if I had found you more stupid than you are we might have worked something out. You think, however, that you are clever. There is nothing so dangerous as a stupid man who believes himself to be clever."

"Oh, cute," smirked Griffiths, deflecting the insult with apathy. "So yesterday you did want the navigation charts and today you don't?"

"No, Lord Emperor. Having refused me yesterday, I didn't think you would give them to me today. More than that, even if you did give them to me, I could not trust that you gave them to me correctly. Most likely you would simply lie to me."

"You know, our relationship really needs a lot of work." Griffiths leaned forward on the throne. "So I have a question for you, Vestis Prime, head-honcho of the Omnet. You came all the way here to ask me a question, now you don't want to trust the answer that I give you. Just what are you after, Targ?"

"Why, you, Lord Emperor!"

"M-me," Griffiths stuttered.

Targ smiled. "Yes, barbarian. You."

In a swift motion, Targ threw the blue lightning ball from his hands. Instantly, the ball expanded, lightning playing along its surface, until it formed a shielding dome around both the Vestis and the startled Griffiths. The TyRen standing at the perimeter of the throne were suddenly pushed backward. They reacted in the following moment, rushing against the shield. Each point of their contact flared with brilliant blue light and crackling streaks of electricity. The TyRen readied their weapons at once but wavered for a time—uncertain as to whether the shield would deflect their various murderous bolts and do harm to the prophet himself.

The assembled crowd gasped in fear below. The Thought-Knights broke ranks and began charging up the stairs.

The thunderous clamor barely penetrated the interior of the force dome.

"I asked you the question while you were on the throne—you could not help but pass it on to the Mantle in that same instant and get the answer as well. You know where the Lokan Fleet went—you can't help but know."

The TyRen opened fire with various weapons on the shield with ever-increasing strength. Their impacts made only distant echoes to the two inside of it.

"Sadly, barbarian, the Mantle by design will only communicate with one sentient being at a time. Even as I state it, you know that it is true. You see . . . I can't trust you to give me the right answer. I need to get the answer directly from the Mantle itself. So long as you live, the Mantle will never communicate directly with anyone else."

Griffiths's eyes went wide. "Oh, shit."

"So long as you live"—Targ smiled again—"I'll never get the answer I need and you'll always be a threat to me."

Targ raised his left hand, his fingers arched into claws pointed directly at the prophet's heart.

Griffiths yelled as he tried to stand up. "Damn it, Merinda! Get us the hell out of . . ."

The bolts formed at Targ's fingertips, joining together instantly in a massive spiral of blinding light. The twisting shaft slammed out from his hand, ripping the air with its passage and boring directly through the chest of Griffiths, whose mouth snapped open in a silent scream. The orange glow of the magical column widened within Griffiths until it occupied a full hand's width of his chest. The power of the bolt continued through the prophet's back, tunneling completely through the back of the Throne of Kendis-dai until finally stopping just short of the frantically flashing shield itself.

The Vestis Prime released the spell.

Griffiths fell forward, rolling slightly as he fell. He came to rest faceup on the floor. Stench-filled smoke drifted from a gaping chest wound so thoroughly cauterized that no blood flowed from it.

Targ barely heard the roar of terror and hatred beating against the shield. He was sweating now, the exertion of keeping the shield maintained and the murder of the prophet having drained him considerably. He had calculated that, he told himself. There wasn't much time before the raging TyRen outside the sphere would finally beat it down. He had to finish before then.

Stepping over the smoldering Griffiths, Targ took a deep breath, turned, and sat on the Throne of Kendis-dai.

What course did Lokan's fleet take, Targ thought. He had addressed the Nine long enough to know that the question always triggered a response. The Mantle had responded to Griffiths's question in like manner. Now it would respond to him.

Targ of Gandri . . . came the voice into his mind.

Targ smiled, his eyes closed.

. . . *You will need to ask your question of Jeremy Griffiths.*

Jeremy Griffiths is no more, Targ thought toward the Mantle of Kendis-dai. He pushed down the panic welling up inside him. *You will answer the question.*

You are mistaken, Targ of Gandri.

What!

A different voice sounded in his ears. "You are mistaken, Targ of Gandri."

Targ's eyes opened and turned toward the sound.

Griffiths, chest still smoldering, turned his head toward him and spoke. "You are mistaken."

Targ pushed himself suddenly out of the chair, grabbing the remains of Griffiths's robes as he knelt. "You're dead, damn you! You're . . ."

Only then did Targ examine the chest wound carefully. To be sure it had passed completely through the body—Targ could see the floor beyond—but the wound itself was filled with protruding metal, broken servomechanisms, cabling, and optical conduit.

Targ tore open the robes frantically, sweat pouring from his forehead.

Two of the arms had been removed but the body itself was unquestionably that of a TyRen warrior.

The replicated head of Griffiths, mounted atop the torso, turned toward Targ and spoke. "Targ of Gandri, you are under arrest by TyRen Seven-gamma-six-nine for the attempted assassination of Griffiths, Lord Emperor and Prophet of Avadon . . ."

Targ stood up, fumbling in the folds of his robes for the transport amulet. He gripped it with both hands to activate it.

Nothing happened.

The blue dome about him was losing color. It was getting smaller. He found it hard to breathe.

He pressed the amulet again.

Nothing.

"By the Nine," Targ gasped.

". . . As such, you will remain under the protected custody of the TyRen until arrangements for your hearing can be made. I have been instructed by the Emperor that you are to be kept safe from the outrage of the populace and treated with respect. He also instructs me that neither of these goals will be easily accomplished."

"Where is he?" Targ growled.

"He has just passed out of range of our telepresence connection."

Targ sat on the throne. Someone had moved Griffiths out of range. Someone had moved the matching amulet out of range as well. Someone had crossed him.

Merinda.

"You will surrender at once," Griffiths's head said at Targ's feet.

Targ bent over on the throne. The dome was closing in on him. Beyond its vague blue outlines he could see the TyRen completely encircling its perimeter, each continuing to press against the shield. Beyond that he could see the hate-filled faces of the petitioners who had stormed the pedestal.

Targ shook with the exertion of holding the shield in place.

There was no place left to run—but he would never surrender.

13

Reversals

INTERSTELLAR VOID.

The word "void" was appropriate if not accurate. The cold emptiness that sat between the burning suns was not completely empty, of course. A few stray atoms drifted lazily through the region. Light energy passed through its expanse unheeding of its dimension and rushing to vacate the space it had just invaded. Such epic events were beyond the sight of an eye or the contemplation of the mind. The scene surrounding it was breathtaking but so, too, was the void itself, for it would rob breath from a living being without a thought, scattering the molecules explosively throughout its entropic volume until the gas had lost any hope or meaning to the sentient creature robbed of it. The void was beyond measure: all things that passed through its infinite space were made insignificant in scale. The void was forever: nothing within its folds outlasted it.

Of course, the interstellar void wasn't entirely universal—in an infinite universe there was infinite diversity. There were uncounted regions in uncounted quantum zones of existence where the void was filled with all manner of interesting things. Some were gaseous and easily breathable. Some were charged with electricity or phlogiston or ether.

Some were entirely aquatic. Yet in this particular zone the stars burned with fierce and steady intensity in the blackness of space—empty and unforgiving.

Scale demands perspective in such infinity and depends greatly on where the observer chooses to stand to bring any meaning to their observations.

Thus, should an observer have been stationed at this particular point of space within the unendingness of the universe, deep between the points of light that gave reference and meaning to the darkness, they would have seen a single discus just over a hundred feet across spinning in silent majesty through the void. The craft gave the appearance of being assembled from a series of different-sized brass dishes—two large ones mounted top to top forming the main body of the ship with two smaller ones bracketing them. The ornate carvings that covered the exterior of the larger disk spun around its axis in purposeful stability while the smaller disks—one above and one below—emitted a pulsing blue glow. The observer would note its incredible speed relative to the stars about it and its purposeful progression toward the distant stars.

He would also note the same craft slamming to an impossible stop, flipping end over end in a blur, stopping once again and then resuming its previous speed without a hint of acceleration. This was followed by a succession of impossible high-speed, right-angle turns which seemed to delineate the outlines of a box before the ship tore once more through space, this time at right angles to its original course as it corkscrewed down its line of flight.

LIEUTENANT ELIZABETH LEWIS, COMMANDER OF WHAT SHE had referred to as "my flying saucer," was beginning to feel slightly motion sick.

The thought angered her. After all the spins she had taken in the NASA trainers, after all the parabolas she had flown and all the disorientation training she had taken in the orbital station back on Earth, she had convinced herself that motion was her friend. She had reveled in it. There hadn't been a roller coaster or cloud coaster at any amusement park on her world that she couldn't tame with a full stomach of bad hot dogs and carnival drinks. Motion, she believed, was her element.

This ride, however, was just a little too much.

"Ellerby!" Lewis choked out. "Stop! Just . . . just stop for a moment!"

"Yes, sir, Lieutenant," Ellerby said at once. The large man released his grip on the control protrusions from the console.

The universe around them began to settle at once.

Thank God for inherent stability, Lewis thought to herself, closing her eyes and hanging on hard to the edge of the console as she waited for the stars to stop revolving around her. After interminable moments, the whining of the ship's drives began to subside overhead.

With minor trepidation, she slowly reopened her eyes. "Is everyone all right?"

Lewis caught the eye of Marilyn Tobler just around the left side of the large glass globe mounted in ornate brass in the center of a wide pedestal. Tobler's face was drained of color but she nodded nonetheless.

"Well," said Ellerby. Lewis could see his slightly unfocused gaze around the right side of the globe. "*That* was quite a rush!"

The universe once again looked safe and, more importantly, stable. Lewis's hands were still gripping the edge of the circular console that was the centerpiece of the command platform. Three clusters of chairs were arranged in groups of three at uniform points along the console's outer edge. The entire assembly sat atop a platform in the center of a slightly compressed sphere. Overhead, a mammoth sphere, matching the one surrounding the console, hung suspended at the focal point of three large cones imbedded in the curve of the ceiling. The platform itself was accessed by three long bridges, each leading to hatchways out of the command sphere and into the labyrinth of the rest of the ship.

Lewis had taken a position at one of the chair clusters, while Lieutenant Ellerby and Dr. Tobler had taken a position at each of the other two. They were three people attempting to run controls designed for nine.

The problem was not that the ship was difficult to handle. Indeed, once Lewis got used to the idea of talking to the ship's newly installed synthetic on a friendlier basis, the ship itself seemed rather pleased to assist in any way that it could. The problem was that the ship was an ancient relic—a ship of the Lost Empire. Its design was unique in the galaxy for it was set up within its hull to handle, in various configurations, every different quantum zone that the ship had encountered thus far. Lewis had expected to encounter some difficulties along the way but, as Mevin, their resident synthetic, had so cheerfully informed them, the ship had yet to encounter any zone which some configuration of its systems could not handle—including many of the magical zones. The ship seemed capable of handling any contingency, but that made its capabilities more than Lewis or any of her fellow crewmen were ready to handle. There were just too many options available.

The console itself was the mounting for a large globe that appeared to be made of bluish glass. The myriad controls that were arrayed on the slanting surface surrounding the globe changed from zone to zone as the ship's configuration changed. Sometimes a control yoke would form out of the console surface. At other times the yoke would melt back into the flat panels only to reappear as a crystal ball or, on one particularly discomforting occasion, a set of humanoid hands.

The real problems cropped up, however, when they entered certain quantum zones that weren't as easily handled as others were. Straight subspace or hyperspace zones were relatively simple for the ship to transit and the controls for the ship were fairly straightforward. This was also true of several of the highly mystical regions they had crossed, where entire other mechanisms emerged from the walls and converted the control sphere into some sort of sorcerer's workshop and they directed the ship by waving their hands through the air in strange patterns. The problem was when zones were mixtures of both the technical and the mystical in a variety of shades, flavors, and mixtures which required all kinds of handles, dances, levers, incantations, knobs, and at least twelve more hands than were available at the moment.

Lewis stood up from the chair, stretching on uncertain legs to try and push the stiffness out of her muscles. "What say we don't try that again right away. Mevin?"

"Yes, Lieutenant Lewis?" came the voice of the synthetic mind from seemingly everywhere in the room at once.

"Is the ship stable and stationary?"

"Yes, Lieutenant Lewis. The ship is stationary and stable relative to the motion of the local stars."

"Great—now all we need to know is where the hell are we," Lewis said, reaching up to rub the bridge of her nose tiredly.

"We are the hell in deep space with the nearest inhabited system being the hell five light years coreward at the hell Leuken system," Mevin replied at once.

"Really, Elizabeth, if you're going to teach the synth to swear, you at least could do a proper job of it," Ellerby said, rubbing his own temples.

"I think it's disgusting," Tobler chimed in, perhaps a bit too seriously. "Mevin's only been awake for seven years. I think you're a bad influence on him, Lewis."

Lewis eyed the brown-haired Tobler as though the doctor had just grown flowers out of both ears. Tobler hadn't been quite right ever since their fine little NASA spacecraft had been brutally boarded by the Irindris what seemed like several lifetimes ago but which, in reality, must have only been a few weeks. She had shown signs of instability then, but Lewis was pretty sure that the woman had gotten over it. Now that surety was waning.

"This isn't getting us anywhere," Lewis said with finality.

"On the contrary," Ellerby said with a sepulchral voice heavy with his own depression, "I thought we were making tremendous progress for being completely lost."

"We are not completely lost!" Lewis leaned over the console and stabbed at a few display protrusions. The room around the platform dissolved into a sphere of grids, stars, symbols, and flashing lines in various neon colors. The course lines were three-dimensional with several of them seeming to pass directly through the air over the instrument panels arrayed before them. Lewis's voice was pointedly triumphant. "See!"

Ellerby raised his head with considerable effort. "Lewis . . . where are we supposed to be?"

Lewis looked up at the chart drifting slowly around them.

"Over there," she said, pointing her right hand at the flashing blue hexagon floating at the end of a deep purple line nearly off the chart.

"And where are we now?" Ellerby sighed.

Lewis squinted slightly as she considered the charts.

"We are here," she said, pointing with her left hand. A red box at the end of a yellow line flashed at the opposite extreme of the chart.

"Exactly." Ellerby nodded wearily, his eyes unfocused as

his brain idled in its own misery. "Right in the middle of Lost. Well, perhaps not exactly in the middle . . . We might be just left of Lost . . . Or perhaps a few miles off a vector from Lost . . . But I'm sure we're pretty close to Lost, wherever we are."

"Hey!" Lewis said, her voice half-cheerful and half-pleading. She knew it was time to rally the troops. "This is a mission of exploration! We're still astronauts and we still have a job to do! We're Earth's ambassadors to the stars. We have a duty to return home and report, to bring back the knowledge we have gained."

" 'Earth's ambassadors to the stars'?" Ellerby repeated in disbelief. "Is that what we were doing on that planet last week? We landed our ship right in the middle of their harvest festival!"

"That was no one's fault," Lewis countered, showing an edge of anger that was never very far from her surface. "The approach sensors said it was an open field—who knew it was a flat tent?"

"They were awfully nice about it," Tobler said more to herself than anyone else. "I thought it was sweet the way they all bowed down and worshipped us."

"They weren't worshipping us," Ellerby corrected wearily. "They were worshipping the saucer."

"I don't know why any of us should feel embarrassed about that," Lewis snapped. "No harm was done. The point is that we had landed for fresh provisions—perhaps it didn't go exactly as we had planned but we did get some very nice fruit out of the deal."

"The point is," Ellerby shot back, "that we haven't got a clue just where the hell we are going! Not only do we not know where we're going"—the frustrated astronaut pointed at the diverging and rather convoluted course lines on the chart—"but we can't even get where we want to go in search of where we're going!"

Ellerby had spoken with such conviction that Lewis took a moment to consider his words carefully, somehow convinced that he had actually said something meaningful. After a moment's careful reflection, however, she realized that he had not. The exercise left her disoriented and confused.

"So," Lewis said after a moment to regain her mental balance, "just what would you propose, Lieutenant Ellerby?"

"I don't know!" Ellerby shouted, "but anything has got to be better than just bouncing from star to star hoping to run into our little planet out there!"

"Better?" Lewis shouted back. "Perhaps you would like to send out an SOS over your little Boy-Scout shortwave radio set . . ."

Tobler's voice was quiet. "Well, maybe we could . . ."

Lewis was in full tirade now: she didn't even hear Tobler. ". . . Or perhaps you would like to flag down a passing spacecraft with your towel . . ."

". . . Er, I heard that might work in some alternate quantum indexes," Tobler persisted in trying to cut into the conversation, "but what I really had in mind was something simpler . . ."

". . . Or perhaps," Lewis continued venting at the reddening face of the large man before her, "you would like to consult some crystal ball for a heading and direction, Mister Ellerby, big shot astronaut . . ."

Tobler tried raising her voice a little more. "Actually, that would work on the last planet we visited, but what I actually thought was . . ."

". . . But until you come up with something better than what I'm offering . . ."

"Lieutenant Lewis?" Tobler insisted.

"*What!*" Lewis screamed.

The sound shocked Tobler so badly it made her flinch. For several moments the only sound in the command sphere was Lewis's ragged breathing.

Lewis regained control of herself, took a deep breath and spoke as evenly as her breath would allow. "Dr. Tobler. What do you want to say?"

"I've been thinking . . . Well, I just think we should ask for directions."

Lewis was suddenly convinced that this poor woman standing before her had, indeed, gone completely over the edge of sanity. In sudden compassion, Lewis put her arms around the woman and patted her on the back as she spoke kindly into her ear. "Tobler . . . Marilyn . . . we can't just pull over to a gas station, dear."

"Well, I know that!" Tobler said with indignation as she stood awkwardly in Lewis's embrace. "I mean, why don't we just ask Griffiths?"

Lewis still held the woman but suddenly quit patting her soothingly on the back. "Griffiths?"

"Of course, Griffiths!" Tobler said. "He's the one who talks to that Mantle of Wisdom device. He said himself that it's as old as that Kendis-dai legend they kept talking about . . ."

Lewis's eyes went wide. She looked with sudden enlightenment at Ellerby.

"My God," Ellerby murmured. "She's right! That synth does date back to Kendis-dai!"

"And Kendis-dai knew where Earth was!" Lewis suddenly smiled. She grabbed Tobler's head with both hands and planted a kiss on her forehead. "You're right! Why didn't we think of it? We don't have to go searching the stars for Earth—Griffiths can tell us exactly where to find it!"

Ellerby smiled. He suddenly had hope that he might yet make it back to his wife and children. "How are we ever going to explain that it took this long for us to come up with this?"

"Don't worry, Ellerby," Lewis said, seated again at the console, "we'll fix the whole thing in the ship's log and no one will ever be the wiser. Mevin?"

"Yes, Lieutenant Lewis?"

"Turn this oversized lunch-plate around! We're going back to Avadon!"

ANOTHER STAR. ANOTHER WORLD. BOTH WERE NOT SO FAR removed from Avadon as pertained to the measurement of the heavens, but far enough removed in the minds of those present who contemplated such things.

Another fleet. Another ship.

The lights faded at her approach. The panels dimmed their displays in reverence. She walked with confident gait onto the bridge of the planetary assault ship *D'Rapiene*, the edges of her cape barely whispering above the polished floor. Each source of illumination turned from her, draping her cloaked face in shadow. To either side of her, several islands of instrument consoles dimmed as well; the chairs situated before them were empty and useless. She climbed the three short steps up to the elevated platform in the center of the bridge, its elegant and luxurious chair falling into darkness as she settled into it.

She was a Sentinel. Darkness was her due.

A great panorama lay before her through the long curve of the observation portal. Her practiced eye could see the fleet arranging itself before her—to her very will, she thrilled at reminding herself.

Two TyRen warriors approached the throne she had created for herself. Each was finished in jet-black, a mark of shame that they had taken upon themselves. Many of their brothers had fallen prey to the wiles of the evil ones and the lies of this so-called Mantle of Kendis-dai. Those who remained true to the faith of the Order were mortified that their brothers should so easily have been persuaded to abandon the promise of free will and had banded against them in defense of the false prophet Griffiths. They wore their new colors in bereavement, vowing to avenge the wrong done to their honor, and believed themselves alone to be the true TyRen.

"Mistress Sentinel," rumbled both TyRen in unison. "You have summoned us. We live to obey."

Neither found any contradiction between their unquestioning obedience and their desire for free will.

"What is the news from Avadon?" came the sultry voice from the shadowy folds of the robe. "Has Targ of Gandri completed his mission?"

"No, Sentinel."

"*What?*"

"Targ of Gandri has failed to take control of the Mantle and has failed in his attempt to destroy the false prophet Griffiths," the TyRen continued, unheeding of the anger which his words had aroused in the Sentinel. She had demanded the information; it would have been impossible for the synthetic mind of the TyRen not to provide it.

The Sentinel leaned back once more in the great chair. "So, Targ seems finally to have met his match. This was— not unforeseen, my children. It was not probable, but it was anticipated. Had he succeeded, then the Sentinels were in place to take advantage of his success. We now must succeed where he has failed."

Silence filled the bridge.

"What is your bidding, Sentinel?"

"Inform the fleet," she snapped. "We are leaving at once for Avadon."

TARG OF GANDRI SAT ON THE COLD FLOOR, HIS HEAD AGAINST the damp stone wall. The sorcerer's hands were shackled, secured to great loops in the wall by long chains. He could move about the cell in a limited way but never quite reach the heavy metal door that was the sole exit from the tomb.

Not that Targ minded that much—he was still alive, and while there is still breath left in a sorcerer, there is the promise of escape. He had been completely spent from the fiasco at the Cathedral of the Mantle three days before. When at last the shield had collapsed around him, the TyRen had surrounded him. He was certain at that moment that his death would be reasonably swift. Yet the TyRen had not dispatched him at once, as he had assumed they would, but had instead surrounded him—protecting him from the screaming mob that no doubt would have been more than happy to fulfill his expectations of imminent demise. They brought him here, half carrying through and half flying above the crying, hateful mob that had suddenly filled the streets in search of his blood.

The TyRen had brought him to the dungeons below the Towers of Justice. The structure was magnificent, standing at the third apex of a triangle of streets surrounding the cathedral. Its lines were sweeping and highly ornamental, graceful and symmetrical. It seemed far too beautiful a building for its obviously grim business.

The interior, however, was in stark contrast and did not disappoint his original expectations. The dungeon was well below the level of the street, lit only dimly by passive optical conduits. Here, in the forgotten depths of a forgotten city, the TyRen chained him, and then they left him to await his fate.

Three days passed. Each day the TyRen entered the cell, brought him food, and cared for his essential needs. When they were finished, they left. Targ remained quietly hopeful through it all, for with each passing day the strength of his magic was returning, and with it, his hope.

The priests, he felt sure, must already have been busy summoning the demon-god Gnuktikut. Well, he could handle that. Targ remembered that Griffiths had banned the horrid creature as a means of acquiring information but Griffiths was now gone.

Gone, indeed, Targ thought to himself. Gone for three days now. With Neskat piloting, he could be nearly a quarter of the way across the galaxy. The Vestis Prime could feel the man's trail growing colder by the moment.

Targ closed his eyes. He looked within himself, felt the strength of the power within and knew that he had rested quite enough. It was time.

Targ's eyes opened. He smiled.

Never leave a sorcerer time to recover, Griffiths, he thought grimly. Strike one and it always has to be a death-blow. Leave him breathing and he will always have his day.

Targ leaned back against the wall once more, relaxing himself with the repetition patterns he conjured up in his mind. He could feel the power of the stars flow through him. He recognized the ether peculiar to the region of this world. He could touch it with his will, bend the elements of creation within it and order it to his liking.

Slowly his flesh began to fade against the background patterns of the stone in the wall, the outline of his body taking on a golden, luminescent hue. With a sudden rush of air, his gaseous self rushed out from the collar of his robes. The chains that once bound him crashed to the floor amid the pile of cloth.

The golden cloud held its human form in the midst of the room for a few moments, floating in the air and looking about itself. Then it began to thin itself throughout the confined space until it filled every corner of the cell. Nothing was left to be seen except the faintest of golden tint in the air.

14

Detours

"WE'RE COMING UP ON AVADON!" ELLERBY STRAIGHTENED UP from his console and turned toward Lewis. "The mystic impeller drives should cut out in about four minutes and we'll be dropping back into normal space—as if I knew what normal space meant anymore."

"Don't worry, Brick." Lewis grinned as she used her favorite nickname for him. "If this works, then we'll have you parked on the White House lawn within a week. Still, I don't think any of us will be able to look up and think of space as being normal ever again."

Ellerby smiled back at her. He had left wife and children to come on this mission. Heaven only knew, Lewis thought, just how much he wanted to get back to Earth and erase the words that were, no doubt, already put on his tombstone.

The *Phoenix* continued to hum through the stars. The stillness of the ship's interior belied the incredible speed with which it now sailed across the interstellar void. There was little left to do except wait. The ship was on course and stable.

"Say, Tobler," Lewis asked casually, "have you been able to get in touch with Avadon yet? You've gotten that com-munication panel all lit up but so far no sound."

"I think it's working, Lieutenant," Tobler answered, her

brow set with minor frustration. "I've followed the sequence down through the hierarchy of menu items several times, but so far no joy."

"Well, keep at it." Lewis leaned back in her chair and stretching luxuriously. "If we can get in touch with Griffiths over that comm-system, then perhaps we won't even have to go to the bother of landing this thing."

"Gee," Ellerby said as he leaned over his own panel and scanned the instruments once more, "and I was just getting the hang of it. About two minutes to go now."

"I was just thinking," Lewis said, swiveling her chair idly. Her eyes were closed, with both her hands resting comfortably atop her head as she moved. "Is it an innate need or is there something about NASA in particular that demands we count down for every big event in space? I mean, it's not like one has to hold their breath or—"

"Hey, I've got them!" Tobler shouted, nearly jumping out of her chair in her excitement. She quickly began jabbing her fingers at the various controls arrayed before her. "It's graphics imaging rather than audio, but it's definitely them!"

Just above the central control pedestal an image sprang into existence. Elegant letters of glowing gold flowed into a three-dimensional display slowly revolving above them.

" 'Honor of Valkiron, Ship of the Grand Emperor,' " Lewis read as the display continued to grow. " 'Welcome again to the true world of Avadon, and the Imperial City of Light.' Well, that's pleasant enough! At least it seems to know who we are."

"Can you get through to Griffiths?" Ellerby asked quickly. "We've only got a minute left until we drop out of this alternate-space drive thing."

Tobler's brow furrowed again as she worked. "There doesn't seem to be any response. This could be an automated message."

Lewis continued to read the message aloud. "Listen to this: 'Our skill we gratefully extend to you. The winds that drive you home are calmed by our glory. In our caring hands shall we bring you home.' "

"Wait a moment," Tobler said suddenly. "There's a sub-carrier that just appeared here. It's affecting the control systems!"

Lewis looked up. If anything, the ship was moving far more steadily that it had before. "I get it," she said, nodding. "It's an automated approach, Tobler. We triggered their automatic landing system . . . and a rather chatty one at that! Too bad, Ellerby, looks like you won't get to land the ship on your own this time."

"Thanks, all the same," the big man responded. "I'll get more practice in later. Drive controls now read on automatic. Thirty seconds indicated for stardrive to shutdown."

The glowing, beautifully crafted letter continued to form overhead. " 'Death and war encircles our peace. Fear not, for the protecting hand of Kendis-dai and the world of his majesty are with you.' Well, that is . . . just what the hell *is* that all about?"

"Shutdown," Ellerby called out.

Somewhere outside of the command chamber, Lewis heard the ship's drive systems begin to spin down. "Are we still on automatic?"

"Near as I can tell," Tobler replied, glancing across the instruments. "The ship is turning slowly . . . Now it's accelerating. We seem to be on course."

"The approach graphics just came up on my monitor here," Ellerby said.

Lewis stifled a yawn. "Well, everything seems to be in order. Mr. Ellerby, would you be so kind as to turn on the external imager so that we can watch this approach? Instruments are fine, but it's always nice to see where you're going."

"Yes, ma'am," Ellerby responded casually as he reached across the console to press the contact. "External visual on."

The dome over the command console appeared to vanish.

Lewis nearly jumped out of her chair. "God *damn!*"

The sky was on fire. That was her first thought. It was as though the stars themselves were ablaze all around Avadon. Bolts of energy laced across her vision, erupting into rolling waves of exploding gas, air, and fuel as they found their mark. Dark shapes trailing long plumes of rainbow fire streaked past them.

"They came back!" Tobler cried out. "The Sentinels came back."

They sailed smoothly and quietly through the chaos exploding around them. No sound intruded on their panic. The ship didn't waver in its course.

"Ellerby," Lewis barked, as she reached for her own control console, "get us out of here!"

"Sorry, Lewis, but the autolanding sequence won't release us," the big man said, looking quite pale. "I keep getting a very polite message about Avadon security and to just sit back and enjoy the view."

Three shadows dashed across their path, followed quickly by five more, each spewing balls of destructive plasma at their prey.

"Damn it, I can't disengage the comm-system," Tobler growled.

"Talk to me, people," Lewis said hopefully, as she punched at her own useless console. "What do we have that *is* working?"

"Proximity display is on-line," Ellerby replied. "There are . . . ah . . . I can't tell how many ships in our immediate vicinity. Their icons crowd the screen. Each of them appears to be hostile in one form or other. It's . . . well, it's pretty confusing out there. It's hard to tell just who is shooting at who."

Lewis looked up into the clear dome. "Those off to starboard are wraith ships. I recognize the Irindris city-ships, but what the hell are those large ships with the superstructure and sails?"

A shattered hull suddenly fell across their view, blotting out the sky. Flame and atmosphere gushed from its ruptured plates as it tumbled past them.

"There must be something we can—oh, shit!"

Tobler and Ellerby both followed Lewis's gaze up into the dome. One of the huge ships with the sails was slowly positioning itself directly in their path.

"Has the *Phoenix* altered course at all?" Lewis gasped.

"Course, speed, and attitude all remain unchanged," Tobler said, her voice quivering. "Wait! We're accelerating!"

"Accelerating?" Lewis and Ellerby squeaked at nearly the same moment.

"Yes . . . I don't . . . so far as I can tell," Tobler replied, "we're still on what must be a standard approach vector to the city."

The warship continued on its course, determined to prevent the *Phoenix* from making landfall on the planet. In moments, Lewis could see the individual windows glowing from the superstructure.

"Brace for impact!" she cried, knowing the act was utterly futile.

Suddenly, a column of coherent energy erupted through the hull looming before them. In moments, three—then five—more similar columns of force sliced through the hull and decks. Their brilliant shafts lanced around the *Phoenix*, never touching her. The atmosphere and power the hull had held in check exploded in blinding light—a light into which the *Phoenix* continued to drive.

Instinctively, Lewis covered her eyes, then forced herself to look again.

The hull was broken in two. The *Phoenix* sailed smoothly between the two halves of the ruptured ship.

"Where did *that* come from?" Tobler yelled.

"It came from the planet," Ellerby said, shaking his head as he still tried to accept what his readouts were telling him.

"The planet is armed?" Lewis gaped.

"Apparently, Avadon can take care of itself," Ellerby answered. "Looks like we'll be landing on schedule—right in the middle of a war-zone."

THE COLUMNS OF LIGHT WERE STILL CUTTING INTO THE SKY AS the *Phoenix* landed. Several of the buildings around the perimeter of the city—tall, crystal structures with elegantly sweeping lines—were glowing with the same brilliant light as the weapons. The beams themselves, however, seemed to have their point of origin far overhead. Lewis had pondered this during the approach, then realized that beam weapons would have been diffused and weakened if they had to be projected from inside the atmosphere. Apparently the ancients had figured out a way of having their weapons start where their atmosphere ended—a rather convenient trick which Lewis thought might have some other intriguing applications.

The *Phoenix* settled gently back into her landing bay—the same landing bay, Lewis ruefully noted, that they had left some weeks before. "It's déjà vu all over again," she said as she extended the landing ramp. She stepped through the air-lock hatch . . .

. . . and found herself facing a nearly solid wall of Thought-Knights, their bruk weapons leveled at all three humans.

Ellerby slowly raised his hands over his head. "You were saying, Lewis?"

The foremost of the Thought-Knights spoke, her voice cold and edged with anger. "We arrest you in the name of the prophet! Thine lives shall be forfeit for the darkness of your sins, vile and scurrilous creatures!"

Lewis was also slowly raising her hands over her head, some part of her mind wondering if doing so was also considered an act of surrender in this culture. Not only that, but why was everyone talking as though they were out of some old movie? "Fine. We're under arrest. What is the charge?"

"You wish us to charge?" the Thought-Knight asked in surprise.

"No!" Lewis said. How was it that the biolink seemed to make translation mistakes only at the most inopportune times? "What is the crime that we are supposed to have committed?"

"Ah, thine words are clear once more to my ears," the Thought-Knight responded gravely. "Thou art arrested upon our belief that thou hast conspired to murder the prophet of Avadon, yea, even with savagery and malice. Further, thou art numbered with our enemies who do now wage war against the holy world of our destiny!"

"Murder?" Tobler squawked. "Griffiths is murdered?"

"Praise the ancients, nay," the Thought-Knight responded. "The prophet lives on. He has flown to the stars in pilgrimage, now safe from your wicked and unrighteous designs."

"Nuts!" Lewis exclaimed. "He's flown the coop! Now we've got to go and find him."

"Thou shalt not live to attack the prophet again!" the Thought-Knight cried out. "Brother knights! Destroy the infidels! Destroy them!"

The Thought-Knights leaned into their weapons. Lewis caught her breath, slamming her eyes shut against the imminent pain.

Nothing happened.

She waited.

Nothing happened.

Lewis opened one eye.

The Thought-Knights stood frozen before her.

"Lewis," Tobler asked timidly, "what's going on?"

The air between the astronauts and the Thought-Knights began to shimmer and coalesce.

"I don't know," Lewis responded.

In moments the air before them began to take form. Suddenly, a tall, robed man with shockingly white hair appeared before them.

"Out of my way," he said, then pushed his way past them through the airlock hatch and into the *Phoenix*.

Lewis looked at her crew. They appeared to be as baffled as she was. She then turned toward the still-glaring Thought-Knights.

"Excuse me," she offered.

There was no response.

"Would you mind if we just stepped back into our spaceship for a few moments?"

There was no response.

Lewis wheeled and leaped back through the airlock. "Come on!"

The three humans quickly secured the airlock and dashed hurriedly through the sweeping corridors of the ship.

"Let's find the old guy, get him off the ship and get the hell out of here," Lewis puffed as they ran toward the control sphere.

"But we've got to find Griffiths!" Tobler wailed.

"Didn't you hear those goons outside?" Lewis barked. "He's not here! We've got to find him!"

"We couldn't find the entire Earth," Ellerby rejoined. "How are we supposed to find Griffiths?"

They entered the control sphere. The tall, robed man was there, hunched over the control console.

"Well, at least we've found someone," Lewis observed.

The man turned, his white hair appearing somewhat disheveled. "Lewis. Tobler and . . . ah . . . Ellerby. The astronauts from Earth, I presume."

Lewis was stunned. She glanced at her companions, both of whom looked as though the slightest breath of wind might blow them over.

"Yes," she answered tentatively.

"How fortunate for us both," the man responded. "I require your assistance."

"You *require* our assistance?" she echoed, somewhat sarcastically.

"Yes, there really isn't a moment to lose. Your companion—Griffiths—he's left the planet. I need to get some information from him—vital information. I need you to take me to him as quickly as possible."

"We don't know where he is." Ellerby shook his head doubtfully, wondering where this conversation was leading.

"Oh, I know where he's going . . . or will shortly. However, if we're going to catch him, we can't waste any time."

Lewis looked skeptically at the robed man.

"You want to find Griffiths, I presume," he said. "So do I. Allow me to introduce myself. I am Targ of Gandri."

"Yes?" Lewis realized from the man's tone that he believed his name alone was full of some meaning to which Lewis had no clue. "And?"

"And if you'll follow my directions, I think I can find Griffiths for us both."

CAPPA:

LOG

OF THE

BRISHAN

15

Interstellar Flight

"... FLEEING FROM K'TAN TYRANNY. THIS IS KA'ASHRA OF Marris with the IGNM NetcastNow update for sidereal 11.2, 3247 ..."

Griffiths slumped in the command seat on the bridge of the *Brishan*. It was almost too comfortable, for without an effort of will—or, at a minimum, instructions to the ship's synth Lindia to make the chair slightly uncomfortable—he would easily have dropped off into yet another blissful nap.

"... Crystal ships of the Zharythian empire have occasionally engaged the K'tan in open battle with mixed results. In other news ..."

Griffiths yawned in spite of his better judgment, and gazed again up into the stars rushing past the clear dome around him. The *Brishan* was moving again. It was yet another quantum zone, the astronaut reminded himself, and therefore, yet another complete set of physical, temporal, and mystical laws that the ship had to address or it simply wouldn't fly. He laughed softly to himself at the thought of Earth science—he had never supposed before just how myopic humanity had been. Everything from Newtonian physics to advanced quantum mechanics had been based on the accumulated scientific observations of centuries, yet no one had seriously considered that physics might have been a local condition only.

It was rather like sitting on a South Sea island and saying that the entire universe consisted of palm trees, coconuts, and ocean. Snow, deserts, and sprawling plains would never have been considered. Earth scientists had looked out from their little island and said that the entire universe consisted of nuclear physics, biology, and chemistry. Mystic forces, etheric conductivity, and sorcery were interesting mental exercises of the imagination but had no real relationship to the physical and "real" universe of scientific observation— regardless of how limited the perspective.

So, those same vaunted scientists had pooled all of their observed knowledge and created a wonderful spacecraft embodying all the best that their wisdom had to offer. They then stuck Griffiths, along with a number of people who were also either very brave or very stupid, at the top of their heap of collected technology and merrily launched them out among the stars in search of new discoveries which, they were confident, would confirm their old discoveries.

The first thing that they had discovered was that their scientists had it all wrong. The universe was not one great homogenous sameness but a collection of pockets of unique mixtures of the logical and the illogical. Whatever worked within the context of its immediate vicinity was law so far as that region of space was concerned—and the first region they had entered simply didn't recognize nuclear isotopes as being anything particularly powerful or dangerous.

That little fact had turned what they had considered the pinnacle of human technological achievement into a drifting tub of directionless metal. Then an Irindris boarding party attacked them, of course . . .

Well, he sighed, leaning further back in his invisible chair, that was another story.

"... Objected to Aendorian totems being used during the negotiations. The Kalikari continue to insist on utilizing their own mystic sages for the duration of the treaty negotiation ..."

Griffiths shifted slightly in order to stay awake. He was having trouble concentrating on the Omnet netcast—something that Merinda, in one of her few waking moments, had insisted that he do. He wished that she had been more specific with the "why" as opposed to the "what" in his task. The netcasts took place once every fifty minutes, although he wasn't sure why that particular interval had been decided upon.

It was amazing to him still that things could be so diverse in the universe and yet so much the same. Take the netcasts, he thought. They were essentially the same kind of thing that one would hear on Earth except on a much grander scale. The top stories repeated pretty much through every day period, with slight variation as the focus and importance of various stories changed. Worse yet, many of the stories were about faraway empires and nations with which he had no mental connection at all. It was one thing to hear a story about the psionics of Prathos and their struggles with other cultures—but an entirely different matter to know just where Prathos was in any meaningful relationship to himself.

For three days now he had patiently listened to each netcast as they rushed from zone to zone. They had made planetfall once for refit—a rushed thing that Seven-alpha-three-five had overseen personally. Griffiths had hoped to walk about the streets of the starport there. The natives looked inviting enough and he would have liked to have sampled some of their local culture—no, he admitted to himself, he just wanted to get out of the ship for a while and breathe air that he hadn't breathed before. Yet the TyRen had insisted that there hadn't even been time for that. The moment the loadout had been completed, the *Brishan* once more rose into the sky. They had passed through six separate quantum zones since then—the last one requiring that the TyRen leave the ship in deep space and rig some sort of gigantic lure to snag some kind of deep space creature to transit their current zone. He had offered to help but the TyRen had refused, saying that what Griffiths was doing was too important for him to leave it right at the moment.

Of course, the TyRen didn't say why it was important, either.

". . . Of Prathos. More news on this story to follow in the next netcast. The Valdori have opened a branch of their Valdori Enchantment Research Institute in the Oltearian Empire, representing the first such exchange of mystic technologies between those two nations . . ."

Jeremy Griffiths turned the command chair toward the sound of the bridge hatch activating. In a moment, the massive form of the TyRen smoothly maneuvered through the opening in the clear cylinder and bowed respectfully.

Griffiths shook his head as though to ward off a chill. It was bad enough that the designers of those things had left them with four arms but the lack of a head continued to unnerve him. He wondered for a moment if he would ever get used to it.

"Lord Emperor, Prophet of the Mantle and Master of all Wisdom," the TyRen intoned solemnly.

Griffiths rolled his eyes back in his head. *Don't these guys ever lighten up?* "Yes, Seven-alpha-three-five, what is it?"

"Lord Emperor," the TyRen rumbled, "I have re-dressed Merinda Neskat's wounds. I regret to inform you that they are not healing well—my own skills being limited to the destruction of human life rather than its preservation. I once again submit myself for termination on the charge that I failed in my duties. I will gladly act as my own prosecutor, should any form of trial be required."

Griffiths smiled at the words and wondered if there was anything worse than a TyRen with a guilt complex. Seven-alpha-three-five just did not want to let go of his self-blame. "I appreciate your honor, Seven-alpha-three-five. However, you are desperately needed on this ship."

"To what purpose am I needed? Tell me, that I may perform the task."

"Merinda Neskat instructed you to take me and this ship with all haste to some backwater core world called Tsultaki, correct?"

"Yes, Your Eminence."

"Yet you don't know how to fly this thing, do you?"

"I am a warrior, Eminence, not a pilot."

"Well, I am a pilot, Seven-alpha-three-five—though I probably couldn't fly this thing without the substantial help of Lindia . . ."

"Thank you, Jeremy," the ship's synthetic chimed in with a deep female voice.

"So," Griffiths continued over the interruption, "the only one who's going to get us to the paradise-planet we're all rushing to is going to be me. On the other hand, you haven't even told me why we are in such a hurry to cross almost a quarter of the galaxy, have you?"

"No, Your Eminence."

"And why haven't you?"

"I have not told you because I do not know."

"Ah, progress at last." Griffiths rubbed his tired eyes.

"Merinda Neskat was quite adamant about the destination and that we travel with all possible speed."

"Well," Griffiths finished tiredly, "I'm not terribly adamant about either our destination or our speed. So, the only reason we are continuing is because you are enforcing Merinda's wishes. Therefore, your job is to force me to continue on this course. If you terminate yourself, I'll fall asleep, the ship will stop, I won't get to this Tsultaki place, and

Merinda's wishes will go unfulfilled. See how important you are?"

"As you will, Your Eminence."

Griffiths shook his head. He hoped Merinda knew what she was doing. He would have preferred to find some healers along the way that could take care of her. She wasn't doing well from the wound; Griffiths was sure she should have been improving by now. Perhaps there was more to that assassin's blade than met the eye—something they had overlooked. Whatever it was, Merinda had been specific about their destination and the urgency of getting there with as little contact with other worlds as possible. Perhaps Merinda knows what's wrong with her, Griffiths thought, and that is why we're going to such lengths.

More troubling to Griffiths, however, was the fact that Tsultaki was a name familiar to him. He had seen it in his mind quite clearly on a map he knew to be thousands of years old. Though he hadn't told Merinda yet, he knew it was a world associated long ago with the Lokan Fleet.

". . . The loss of many sentient lives. Searcher ships from New Asgaard continue to patrol the lanes in the vicinity of the incident in hopes that additional clues as to the carrier's disappearance will become evident . . ."

"Your Eminence? How may I serve you?"

"Well," Griffiths yawned. "You might take the bridge for a while."

"Your Eminence, I am a warrior, not a pilot."

Griffiths smiled to himself once more. If he didn't know that synthetics were without volition he might wonder if the TyRen was taking some sort of fiendish pleasure in being clever. Not that it would bother Jeremy Griffiths, he reminded himself. The TyRen had undoubtedly saved his life by constructing a duplicate Griffiths out of another TyRen warrior. That officious Targ and his little whelp assistant

J'lan had plotted an attempt on both Merinda's and Griffiths's lives and would almost certainly have succeeded if Merinda hadn't stayed one move ahead.

"Then keep an eye on Merinda—er, Vestis Neskat—for me and let me know if there is any change in her status."

"I will enforce your will with pleasure, Lord Emperor," the TyRen rumbled as it moved toward the hatch.

". . . Of the Valdori announced from their home world of Shandrif that the government enacts stiff new penalties against conjury in the outer provinces. Speaking out again . . ."

"Just the usual, you know." Griffiths tried desperately to stifle a yawn as he spoke to himself. "This empire is at war with that empire. There's a quantum hurricane brewing somewhere coreward of the K'tan Empire while everyone bordering them wonders why it couldn't be brewing inside the K'tan Empire. Trade deals were signed; others were broken—the usual."

". . . The two-hundredth and seventy-second Psionicad continues today on Ulik. Hunis Zhakandia-tek was awarded his fourth ethereal pendant for his first-place finish in the astral projection steeplechase, tying the record formerly held by Pukai Olivan of Sechak IV. Hunis will face stiff competition tonight in the 400-meter lodestone levitation where Helgin Garuntha is favored to win . . ."

The stars cascaded around him. Griffiths shook his head violently, trying to blink the fatigue away. Merinda, he thought, what are you up to?

". . . With the quarantining of the Irindris fleet. A squadron of the Omnet Centirion has deployed around the city-ships . . ."

"Wait a moment," Griffiths said aloud. "Lindia, are you monitoring this?"

"Yes, Griffiths."

"... And is currently engaged both in quarantine operations and in offering assistance to the city-ships where possible. Prophet Belisondre said earlier today in a prepared statement . . ."

"Belisondre!" Griffiths gasped. "Belisondre is dead! I took his place! I'm the prophet now."

Yes, Lindia spoke into his mind. *It would seem that the report is in error.*

" '. . . Gratitude of the chosen people.' In a related and troubling development, Vestis Merinda Neskat of the IGNM Inquisition is currently being sought for questioning . . ."

"Here it comes," Griffiths said quietly.

". . . Following her unauthorized departure from the infected Irindris colonies three days ago. Sources in the region . . ."

Griffiths smiled. Targ, he thought, he must have escaped somehow. He's engineering this.

". . . Report that Vestis Neskat's actions of late have been under scrutiny by IGNM internal security forces. It is not known whether she is involved in planting the Irindris plague outbreak or not. Vestis Neskat is most likely suffering from the deleterious effects of the plague virus at the current time. For her own protection, Omnet Central has revoked Vestis Neskat's diplomatic status and her Inquisition authority until the matter has been resolved. If discovered, local authorities are urged to detain Vestis Neskat with extreme caution."

"WELL," MERINDA SAID DRYLY, "THAT SHOULD HAVE JUST increased the bet considerably."

Griffiths knelt next to the Vestis's bunk. Her forehead was glistening with sweat but the latest fever had broken. Jeremy could see, however, that whatever was taking Merinda wasn't letting up. Still, she had insisted on being told of any netcasts that were unusual. Griffiths had not thought that any he had heard thus far were important enough to warrant bothering her rest—until now. That fact, however, had not stopped him from occasionally standing in the doorway of her quarters and worrying about her as she slept.

"What does it mean?" Griffiths asked hesitantly.

Merinda turned toward him again, her bright eyes locked on his own. "Was there anything in that last part of the broadcast that was true?"

Griffiths snorted at the obvious. "No!"

"Exactly. The Omnet Vestis is the guardian of truth and fact across the galactic disk. Our motto is burned into our minds: 'Factum Primum est'—Truth is above all."

"Excuse me?" Griffiths held a hand up as he interrupted. He couldn't quite believe what he was hearing. "I may not be that experienced in this old galaxy of yours, but in the little time I have spent here, I've seen the Vestis threaten, subvert, beat their enemies into submission and—yes, Merinda— even lie."

Merinda shook her head. "No, Griffiths, this is different. We use all those things as tools to uncover the truth, never to bury it."

"Well, isn't that convenient! So, it's all right for you Vestis to lie so long as we don't lie to you?"

"I don't have time to banter semantics with you right now," Merinda said, a thin chill of ice on her weak words. "The point is that Targ has lied to the Vestis. He is covering up the truth—the very truth that the Omnet has been searching for over the three centuries of its existence. He sees the Nightsword as something to do with his destiny— and that frightens me. The legends of Kendis-dai universally refer to his returning to reunite the galaxy in some future epoch when it is in desperate need. Targ seems to think that it's his destiny to fulfill that legend and become Kendis-dai in our own age—apparently with or without the benefit of the Mantle of Kendis-dai."

"You mean he thinks he is Kendis-dai?" Griffiths asked incredulously. "He's nuts!"

"Yes," Merinda nodded sagely. "I believe he is, as you put it, 'nuts'—if I understand you correctly. Despite that, he still holds enough power to reach out and strip away my authority from this far across the stars. Do you understand what that means?"

Griffiths shook his head slowly.

"It means that no one—not the Vestis Dictorae, not the Interion, not the Marshals of the Fleet Centirion—no one knows that he is, as you say, nuts. No one will try to stop him," Merinda concluded.

"No one," Griffiths said, his mouth suddenly dry. "No one except us."

Merinda nodded as she closed her eyes against the pain. "No one—except us."

16

Tall Man

HIS NAME WAS EVON FLYNN. THE TSULTAK CALLED HIM Tall Man.

He was tall—far taller than were the others who worked around him. The E'knari—the major work force on Tsultaki, having been one of their early interstellar conquests—were not known for their great height. It was therefore easy to spot foreigners who came from the Rim Territories, as they were so often called locally.

The human's height identified him quickly as someone from distant parts, but this in and of itself was not a thing of concern. The starport was, after all, a nexus for all kinds of interstellar travel. People and creatures from various distant stellar systems and quantum zones could be found hanging around the bays, working odd jobs for the freighters as they came in. Occasionally they were official docktenders whose job it was to guide in the ships. Frequently they were just hangers-on who stood about waiting for some odd work from the crafts as they landed. More often than not they simply presented themselves as nuisances to which each of the various captains would have to firmly—and occasionally violently—explain the meaning of "no."

Flynn, however, wore the livery garb of the Tsultak Port

Services—or at least the remains of what had once been a deep maroon tunic with navy-blue trousers. The maroon was worn to a pale imitation of its former vibrancy—its once stylish lines marred by long-unchallenged stains and several long swipes of black soot and grease. The navy color of the pants had been worn to a flat tone that could hardly be seen from under the dust that caked its surface. The fabric was torn and frayed at both knees. The shoes were worn and appeared comfortable although they certainly had not been issued as part of the ensemble.

Flynn paused for a moment, his most immediate task complete, to watch the ship's departure. Looming over him, the massive, crystalline, angled lines of the Zharythian transport schooner drifted slowly away from him, flipped over and began to accelerate. His eyes followed the ship as it rushed out through the port bay entrance into the blistering air outside. The crystal of the ship flared painfully as it emerged into the sudden brilliance of the sun. The bay entrance was one of thirty such openings—a gaping maw in the face of a nearly vertical cliff. Far below, and for as far as his eyes could see, lay the great Sand Sea, painfully dazzling beneath an emerald sky.

Flynn pondered what the tour pamphlets described as "the breathtaking wonder of the world of Tsultaki, hub of power for the entire Tsultak Majestik and foundation of the throne of Tsulandis Marcondis Eternicas, Lord Master of the K'dei and Arch-empiris of the Majestik Sphere."

He shrugged. Big deal.

He turned to the newly arrived wooden cart behind him. Four centaurs—another early conquest—drew it. Evon was considerably shorter than any of them, of course: the centaurs were nearly eight feet tall. He recognized two of them as drinking acquaintances that he occasionally met after their collective shifts were over. He remembered their names as

Hwnos and Whilm. They stood in harness with two other centaurs that the man had never seen before. Hwnos was arguing a point rather strongly with his companion who now wore a rather dark and glaring countenance. The man knew that Whilm was something of an angry drunk and made a mental note to leave the bar early after work before Whilm worked himself into lather.

The oversized cart contained a number of tightly woven baskets. Each was filled with export goods clearly marked for destinations in the more civilized areas of the galactic disk. The names stenciled hurriedly on the sides of the crates evoked images of distant worlds and lands—of art and life, beauty and poetry, grandeur and refinement, that were somehow lacking in every aspect of the dusty wilderness on Tsultaki.

Flynn read the names of those faraway places across the stars. He had visited many of them, tasted their fruits and meats, and basked in their gentle breezes. Now they were only names to him of places he had left behind. His old life out on the rim was like a bad dream, and he had no desire to return. He had another trade—one which he had kept to himself these last two months in port—which offered him much higher rewards and far fewer questions about his past. It was exciting, it was dangerous, and it offered little opportunity for too much introspection. Unfortunately, it required that he come occasionally into the Tsultak port in order to learn just where opportunity would present itself.

He grasped the handles in his strong hands and pulled the crating free of the cart. The strain of it showed in his face but he uttered not a single sound, bearing the weight on his own while it took two of his E'knari companions to equal his load. Looking up, he could see the Aendorian ship bobbing slightly in her moorings, the carefully carved totems lining the trunk of her hull. She was a long ship; her branches slowly shifting the acceleration matrix of her leaves. She was bound for Aendorian space and there was almost certainly a consignment of yardow aboard her—a cargo whose ransom could be counted in the worth of entire continents. Indeed, the thought crossed his mind that the very container he was laboriously moving toward the hands of the waiting crew could be that same consignment. It was an idle thought, however, and he knew it.

His job was to send others on their way. He never joined those shipments on their cross-stellar treks. He helped to load the wealthy and bored who were all on their way to nearly mythical worlds far from the core frontier. He loaded them efficiently—but was never counted among them.

They were all headed back toward that "other life" as he had come to think of it. It was not a direction that he cared to take. Tsultaki was the last gasp of civilization on the verge of the Maelstrom Wall and all of the lawlessness that the place implied. One could hide in such a place, and he rather liked the comfort that anonymity gave him.

"Tall Man," rumbled the cultured, resonant voice behind him. "We crave your attention on a matter of some concern to us."

Flynn turned. His words were tired and flat—a litany that he had performed all too often. "I hear and direct my thoughts and being to your words, Master of the Port. My spirit is directed to your will."

The Tsultak port master was a massively impressive dragon, even for one of his kind. The wings were folded back modestly against the beast's vibrantly blue doublet. The shirt beneath was a brilliant, and nearly painful, white whose multiple-ruffled front blended with a massive cravat pinned tightly just below the dragon's head. All Tsultak wore long, splayed kilts over their hindquarters. The pattern of the port master's kilt was woven to represent scales of his clan. Titanium chains, bracelets, and bands adorned the entire length of his tail, while a massive golden pendant swung suspended around his long neck. Flynn noticed that the multiple rows of horns crowning the dragon's head were carefully filed and manicured. He could even swear that the beast was wearing eye shadow. The effect was something of a fashion overkill.

The man could see the E'knari workers sitting down on the cart. The Tsultak had not addressed them directly, but they were required to stop work and listen whenever a Tsultak addressed anyone in their group. They at least got the "stop work" part correct. When a Tsultak started talking, the end of the conversation could be a long way off.

"Tall Man, we would address you concerning your appearance and uniform. The Lord Master of the K'dei and Arch-empiris of the Majestik Sphere, may the celestial spheres shine forever on his magnificence and wisdom, praise to his righteous reign and blessing upon his clutch and brood, has decreed that the starport stevedores should be liveried in fabrics of good repair. It is with my heartfelt regrets that I present to you this admonition of rebuke on your appearance and a challenge of demand that you purchase new livery within the ten-day."

Flynn put both fists on his hips as he looked up at the thirty-foot-tall dragon. "Would Your Lord Portmaster be paying for these new clothes that I'm supposed to buy?"

The dragon gazed down at him with his solid black eyes. "Your response is outside of the protocol for this conversation, Tall Man—as you well know."

The man sighed with resignation, and picked up the litany once more. "I hear your admonition, Lord Master of the Port, and shall comply with your challenge of demand within the prescribed ten-day. Might I offer you and your clan my sincerest humility and groveling at your discountenance from my actions." Damn, he thought, this is going to cost me a week's pay. I wonder if I can get off-planet before then and save myself the trouble?

The Tsultak dragon pulled his head back, his eyes narrowing in satisfaction. His words purred sweetly. "Your compliance is acceptable to us. We are appeased. We admonish you to continue with your duties at this time, that the clan may prosper and you may find fulfillment in your contribution to the collective." The master of the port sniffed and shifted on his four clawed appendages. "I beg your pardon now as I have other duties to attend to. I shall return within the ten-day and see to your compliance. As your shift is nearly completed, I admonish you to complete your loading of this tree-ship at which point we do magnanimously release you from further labors for the duration of this shift. Live well, Tall Man."

Flynn watched the foppish dragon lumber off in the direction of the larger Tsultak fleet bays.

New livery, he thought as he reached for another container on the cart. I've just got to get off this planet soon.

"All I need is one good prize," he grunted to himself as he lifted another large container. "Give me just one and I'll be on my way."

FLYNN EXITED THE STARPORT CAVERNS, HIS LIVERY ALONE being his passport back into the center shaft of the volcano. The crowds were heavy on the wrought-brass promenade that encircled the throat of the cone at the port level. He pushed his way across the wide platform to lean against the ornamental railing and gaze over the side. Despite the Tsultak's generous offer of an early duty release, the Aendorian ship had taken too long to load and he found himself exiting at the worst moment during the shift change. He really didn't have anywhere he had to be, and he preferred to get there without such a large crowd.

Looking down over the edge, he could see the warrens below. His own billet was down there somewhere, he knew, though he rarely spent much time there. One could pretty well pass out anywhere in the myriad bars and taverns in the Pleasure Warrens and not attract too much attention. Hygiene was a factor that one could ignore for several days if one worked hard enough at it. He bathed when convenient. Truth was, it didn't pay to be too clean in his line of work. Someone who was fastidious attracted too much attention on the docks.

He leaned over the rail slightly. Darkness and distance obscured the depths of the shaft, but he could make out the seething red dome of the magma cap far below. The Tsultak wizards had woven that spell centuries ago and had continuously refined it since into something of a commercial artform. A column of deep-red energy rose from the top of the dome the entire length of the shaft. The man's eyes followed it up above his head to its termination point—the massive Tsultak palace overhead. Seven huge support buttresses rose from the walls of the volcano, holding the palace directly over the shaft. It stood in the volcano's original caldera. The towers of the mammoth structure shone in the sunlight that never reached the lower warrens.

Light never gets down here, he thought, and it comforted him. It was time for him to find his way to somewhere a little darker and disappear from himself for a while. It's bad when you don't even like your own company.

The crowds were thinning. He remembered the centaurs were going drinking and thought their brawling would make for a good show—at least for a while. He pushed himself away from the railing and headed for the Pleasure Warrens.

OPHID'S WAS ON THE LOWER LEVEL OF THE PLEASURE WAR-rens. It wasn't fashionable but it was fairly well patronized. There was no entertainment except that which was provided by the clientele—and that was often well worth the price of a drink or two or twelve.

Flynn passed through the large, rough-hewn entrance. The Pleasure Warrens were always in shadow and Ophid's was a darker place amid the darkness. The man could barely make out the shapes of the long bar and the various alcoves situated around it. Hwnos and Whilm were already at the bar, bending down over their drinks and getting louder by the moment. Whilm was already starting to scrape at the flooring with his left front hoof, a sure sign that the argument was not going in his direction. Flynn figured he had about half an hour before the real fight began. Time enough for a few drinks, he decided.

Flynn moved to a side alcove. An E'knari lay with his head down on the table. Evon pulled the small figure up by his collar, determined the creature to be passed out cold, and then calmly dragged him out of the chair and onto the floor. The E'knari never moved a muscle as the tall man slid into the alcove and sat at the table.

The barmaid was a centaur, Flynn noted with satisfaction. It was a good thing since the female centaurs were generally much better in a fight than the males. She could, no doubt, handle his two noisy coworkers when the time came.

"What is your desired beverage, sire," the centaur asked, her voice gravelly and loud.

"What have you got?"

"Sartagon grog," she responded. "We have hot Sartagon grog which isn't that hot; we have chilled Sartagon grog that's a bit on the warm side; we have spiced Sartagon grog though you can't taste the spice all that well; we have . . ."

"Ah," Evon interrupted, "I think I'll just have the Sartagon grog."

The female centaur nodded, her unruly mane shifting

with the movement. "Glad to be of service," she said as she clomped off.

The grog did prove to be nondescript. Sartagon grog was something of a generic term. It didn't refer to any particular recipe but more to a generic class of hard drink whose primary qualifier was to help the person drinking it into a blissful stupor with as little fuss as possible. Efficiency was the prime qualifier of Sartagon grog. Taste and enjoyment were factors that were somewhat down the list.

By the second glass, Flynn had determined, first, that it was time for him to settle on a ship to leave this world on and, second, that this brand of grog was particularly efficient.

"A ship," he mumbled into the second, now-empty grog stein before him. His voice sounded back to him from the depths of the stein. "A ship; I've got to find myself a proper ship."

Flynn lifted the stein up in search of the last drop of the Sartagon grog. Through the glass bottom of the stein he could see the grog-shrouded form of a human male in a blue uniform approaching him. The uniform stepped across the still motionless body of the E'knari on the floor and stood before the booth.

Flynn replaced the stein on the table and gazed up at the man, trying to focus on the uniform. "A ship," he said at last, looking back into the stein, "I need to find a ship."

"Well, you won't find one in there," the uniform said. "But I think I might be able to accommodate you—if you're the man I'm looking for. My name is Jeremy Griffiths. Someone needs your help."

Flynn looked up again from the stein, straining to make out the face above the uniform. "Who sent for me, Master Tight-butt Jeremy Griffiths?"

"I'm not supposed to say," Griffiths said, glancing around the dim bar. "She said to bring you back to the *Brishan*."

Suddenly, Flynn leaned back in the booth and slapped the table, pointing at Griffiths. "Merinda Neskat! Witch-queen of the universe! What in all the hells is she doing out here?"

Griffiths leaned over the table and pulled the tall man out of his chair. He didn't resist. "Evon Flynn, would you believe she's come looking for you?"

"Oh, how lucky for me!" Flynn said, just before his knees buckled and he fell unconscious to the floor.

17

Familiars

THE TYREN PULLED FLYNN'S HEAD CLEAR OF THE TROUGH, spraying water all about the promenade. Flynn gulped air as the mechanical warrior, all four appendages grasping the tall man at various points about the back, head, and shoulders, slammed him for the third time headfirst deeply into the murky water.

"That's enough, Seven-alpha-three-five," Griffiths said, his arms folded across his chest as he eyed the scene critically. Griffiths stood somewhat toward the wall of the promenade. He was an astronaut who, ironically, could fly just fine but had a rather unreasonable fear of heights when standing on the ground. "Put him down."

Griffiths wasn't sure, but the TyRen seemed to perform his bidding with some reluctance.

Griffiths leaned forward as much as he dared. The volcanic shaft before him seemed to be beckoning him to his doom, and he didn't want to get too close to its siren call. "You are Evon Flynn, are you not?"

Flynn slid down to the ground, the water streaming off of him through the metal grating of the promenade sounding like a gentle rain. He shook his head, the shower of spray from his long hair creating a nimbus around his head. He immediately regretted the action, pressing both palms against his temples. He looked up.

"I most certainly am Evon Flynn," he said of himself from the large puddle in which he sat. "I am one of the finest Atis Librae ever known. A stellar researcher and an intuitive genius when it comes to unrelated data, legends, and lore who is currently employed as an I-don't-give-a-damn space-dock bum—at your service. Thanks for the bath. Now, go the hell away."

"Glad to find you at last, Mister Flynn," Griffiths said disdainfully. "TyRen?"

"Yes, Your Eminence."

Griffiths winced. "You are to refrain from using that form of address with me until further notice. We are trying to keep a low profile!"

"Yes, Your Magnificence," the TyRen replied.

Flynn thunderously belched his approval.

Griffiths shook his head. "Whatever! Please take the heroic figure of Mister Flynn here up to the dock of the *Brishan*. Let him use his own feet, if he is capable; otherwise, I don't care how you get him up there but do it."

"Yes, Your Immenseness."

"This is no way to start a relationship," Flynn mumbled as the TyRen picked him bodily clear off the floor.

"MERINDA NESKAT," HE SAID AT LAST, SMILING THROUGH THE pain throbbing through his head. "It's been a long time— but not long enough."

"Hello, Evon," Merinda replied hoarsely from her bunk. "Great to see you again, too."

They were in Merinda's small quarters aboard the *Brishan*. Indeed, the room seemed barely large enough for one person, let alone three of them at once. Griffiths found himself uncomfortably wedged into the corner of the space as Flynn knelt down next to the bunk. Flynn was tall to begin with and the dock work had apparently agreed with him; the muscles of his arms were obvious even when fairly concealed by the dockworker's tunic he wore. More irritating yet, so far as Griffiths was concerned, was that his health showed through a remarkably handsome face with well-chiseled features. Flynn approached, if not attained, an Olympian ideal for the masculine form.

Griffiths hated this man more every minute.

Flynn shook his head slowly, smiling to himself. "Still the same old Merinda. Humility never was your strong suit."

"Responsibility was never yours, either," Merinda responded, no sign of emotion in her voice.

Flynn smiled sadly once more. "Ah, Merinda, you always did have a way of talking to men. Always had to put me in my place, didn't you Merinda? Never much of a word other than criticism. Your reach was always longer than your grasp, Vestis. I've no use for the Omnet any longer—and it has no use for me. You want to play your little games and run everyone else's empires like a god with puppets then, please, be my guest. Just don't come around here with that Omnet-ethic attitude and expect me to roll over and whimper anymore."

"*This* is the guy we crossed most of the galactic disk to find?" Griffiths said incredulously. "*This* is the guy you're turning to for help?"

"Quiet, Griffiths!" Merinda snapped. The effort took more from her than she expected. She lay back against the pillows of the bunk, closed her eyes, and rested for a moment.

"Relax, star-jock," Flynn said sarcastically to Griffiths. "Just stand there quietly and enjoy the show. I know I am."

Griffiths seethed. "You muscle-brained asshole! Can't you see the woman needs help?"

"Since when did a Vestis need any help from anybody?" Flynn whined back.

"Since now," Merinda said quietly.

Flynn turned back toward Merinda. "I'm nobody, Merinda. I've worked hard to become nobody and I intend to remain a nobody. You've come to the wrong guy, Merinda. It was you that taught me how wrong it was to tamper with the stars. I learned that on Tentris. The Omnet is no friend of mine—and I'm no friend to the Omnet."

Merinda reached up and grasped Flynn's hand. A look of surprise crossed the stevedore's face.

"That is exactly why we are here, Evon," she said as steadily as she could manage. "Listen to me, answer me! How long does it take the netcasts to arrive here from Central?"

Flynn frowned, still suspicious of her. "The netcasts that reach us come by packet along the trade routes. They're usually about twenty days behind the local calendars—why do you ask?"

"Griffiths, how long have we been in flight?"

"About twelve days," Griffiths answered, folding his arms across his chest.

"Then we've got about eight days before the news reaches court here," Merinda said. "It might be less if someone is tracking us."

"Tracking you," Flynn said, his eyebrows raising.

"Evon . . . Targ tried to kill us."

"Targ? Targ of Gandri?" Flynn sputtered. "E'toris Prime who-runs-the-whole-*drig*-Omnet Targ? THAT Targ?"

"Yes," Merinda sighed, her words becoming slurred and disjointed the more she spoke. "I didn't see it coming. I should have seen it but I didn't. A Vestis assassin tried to take me out—not one of the Interion assassins from internal security but a Novus of the Inquisition. The boy was green but he was talented. He nearly took me out with a T/S kris. I think there may have been something coating the blade—I haven't been able to get the wound to heal at all. I seem to be getting weaker although . . . although it could just be . . ."

"Let me see," Flynn said sharply.

"What?" Merinda suddenly couldn't seem to focus on the question.

Griffiths realized that she hadn't spoken this many words during their entire rushed flight here. "She's tired, Flynn. She needs her rest."

"Where did he knife you?" Flynn leaned over the bunk, ignoring Griffiths. "I've got to see it."

"I'll show you mine, if you'll show me yours," Merinda said, tittering, her eyes bright but unfocused.

"Very funny, Merinda," Flynn said, a hint of anger in his voice. "Now be a good little Vestis, and show me!"

"I told you, Flynn," Griffiths said emphatically, "She needs to rest!"

Merinda closed her eyes again and rolled over on her right side, tugging feebly beneath the covers. Flynn pulled over the bedding and gingerly lifted the heavily stained camisole. The smell was suddenly overpowering. Griffiths looked away.

"By the Nine," Flynn breathed.

He turned quickly toward the water basin opposite the bunk and soaked a cloth. He began cleaning the wound, alternately turning back toward the basin. The water rapidly became dark and cloudy.

"You, star-jockey!"

"The name's Griffiths!"

"Fine! Whatever! What do you call the synthetic on this ship?"

"Lindia, but . . ."

"How may I help you," Lindia chimed in at once, having heard her name voiced aloud.

"Lindia," Flynn said as he continued to clear the wound, "find that floating synthetic nightmare that nearly drowned me earlier and have him go to my quarters."

"Please specify the particular floating synthetic nightmare to which . . ."

"He means the TyRen," Griffiths said sharply, feeling more and more helpless trapped against the corner of the room. Flynn was working between him and the door. There was no graceful way for him to make an exit.

"Seven-alpha-three-five," the synthetic confirmed, "has been located on the starboard deck three."

"Fine," Flynn continued, his hands moving skillfully across the clotting of the wound and the discolored flesh. "Instruct that monster to go to my billet down in the warrens—sublevel Claw-breadth, billet Phalanx Prima Dorsal Scale. Have it ask any constable in a bright blue doublet what those directions mean—although they'll probably run at the sight of it. The door isn't locked so please ask him not to break it down. In the sleeping cavern to the left there is a shipping container. Inside it will find a black bag about twice the size of Griffiths's head here."

The astronaut bristled.

"Have the headless brute bring it back to me as fast as he can fly."

"Yes, Evon Flynn," the synth answered.

"Now, Lindia!" Flynn roared.

"Seven-alpha-three-five is currently en route per your specifications," Lindia answered evenly.

Flynn reached up and pressed his fingers against Merinda's neck. His face looked suddenly grave. He quickly tossed the soiled cloth back into the basin and clapped his hands together. Flynn's lips began moving as his fingers moved rapidly in their clasped grip. Suddenly he spread the hands into a cupped shape, palms down. They seemed to hold a yellowish ball of light. Threads of gold, green, and brown seemed to lift from Merinda's flesh, spinning and gathering inside the glowing yellow orb. Quite suddenly, the globe flashed with a thunderclap. Flynn was pressed backward against the opposite cabinet, rocking the basin.

"Void Stars!" he cursed. "What a job they've done!"

"Can you help her?" Griffiths's words were urgent and pleading. "Can you heal this thing?"

Flynn scrambled back to his feet, reaching again for the cloth in the basin and wringing it out. "Yeah—I think so. I've seen worse out at the Maelstrom Wall but not by much. Whoever did this wasn't taking any chances. Dead now or dead later, they were determined to kill her one way or the other. What's all this about, Grissif?"

"That's *Griffiths*!"

"Yeah, Griffiths, whatever," Flynn said, turning back to Merinda and starting the cleansing again. "Why does Targ want her dead?"

"It's not just her," Griffiths said, gazing down at Merinda's now still form. "He wants us both stone cold."

"You, too?" Flynn scoffed. "How do you know that?"

"Targ himself tried to kill me!"

"Targ? The greatest Vestis there is tried to kill you?"

"He certainly did!"

"So what happened?"

"He succeeded!"

Flynn stopped what he was doing and looked at Griffiths out of the corner of his eye. He raised an eyebrow. He took in a breath to ask a question but then thought better of it. He just shook his head and continued with his healing arts.

18

Courts of Tsultak

THE TSULTAK DRAGONS HAD A STRICT PROPENSITY FOR ORDER in all that they did—unfortunately they were never very comfortable with numbers. In the ancient days, so it was whispered among the E'knari stevedores, the Tsultak didn't understand numbers at all beyond the concepts of "few," "many," and "none." To the humanoid mind, this would have been a contradiction: fanatical devotion to sequence and order without a clear understanding of counting—but it made perfect sense to the Tsultak dragons. Their sequencing was all bound in their complex language forms, which often were tied to mutually accepted hierarchical forms of the dragons' types, colors, categories, and various body parts. Travelers were often dismayed by this fact, for directions to various places—from the deep warrens to the massive court complex of the lofty caldera—were invariably confusing to all but the savviest new visitor.

For this reason, so far as the Tsultak were concerned, the *Brishan* was cradled at the Wyvern Portwing Dewclaw dock in the cavern Dragon's Eye. With the yardow bulk-freight ships coming and leaving many times through the day, the relatively small size of the *Brishan* hull was of little concern to the local dock authorities. The casual observer quite easily missed it as it rested under the massive shadows of the merchant fleet.

For this same reason, another landing was taking place in relative anonymity in cavern Dragon's Lair Starboard Cresthorn. Its small, compact form was quickly steered out of harm's way from the moving larger ships and directed to a remote berthing at Wyvern Starboard Wing Clawtip dock. The lines of the new ship's hull were unfamiliar to the port director—a relatively young dragon of only two hundred and thirty-five years. However, the procedural ceremonies required for accidents in the port were so long and tedious that he preferred to simply get the small ship out of the way rather than examine it further.

The hull was black—polished to a mirrored finish. Its general lines reminded one of an enormous, elegant insect, being comprised, as the ship was, of rounded components easily classified as a head, thorax, and abdomen. The ship slipped silently through the massive cavern. At one point it narrowly avoided a hulking transport with Aendorian markings that was just then lumbering out into the main exit pathways from an elevated departure dock. Dim red mooring lines of force extended from the ship to the cleats on the dock as it slid silently to a halt.

Stevedores—both sanctioned and unsanctioned—swarmed the dock at once. The ship was elegant, small, and obviously of distant construction. Any one of these factors would have signaled money and opportunity to the dockyard workers anxious to bargain a better wage for themselves; to have all three present in a single craft was an unprecedented opportunity. In moments the dock was filled with clamoring, excited E'knari as well as a smaller mixed bag of other races, each trying to determine where the hatch on the seamless hull could be located. Each creature there hoped that they might be the first to offer their service to the important—and undeniably wealthy—person aboard.

No hatch opened. The figure simply slid through the hull of the ship to appear before them.

A collective gasp breathed through the crowd.

It was a tall, thin figure—tall enough to be human—though it was difficult for anyone present to tell. The long robes concealed the features of the creature. Its face lay completely hidden under a massive hood.

Worse yet, a globe of darkness surrounded the figure, whose very presence inspired fear and loathing in all that were present.

The dockworkers closest to the dark figure pressed hastily back against the crowd. Shouts of alarm were raised from the back.

The figure drifted silently toward the dock, never touching the ground.

The crowd turned in panic. There was no reason in their desire. The approaching darkness was beyond reason and beyond thought. Still the back of the crowd remained unaffected and refused to move.

The globe of darkness touched the first rank of the stevedores. Their cries rang only for a moment before they dropped to the planking of the dock, unconscious and unmoving. Rank after rank in the crowd fell before the gray perimeter of the robed figure's passage.

The back of the crowd at last realized what was happening. Those stevedores still moving vanished as quickly as they had arrived. In moments the only figures remaining on the dock were the still forms of those dockworkers who had the misfortune of being the first to arrive—and the robed figure of darkness that silently drifted over them toward the promenade.

Suddenly, a mammoth dragon appeared in his path. Its bright red doublet and ruffled shirt were impeccably tailored. The chrome helmet fitted over its thorny crest seemed somewhat redundant to its fierce demeanor. The dragon was ancient, massive, and had almost surely seen service in the early wars of conquest during the Tsultak migration seven hundred years earlier. He towered over the robed figure menacingly.

"Unknown man! We demand your attention to our inquiries as we are an officer of peace and justice duly recognized and accredited by the Lord Master of the K'dei and Arch-empiris of the Majestik Sphere, may the celestial spheres shine forever on his magnificence and wisdom, praise to his righteous reign and blessing upon his clutch and brood! In his name and in the name of the Tsultak nation whose security I guard, you shall forthwith identify yourself, your ship, and your purpose in walking the ancient halls of the Tsultak sanctuary! Speak now or answer the consequences of Tsultak wrath!"

The robed figure listened to the litany with detachment until a long pause ensued.

"Oh, were you speaking to me? Are you finished?" the figure demanded after a few moments.

"Your impudence shall not go unnoted in my rehearsal of all facts before the Council of the Nine! You shall respond as decreed by the Law of Challenge or be held accountable!"

"Oh, very well," the robed man said, hovering in the center of his darkened sphere. "Ahem—now please pay attention, I only want to do this once. Let's see—how does that go now? Oh, yes—I hear your admonition, Lord of Port Security, and shall comply with your challenge of demand as is within my desire to do so. My name has been challenged: I refuse to give it for it is of higher station than your own and therefore is not yours to demand. My ship's business is my business and therefore also my own. As to my purposes in arriving upon this world, I have come to demand an audience with the Lord Master of the K'dei and Arch-empiris of the Majestik Sphere—may the celestial spheres shine forever on his magnificence and wisdom, all praise to his righteous reign and blessing upon his clutch and brood. I further demand, as you are my inferior, that you take me before the Courts of Tsultak in the Palace Aerie at once."

The massive dragon blinked. Not only had this strange human that hovered literally in the shadows responded with entirely proper Tsultak protocol, but he had effectively placed himself above the security dragon on the social sequence. The dragon hardly thought it possible, but this little morsel of a human had the gall to place himself above the dragon of all security! The Tsultak momentarily considered simply eating the impudent little snack. Two thoughts, however, stopped him: one, he could not think of any justification for the action under the New Code which had governed all Tsultak for that last seven hundred and thirty-two years and, two, it occurred to him that the human might be right.

In any event, the dragon reasoned, if he brought this robed fool before the Council, perhaps, *they* could come up with a legal protocol whereby he could kill the man.

THE TSULTAK MAJESTIK WAS A VAST STELLAR EMPIRE BUT IT had not always been so. In the ancient times beyond the memory of even the eldest Dragons of the Mystic Circle, the Tsultak dragons lived on a distant world now forgotten. The sun that had spawned them, however, ultimately failed them, for the Tsultak had divined that their celestial neighbor had become unstable. The Seers of the Mystic Circle prophesied their impending doom—and thus was their entire race thrown into the stars.

The catastrophe came at a most fortunate period in the Tsultak history, if one could consider any such cosmic horror as coming at a good time. The Tsultak warriors had subjugated a number of neighboring suns and conquered the native races living there. The Tsultak were not, therefore, completely without options in the saving of their race and their culture. The Great Fleet was undertaken as an interstellar imperative. It is one of the greatest moments of Tsultak history that the fleet was almost eighty percent completed and operational by the time the Tsultak sun finally exploded into oblivion.

One of the legacies of the Great Fleet was the New Code. The evacuation of an entire race of dragons from their home world was an organizational and logistical behemoth. Careful planning and organization, beyond an order of battle, ran counter to the warrior culture of strength and dominance which had pervaded their society up to that point. However, Grashna the Philosopher, a young dragon of the Tailblade clan, proposed a revolutionary restructuring of their entire society through a set of organizational, procedural, and ceremonial structures. Grashna had actually taken the time to study several of the cultures which the dragons had crushed and come to the conclusion that many of their ideas might further Tsultak society.

Faced with the question of either changing their old warrior code or dooming their race to extinction—the Tsultak naturally fell into lengthy debate. The Mystic faction, led by the elders of the Mystic Circle, held that for the race to die off entirely in a cataclysmic flash of energy from their suicidal sun would be a valued death honored in the halls of the ancients. Indeed, they held that such an event might well represent the crowning achievement of their entire race. The Grashnak faction, on the other hand, argued that there would be no songs sung of such an achievement, and therefore it would be of no value in the ancient warrior code. Further, the Grashnak argued that as their empire expanded even marginally out from the galactic core, the races they encountered were demonstrating both power and civility.

For the protection and furthering of their race, survival in a more civilized galaxy required that they change their ways.

These debates were short-lived—only seventy-three years—before the Mystic Circle conceded the argument in an elaborate ceremony. In that act, the Great Fleet was born and with it, the New Code.

The New Code governed nearly every aspect of Tsultak life. It was the way of the Tsultak and, as such, was the only way anything was done. In their rush toward both the organization and the domesticity that they found in other starfaring races, they took on all the trappings of civilization without a deep understanding of the reasons behind it. Their ceremonies were endless and omnipresent. There was not a single act in the day of any Tsultak dragon that did not involve a prescribed and rigid procedure and code to be followed. They wore outlandish costumes because the code dictated it. They affected elaborate speech patterns because the code required it. Nothing short of their honor was at stake. It had been ingrained in every Tsultak that participated in the Exodus of Tears. It was woven into the teachings of their young. The old ways were being stamped out—quite systematically—by the New Code.

And yet . . .

Each Tsultak wore the prescribed garment but it was as much of a shell as the New Code itself. Each Tsultak offered meditations at the prescribed time but no regulation clearly dictated what thought dragons should meditate upon. For beneath the foppish clothing and behind all the ceremony, there still beat the heart and soul of a conquest-centered, battle-blooded dragon.

It was prudent for those who dealt with them to remember that fact from time to time.

———

"... THE MASTER OF THE HOUSE OF KIPCHIK, WHOSE NAME was great before the Battles of E'knar Prime and whose deeds are sung still beyond the outposts of Thebindara . . ."

The shadowed man drifted slightly in the center of the Hall of the Nine. All the ruling elders were present, each lounging on a massive fainting couch, their tails draped around the furniture in the prescribed manner. Each was set in his own alcove on a level high above the polished marble floor where the man hovered.

The man seemed to right himself suddenly, as though his concentration had somehow lapsed in the midst of the litany and he had only now recovered himself. Dealing with the Tsultak could often be a matter of patience beyond endurance.

The cloaked figure had endured enough.

". . . When, in the midst of our trials, did my ancestor side with the blessed Grashnak, may all honor be unto his name and to his descendants all glory . . ."

"Excuse me?" The hooded man raised his hand from within the globe of darkness about him.

"The reading of greeting is not yet complete!" said the rust-red dragon from an alcove to the man's right. "We cannot deal with the complaints lodged against this creature without a full reading of greeting and an establishment of our jurisdiction over this complaint!"

"Agreed," responded the cobalt-blue dragon languidly from her alcove behind the robed man's position. "The New Code is clear on these protocols and must not be violated."

"I quite agree with you," said the robed figure loudly from his place below. His voice resounded through the overly ornate hall.

The heads of nine dragons turned toward him as one.

"Without a reading of greeting and jurisdiction, you

cannot adjudge me nor rule on my requests officially as the Council of the Nine. However," the robed figure said clearly, "if you will indulge my ramblings for a few minutes— simply listening in silence while I allow my thoughts to take form through my words—I believe that your selection of protocols and processes may be much different and to the greater benefit of the Tsultak Majestik."

The robed figure waited.

The dragons watched him—in silence.

The robed figure smiled to himself.

"I am a Sentinel. I represent a great and holy movement far across the stars. Our goals are one with the Tsultak Majestik. Your race was anciently wronged by the passing of a terrible and cursed soul known to us as Lokan. With him came the power to conquer the stars—through him was even the mighty Tsultak brought to its knees in disgrace."

The dragons shifted slightly in their anger.

"Yet," came the clear voice from the globe of darkness, "should the Tsultak choose to join with us, we believe we have the means to deliver the power of Lokan into your hands—er, pardon me, claws. The Tsultak will be mighty again for none should stand to stop them."

Once again, the Sentinel smiled at the silence.

"I am a Sentinel; would you hear my thoughts?"

19

Cold Trails and Old Tales

GRIFFITHS SAT QUEASILY IN THE BAR DEEP WITHIN THE WAR-
rens. Flynn had brought him back here after he had finished
working the healing arts on Merinda. It would take time
now for his ministrations to take effect. Flynn had insisted
that an otherwise empty ship guarded by the TyRen might
afford her the best chance of healing. Besides, Evon seemed
anxious to talk. Griffiths, on the other hand, was still very
much in the dark as to where they were and, more particularly, why they were here. When Flynn offered him a drink,
therefore, it seemed like a mutually beneficial deal.

Who knew, Griffiths thought miserably, that the spacer
would lead them right back to the same grubby tavern deep
in the bottom of the volcano where he had found him in the
first place?

"A Sartagon grog for my friend and myself," Flynn cried
out to the barmaid who, to Griffiths's astonishment, was a
bare-breasted female centaur with an enormous, firm chest.
"And make them hot!"

The centaur looked back at them through suspicious eyes.
"You have money, Flynn? You're far behind on your tab
now!"

"Not mine, old filly!" Flynn bellowed across the cavern.
"My old friends have come to buy me a drink."

"Hey," Griffiths said under his breath, "I don't have any money!"

"You don't!" Flynn said with mock surprise. "Well, I'd say that's terribly inhospitable of you, friend! You invite me out for a few drinks . . ."

"I did not invite you out!"

". . . And here I've come to find that you aren't even paying for the rounds! Well, never mind. We'll charge it up to the bay and Merinda can put in on her expense account. I'm sure the Omnet isn't going to miss the price of a drink or two at their expense."

"I'd think you might have a hard time selling that line to the owners here," Griffiths said dubiously. "I'd bet a month's pay that they've heard that dodge before."

"Not at all, boy! I borrowed Merinda's baton of passage. Careless of her to just leave it lying around her cabin like that. Such a valuable instrument should never go unguarded. Did you know that this little beauty could act as credits just about anywhere that the Omnet is recognized? Even in this sorry excuse for a drinking facility, old Ophid will no doubt part with quite a bit to get a credit impression from the base of this little jewel! Of course, it probably won't be worth a damn once word from Central gets here that her baton has been recanted. Still, as Merinda is fast enough to outrun that information for the time being, this baton is a prime target. Such a device shouldn't be left lying around where thieves and cutthroats might use it for their own nefarious purposes." Flynn slipped the baton back into the open folds of his tunic. "Best if I keep an eye on this until she regains her strength."

"I'm sure," Griffiths said with open contempt. "Look, you might just have some trouble using that . . ."

Griffiths let his voice trail off as the barmaid returned with the soft clatter of hooves. She leaned over the table, setting each steaming drink down before the humans. Griffiths just couldn't take his eyes off the centaur's chest.

"Are you feeling all right?" Flynn said with what seemed to be genuine concern. "You don't look very well."

"I've . . . I've never seen anything like that," Griffiths gaped. "They're huge but they, well, they don't sag at all!"

"What's huge?" Flynn puzzled, sitting back in the booth and putting his feet up on the small table. "What are you talking about?"

"The barmaid!" Griffiths said. "Her—you know!" Griffiths held both hands out in front of him, cupping his hands symbolically.

Flynn puzzled over this for a moment. Suddenly his head fell back, his laughter roaring throughout the cavern. "Her breasts? Of course, they don't sag, you idiot! She's a centaur. By the Nine, where are you from, Griffiths?"

"It's . . . well, it's a long story," Griffiths said, half to himself. He reached across the rough-hewn table and pulled the massive, steaming flagon towards him. Things weren't working out quite as he had planned. "Look, the fact is that Merinda's expense account isn't going to be of much use for very long. We're . . . well," Griffiths let his voice drop below low, hoping to keep their conversation private. "We're fugitives from justice!"

"What?" Flynn's voice echoed from the distant recesses of the upturned flagon. "Fugitives from what?"

"Fugitives from justice," Griffiths repeated from between clenched teeth. Damn these biosynth translators, he thought. Why don't they work right when you really need them? He tried several other phrases, hoping the translator in his head would catch up with his words. "We're on the lam. We're running from the law. We're wanted criminals."

Flynn slammed his flagon on the table—the force of the

noise attracting irritated looks from several of the bar's customers. "Wanted criminals!" he yelled.

"Geez." Griffiths shuddered, glancing furtively around him as he cradled his drink. "Keep your voice down, will ya!"

"You and Merinda?" Flynn bellowed, laughter spilling between the words. "Fleeing from the law? Hah!"

"Shut up, damn it!"

"Oh, you wet-nosed little pup," Flynn laughed as he tousled the astronaut's straw-blond hair.

"Stop that!" Griffiths squawked indignantly.

"Just where do you think you're drinking, anyway? This isn't some haunting lounge on Ja'lel! None of the constabulary comes within five levels of this part of the warrens, and you're equally unlikely to find any company in this place that hasn't had more than one run-in with the law in some part of the stars or another. Look here," Flynn said, standing up in the booth and suddenly addressing with a booming voice the meager crowd around them. "May I have your attention, citizens of the empire! I find myself at the same table as a wanted criminal, a desperate, fierce creature who would just as soon kill me as look at me! Won't someone please call for the local watch? Who shall come to my rescue in this time of peril?"

The level of apathy, rampant in the room, remained unchanged. Of the twenty-odd patrons in the cavern only four or five faces turned toward Flynn's impassioned, loud speech in the vague hope that they might find it entertaining. They looked disappointed.

"What shall I do?" Flynn went on with overblown, melodramatic flare. "I am undone! Please, bold adventurers of Ophid's Tavern! Do not let me meet such a foul end in the dark Pleasure Warrens!"

The centaur barmaid turned toward Flynn wearing a puzzled expression on her face. "Flynn! You haven't had enough yet for such antics! Sit down and shut up, will you? All this talk about constables is annoying the customers—and me as well!"

Flynn shrugged an apology and sat slowly back down in the cavern booth. He turned his smug face back toward Griffiths. "As you can see, there really is little interest in hauling either of us before any magistrate you can name. So what if you're a wanted criminal? So what if you're fleeing the law? Half the people working the docks here are wanted creatures by some government and the other half are lying about it. Relax, drink your grog while it's hot."

"Yeah," Griffiths answered, gazing down into the foamy flecks roiling at the top of his drink. "I guess you're right. How long until Merinda comes around?"

"Ah, the fair lady Merinda Neskat?" Flynn said, sitting back suddenly in the booth, an equal mixture of disdain and regret in his voice. "She should be up and around in a few days . . ."

"A few days?" Griffiths said suddenly, leaning forward over the table. "We haven't got that long. Once word reaches here from the Omnet, they'll shut us down quicker than you can say . . ."

"Didn't I just tell you to relax, boy?" Flynn said, laying his large hand on Griffiths's generic jump suit to calm him down. "We'll take care of Merinda—and you, too, while we're at it—all in good time. You've come for old Flynn's help and here I am to give it to you. So, tell me, what could be so important as to make such a fine, upstanding citizen as yourself into a fugitive from the Omnet?"

"I don't know," Griffiths said hesitantly. He had only met the man a few hours ago and nothing he had seen thus far gave him any reason to trust him. Indeed, there was something about him—in his smile that was too bright and inviting, or his mischievous eyes—which Griffiths just could not bring himself to trust. On the other hand, argued the more methodical side of his brain, the man was the one Merinda had specifically come to see. It was obvious that they knew each other in the past and Merinda certainly seemed to trust him. On the other hand, their relationship had been long ago and people do change over time. Merinda just might be wrong about this Evon Flynn. On the other hand—he realized that he had already used three hands in his argument.

What he really wanted, he thought, was a drink.

Oh, he realized, he already had one.

Say, the fumes from the grog are pretty enticing.

"Just relax," Flynn smiled. "You take a drink, sit back and take your time. Old Flynn will be more than happy to listen to your little tale. That's what us Librae are supposed to do best, you know!"

Somewhere in his head he had a nagging suspicion, but it wasn't nagging him loudly enough. Besides, Griffiths had always held his own in any officers' club on Earth. This local ale couldn't be so bad.

Griffiths tipped the flagon back. The amber liquid—warm and delightfully bodied—coursed down his throat. It seemed to spread itself to warmly enfold him in its embrace, its warm fingers traveling upward toward his face. He began gulping the sweet liquid.

Bang!

He was staring at the underside of the table. The back of his head hurt, but that was all right, since the colors the pain made were so pretty and added to the moving patterns that made up the table overhead. He could see wonderful images emerging from the underside of the table. Oh, look, a horsy! He smiled. Over there is a dragon! Ah, isn't that cute! That one over there is a grik-looper! He had no idea what a grik-looper looked like but he was convinced at the moment that it looked just like what he saw.

The table started to move against his will but his own

mental powers seemed incapable of stopping it. Griffiths cursed the fact that he had never completed mental telepathy college, though he could not remember ever enrolling in the nonexistent school. Suddenly the face of a female centaur was leaning over him and speaking from high above him. She was a giant of amazing size.

"Is he going to be all right?" her gigantic voice thundered.

"Aye, he'll be fine," came the voice of a second giant, only now coming into view. It was Flynn the Giant. "He just doesn't get out much."

"Well, make sure he's got the coin to pay for this," the huge centaur replied, drifting out of his sight.

Flynn the Giant picked him up and sat Griffiths back upright in the booth. The perspectives began to settle down to normal size. Griffiths seemed to find it difficult to focus either his eyes or his mind.

"Good Lord," Griffiths said shakily, "what was that?"

"Are you feeling a little better?" Flynn asked in a most friendly voice.

"Well, yes, actually, I do." It occurred to Griffiths that he wasn't feeling anything at all.

"Well, there you have it then!" Flynn said, carefully slapping Griffiths on the back, so as not to propel him too far forward. "So, Spacer Griffiths, what brings you and my good friend Merinda Neskat to this dirty hole in the middle of nowhere?"

"We're in search of the Lokan Fleet." Griffiths looked at Flynn as though he had to explain the obvious for the hundredth time. "Isn't everybody?"

"Yes, they are," Flynn laughed, "but none have ever known where to look for it."

"I do."

Flynn turned slowly toward Griffiths. He eyed the man as though he had just seen him for the first time. "Do you now?"

"Sure," Griffiths said. He couldn't stop talking about it. It seemed like the neighborly thing to do. "I've got the entire map of their course right here in my head. Got it straight from the Mantle of Kendis-dai." Griffiths reached out to grasp the front of Flynn's tunic but was having trouble gauging the distance. He was relieved when Flynn grasped Griffiths's groping hand and planted it where Griffiths had aimed. Griffiths could then pull Flynn closer and speak conspiratorially. "I know where the whole thing is—the fleet, the Nightsword—all of it."

"That's a grand prize, indeed," Flynn whispered back in a rough voice, half to himself. "With that Nightsword, a man could rule the stars—there would be no price high enough. So, when do you figure on going after it?"

"Can't." Griffiths nearly cried as he spoke the word. He was overwhelmed with disappointment.

"There, there now," Flynn said with a comforting pat on the astronaut's back. "Tell old Uncle Flynn why not."

"Well," Griffiths sniffed, a little unsure as to why he was acting this way. "I know where the map leads to—I just . . . I just . . . I just don't know where it starts!" Griffiths suddenly broke down sobbing into Flynn's shoulder.

"Ah, there, there, now," Flynn said, cradling Griffiths in his arms and rocking him back and forth slightly. "I'll bet old Flynn could help you out with that one!"

"Could you?" Hope, it seemed to Griffiths, exploded like a nova just a few feet above them. Quite suddenly, he couldn't remember what he had just been talking about, but the pain in his head was growing to Olympic proportions.

"Sure I can help you!" Flynn said confidently. "I know these stars better than anyone you'll find. I haven't been just picking up dust here in the docks. This is just part-time employment. We just need to get connected to the right people and we'll make sense of that map in your head!

When we do—by the Nine!—we'll find old Lokan's fleet yet!"

"Did I . . . did I tell you about the map?" Griffiths asked, his eyes wide.

"Of course you did, Griffiths!" Flynn said through a grand smile as he turned back to the barmaid.

"Bruthn! Two more hot Sartagon grogs!"

20

Minister of Peace

DEDRAK KURBIN-FLAMISHAR LAY ON HIS STOMACH, THE MAS-sive doublet open, his wings spread relaxed across the expansive polished marble floor. Columns surrounded him, each one finished in brilliant blue enamel and defined brightly by inlaid gold and jewels. These supported a coffered ceiling finished in a fresco of armored dragons flying in a cloud-streaked sky. Beyond him, the platform of office was left empty, its ornamental alcove abandoned for the informality of the floor. A gentle breeze drifted through the massive arch at the left of the chamber, which opened onto a balcony, beckoning flight over the volcanic peaks beyond. It was a picture of draconian repose, but it was a studied picture composed with great effort. Dedrak Kurbin-Flamishar was anything but relaxed.

"This entire business makes my tail twitch," the dragon rumbled to himself. Indeed, his tail was twitching behind him, flipping his elegant kilt this way and that, causing the fabric to fall about his haunches in a most undignified manner. Each of his wives knew that it was the first sign of something troubling him, and each of them knew better than to disturb him when his work had become such a mystery. Dedrak was the Minister of Peace for the Tsultak home world. It wouldn't do to have him upset in public.

Dedrak's head lolled over a massive pile of scrolls of various sizes heaped unceremoniously on the floor before him. This one contained a deposition. That one contained a testament. Still others contained reports, witness statements, transaction records, port records, and a host of other minutia which had, thus far, failed to yield a clear picture of anything except the dragon's own deepening perplexity. At last, with a deep rumble, Dedrak let his head fall to the cold floor with a rush of wind. Papers and scrolls floated lazily amid the scarce dust particles as they settled once again toward the floor.

"*Draf!*" Dedrak swore loudly under the assurance that none of his wives were near enough to hear him. "Humans! Can't live with them; can't eat them!"

The cascade sound of chimes caught his sudden attention. He was struggling to get to his feet and put himself in some sort of more dignified posture when he noticed who had entered the large official suite his office afforded him. He relaxed once more down to the floor.

"Ah, Celdric, it's only you."

"Only me," the massive blue dragon returned with a glint of humor in his eyes. He was an ancient one. His rows of crowning horns were well-worn and, in many cases, cracked and broken. He had seen service before the migration. "Such disrespect towards an elder of the clan! I should turn you in for violations of the New Crud!"

"That's 'New Code,' Celdric," Dedrak warned solemnly. "You should remember that it is also a violation of that self-same body of law to disparage the New Code verbally either in public or in private."

"You going to detain me, Minister?" the blue countered, closing one eye tight while ogling Dedrak with the other.

"Me? I think not," Dedrak snorted. "By the time I was finished reading you the formal charges, you would probably be dead anyway."

Celdric trumpeted his laugh. The sound was earsplitting and sincere. The enormous sound shook the pillars in the hall. It was an honest, terrible laugh which entertained Dedrak completely and would have struck terror into the hearts of any other creatures present who were unfamiliar with the Tsultak ways.

"Only too true, my young friend," Celdric replied, his jowls curling upward as he smiled, baring his yellowed rows of sharp teeth. "Even so, the life I have lived is honorable and filled with all the joys this life can bring. You've a long way to go before you will enjoy my happiness!"

"Am I not aware of it?" Dedrak said, a weary sadness creeping into his deep voice. The Minister of Peace reached up without thinking and tugged at the high collar of his ruffled shirt, which, unfortunately, was about half a size too small. "You lived in the days when our kind were warriors. You knew what it was to fly naked in the sky. You hunted the hunt. You had only one wife."

"You would go back to such a time?"

"Ah, Celdric, those were the days when dragons were dragons. We were the rulers of all within the flight of our wings. Now, what are we?" Dedrak gestured with his open claws at the paperwork arrayed before him. "Now I get fat lying within these castle walls doing human work! You know well that my position was once known as the Bloodmaster. Now, in our more enlightened time, I am the Minister of Peace, playing at idiotic diplomacy with a human emissary. The fool thinks he is frightening because a globe of darkness surrounds him everywhere he goes." Dedrak shook his massive wings and sneered in disgust.

Celdric's head was weaving from side to side in disapproval. "It is a human galaxy, Dedrak. They are the dominant species now, whether we like it or not. If the Courts of Tsultak are going to ever have any prominent say in the affairs of the stars surrounding them, then we must learn this unpleasant fact."

"Yes, Celdric," Dedrak said with resignation as he absently pushed his foreclaw through the papers on the floor. "So it has been explained to me in no uncertain terms by a representative from the council herself. I would it were so, however, that these humans were a bit more combative and a great deal less cunning."

"What is it?" Celdric asked, stepping slowly around his younger master to get a look at the papers. "What is troubling you?"

"This Sentinel, as he calls himself." Dedrak shifted slightly in his discomfort. "He comes from a distant part of the stars—more distant than any I have yet encountered in my offices. He claims to represent a mighty political movement which challenges the authority of yet some other human entity known as the Omnet."

"Have I not heard something about this Omnet?" Celdric pondered aloud.

"It is quite possible you have heard their name before. They arrived here with the early trade ships, offering knowledge of distant stars. They still packet their information entertainments to us regularly, although there are few of our own kind who pay any attention to them. The council has someone to watch these briefings—or whatever they are called—and decide if there is anything useful in them. Their information is almost entirely human-based, however, and has only passing use or interest to us in general."

"Are the humans fighting the humans?" Celdric asked with perhaps a little more hope in his voice than the New Code would allow.

"Well, the fact is that the humans are always fighting the humans, so far as I can tell. They must not be very good at it, however, since no clan in particular has ever completely destroyed their enemy. So far as I can tell, their wars are always taking place and never fought to any real conclusion. What is the point of conquest if one does not conquer?" Dedrak shook his head. "I'm never going to understand humans."

"So what does this Sentinel want?" Celdric asked, shaking his massive head and causing the various gilded chains decorating his horns to jangle sweetly. "He is far from his clan and can present little threat to us."

"He is a masterful wizard, Celdric," Dedrak cautioned, "and should not be underestimated. However, he has not come for the purpose of war—he says—but on a mission of atonement."

"Atonement?" Celdric blinked.

"Indeed." Dedrak stretched and stood at last. "He claims that humanity has robbed our noble race of its destiny in the galaxy. We were wronged anciently by one of his ancestors and he has come to ask our help in making amends for his clan's former indiscretion. Worse yet, he claims that another of his clan has preceded him here. He wants us to apprehend this second individual so that he may obtain the knowledge necessary to complete his quest."

"He uses us, Dedrak," the old dragon said.

"Yes, indeed, he does use us and his motivations are unclear." Dedrak nodded. "Yet what he offers in return may well be worth our turning our eyes toward the sand rather than the sky."

"Nonsense!" Celdric raised his head in pride and disdain. "No human has anything to offer our clan!"

"This one might," Dedrak replied as much to himself as to his older friend. "He says that an ancient member of his clan robbed us of our destiny some three thousand years ago. A warrior who brought a bright blade through the heavens and . . ."

"In the Name of the Fathers!" Celdric coiled his body back. "I know that story well! Star-sunderer!"

"Yes, Star-sunderer indeed."

"It was a myth!"

"Perhaps, but the very possibility that such an artifact could be put in the hands of the council was enough to gain its support. I have been going over the documentation presented by this Sentinel for the last six days and he presents a very interesting case, though I cannot say that I am altogether convinced. The Sentinel presents himself as a powerful being but he is, after all, merely a human, and a cunning one at that. I certainly do not know what his true motives may be, but the council says that I am to support him. Support him, then, I must." Dedrak rose up suddenly, his wings extending as he reared back in his rage. "Me, Minister of Peace and Master of the Home Fleet of Tsultak, searching through transit records at the behest of a weak-robed human!"

Celdric waited until his friend calmed himself. Dedrak finally lowered himself to the floor again. Puffs of threatening smoke drifted from his nostrils.

"You know," Celdric said at last, as he absently ran his forward claws across the polished marble floor, "it is still a great thing to dream about."

"What are you talking about, Old One?"

"Well," Celdric said cautiously, "it's just such a delightful fantasy. The Star-sunderer of L'kan caused the ancient ascendancy of humans. It was the means by which humanity nearly destroyed everything that was not in its likeness and assured that they would remain in power for the last three thousand years."

Dedrak listened to his old friend intently.

"Would it not be wonderful," Celdric continued, "if that selfsame artifact were to surface again—say in the hands of some clan other than the humans?"

Dedrak looked up at his old friend. "What you are suggesting is as devious as the humans themselves."

"Not devious—but perhaps not as delicate as the New Code would have it. Perhaps it is not a question of being devious but simply knowing when it is time to strike." Celdric held up his right foreclaw to stave off the minister's comment for a few moments more. "We have cultivated the New Code well in our attempts at ingratiating ourselves into the society of humans. We have even taken on their clothing after our own style. Do you not also long for the open sky, Dedrak? Would you rather that sky be filled with human stars—or those of your own clan?"

Dedrak turned his massive head toward the ancient blue dragon. "That is, I believe, the intention of the council."

"Then we are all of one mind," Celdric said pleasantly.

"Indeed," Dedrak returned. "If the Sentinel does indeed wish to atone for his clan's injustices, then we shall dutifully assist him in finding this valued missing person. I believe I see your point in all of this, Celdric. Should he then subsequently lead us to the Star-sunderer of L'kan—this 'Nightsword' as his clan calls it—then he may complete his atonement by delivering the prize to us."

"What if he is not that penitent?" Celdric replied.

"In that case"—Dedrak smiled wickedly—"he shall forfeit his life. Either way, we would be well on our way to ruling the stars once more, with humanity well back in its place."

21

Cartographer

"ARE YOU SURE YOU KNOW WHERE WE'RE GOING?" GRIFFITHS said yet again. He could barely see. The few signs that he had been able to make out seemed to indicate that they were on sublevel Heel-spike, which meant absolutely nothing to Griffiths. All he knew was, it was the darkest part of the warrens that he had been led into yet by Evon Flynn. Through an occasional break in the coarse wall, he could make out the lighter regions of the volcanic shaft above him. Such glimpses beckoned him upward toward cooler and more pleasant surroundings. The shaft at this depth was rough. The promenade here was a tortuous route winding around massive protrusions from the wall itself. It was poorly maintained, in any event. He felt as though he were working his way down through Dante's hells, certain that only the damned would be found this far down.

"For the last time, Griffiths," Flynn said with a bit too much cheer, "I've been here before."

"I'm sure you have," the astronaut retorted, "but I still don't see the need. There was a huge Cartography Merchant on the main promenade. Why couldn't we have just gone there?"

"Because the map we're looking for isn't in a fancy

guild-merchant store, barbarian," Flynn said, smiling at him just before disappearing around another rock.

Griffiths wanted to push those glowing teeth down the dockworker's throat. Instead he continued to follow the stevedore through the gloom.

"Every merchant and would-be frontier explorer that passes through Tsultaki goes in that guild or one of a dozen on that same level just like it. The conversation is always the same," Flynn went on, picking his way along the catwalk that passed for the promenade at this juncture. He spoke as he moved through the darkness, his voice suddenly shifting between a mocking falsetto and a deep bass as he acted out the parts of his little drama. " 'Excuse me, big master frontier guildsman! I'm looking for something really special in a map!' So the guildsman says, 'Of course, I will be glad to help you. What do you have in mind?' 'Oh,' says the idiot adventurer, leaning over the counter and whispering too loudly, 'I seek the treasure of Fu-bar-boo!' 'Ah,' says the guildsman, 'no living creature knows where that great treasure is—but for you, I have a map! A chart that no man has ever seen. But for you—for you I would be willing to part with it!' "

"Fine," Griffiths responded, ducking just in time to miss an outcropping of rock. "I get the picture." Griffiths pushed back images in his mind of Satan tapping him on the shoulder amid the sulfur-laced gloom around him.

"There isn't a counter up there that doesn't have a map to every known treasure rumored to be scattered out on the Maelstrom Wall as well as a good number that no one is supposed to have heard of. Making those maps is a major cottage industry here, Griffin . . ."

"That's Griffiths!"

". . . And while they might have enough information to get you from one star to another, they almost certainly have nothing whatsoever to do with finding any actual treasure, no matter how outlandish the claims of the nice creature behind the counter." Flynn stopped with satisfaction before the closed metal door, set, it would seem, to fit the rough contours of a cavern in the sheer rock wall. "Ah, here we are at last!"

The door looked ludicrously overmassive to Griffiths's critical eye. Massive bolts affixed wide, rough-hammered bands across its gray surface. "Someone appears to be a little over-security conscious," he remarked.

"You said it," Flynn replied as he knocked on the steel plate five distinct times. He waited for a moment and then knocked three times more before standing back.

Griffiths, too, stood back before the massive door, waiting for something to happen.

Nothing did.

"It's not moving," Griffiths said at last.

"Of course not," Flynn responded. "Give it a moment, will you?"

They waited.

"What are we doing . . ."

"Quiet!" warned Flynn.

From behind the massive metal door, there came two faint knocks followed by a third.

"That's it!" Flynn said with a smile. "Come with me!"

Griffiths was suddenly caught off guard. "Go? But we just got here!"

"Not a moment to lose," Flynn said as he moved quickly across a second catwalk and vanished around the corner of yet another outcropping.

Griffiths quickly moved to follow. He rounded the corner and found himself facing the end of the catwalk at a rocky ledge—with his companion nowhere to be seen.

"Flynn!" Griffiths called out in a sudden panic. "Flynn,

where are you?" He turned around quickly, looking for some possible means of escape from the dead-end rocky alcove he was confronted with. Above him the slope was precipitous and wet—certainly impossible to scale. There was only one other place his companion might have gone. With trepidation he leaned over the shaking railing to gaze into the steaming depths below him. "Flynn!" he called loudly. "Are you . . . ?"

Two large hands reached out for him from the rock face itself. In a moment, the strong grip pulled Griffiths backward through the cliff and into the darkness.

Griffiths began screaming. He couldn't help himself. He had made the descent into hell and now the demons had gotten him! Images of brimstone and horned devils floated unbidden into his dark-enfolded mind. He shook uncontrollably; barely able to hear the voice that was speaking insistently to him just a few inches away.

"Will you be quiet, Griffiths! Stay your mind to a cleat and stop your noise!"

"What?" Griffiths said at last, struggling to make sense of his surroundings.

"It's a secret entrance, fool!" Flynn said, still holding onto the man to make sure he didn't lose his nerve again. "The rock face is an illusion—not real."

"Secret?" Griffiths stammered, his heart rate finally dropping to tolerable levels.

"Of course it's secret." Flynn rolled his eyes in disgust. "These friends don't want just anybody to come visiting whenever they please."

"But what about the big metal door?" Griffiths gasped.

"That's no door!" Flynn said, finally releasing Griffiths and turning to face the dim flickering light around the bend in the tunnel. "You could cast columns of fire down on that metal plate all day and never even scratch the paint. That's just there to distract the tourists."

Great, Griffiths thought to himself, I was a barbarian and now I've worked my way all the way down to tourist.

The rock corridor wound its way back into the mountain. Small side chambers branched off from the main tunnel, each lit by glowing balls of pinkish light. Flynn continued to move ahead, however, as though the way were well known to him.

"Look," Griffiths said as he followed the large spacer. "Merinda said we needed to be back inside of three hours or she would come after us. It's taken us nearly half that time just to make our way this far. Merinda is in no shape to mount a rescue mission."

"She's doing just fine, barbarian," Flynn said, moving with an easy gait further into the heart of the mountain. "It's only been a six-day now and already she's walking the decks. She's just a little weak still, that's all. It will pass soon enough."

Griffiths continued along in silence for a moment. This was a complex series of tunnels and, he suddenly realized, potentially quite vast. "Say, Flynn, it seems strange to me that such a secret place would be left so unguarded. Why isn't someone watching us?"

Flynn snorted. "Who says they aren't?"

Griffiths was trying to think of an answer to this question when Flynn came to a halt before a ragged curtain. Light spilled into the corridor from the room beyond.

"I have someone special I'd like you to meet." Flynn smiled as he pulled the curtain aside.

The room beyond was a magnificent cavern, brilliantly lit by several carefully placed floating globes. Ornately carved bookcases were fitted to fill every possible space around the cavern walls. The cascade of items had exceeded even their prodigious capacity, however, and covered nearly every flat surface available. Books without shelf space stood stacked between five and twenty deep in places. Scrolls in excess of the storage lay curled in soft mounds either on the floor or atop the bookcases. Maps seemed to explode out of their assigned drawers, spilling across several standing tables in disordered layers. In the center of this frozen hurricane of information sat a single figure atop a tall stool, his back turned toward them as they entered. He was a short, balding creature, leaning intently toward a massive and ornate drafting table. Pen in hand, the little creature was carefully drawing something on a large piece of parchment.

"Here he is," Flynn said with something of a cross between a smirk and honest pride. "This is the person I've brought you to see!"

The small creature turned around to look at them.

Griffiths was stunned. He had followed Flynn down into the heart of the volcano just to meet some sawed-off, pint-sized little shrimp of an alien?

"Yoda?" was all Griffiths said, pointing incredulously at the diminutive creature before them.

"Yo-dah back at you," the small creature said, mimicking Griffiths's expression and pointing back at him. "Bizarre custom have you for greeting, barbarian, but figure I to please a guest you can't go wrong in trying." The gnomish little man turned to Flynn. "Guy is this you want for me to work with, Evon?"

"That's right, Scrimshaw," Flynn said, folding his arms across his chest and smiling as he leaned back against a disorderly table. "Thought you might help us out with a little stellar cartography problem."

"Help you I can, but pay me you must," the little man said, his long pointed ears flapping in anticipation.

It wasn't until that moment that Griffiths realized what had happened. The biolink had done it to him once again. On Avadon, Griffiths's perceptions of the people there had caused the biolink to translate their language as though they were from some Biblical epic. His impression of this creature at first led him to remember a character from a classic science-fiction film he had seen when he was a boy. Now, no matter where he went in the universe, whenever he encountered another of this dwarf creature's race, he would hear that annoying voice in the translation.

"Well, I happen to have the passport to your dreams right here in my hand, Scrimshaw," Flynn said, casually twirling Merinda's small baton in his right hand.

"Hoommm! An Omnet payment wand you have!" The wrinkled, green dwarf's eyes grew large. "Payment you will make. Service render well I shall."

"Yes, but at the agreed price, you little *druk*!" Flynn said, suddenly snatching the baton away from the outstretched hand of the small creature. "A chart to our specifications. If you do your job well, then you will have our grateful payment plus a good bonus for your trouble."

"Hard is your bargain," the green dwarf said. "Difficult to accept. Rich I shall make you and poor here in this cave shall I be."

"You'll be rich enough while we challenge the Maelstrom Wall, Scrimshaw," Flynn snorted. "Of course, you could come with us on the voyage. Your experience would be most valuable . . ."

"Away with your offers," Scrimshaw gasped, holding his oversized hands in front of his face as if to ward off an evil standing before him. "Safe will I be while dead you shall in space be floating."

"As you wish it." Flynn shrugged, stowing the baton in his tunic pocket and turning back toward Griffiths. "I suppose we could go over to One-eyed Huka. He'll make your chart for you . . ."

"One-eyed Huka!" The dwarf's voice went suddenly shrill and ugly. "Over the wrong eye did he put his patch, yes? Cartography his skill it is not! Star-map a chart only is not. Knowledge. Legends. History. These things a proper chart does make!"

Flynn turned back toward Scrimshaw. "Then do we have a deal?"

The pointy-eared dwarf sighed. "Deal we have. The barbarian you are bringing over here."

Flynn gripped Griffiths by the upper arm and began pulling him into the center of the room. It was all the astronaut could do to avoid stepping on the scattered tomes, scrolls, maps, and books strewn everywhere across the floor.

"Hey! What are you doing?"

"We need the map. The map inside your head," Flynn said simply. "We just need to get the map from the inside to the outside."

"Here you may sit him," Scrimshaw cackled, indicating a tall stool next to his large cartography table. Griffiths noticed that in addition to the paper items, a number of cables and odd pieces of equipment were situated around the table. Each had a rather sinister, torture chamber look to them.

"But . . ."

"Nothing to worry about." Flynn gripped his companion firmly by both shoulders and sat him roughly down on the stool. "Just a simple process of mental transposition of thought. Doesn't hurt a bit. You'll find it quite interesting and a wonderful story to tell your children in the years to come."

Scrimshaw reached among a pile of papers and withdrew a large crown of blue-black steel. A massive cable was attached at its peak, connected at the other end to a globe containing green lightning. The gnome jammed the crown down on Griffiths's head. "Wear this you will. Protect you it can!"

"Protect me from what?" Griffiths squawked.

"Nothing, really!" Flynn assured him. "Just relax."

"Relax?" Griffiths turned to look at Flynn, standing so

smugly next to him. The crown did not fit Griffiths well. It had apparently been made for someone with a much larger head. The only things keeping it from slipping down over his eyes were his ears, which were now painfully bent. "Are you sure this is the right guy?"

"He's the best I've ever met. Many maps made by his own hand are a coveted feature in the shops on the promenade."

"Really?" Griffiths said. "So this is the guy that makes the true maps?"

"No," Flynn replied with a sly smile. "This is the guy who does all the forgeries."

"What?" Griffiths quickly rose from the stool but was suddenly held down by a gnarled hand on his shoulder.

"Concerned you not be," the dwarf said as he pushed the confused man back down onto the stool. "Forger I am, it is true, but more skill than a forger you will not find. Know we must truth that is lost. Knowledge. Legends. History. Forgery that is good must be mostly truth or fool no one it will. Map you have that tells you where to go. Where to begin, this you know not! Trust in Scrimshaw. Place to start will he give you!"

The old gnome returned to his own stool on the opposite side of the massive drawing table. With surprising deftness, the small creature pulled out a large, yellowing sheet of blank parchment paper and laid it carefully flat on the smooth surface.

Griffiths looked at him miserably from under the massive helmet pressing down on his ears. "So what do I do? Use the force?"

"Clear your mind and think only of the map you have seen," said the gnome. "Let the haunting projector do its job and soon the map in your hand you will have instead of in your head."

Griffiths sighed and slumped slightly on his stool. He closed his eyes but was haunted for a time not by the chart swimming in the back of his consciousness but by the image of Evon Flynn still standing before him grinning from ear to ear.

"IS THAT IT?" FLYNN SAID AT LAST.

"Completed the map is," said Scrimshaw, the gnome's voice weary from the exertion, "though little is the good it may do you."

Griffiths winced against the stabbing pain that was shooting through his temples. He struggled off the stool that he had for so long sat upon with increasing discomfort. "Can you take this thing off my head now?"

Flynn smiled again his roguish grin, making no move to help the astronaut. He moved to examine the chart more carefully. "Now that is one of the most intriguing maps you've ever done, Scrimshaw. Just where did you get all that ornamentation around the edges?"

"Dreamed it his mind did," the gnome said pointing with no small amount of accusation toward Griffiths.

"From his mind, you say?" Flynn moved in closer toward the newly rendered chart. "Naked women and mermaids cavorting amid windswept surf?"

"The mind a strange place often is." Scrimshaw jumped down from his work stool and moved quickly over toward where Griffiths was struggling with the headpiece. "Details I was concentrating on. Difficult is the human mind to keep up with. When busy I was, idle thoughts he brought up. This idea of a treasure map, his it is."

The helmet on Griffiths's head came loose with a sudden sucking sound. "Ouch! Is that it?"

"Finished I am; pleased you will be," Scrimshaw cackled once again.

Griffiths stood up quickly and rushed around the drafting table. The great parchment that had not so long ago been a blank surface had been transformed under the small gnome's hands. The whole of it was framed in beautifully detailed ornamentation with great curling waves and beautiful figures. Fine lines of ink were traced with precision across its surface. Impossibly perfect circles and dots designated the various stellar systems. Vast areas of dust clouds and nebulae were drawn in exquisite detail. A single black line wound its way with increasingly convoluted turns into the center of the galactic spiral. It was perhaps a bit more gaudy than he remembered it in his head—but it was complete in every detail.

"Exquisite calligraphy," Flynn said, reaching down and tracing the newly dry figures with his fingers. "What does it mean, I wonder?"

"You can't read the map?" Griffiths asked as he peered at the details laid out before him.

"Scrimshaw just drafts what you see in your head," Flynn said, studying the map with equal interest. "These symbols are apparently from the Lost Empire, which means that all the symbols are . . . wait! Are you saying that you *can* read these symbols?"

"Of course," Griffiths said. He pointed down at several of the groups situated at various points on the course line. "This says Gates of Darkness. This one over here says—let's see—Siren Shoals, I think. Mardeth's Turn, Star of the Ancients, Here Be Dragons . . . it's all pretty plain. There are lots of course and timing numbers scattered over the thing but they don't make much sense to me. Well, you can see for yourself!" Griffiths gestured casually at the map.

Flynn's eyes narrowed in concentration. "I can't read it. Scrimshaw, what about you? Can you read these symbols?"

The old gnome snorted from where he stood coiling the cables from the helmet for storage. "Read them I cannot. Nonsense they are."

"There must be something wrong with your biolink,"

Flynn said to Griffiths. "Once a language is learned, the link automatically transmits the translation to all biolinks that are locally in use. It's the backbone of galactic communication."

"Well, I'm understanding you just fine and it seems to be working well enough on the little guy over there," Griffiths snapped back.

"So why are you the only one who can read it?"

"I don't know," Griffiths said, turning back toward the chart. "It's an ancient imperial language form. I understood it when I first saw the image through the Mantle of Kendis-dai. Perhaps there's something about ancient imperial language that prevents TFPs from propagating any translations."

"Great!" Flynn roared. "Now we have the map but we still need you to read it! What good does that do us?"

"Much good it does you," Scrimshaw cackled again. "Read it we cannot but familiar it is."

Both humans turned toward the gnome, Flynn being the first to gain his voice. "What are you talking about, old one?"

The gnome shuffled hurriedly across the floor, kicking an occasional book that was in his way in his haste. The small, ancient figure pulled several books from the shelf, discarding them almost carelessly until he found the passage he was looking for. "Ancient maps have ancient names! Places you have read. Know them I do! Others can you recognize once you go there! Said you this place Siren Shoals, Griffiths-man?"

"Yeah," the astronaut responded, pointing back to the map. "It's right here, this sliver between these dark areas."

"Not always by that name was it known," Scrimshaw said, wagging his finger as he balanced a massive open book in his hand. "Many warriors followed Lokan into the core. Many died among the Shoals. Name changed it did."

"What do we call it now?" Flynn asked without patience.

"Bonefield Narrows," Scrimshaw replied.

"Bonefield Narrows?" Griffiths repeated. "Well, then we have it! We know where to pick up the trail!"

Scrimshaw's cackle was beginning to get on Griffiths's nerves. "Have it you do not! Know I not where to find this legendary Bonefield Narrows. Do you, Griffiths-man?"

"No, he doesn't," Flynn said through a huge smile. "But I believe I know where to find a man who does!"

22

Last Stand

"WHAT A BREAK," FLYNN SAID, STEPPING LIGHTLY DOWN THE maze of tunnels leading back to the volcano's throat. "I worked passage on a ship a few years ago. There was this old man aboard who used to tell all kinds of tales. I used to think the captain kept him on just to listen to the crazy old fool spin his yarns. He was always going on about the Bonefield Narrows and how he'd been there. Last I left him, he was coreward, on one of the New Territories—down on his luck and more willing to talk than ever. If we find him, then we know where to start!"

Griffiths was tired from the mental exertion of making the map. All he really wanted to do now was sleep. "Fine. We know where to start. Hey! Slow down!"

Flynn was already striding down another tunnel, weaving rather jauntily along its path through the larger boulders jutting out of the wall. "Come along, Captain Griffiths! We have places to go, things to do! Provisions for the ship may be in order, although if I know Merinda, the ship is already stocked for an extended voyage. We'll need some departure clearances, but I'm sure that Merinda can get us those, as well."

"Flynn! Hold up, will you?" Griffiths picked up his pace.

Flynn was already nearly out of sight among the rocks and turning down yet another branching tunnel. Without Flynn, Griffiths suddenly realized, he would be hopelessly lost down here. "What's the big hurry to get out of here?"

"Ah . . ." Flynn stopped, but the spring was still in his step. He was fairly dancing with anticipation. "One happens upon a chance like this only once in a dozen lifetimes, Griffiths. In my trade, that means that for every one person who gets this chance, there are eleven others willing to kill you for the chance they will never get. That's not the kind of thing that one wants to stand still over. Opportunities can vanish as quickly as they appear in your hands."

Flynn brandished the map. Then, with a smile, he quickly rolled the parchment up and slipped it into a leather map case. "You see, lad, I figure that as there are three of us now involved, there must be at least thirty-three people looking to kill us." He smiled at his own little joke. "I'd say that's reason enough for a little haste on our part."

"Your assessment is mathematically flawed, Evon Flynn," came a voice from the darkness.

Flynn's face fell suddenly as he turned around, tense and wary. In the next moment, however, he relaxed. "What are you doing sneaking up on men like that, you piece of scrap metal? And how did you get in here?"

"I am Seven-alpha-three-five," the TyRen replied. "It is my job to keep the prophet safe from harm. As Merinda Neskat suggested that the prophet was overdue for check-in, he may be in need of my assistance. Apparently she was correct in her assessment, considering your recent conversation. As to my getting into this secret location, that is part of my training."

The distraction gave Griffiths a chance to catch up to Flynn. "So you've been eavesdropping?" he asked as he joined the other two.

"I have been monitoring your conversations for the last seven minutes. As your communications seem to indicate danger in the immediate—Just a moment."

Both Flynn and Griffiths looked up sharply at the change in the TyRen's speech pattern.

"There are five large creatures approaching from various vectors. They are Tsultak dragons. Their coordinated patterns indicate that they are trained warriors. That they are continuing to approach rather than attack from a distance indicates that they mean to capture us rather than destroy us."

"Escape options?" Griffiths asked.

"Follow me," the TyRen responded.

The headless torso of metal and multiple weapons appendages suddenly illuminated the tunnel in a brilliant light. The TyRen turned and floated quickly down a side corridor, its own light illuminating the way. Despite his fatigue, Griffiths quickly settled into a run behind Flynn. "Where is he leading us?" he huffed.

"I don't know," Flynn replied. "I've never been here before."

"Well, *I* certainly haven't been here! I'd be willing to bet that TyRen hasn't either." But Griffiths continued to run after the guardian machine.

"Threat targets are closing," the TyRen announced. "Three additional targets detected. Two are Tsultak dragons. The third is a humanoid form. The humanoid's signature is obscured by mystic protections."

The TyRen rushed toward a solid wall of rock at the end of the tunnel. The face was clearly lit by the TyRen's own illumination.

Suddenly the light vanished. The tunnel was plunged into darkness. Griffiths tried to stop but his footing slipped on the sand and loose stones scattered across the floor of the tunnel. He slid in the darkness and suddenly emerged back into the TyRen's light.

Flynn emerged from the illusionary wall and stumbled over the supine Griffiths, nearly falling in the process. "Which way to do we go now?"

The TyRen held still, the beam of light fixed on the end of the tunnel.

Griffiths dragged himself painfully to his feet. "Well, Seven-alpha-forty-two! Which way now?"

"I am Seven-alpha-three-five," the TyRen responded in a voice just barely loud enough for Griffiths to hear. "We are surrounded. Please hold still for a few moments while I finish my threat assessment."

"Surrounded?" Griffiths squawked. "What the hell kind of a guardian are you, anyway?"

"I have studied the Tsultak attack patterns. This situation offers us the best possibility for escape."

In the distance of the tunnel, huge shapes could be seen moving at the edges of the TyRen's light. The openings to two other tunnels remained dark, but Griffiths could hear ominous sounds of approach coming from those, as well.

"Flynn, you must get the prophet to safety," the TyRen intoned. "You must take him off-world as soon as possible."

"How?" Flynn asked.

"The wall directly behind me is also an illusion. It leads to the catwalks surrounding the lower warrens."

"Great, then let's just—"

"Do not pass through there at this time. Two of the Tsultak dragons lay in wait beyond the illusion to take the prophet captive. When the time comes, however, take the prophet through and get him to Merinda Neskat's ship as soon as possible. You will need to depart at once, as I believe your best hope for safety lies off this world. Threat assessment continues."

The heads of the approaching dragons could clearly be seen. Griffiths wondered how such huge creatures could so easily move through such a confined space.

"Halt!" the TyRen cried out in a booming voice. "Identify yourselves and your purpose!"

"We are the minions of Dedrak Kurbin-Flamishar, Minister of Peace," rumbled a voice in return. Its sound shook stones loose from the ceiling above Griffiths and his companions. "You are commanded to surrender yourselves to the questioning of the minister and his authorized counsel."

"His counsel?" Flynn said to Griffiths, puzzled. "The Minister of Peace has no counsel."

The TyRen overheard the remark. It called out a second challenge. "We do not recognize the counsel to your minister. Identify this counsel!"

The dragons were close. Griffiths could feel the lead dragon's hot breath as it spoke.

"The counsel is an emissary of the stars," the dragon replied. "A wizard from a new kingdom of the Outer Rim. He is a master of the Darkness and leader of wraith fleets."

Griffiths started suddenly. "My God! It's a Sentinel!"

Flynn took in Griffiths's fear. "Sentinels! *Those* Sentinels? The we-destroy-life-at-the-drop-of-a-stone Sentinels? They're after the map, too? They'll eat our hearts out, Griffiths!"

"I see you have some experience with them," Griffiths said dryly.

"The counsel is approaching," the dragon hissed.

"We've got to get out of here *now*," Griffiths breathed. The walls of the tunnel seemed to be getting closer.

"Threat assessment is complete," the TyRen replied. "How much time does the prophet require to reach the ship and escape the planet?"

"Fifteen minutes," Flynn responded at once.

"I can give you twelve minutes," the TyRen said quietly.

"We'll take it! What do we do?"

"When I tell you," the TyRen said softly, "you must run for the exit."

"When?" Griffiths asked, panicked.

"Now!" the TyRen shouted loudly.

In a fluid motion, the TyRen rotated. All four of its appendages rotated open, their weapons brandished and focused toward the illusionary wall. A hail of fire erupted from all four weapons mounts, their deadly effect carrying through the false barrier to their targets beyond.

In that instant, Griffiths and Flynn dashed for the wall, as well. The murderous discharge streamed between them, each bolt and bullet aimed with incredible precision so as to avoid either of the humans in their flight.

Behind the TyRen, the dragons roared their anger.

"I AM SEVEN-ALPHA-THREE-FIVE!" the TyRen shouted over the thunderous cacophony of sound. "DEATH TO THE ENEMIES OF THE PROPHET! I AM SEVEN-ALPHA-THREE-FIVE!"

The TyRen then rotated its weapons upward.

GRIFFITHS AND FLYNN RAN THROUGH THE ILLUSIONARY WALL only to find themselves crossing a thin catwalk rimming the volcano's throat. Griffiths tried to stop but slammed painfully against the safety railing. For a moment, he was concerned that his impact would break through the chains restraining him, but they held.

A strong hand grabbed Griffiths's upper arm. It was Flynn, pulling at him. "Come *on*! We haven't much time!"

"Where are the dragons?" Griffiths gulped.

"Still falling down the volcano shaft, if that TyRen did his job," Flynn shouted. "Now get moving!"

Griffiths extracted himself painfully from the railing, gasping for the breath that had just been knocked out of him. He stumbled under Flynn's insistent grasp, finally getting his feet under him.

Suddenly the catwalk began to shake. Griffiths grabbed the railing and held on for life. He looked back.

The face of the rock wall behind him exploded. Rock jetted out, trailing dirt and debris in great cascades. Slowly at first, and then with increasing momentum, the rock face above the opening began to slide.

"Avalanche!" Griffiths cried out.

"The exit!" Flynn yelled. "Your friend has sealed it! What a metal miracle that beasty was!"

Under his feet, Griffiths thought he could still feel more weapons being discharged through the rock below.

"His name was Seven-alpha-three-five," Griffiths said quietly, then pushed himself angrily from the rock wall and began to run after Flynn.

23

Followers

FLYNN THREW OPEN THE AIRLOCK DOOR, NOT WAITING FOR IT to stop moving before leaping through its airtight frame and into the *Brishan*'s main bay. Griffiths was not so quick, catching the heavy door as it rebounded, nearly knocking him over.

"Hey, Flynn!" he shouted as he tried to keep up with the tall man. "Watch what you're doing!"

Flynn seemed to take no notice. He crossed the packed bay quickly, his eye seeming to take rapid inventory of the extensive equipment filling it. Names for each piece of equipment fell from his lips as he walked as though checking each off in his memory. "Bestran inversion drive . . . Cannon Projector . . . Oracle crystal apex . . . etheric dynamo armature . . ."

"Flynn," Griffiths called out again, scrambling over some translucent tubing that pulsed with a soft yellow light. "Wait!"

The tall man passed quickly through the iris hatch on the port side of the bay and stepped at once into the selective gravity tube, dropping down to the deck below. Griffiths had a pretty good idea where the man was going and wasn't convinced it was a good idea. The astronaut followed suit and dropped to the next deck just as the iris valve to the bridge closed behind the spacer.

Griffiths strode toward the now-closed hatch and ran into it. It hadn't opened for him. Fury welled up inside him. He balled his fists and began beating on the door as he yelled. "Flynn! Open this hatchway right now, Flynn!"

"Griffiths?"

The astronaut turned suddenly toward the words in his right ear.

"Merinda!"

She stood in the hatchway off to his right in what seemed like a casual manner. Griffiths noticed, however, that her fingers were white from the strain of her grip. Light beads of sweat glistened on her forehead. He had forgotten that the captain's cabin was situated right off the bridge. Now, confronted with her suddenly so close to him, he seemed somewhat off guard. Damn, he thought, why can't I get a grip on myself around this woman?

"Startled to find me here?" Merinda said easily. "There is a reason why they call it the captain's cabin, you know. What is all this noise about?"

Griffiths regained a small measure of his composure. "I think we're being hijacked!"

Merinda eyed him closely, as though squinting her eyes would somehow improve her hearing. "What did you say?"

"I said, we're being hijacked! That idiot Flynn has just . . ."

"Flynn?"

"Yes, your old pal Evon Flynn just dashed off to the bridge and shut the door in my face!"

"Well, while that might qualify as rude and unthinking I hardly think . . ."

Merinda suddenly cocked her head at the whining sound that was building in pitch and intensity down from the direction of the ship's main bay.

She turned back toward Griffiths. "On the other hand, those are spindledrive lifters spinning up the main drive. Perhaps we should ask Master Flynn what it is he's doing with my ship."

"Be my guest." Griffiths slammed his fist into the closed hatchway again. "He's just on the other side."

"Well, did you try opening the door?" Merinda said tiredly.

"What do you mean?" Griffiths said irritably. "Of course I tried to open the door! It's always opened for me before!"

"Lindia," Merinda said with effort, "open the bridge iris hatch."

The closed iris rotated quietly to its open position. Griffiths grimaced, giving the hatchway a glance as though it had purposefully made him look foolish, and stepped inside. Merinda followed him through a bit more languidly. The massive captain's chair was situated well forward in the bridge space. It was mounted on a protruding section of the deck that extended out into a large clear bubble. Flynn was already seated in the chair, his hands working quickly over the control surfaces that covered the hovering crystal panels arrayed in front of him.

"Tsultak Departure Master," Flynn bellowed, apparently to no one in particular in the room. "The *Brishan* of the Wyvern Portwing Dewclaw dock in the cavern Dragon's Eye! Our technological drive system has reacted badly to the local spiritual quantum index and is threatening to go critical. We are declaring an emergency . . .

"We are?" Griffiths said.

". . . And demand immediate clearance for departure as a precaution for the safety of the greater Tsultak Majestik," Flynn continued without missing a beat. Even as he spoke, he continued working the panels about him. Suddenly, the moorings loosed the ship. Griffiths could see it rotating away from the dock almost at once.

"Now wait just a minute!" Griffiths said, moving quickly across the bridge.

"Lindia!" Flynn said, still working the controls. "Set battle condition one-delta. Assign Griffiths to defense." Griffiths suddenly was lifted into the air, surrounded by an all-too-familiar glowing globe of light.

"Greetings, Captain Jeremy Griffiths!" said the sickeningly cheerful voice. "This is Fisk, your on-board defensive systems synthetic mind. May I take this opportunity to say how good it is to be working with you again as we defend our ship and our shipmates against imminent death and destruction."

"Fisk!" Griffiths yelled as he clawed hopelessly at the air around him. "The ship is NOT in any danger! Let me down at once!"

"Oh, I am sorry, Jeremy Griffiths," Fisk said with only a slight measure of disappointment in his synthetic voice. "Our current defensive condition has been set at one-delta which means that attack, while not registering on any of the ships sensors at the moment, is nevertheless expected. Caution dictates that you remain at that station until the defensive condition is reset." The chipperness returned to his voice almost at once. "However, this does not mean that we cannot entertain ourselves with a few simulated battle drills until such time as true death and destruction are hurled our way!"

Griffiths clawed his way about in the air until he could face the command chair again. "Flynn, damn it! Let me down!"

"Relax, Griffiths," Flynn said without taking his eyes off of the instruments. "Play a few games with the nice synth."

"Evon," Merinda said, pulling herself with obvious difficulty onto the bridge. "What has happened? Where's the TyRen?"

"He's buying us time," Flynn said. "It's time we need."

The view out the main portal stopped swinging. Griffiths could see the enormous cavern that housed the ships from all across the stars. In the distance was a single, brilliant sliver of light. Suddenly the *Brishan* surged forward. Uncounted docks and ships slid past their view as they rushed with increasing speed toward the distant light at the far end of the cavern.

"Merinda," Flynn said as he continued to furiously work the controls, "do you remember the story of Baldor the Jester of Kendis-dai?"

"Of course," Merinda said as she sank gratefully into a force chair forming to catch her as her strength waned. "He stole the Book of Truth from the halls of his master so that he could gain power over others in the court and reign over them. Upon reading only a few lines, however, he discovered that he knew the sum of all truth, far more than he had set out to learn. The knowledge eventually proved to be his undoing. If the legends are true, the remaining members of the court killed him for the knowledge of them that he possessed."

"Well, whether the legends are true or not," Flynn said as he gripped the controls, pressing the ship faster through the cavern, "I have just taken a peek at the Book of Truth. Truth is the hardest thing of all to run from, Merinda—and I'm just hoping to give us a head start."

The *Brishan* suddenly emerged from the cavern. Brilliant sunlight glanced off her hull. The *Brishan* shot across the enormous Sand Sea for over a hundred leagues before rising quickly into the sky.

THE SENTINEL MOVED QUICKLY AT THE HEAD OF A COLUMN OF dragons, darting down the dark quays of the cavern with little regard for the dockworkers or spacers which blocked their way. Indeed, such creatures as may have stood before them rushed to open the path. No one wished to challenge the Sentinel—especially when he was backed by the Minister of Peace and a squad of dragons quaking the docks behind him.

"You are sure of what this Scrimshaw told you?" the Sentinel intoned from the dark folds of his hood.

"Yes, Sentinel," said Dedrak Kurbin-Flamishar, his great head drifting near the floating form of the human as they moved past the ships in port. Dedrak found it difficult to follow the human's words unless he kept his head so near. Humans always seem to communicate in whispers, Dedrak thought to himself. It is the dark nature of their hearts that they attempt to conceal. "The Vestis paid Scrimshaw well, but not well enough to insure his silence. I have instructed him to create a copy of the map for us to his best recollection . . ."

"We haven't the time for that," the Sentinel interrupted at once. "Neskat has the map—that's all that she will need. We cannot allow them to escape!"

"Even so," Dedrak replied, "their craft has already departed five minutes ago."

The Sentinel revolved suddenly. In a quick motion, the robed human reached up and grasped Dedrak by the fifth jowelspur and gave a hard yank.

"Yeeahharoo!" the dragon bellowed, leaning closer toward the human to relieve the pressure on the sensitive ridge thorn.

"You listen to me, Dedrak!" the Sentinel said fiercely into the dragon's ear. He still held the jowelspur firmly in both hands, pulling the dragon's head closer to his own. "I have crossed the stars at great discomfort and expense just so that I might find this woman and her cursed treasure map in this hellish place. I will not be disappointed! Your council has ordered your cooperation in this matter. Now, get me a ship that can track that woman NOW!"

The Sentinel released the dragon.

Dedrak snorted a puff of indignant smoke from his nostrils. "So they have. Here, Sentinel, is our ship."

The Sentinel looked up and, for the moment, was struck speechless.

The towering hull of the Tsultak war barge was a magnificent sight. Fierce in her lines and decoration, she bristled with no fewer than a hundred cannon projectors a side. Her dull gray finish was decorated throughout with ceremonial markings in brilliant greens, oranges, and reds. Dragons roamed her massive decks above, their crews preparing to make way into the stars.

"She has only been gone five minutes, you say." The Sentinel spoke as much to himself as to Dedrak. "This is most satisfactory. Dedrak, how long before the ship can be under way?"

"The preparations have all been accomplished but one, Sentinel," the great dragon rumbled.

"Excellent!" The shadowy figure began drifting up the access plank at once. "I am pleased. Never mind showing me my quarters now. Let's get this ship under way at once!"

"So we shall, Sentinel, just as soon as the launching ceremonies are completed."

The Sentinel stopped.

"Ceremonies?" he asked.

"Surely you, of all visitors, must be aware of our warrior customs," Dedrak said simply. "This is a voyage of campaign. The proprieties must be observed prior to launch!"

"Proprieties!" the Sentinel screeched. "I'll show you some proprieties if this ship isn't moving within the next five minutes!"

"This craft is scheduled to move at the right hind heel of the twilight nod," Dedrak intoned.

"That's seven hours from now!"

"The proprieties must be observed," the dragon answered simply.

"Dragons!" the Sentinel snorted. "I've had my fill of dragons! Everywhere I go—dragons!" The Sentinel rushed back down the access ramp. "I'll take care of this myself."

Dedrak reached quickly out with his large foreclaw and in a swift move quite suddenly pinned the Sentinel to the planking of the dock. Lightning erupted beneath his claw but Dedrak withstood the pain. The dragon pressed closer to the trapped human and, with his mouth gaping wide, roared loudly at the struggling figure. The sound rattled the planks for the entire length of the dock.

The Sentinel held still. The lightning ceased.

"The council has decreed that you shall assist us in this expedition—not the other way around, Sentinel," Dedrak intoned. "The proprieties SHALL be observed!"

24

Star Cross Tavern

"A TALE! A TALE! A TANON FOR A TALE!"

The yarnspinner was old beyond his years, obviously human by his general physique. His every appearance was a chorus of contrasts. His eyes were bright and young, yet set in a craggy, ancient face weathered by hard work and a harder sky. That he had been a spacer was beyond anyone's doubt who knew the type: the very look of his ravaged, tough flesh brought to mind the tall rigging of the core-ship masts and the years of exposure to the stray radiation that passed through the shifting sails, wings, and crystals as they strained to keep up with the unexpected fronts through which they so often passed. He was missing his left arm just below the shoulder, the story of whose passing he was most willing to impart for a few titanium tanons or, at least, the price of a drink. Coarse, iron-gray hair gave a bare acknowledgement to gravity as its knotted, twisting mass struck out on its own from the top of his head. It made his beard, stroked constantly by his remaining good hand, appear soft and inviting. Indeed, his beard was so different from the rest of the hoary mass that one was tempted to think it was fake, a cheap affectation by a wild-eyed sailor of the stars now shipwrecked in this dull and dingy inn.

"A tanon for a tale!" he squawked again.

The tavern keeper looked up a moment and considered whether to say something to keep the old man quiet or just run over and throw him out. Sense slowly returned to him, however. The yarnspinner didn't bother people much with his ranting and—he had to admit—was probably the closest thing to a floor-entertainment as he was likely to get in these parts. Still, he wondered what had set the old man off and looked quickly about the large and mostly deserted room.

Humans, he thought, nodding agreeably at the sight of the pair entering the room. Well, thank the Masters for that. He could deal with a few more bipeds these days, that was sure. Of course, one expected that sort of thing coreward—there were far more nonhumans on the inner frontier than anywhere else in the disk. The tavern keeper didn't know why that was so and, frankly, didn't care. It wasn't up to him why the universe was the way it was—that was just the natural order of things, he thought. Humans ruled; that, plus the fact that he was one of them, was enough for him.

The tavern keeper straightened up, cleaning a glass absently with the dirty rag that usually adorned his shoulder. You run into all kinds at a starport, he mused absently. He'd heard tales of the great starports further toward the rim— seen many of them on the rare netcasts from IGNM that happened his way through transcriptions or hauntings—but he only really knew the sprawling, vacant complex here on his own world firsthand.

The couple both wore cloaks with hoods to ward off the chill air outside. Their layered clothing apparently wasn't up to the task, as the male of the pair was both rubbing his hands together and blowing on them. Wrestling his face into a semblance of a smile, the tavern keeper approached them.

"Greetings, sentient! Welcome to the Star Cross. Mighty chill night to be about," he said with as much cheer as he could muster on such short notice. "No doubt you be off that starship I heard down to port just now. What might I do for you tonight?"

The man looked up cautiously, "What do you have that's warm?"

"Warm is it?" The tavern keeper laughed darkly. "Well, now, you'll be wanting a large flagon of hot Sartagon grog, to be sure!"

The grizzly-faced human seated before him nearly shook with a sudden rage. "I most certainly do NOT want any of that . . ."

"Two hot Sartagon grogs," the woman next to him quickly said, placing her hand on his arm in a move that quite effectively restrained him from rising. "It will warm us well."

"Aye, madam, as you wish," the tavern keeper said with slight emphasis through his smile. He then turned sourly toward the man again—an expression to which he was more accustomed. "Will there be anything else, master?"

"Yes," the man sighed. "Your sign's falling down."

"Master?"

"Your sign," the man repeated. "The one outside. It's falling away from the building. I just thought you'd like to know."

"Aye, master," the tavern keeper said without much commitment. "Paint don't stay put here like on them grand starports to rimward. Here we mostly just wait out the dirt and the smell. Loneliness—aye, we have plenty of that, too. Now and then some terrifying roar descends on us carrying who-knows-what-kind of horror into our backyard and then leaves us be again—beggin' your pardon, master, but this here is a wild place, not fit for the likes of the young lady here. It be terrible enough for the old likes of me, that be sure!"

The man only shook his head, the look of smooth-skinned incredulity belying his refinement and the fact that he did not belong in this place. "Why don't you leave, then?"

"What? And give up space travel?" The tavern keeper snorted as he turned away. He drew two large flagons from behind the bar and crossed the room to the great black cauldron bubbling ominously above the fire. Some people, he thought to himself sadly, just don't understand the romance of the stars. Take these two, for instance; here they come straight off some ship or other after plying the night and all either of them wants to do is visit this old groundling tavern and forget all about the stars. Criminal it is.

He turned with his flagons, somewhat determined to set these strange folk straight with a piece of his mind. These two travelers were far beyond the pretty life they had obviously been raised in. Tourists, he thought with a snort. Well, best he gives them some good advice so that they might keep their heads. He didn't much care for the young man—too cocky, he thought—but the woman was someone he might think twice about before contributing to her death.

"Here you be," the tavern keeper said, setting both flagons precipitously on the rough-hewn table. He straightened up and when no further conversation was forthcoming, he uttered what he considered to be the smoothest and largest understatement he had ever uttered. "You be not from these parts, eh?"

"No," the woman said over the top of her steaming mug.

The tavern keeper waited somewhat awkwardly for any further clarification. When none was forthcoming, he tried again. "As I thought, for certain. No doubt some pressing business brings you to this gods-forsaken core of the universe." The statement hung as a question in the air.

"No."

The tavern keeper would have frowned more deeply, were that possible. He wasn't terribly bright to begin with and riddles made him feel both confused and suspicious. "Ah, of course, then, it would be a government posting, now, wouldn't it? No doubt your ladyship and master are establishing that there righteous law of the Tsultak dragons through the local stars once again. I can't say that I'd be finding your rule of law to be unwelcome in these . . ."

The young woman was holding up her free hand as if to stop the tavern keeper's litany.

"Er, what I'm meaning to say, is that them godless Tsultak really have no business interfering in the free-trade affairs of enterprising . . ."

The woman shook her head slowly, as she set her flagon down.

The tavern keeper's face glazed over in crimson frustration. "Well, blast it all, woman, whatever business would a fine lady and gentleman like yourselves have being out and about in this lawless frontier of . . ."

"Adventure!" cried out the yarnspinner. "Adventure and treasure and blood, no doubting it!"

The tavern keeper turned suddenly on the craggy old sod struggling to his feet. "You keep out of this, you old *kredge*! And don't you be bothering this fine woman or I'll have you back out in the mud, hear me?"

"Hear ye?" the yarnspinner cackled back at the man as he navigated an unsteady course toward the table. "Aye, hear ye I do, as I've the ears for it! Yet see if I'm not right, Master Thembris! These two have the look of the hunger in their eyes! Have ye not seen that before, Thembris? Are ye so dead yet that ye can't smell it in their very breath?"

" 'Tis a sure thing that your own breath is . . ."

The yarnspinner smiled, the skin of his face contorting into craggy delineation of every muscle beneath it. His voice was soft as he spoke. "Thembris, good taverner! These be mates of mine—heart and soul. You wouldn't want me to be cursing this place, now, would ye?"

The ruddy face of the tavern keeper suddenly drained of all color. Spacers of the core were a wild lot and not a few of them quite powerful in the dark arts. It was part of the craft. Only the bravest or most foolish dared cross a spacer. The tavern keeper fit one of the categories fairly well, although he was mistaken about which one. "You'll not be practicing any of that star-sailor's deviltry in my tavern, Thom, or I swear I'll have the mystics in here enforcing you before . . ."

"It's all right," the woman said, smiling at the tavern keeper, but her eyes were on the old spacer. "He's quite correct after all. We do seek treasures, in a way. I collect tales as I travel. The greatest of treasures are stories and songs which . . ."

"Stories!" The yarnspinner danced suddenly with delight, his good hand snaking through the air, caressing memories that drifted unbidden into his mind. "Aye, lady! I'm an old spacer come to no good end at this here tavern. I've only my tales to tell and memories to live on, sweet mistress. I've seen more, heard more, and tell more than your mind has ever dreamed."

The man put his hand on the woman's shoulder. "We haven't much time. I don't see how we are ever going to find this man in time, let alone get him to tell us what he knows. Besides, even if Flynn did give you instructions, I don't see what all the rush is to get back to the . . ."

"Aye, back indeed," the yarnspinner cackled. "Back to your pretty ship and its important journey taking your fine pretty people from here to there among the stars. Ye see the lands and the planets and the stars—but the space? Indeed, lady, the space itself harbors many a tale that is overlooked in the rush from departure to arrival."

The man interrupted again, rising as he spoke. "We really haven't the time . . ."

The woman placed her hand again on his arm, gently pressing him back into his seat.

"We have time enough," she said, her eyes fixed with amusement on the old yarnspinner. "Flynn says he has much to do before she'll be ready to leave again. We have time enough. Tell me, old one, is your tale a true one?"

"Aye, lady," the yarnspinner murmured. "True as the stars themselves."

"And is it a tale of adventure or romance?"

"Both, lady, truly both!" The old man nearly spit with the excitement of his words. "A tale of haunted ships and ancient betrayals . . ."

"Indeed," the woman said, leaning closer across the table as her companion reluctantly returned to his seat. "Tell us this tale, old spacer."

The firelight danced in his eyes as the yarnspinner began his tale. "Once, long millennia back, these stars about us were ruled by the Dysday emperor. Great was he in that time, lady, as well ye know. His word spread across the stars like a quantum gale. Where it was heard, there was law.

"He brung the rule of humankind to all the heavens, he did. Afore that time, the disk was a wild place, filled with all manner of heathen creatures a-writhing and a-wriggling their way about. 'Twere a maddened time. Yet ol' Dysday said that man were in his image and that were that! He pulled out his sword—aye, that be the Nightsword that ye heard tell about—and wherever he turned that black-craft magic that were in the sword, whatever he thought to be true, were true. If he were to think that water was turned to yardow, it were so! Aye, as unlikely as you please and he could make it happen. So, one day he thought the thought and drew his sword and passed among the stars in his great

CAPPA:
LOG
OF
THE
BRISHAN

ships. He passed through the disk with his sword drawn and thought a thought about how all greater life should be in his own image and wherever he passed it were so! Many thoughtful heathen creatures were changed in that day, great lady! Many worlds were forced under Dysday's sword to forsake their past and become human like us.

"Yet did he have his weakness, as all the great do. For Dysday loved without bounds his wicked queen, Shaunki. It seems that the wicked Queen Shaunki had been seduced by the emperor's brother, Obek, and fallen into the stars right here—yes, good lady, these very stars above us, and into the center of the disk! Can you imagine it, good lady, gentle sire! Shaunki, cold beauty of the night sailing into the heart of chaos, the madness tearing at her every thought!

"It were too much for Dysday. The emperor abandoned his glorious throne and fell into the maelstrom core in search of her and his brother . . ."

"We've heard this one before," the man said to the woman, ignoring the yarnspinner as he looked about the tavern in search of a face or look that would signal to him the man they were supposed to meet here.

"Aye! No doubt you have," the old spacer said, without missing a beat. He'd been at his trade long enough to know when to switch tales. "Yet do ye know what happened to that selfsame Nightsword? Do ye know the tale of its fate and its doom for all who seek it?"

The woman smiled. "No. Would you tell us?"

The man shook his head. "Merinda! We've got to find our contact! We really don't have time for this . . ."

"We'll take time," the woman said, smiling at the old man, "and make it worth your while, spacer."

"Aye," the old man's eyes flashed in the dancing light of the fire. "And such a tale I have to tell . . . about a young lad named L'Zari who sailed the stars with his father, looking for that selfsame Nightsword ye've heard tell about and how they both came nearest to claiming that prize as any in the tales that have been told!"

The young man turned suddenly, looking at the spacer as if seeing him for the first time.

"Him?" the young man said, gasping.

"Him," the woman replied with a smile.

The young man turned to the old spacer, with new interest. "Who are you, old man?"

The woman, however, reached across the table with her strong but gentle hands. "Please," she said soothingly, "tell us the tale of this L'Zari and his quest for the Nightsword."

The old spacer smiled, anticipation of his reward already gleaming in his eyes. He quickly warmed into the performance. His words breathed life and color into the tale, conjuring images in the mind as well as a host of associated sensations all playing on his expertly crafted words. L'Zari, the boy who had found his father, walked again the decks of their minds. The boy struggled among the stars for his father's approval only to discover the ancient, secret knowledge that could lead him to the Nightsword and, through it, all his heart's desires. There, within the tavern, was Kip's crew foully murdered. There floated the ghosts of the ancient Settlement Ship amid the smoke of the fire in the hearth. There, too, in the darkness, did L'Zari lose his father to an unknown fate.

Time slowed over the Sartagon grogs. It swam lazily through the smoky, thick air of the tavern. The yarnspinner wove images that were brilliant and frightening, a craftsman with images of the mind. At last, the tale was told and time resumed its course.

"What a magnificent tale," the woman sighed, gazing with deep intent into the eyes of the yarnspinner. "If only it were true."

"True?" The yarnspinner gaped. "True it is as I sit here and breathe!"

"Oh, really now!" The woman's dark laughter was warm and playful. "How would you know such a thing?"

"I were there, ma'am! Swear by the stars, I were there!"

"You?" The woman laughed again. "I thought you said all the crew died?"

"Aye, that they did for a fact, ma'am!" the yarnspinner protested. "I weren't part of that crew. That L'Zari's family took me on to find the boy. 'Twere I that led them into the Narrows, it was!"

"Were it now?" the woman asked coyly.

"It were indeed, ma'am!"

"Then, yarnspinner, you shall have that privilege again," Merinda said, smiling.

"I'll not be going back to that place again," the yarn-spinner cried out. Reality was beginning to settle on his fogged brain. "It were forbidden! If that boy's family were to find out—or worse, that L'Zari himself—I'd be good as dead!"

"You'll be a good deal better than dead if you don't help me!" Merinda suddenly reached across the table, grasping the old spacer by his beard and pulling his face close to her own. "I've been chased halfway across the disk and I will not be giving up now. I am a Vestis Inquisitas of the Omnet. Now you will tell me what I need to hear and you will show me the way to the Boncfield Narrows because even thinking that there will be an alternative will cause you incredible pain!"

"Ye . . . ye be wanting me to show ye the way to the Narrows?" the yarnspinner squawked.

"Yes! Now!"

"But ma'am, I'd have thought ye knew . . . being a Vestis and all." The yarnspinner swallowed. "What with him being your master and all."

"What are you talking about?" Merinda said, letting go of the old man's beard. "What master?"

"Well, that L'Zari never did take his father's name. The family were powerful and propertied beyond avarice. He took his mother's name and was taken back to his home world on Gandri. Made quite a name for himself, he did, though he dropped the use of his first name."

The young man sucked in a deep breath. "No!"

"Aye! Perhaps you've heard of L'Zari Targ—of Gandri?"

25

Gales and Tides

THE DISPLACEMENT DRIVE SUDDENLY FAILED.

"By the Nine!" Merinda slammed her hand down on the command console, another in a series of blows she had inflicted upon the continuously offending instrument. "Now where are we?"

"We are four parsecs rimward of the Blood Tide Archipelago," Lindia stated clearly. "The quantum index has shifted radically. Current Q-dex indices indicate the strong probability of phlogiston with ether content. Harpies with both sorceress and psionic abilities highly probable. Mystic drives in the 82.76 range recommended for this environment. Recalibration of drives will require thirty-six minutes."

"How long can we go on like this?" Griffiths asked, seated tiredly to the starboard side of the bridge. Lindia had formed a comfortable reclined chair out of the malleable wall for him, though he was feeling anything but comfortable at the moment.

"The last drive failure occurred twenty-three minutes ago," Lindia added cheerfully.

"Well," Flynn said as he leaned casually against the bulkhead at the back of the bridge, "that's about ten minutes less than last time. I suppose we will get there eventually."

"Eventually is not good enough, Evon," Merinda responded as she reconfigured the command console to display and control the new drive configuration. "Targ is out there. He's free and has the entire galaxy looking for us. I'd bet good tanons that he also is personally on his way here looking for us. We haven't got the luxury of time."

"Well, you'll never stay ahead of them at this rate," Flynn snorted as he folded his arms across his chest. "Besides, I'd be more worried about that Sentinel than Targ. That wizard not only got here from the outer rim nearly as fast as you did, but he also knew exactly where to look for you. I can't even fathom how that is possible."

"The Sentinels are still powerful in the galaxy despite recent setbacks." Merinda continued to reconfigure the controls of her command chair as she spoke. "There are no doubt many synths that are still infected with their faith virus. We may have left a trail for him to follow without realizing it. In any event, I wouldn't count Targ out of the equation just yet. If anything, I think he may be more dangerous now than he was before."

"You do?" Flynn said, folding his arms casually across his chest.

"Absolutely," she replied, as she struggled with a set of newly formed control surfaces on the consoles around her. "I thought all this was just some maniacal bid for power on Targ's part—as if the office of Prime weren't enough power for one man. After that story we heard from that old spacer, I think it's worse: I think that for Targ this is personal. Perhaps he's out to prove something to himself. Perhaps he's out to prove something to his dead father."

"If his father's dead," Griffiths interjected.

"Well, either way it makes Targ unpredictable," Merinda concluded as she stabbed her fingers at the sequencing buttons once more. "If you do not understand a man's motivations, then you cannot hope to anticipate his moves. If we only knew what Targ—damn! The etheric motivators don't work at all here! We'll have to try another drive!"

"Hmm." Flynn's voice sounded almost bored. "Have you ever flown the core before, Neskat?"

Merinda rotated the command chair back to face him. Her voice had a cold edge to it and was more than patronizing. "No, Flynn, I have not flown the core before."

240

"Well, that, I'm afraid, is obvious." Flynn flashed his brilliant smile and looked down at the floor planks for a moment before continuing. "Merinda, you are an experienced Vestis but you obviously don't know anything about sailing the core. This ship of yours is a technological wonder. It's loaded with all the right bells, whistles, and gizmos to take you through just about any conceivable quantum zone that you would run into. Unfortunately, while your ship would run circles around just about anything the rim has to offer—here in the core it's just the wrong choice."

Merinda folded her arms across her chest and flung a defiant look at her old friend. "Fine. I suppose you have an alternate suggestion."

"Yes, as a matter of fact I do," Flynn said, his own arms crossed as well. You're used to pointing your pretty little machine in the general direction you want to go, giving the order, and getting there. Sure, you use the prevailing quantum weather conditions and plot your course accordingly but that's mostly a matter of convenience and economy rather than necessity. Here you can't just bully your way through the weather with brute force. You've got to be a bit more humble in the face of the universe here at the core."

"You're saying I should use the weather rather than work against it." Merinda sniffed stiffly.

"That's the way we do it here," Flynn said stepping forward as he cocked his head upward to address the synth. "Lindia, please give me the navigation chart for this region.

Include our course to date and our projected course as we explained it to you earlier."

In an instant, a glowing cube a yard square on the side appeared before Flynn. It was quite suddenly filled with stars, wave fronts, nebula clouds, and navigation markings. Griffiths gazed at it with increasing anxiety. He had used similar charts navigating out to the Tsultak region—with a great deal of help from Lindia—but this chart was far more complicated than any he had looked at thus far.

"Here's Tsultak and here's our course thus far," Flynn said, reaching into the illuminated cube and pointing at the point of light and the glowing lines projecting from it. "As you can see by these benchmarks, the distance we are traveling per unit of time is getting shorter and shorter—we're making less headway. However, if we make our way over to the prevailing trade routes here," he pointed downward toward a milky band below, "just off Griffin's Turn, then we have some pretty clear lanes down to the Maelstrom Wall— and hopefully the Bonefield Narrows as well. We could be there in days rather than the months it will take us to wallow through these choking little quantum variances."

"That sounds good to me," Merinda said, studying the chart. "So what's the downside?"

"Well," Flynn shrugged, "the downside is that the lanes get pretty congested in places. It's not that there's a great deal of traffic. The armed merchant freighters certainly won't bother us. The problem will be the pirates."

"Pirates?" Griffiths suddenly chimed in.

"Yes, Griffiths, pirates," Flynn said, with a bit of a twinkle in his eyes. "They know the lanes far better than the merchant pilots do. They know just where to wait for prey and they'll pounce if they have a chance. However, I don't think we have much to worry about from them. In most cases we should be able to outrun them. Even if we can't shake them, we could just surrender, let them board us, strip us of some equipment, and then they'll be on their way. We probably don't have much that would interest them in the first place. They hunt yardow mostly and that's not part of our manifest."

"Well," Merinda said, "pirates or no, we've got to give it a try. We can't afford the time. Is there any alternative?"

"I could try to get you a better ship," Flynn suggested.

Merinda eyed him coldly.

"Sorry. Your ship may be a wonder to behold in the outer territories but here at the core it's an accident that hasn't happened yet."

"Thanks, Flynn. Lindia?"

"Yes, Merinda?"

"Plot us a new course to the Griffin's Turn. We're going to make a run for the prize."

THE RAINBOW PHLOGISTON DRIVES BROUGHT THEM SMOOTHLY around the Griffin's Turn and solidly into what Flynn cheerfully called the Widower's Throat. The prevailing trade weather held for them, bringing them within eight hours to Gibbon's Point. They reconfigured then for a time-front pressure drive that operated without difficulty nearly the entire length of a spiraling, twisting corridor of space which was known as the Devil's Gut.

Griffiths wondered if he would be able to read a map of the local region and keep his lunch down at the same time. As it was, he watched the chart of their course in the little chart cube on the bridge with puzzlement. It was true that they were making much better headway toward the Maelstrom Wall—a place that he decided was some sort of natural boundary keeping people out of the very center of the galactic core. However, the course that they were taking was remarkably bizarre. It curled in and around on itself multiple times in a dizzying projection of angles and lines. They were covering four times the distance but at least they were progressing toward the Wall.

There was just something nagging at Griffiths that he couldn't put his finger on.

MERINDA STOOD ON THE OBSERVATION DECK AND GAZED languidly through the clear dome that stretched both above and before her.

The stars of the core were a marvel to behold. The density of their light nearly filled every available space in the dome about her. Never before had she seen so many stars. Many of them stood in sharp relief against the feathery backdrop of dust clouds, which themselves were outlined starkly by the grouping of stars beyond them. It was a glorious sight. Merinda wondered, however, how many other such sights she had simply let go during her life. She had spent much of that life trying to atone for a terrible wrong. Her own guilt had consumed her and robbed her of any true life, but it also was a large part of what motivated her. Now she was free of that guilt and, quite often, missed it. Yet in moments like these she thought that perhaps the greatest crime was in the things she had missed. So consumed with introspective hatred that she had never looked beyond her work and her own pain: what had she missed along the way?

"Where are you, Merinda?"

Evon. A voice from her past that no longer hurt.

"Far among the stars, Evon," she replied. Her Vestis training made her aware of him as he fell quietly up the access chute and stepped onto the soft carpet covering the deck. There was no need for her to turn from the view. She knew he was approaching her and, somehow, here beneath the flowing stars, she didn't mind.

"We are a long way from home, Merinda," Flynn said. She could feel the brush of his breath through her hair. He was close behind her. "A long way, indeed, from those days back on Brishan."

"Yes." She laughed and was startled by the sound—so free and light. It reminded her of someone long ago. "Those were good times, Evon. I remember you and your little grav cart going into the city and hauling fresh vegetables all the way back up the canyon so that we could have something decent to eat. You were a wonderful cook, Evon."

"Hey, I am a wonderful cook!"

They both laughed.

He easily slipped his arms around her waist.

She relaxed backward into him, folding her hands down over his.

What else have I missed, she thought.

"I may have been a great cook," Flynn said, pulling her closer to him from behind, "but let's not forget that I was the best sifter in the entire Citadel, if not the sector itself."

"Yes, Evon, you were all that," Merinda said, smiling into the stars. "You were that and I suspect a good deal more."

His arms suddenly relaxed slightly and he seemed to move away. Something she had said had touched a nerve. Some part of her knew that she had tread on dangerous ground and that she might be better off not pursuing him on the subject. Yet Vestis she was and would always now be. She could not leave well enough alone.

"Evon, what have you been doing these past years?"

No reply.

She turned to face him, his arms still around her, though they now seemed somehow awkward in how they held her. She looked up into his face. "Evon, please. It was long ago. What brought you here?"

A shadow crossed his face for a moment, only to be banished by the flash of a brilliant smile. "Why, you brought me here, Merinda! I just came up the chute and here you were."

Merinda shook her head. "You always were one with the ladies." Her words were casual but her hands moved awkwardly around his waist. It had been a long time indeed.

"Yes, Merinda, but I always had my eye out for you. Even back then. Even when you were so set on . . ."

Words suddenly failed them both.

Merinda suddenly realized that they shared something. They both shared the pain. She looked up into his clouded face and spoke. "Yes, Evon. Even then, and I do remember— even though it was a long time ago."

He looked down at her.

His face moved closer to hers.

"Yes," he murmured. "And terribly far away from here."

"HEY!" yelled a voice at her from far too nearby. She jumped at the unexpected sound, pulling out of Flynn's arms and shaking as she stood.

"Excuse me! Sorry to interrupt!" Griffiths's face was red though Merinda couldn't tell if it was from embarrassment or some other cause. It was obvious, however, that he was not sorry for the interruption at all. "We have a proximity alarm going off down on the bridge. There's someone out there and they're closing on us fast."

"Well, why didn't you just call us over the com system?" Merinda sputtered. She realized that her own face was growing flushed as well, but could do nothing about it.

"I did call you over the com system but Lindia seemed to think you needed a little privacy," Griffiths's emphasis on the last word was filled with distaste. "She said we should just handle it ourselves!"

Merinda was already running for the chute. "So why didn't you just handle it by yourselves!" she scolded.

"Well, excuse me," Griffiths yelled down the tube as Merinda vanished down into the ship's depths, "but I thought the captain of the ship would have liked to have known we were about to be attacked! Hey, you can't get out of this that easily!"

Griffiths jumped down the chute after her.

Meanwhile, on the observation deck, Flynn stood contemplating the events that had just so suddenly taken place. What was happening outside the ship, it seemed to him, wasn't nearly as complicated as what was happening inside the ship. He shrugged once and made his own rush for the lift chute.

26

Boarding Action

"LINDIA, DAMN IT, WHY DIDN'T YOU GIVE ME A PROXIMITY warning?" Merinda yelled, bursting onto the ship's bridge. She was embarrassed and confused and neither sensation was one that she was either used to or comfortable with. More troubling still was the fact that she didn't know why she should be embarrassed and confused. The more the thoughts looped through her mind, the angrier she became, both with herself and the universe in general.

"Captain Griffiths was on the bridge at the time," the ship's synthetic mind said calmly. "He instructed me that the message was better delivered in person."

"Well, he was wrong," Merinda spat, grabbing the back of the command chair and leaping into it. "Next time, you just tell me over the com system. There is nothing so important that you cannot do that, do you understand?"

"Well, then, next time man your own damned bridge," Griffiths said as he moved to his own station on the starboard side of the compartment. "I was just doing my job."

"Badly, Griffiths," Merinda shot back. "You were just doing your job badly—as always!"

"Now just what do you mean by that!"

"You know what I mean!"

"Wait, please!" Flynn entered the bridge wearing a

surprised look, as though he had just walked out onto a weapons testing range. "I don't know what's going on here, but there is a ship chasing us and I don't think this is the time to . . ."

"Hey," Griffiths yelled at Merinda as he sat down roughly in the force chair Lindia had formed for him, "I didn't ask for this! I had everything under control until you insisted that we pick up your boyfriend!"

"My what?"

"Your boyfriend!"

"If it hadn't been for Flynn, I'd be dead by now!"

"Hey, I was taking care of you! We didn't need that drunken spacedock freeloader along for the ride! But, no, you insisted that I go down to the bar and fetch him."

Lindia chimed in calmly. "Proximity alarm. Vessel approaching is identified as a Class D Aendorian design trailing a large red banner indicative of the Marren-kan pirate flagship. The ship is approaching at 201.4 degrees true vector minus 15 degrees. Time to intercept is eight minutes."

"By the Nine!" Merinda shook her head in mocking wonder as she swiveled the command chair forward and stabbed at several display controls with a vengeance. "Is your entire race of males so full of their own testosterone that they cannot see anything in more than sexual relationships? It's a wonder your people ever got as far as space travel in the first place!"

"My people have done just fine," Griffiths shouted back at her. "And we certainly know a good deal more about some things than your so-called advanced civilization!"

"Excuse me." Flynn tried again to inject his thoughts into the conversation. He was staring at an ominously flashing readout panel on the wall. "We're losing cohesion in the stellar sails. We're coming up on another wave front."

"Advanced civilization," Merinda mocked as she swung the chair around. She leaped up and moved at once toward

Flynn's panel, pushing him out of her way as she continued to speak. "Advanced at what, barbarian—rhythmic drum-beating? Basket weaving? Did your people actually construct a spacecraft or did you just carve it out of an old log?"

"We could show you people a thing or two!" Griffiths grumbled as he turned back to his console, stabbing his finger at a few controls of his own. "At least we know something about loyalty!"

"Loyalty?" Merinda continued to reconfigure the drive system for the local conditions, her hand flying across the control surface before her as she spoke. "Loyal to what? You wanted to get out of your blossom-scented luxury as the big prophet to the Irindris. Where was your loyalty when you walked out on them? You wanted your little fling in the universe and now you've got it. I nearly died paying for it . . ."

"Oh, great." Griffiths threw both hands up in the air. "You're the one who wanted to dash off and find this Nightsword thingy. Now I'm supposed to go on a major guilt trip simply because you nearly got yourself killed . . ."

"Hey, both of you!" Flynn said, his own anger beginning to rise. "Stop this! What's the matter with you two?"

"Just stay out of this, Flynn!" Merinda warned in a voice that brooked no question or insubordination. "Perhaps I did nearly get myself killed, Griffiths, but I did it because of your bizarre little plan that didn't make much sense at the time and, in hindsight, may have been a big mistake in the first place!"

"Great! So now I'm a mistake?"

"I didn't say that!"

"Yes, you did!"

Linda chimed in once more. "*Brishan*'s speed dropping. Time to intercept revised to five minutes."

"Lindia," Merinda yelled even though the synth could hear her perfectly well. "What's the problem?"

"We have moved through a minor quantum front and are now in a class three-eight quantum zone, unsuitable for our current drive situation. Maneuverability is down to twenty-two percent. Propulsion is operating at thirteen percent efficiency."

Merinda cursed again under her breath. What was the matter with her, she thought. Why was she acting this way? Griffiths had walked in on Flynn and her on the observation deck. Why was she so upset about that? Worse, where was the titanium-eyed, clear logic that had dominated her life since the accident on Tentris? The questioned threatened to overwhelm her even as she struggled with the main drive console to find another, more suitable propulsion system.

"Revised intercept time now three minutes," Lindia said a bit too cheerfully for those present.

"I can't get this reconfigured fast enough," Merinda said at last. "We may have to fight them off."

Flynn, who had been casually leaning against the aft bulkhead all this time, suddenly became animated. "Wait a moment, now! Those are pirates we're talking about. They'll treat you well enough if you simply relax, give them some food and trinkets, and let them go on their merry way in search of real treasure, Merinda! Just let them come and be done with it."

"No, I'll never submit," Merinda said determinedly as she moved quickly back through the hatch at the aft end of the bridge. "I won't let them take my ship!"

"Merinda." Flynn followed her, trying with obvious effort to keep the Vestis calm. "They don't want your ship. They just want to rummage about in it for a while. Once they see you're not carrying any yardow they'll just let you go."

"How is it you've become such an expert on pirates out here on the frontier?" Griffiths was right behind him, his voice dripping with suspicion.

They had arrived at a massive hardwood cabinet located where the access corridor curved around to join the lift chute. Merinda spoke quietly as she pressed her palms against the doors. In a moment, both doors swung quickly open revealing a host of handheld weapons all mounted carefully in racks. The Vestis considered for a moment the arsenal arrayed before her, then quickly began pulling several of the more deadly looking weapons down from their mounts. She began passing them one by one to the men standing behind her.

"Look, all I'm saying is that it doesn't have to end this way!" Flynn argued, even as Merinda was pressing an ungainly looking piece of chrome-finished weaponry into his hands. "Just relax, make no sudden moves, do what the nice men in the big scary spacecraft say you should do, and everything will turn out just fine."

"Flynn, shut up, will you," Griffiths whined. He was holding his own weapon awkwardly in his hands, terrified to ask which end he was supposed to point at the enemy. Still, he was willing to talk a good fight. "You sound like you'd rather we surrendered before they got here."

"You're right, barbarian birdman," Flynn returned a little too quickly. Merinda thought the strain was getting to her old friend as well. "It makes no sense to put up a fight when one isn't necessary."

Merinda took it all in with grim determination. She was relishing the possibility of battle. Her blood ran hotter in her veins at the simple act of preparing for it. She was not required to make any decisions beyond the familiar ones of battle. The complexities of human relationships would not cloud her thinking or her judgment now. It was a relief, she realized, that she could leave those gentle complexities behind for a time and simply turn herself over to her training and her instincts. Life and love had not occupied her mind in the years since the accident. No, she realized that wasn't truthful. Her emotions had ruled her actions for many years. Now that she was free of her past, she had to rule her passions rather than the other way around. It was one skill that she had never acquired.

Battle, however, was something she knew very well indeed.

Lindia's voice rang through their ears. "Approaching ship. Proximity alert. Time to intercept sixty seconds."

Merinda shouldered a massive weapon of her own and pulled two smaller weapons into each of her hands. She turned toward the men next to her. "Follow me up to the next deck. They will almost certainly try for the bridge. If they can get to the synth then they have the ship. I'll seal the hatch after us, then we'll take up positions in the main equipment bay just outside the hatch. After that, just follow my instructions and we may get through this yet." Merinda turned toward the lift chute behind her, calling out even as she stepped into the lift. "Lindia, what is the position of the approaching vessel?"

"Ship is coming alongside. Several of her exterior hatches are open. Merinda, we have an access open request at the exterior main airlock. Access denied. Override request denied."

"Don't let them in, Lindia," Merinda growled as she stepped off the lift and opened the hatch to the main equipment bay.

"Subroutine access denied. System access denied. Tracer access denied. Communication access denied," Lindia chanted a litany of sins attempted against her.

Merinda looked out into the crowded equipment bay. There were few clear fields of fire but she knew that she could use that to her advantage. If Flynn and Griffiths could protect access to the bridge, then she would have a chance to go out and do some hunting. The thought pleased her.

"Flynn?"

"No, Merinda, it's me," Griffiths said somewhat sullenly.

"Get down behind that spiritual attractor there." She pointed at the massive black piece of glass. "You'll be able to cover the opening from there. If things get too hot, duck back into the hatch and lay down fire from there, got it?"

"Yes."

"Where's Flynn?"

"Back here, Merinda," Flynn called. "I'm just trying to lock down this iris hatch to the lower level. Give me a minute."

The equipment bay rocked suddenly. The rumble of a distant explosion echoed through the huge bay.

"Aft main access hatch to airlock one has been compromised. Emergency atmospheric envelope in place. Security has been compromised. Intruder alarm. Intruder alarm."

Merinda could see several of the figures moving across the deck through infrequent gaps in the equipment. She raised her weapon.

Suddenly, a hail of green flaming bolts cut just over her head from behind her. She turned quickly toward the unexpected attack.

A plasma-bolt assault rifle was leveled at her with unquestioning menace.

"Sorry, Merinda," said the voice behind the rifle, "but it really is for the best. Surrender your ship and your cargo—right now—and do as I say, or it will go very badly for you."

It was Evon Flynn.

GAMMA:

INHUMAN

CREED

27

Smoke of Battle

GRIFFITHS PRESSED HIS FACE FLAT AGAINST THE COLD METALLIC plating of the deck. There was a time for heroics and desperate deeds but this was not one of them, he quickly realized. Flynn had them covered. He might spare Merinda but so far as he was concerned, Griffiths knew that Flynn would just as soon vaporize, atomize, disintegrate, burn, explode, or visit whatever other unspeakable destruction his weapon could do to him without a second thought.

One thought continued to roll through his head—that they had been taken by pirates. Indeed, he realized he could both hear and feel their rapid approach through the vibrating floor plates. He wondered if Flynn had been at least truthful about the intentions of the pirates. Was looting their only real objective? Would he and Merinda be released after the ship had been stripped?

In a moment the pirates were about him. His face remained pressed to the floor. The voices rang out over him, sinister in his own mind.

"Ahoy, Cap'n Flynn!" A deep, guttural voice sounded. "Sure as we thought of never setting eyes on ye agin and here ye be bringin' in the mark slick as ever before!"

Captain Flynn? Griffiths was quite suddenly glimpsing the depth of what had happened to them.

"Aye, true that be captain!" rang out a reedy voice on Griffiths's other side. "Ne'r were a son of a bilge rat that were more pleased to set eyes on yer tattered carcass."

"I am grateful, Master Kratha." Griffiths all too easily recognized Flynn's voice. "Pass the word to the men: prepare to abandon the prey."

"But yer honor," protested a third voice, "we just boarded her! There be many a pretty piece still laying about her decks that would be profitable!"

"Aye, Cap'n!" the guttural voice chimed in. "Where's the rush to be kickin' this old hulk loose so soon?"

"We have bigger concerns, Master Kratha. Besides, there's no need to bother with the small change when the real prize is at our feet. Master Shindak, would you be so good as to bind and blindfold these two humans and transfer them to the *Venture Revenge*. Gently, Master Shindak, we wouldn't want our prize damaged."

"By your word, Cap'n!"

Black strips of cloth were quickly pulled over Griffiths's eyes and tied behind his head. Throughout the process he wondered about Merinda. She had not said a single word since Flynn fired the shots. She had made no move to oppose him. Indeed, she had simply complied quietly, as he had done. What was wrong with her? Knowing Merinda as he did, he wondered why the woman had not torn out the man's heart by now.

The blindfolds effectively kept Griffiths from seeing anything. A moment later, they were both bound with cords and lifted up. Griffiths wasn't sure just where he was being taken. For a time he felt as though he were being passed around over the heads of various-sized people. Then quite suddenly he was adrift—floating in a free fall he could only guess was outside the *Brishan*'s gravity. He began to panic, only to realize that he could breathe perfectly normally and was reasonably warm. The perception of motion soon died. He wondered as he floated just how long he would be left here in this sightless, weightless void when, quite abruptly, his motion was arrested painfully by a deck that materialized, complete with gravity, below him. More hands—or what he hoped were hands—took hold of him, lifting him up and passing him along for a time. He had the vague impression that he was moving downward into the depths of the pirate ship's spaces. With the creaking of a door, he was tossed unceremoniously into a chamber and came at last to rest. Another thump and bump in the room—which he assumed was Merinda following him—and the door slammed closed loudly.

Griffiths felt with his bound hands the rough planks of the deck under him. He held still, waiting for something to happen, for one of the pirate band to say or make some sort of sign as to what they expected of him. Nothing was forthcoming, however, and after a short while he ventured to move. His hands were tied firmly behind his back. His feet were bound also at the ankles. Yet with some effort he managed to push himself to a sitting position. It was a good deal more comfortable than lying against the floor.

"Neskat," he called out sotto voce. "Neskat, are you in here?"

"Quiet, you fool," Merinda replied. "Hold still and I'll get to you in a moment."

There were a thousand questions burning in his mind at the moment, all of which seemed larger for the darkness that he felt himself engulfed in. Still, he figured that doing as Merinda said was a safe bet. So he sat still on the floor, taking in what he could in the darkness.

The ship had a peculiar smell, something like a cross between sandal leather and old wood. There were other scents that were mingled into it—unidentified spices that seemed inviting and warmly sweet. All together, Griffiths took it for a workmanlike aroma that called up visions of sweat-drenched muscles and oiled deck planks. It was the smell of old ways and long use.

To his ears came the creaking of the wood itself: a low moaning rattle that occasionally groaned under some shifting stress of the hull. A rhythmic banging could be heard in the far distance, muffled by bulkheads and passages. Above it all came the distant, dark voices singing far above them, their voices straining with the tempo as their bodies toiled in unison to some great unseen task.

> *Hang dried on the gibbet, my lady, my queen,*
> *Drunk on the wine of a blade that is keen,*
> *We'll swing to tune of the devil's black song,*
> *For dead-eyes we have closed on the fools we have wronged,*
> *A pox on our past, to our end rush anon,*
> *A curse on the bones of our Lord Marren-kan.*

"Good God," Griffiths murmured in awe. "We've been taken by the Marren-kan!"

"What do you know of the Marren-kan?" Merinda asked, her voice filled with strain as she struggled against her bonds.

"Enough!" Griffiths's hands began working ineffectively against the ropes. The room in the darkness beyond seemed to be closing in on him. "From what that old yarnspinner told us . . ."

"Yarnspinner? Do you believe everything old men tell you in bars, Griffiths?"

"Well, you seemed to think enough of what he had to say to drag us out into this forgotten—and, may I point out, deservedly—ignored frontier of the galaxy so that we can all be captured, drawn, quartered, tortured, or worse!"

"One more remark like that," Merinda said through her huffing breath, "and I may just leave you tied up."

Griffiths considered that for a moment. Yes, he thought, she probably would. No doubt another tack would be required. "Yes, Vestis. So you don't think that these are the Gorgon pirates?"

"Pirates? Certainly. Gorgon—not even the remotest possibility . . . There!"

Griffiths heard the rather satisfying sound of a cord unraveling and falling to the floor. Just stay calm, he reminded himself. You will be free in a few moments if you will just stay calm. Talking seemed to help. "Why not?"

"Because," Merinda said with a strain registering again in her voice, "there hasn't been a true Gorgon seen on the frontier since Marren-kan disappeared. Marren-kan, so the spacers locally tell it, got word of where the Lokan Fleet might be found. He disappeared beyond the Maelstrom Wall and was never heard from again. From that time until the present, no Gorgon has been seen anywhere on any world."

"Well, what happened to them?" Griffiths asked.

"No one knows. That may be something else for us to find out on this little journey of ours."

Another cord fell quickly to the floor.

"At last." Merinda's voice was filled with satisfaction. "All right, Griffiths, hold your head still and I'll get you loose."

In an instant, the blindfold was pulled from his head.

Griffiths stiffened suddenly.

"Neskat?" His voice was half awe and half terror. "Where are we?"

Merinda looked around, following Griffiths's gaze. The compartment had been grown into its shape rather than carved. Its walls were curved, with ribbing supporting the ceiling. A heavy door blocked the only entrance; iron bars had been fitted into a small observation opening. The walls, ceiling, and floor were covered with carvings. Some were small; others were quite large, but they each had a unifying characteristic. Each was of the face of some horrific beast.

"Well," Merinda commented, "I'm not sure of the exact location but it looks like we are inside an Aendorian totem ship. The Aendorian home world is far from here, but their ships would be quite appropriate to the changes in the quantum zones here. They're easy to reconfigure and remarkably adaptable. It's an excellent choice for this area."

"Well, perhaps." Griffiths's eyes were still fixed on the faces all staring back at him. "But why all the faces?"

"Each face represents different types of power associated with different types of quantum zones," Merinda said as she examined the walls of their prison. "It becomes largely a matter of identifying which totem works in which zone to get the ship to operate there. It is a very efficient system in a place where zones change quickly. These, of course, are guardian totems and thus rather stern in their appearance."

"Stern?" Griffiths gaped. "They're horrible!"

"Yes, well," Merinda said as she reached down and began working to loosen Griffiths's restraints. "Still, I think you can admire their craftsmanship. They do their job very well."

"Perhaps, but I'd just as soon not look at them for any length of . . . wait! Merinda! Someone's coming!"

In a moment, Merinda backed silently next to the door. Griffiths struggled, the cords around his wrists not yet loose enough for escape. He looked up at the door. He was seated directly in front of it.

Something was moving on the other side of the barred portal.

Griffiths's mind raced. He had seen any number of things in the galaxy, but for the most part they had been relatively human and often friendly. Here at the core, however, the rules seemed to be different. All sorts of horrors ran through his mind: beasts from his childhood nightmares and terrors from the entertainment videos he used to rent to scare himself. These weren't imaginings, he reminded himself. These were real.

The lock turned. Slowly, the door began to open with a screaming, rusted hinge.

Merinda quickly reached into the opening, grabbing whatever was on the other side of the door. She pulled hard, throwing the large shape directly at the spot where Griffiths sat. The astronaut had no time to react. The massive blur stumbled over him, knocking Griffiths backward onto the floor as it fell heavily against the wall beyond.

Merinda grabbed the door before it could slam shut again. With one foot against the door, she reached down for the nearest available object. It happened to be Griffiths's foot. She pulled the man across the floor until Griffiths effectively blocked the door from closing, then stepped over him to pull their captor up from the floor.

Griffiths tried to roll over, to see the terrible monster Merinda had pulled into their cell, but something grabbed him, pinning his arms against his sides. A massive creature covered in coarse hair lifted him bodily off the ground. Griffiths's eyes went wide with terror. The muscular body was crossed with a thick leather harness ornamented by rows of successive knives. Each knife was sheathed with its handle outward, ready for use at a moment's whim. Griffiths shuddered involuntarily: the creature's stench was unbearable. In moments his face was drawn level with the monster's own hideous muzzle. It was a broad, flat snout, black and wet across its tip. Pairs of curled fangs extended from both sides of its maw. Bloodred eyes gazed back, their massive brows frowning down over them. Horns curled backward from the creature's forehead over a massive mantle of thick black hair.

"Lay to, lubber!" The monster's voice was impossibly deep, its resonant sound shaking his very bones. "The Cap'n has asked that you not be disturbing the lady. We've got special accommodations just for yourself alone. Now, you wouldn't be givin' ol' Kheoghi any trouble now, would ye?"

Griffiths couldn't find his tongue. He only managed to nod his head emphatically. He fervently hoped that the creature understood that he had agreed.

264

28

Perspectives

KHEOGHI LOOKED WITH DISGUST THROUGH THE SMALL VIEW-
port of the brig door. He found humans abhorrent in general
and, for reasons even he could not explain, found this one
particularly revolting.

"Master Kheoghi," came the fluting, high-pitched voice
at the end of the corridor. "What vision so enraptures your
attentions?"

The huge minotaur straightened up from the locked door
as much as the low corridor would allow. It wasn't much.
The flat-faced brute with the brilliant red eyes remained
mostly crouched in the confined space. His horns, curled
downward on either side of his head, occasionally scraped
against the overhead with an annoying sound. "Just givin'
the eye to that thar Griffiths-human, Master Shindak, as per
the Cap'n's orders. Once every eight bells, sir, though it give
me no pleasure to do so."

Kheoghi waited for the elven first mate to approach. Elves
love to make an entrance, Kheoghi thought to himself.
More human-appearing than the majority of the crew, Shindak seemed to curry the favor of the captain—possibly even
along racial types. Most pirate crews were fully integrated, of
course, with little regard to race origins and little tolerance

for prejudice. Still, Kheoghi thought, it never hurt to be realistic. Humans have always promoted their own kind over all other races. Superficial coincidence—such as having no tail or walking like a biped—could often enhance one's career in a human universe.

Elves, Kheoghi reminded himself, were not above taking such an advantage—or any other kind of advantage for that matter.

Still, the OomRamn, as Kheoghi's clan called themselves, were known for their power and prowess. There was little subtlety among his kind. Their history was summed up in the saying "If it moves, kill it; if it doesn't move, kick it until it moves." They were proud warriors, conquerors of the stars, and they had been a terror in their own time, or so their legends said. Their fleets had brought power and glory to OomRamn.

That was long ago, thought Kheoghi sadly, long before the time of Lo-han the Oppressor . . . Lo-han the Destroyer. Three thousand years had passed and still his name was cursed in the remaining halls of the OomRamn. Lo-han: murderer of all unhuman.

Now the great OomRamn Empire was a shadow of its former greatness; a mere handful of worlds backed up against the Maelstrom Wall. The Old-masters continued to debate and brawl in the Arena, snorting and posturing about the greatness of the OomRamn and their destiny, but little changed. Kheoghi had grown tired of the talk and had come into the stars to try to actually do something about valor and glory. He had more or less by accident had his ship boarded by the Marren-kan and discovered, in the process, that blood honor and glory could also be very profitable. He had signed the Ship's Articles—by pressing the inked palm of his left clawed hand to the book and taking up the entire page—as soon as they were offered to him.

Kheoghi watched as the elf glided toward him, seeming to never touch the floor. "You have an objection to our prisoner, Master Kheoghi?"

"No more than I objects to any other human, beggin' yer pardon, sire," Kheoghi replied with a rumble in his voice, "and that be considerable, indeed!"

"Come now, Kheoghi," the elf said imperiously as he stopped to stand before the minotaur. "Surely your clan is not the only clan who would harbor resentments toward the rule of men?"

"We've grudge enough to go around," Kheoghi replied with a curl of his black lips. "I'd be eatin' the raw heart of humanity, given the chance, for what they done to us, and finish the meal with a proper swig of their blood, at that."

"Indeed," purred Shindak with wearied overtones in his voice. "Bold words, as one might expect from a warrior race."

The minotaur snorted clouds through his massive snout into the cold air of the lower decks. The black eyes narrowed, the overhead shaking to his bellowing voice. "Bold enough for you, mate! I've had a bellyful of humanity and their high ways! You seem cozy enough with His Majesty the captain, or do you reckon his being human is more to your liking than those of us that ain't?"

Shindak didn't move a muscle though his face took on an appearance that was several degrees colder than before. The silvery eyes simply stared at the minotaur for a moment, sufficient for him to establish his displeasure and very real threat toward the hulking Kheoghi.

"We of the Tsokon-nukorai live long," Shindak said directly and quietly, his eyes never leaving those of the minotaur before him. "Our memories live longer still within the Collective. We—more than the OomRamn, more than the Tsultak, more than the E'knari or the Uruh or the

Hishawei or the Goromok—more than any other of our outcast brethren, we know the depth of what was done to us!" The elf's blue-tinged face turned slightly upward. His silver eyes lost focus as he stared at something incredibly far away. "The fleets of the Lost Empire were young in those times. I see them as they drove through the stars as though through a dark and rippled glass. Lokan—that same Lo-han in our own coarse tongue—moved with unholy purpose through the night. Each civilization he came upon he judged by his own standard—the standard of humanity! As though humans were the perfect form! As though no other form was its equal or better! Then with his prejudice and his ego he held aloft the Nightsword and bent the quantum weather radically towards his own will. Where the inhabitants were humanoid, the Nightsword made them fully human. Where the local race was too dissimilar, the will of Lokan devolved them into unthinking beasts. That latter was the fate of most of your great empire's conquests, Kheoghi. The former the fate of my own old worlds."

Kheoghi blinked. There were legends in his own culture of the Great Collapse. Lo-han the Destroyer had come with his magic and transformed armies into witless beasts. "He were a terror, that Lo-han."

"Yes, indeed he was," Shindak replied patiently. "Yet do you not see, my friend, what else was lost? Entire histories vanished before him. Cultures, songs, hopes, and dreams all died before him. The converted races that fell before the will of Lokan forgot their former selves and all that they were. They became truly human. Worse than dead—they have forgotten who they truly are. Only those of us who escaped conversion remember the truth that was. Only we know the name of those that oppressed us and took from us the love of our own brothers. We cannot forget. We will never forget."

The minotaur seemed to shrink back, if that were possible, in the corridor, though he had not yet been completely rebuffed. "Beggin' your pardon, Master Shindak, but the Tsokon-nukorai think too much."

"It is our curse," the elf replied calmly, "but one that you will never be burdened with. If you have completed your assigned duties here, I have further tasks for you to accomplish."

Kheoghi pondered the elf's words for a moment, decided that it would be too much trouble to decipher the meaning buried in the words, and concentrated on the last part of the statement. "By the captain's word, I must be lookin' in on that human again come another eight bells."

"The captain's word means a great deal to you," Shindak said, his voice flat and without inflection.

"He be the captain," Kheoghi replied simply.

"Indeed he is." Shindak smiled. He paused for a moment before continuing. "Perhaps you would like to join me in a ration of Sartagon grog?"

"Sartagon grog, sire?" The hulking brute smiled at the thought of a pleasant slam at the back of his head. " 'Twould be an honor, Master Shindak."

The elf had already turned and was moving down the curving corridor toward the third lower ship's hold. "Then please come with me. There are a few things which we need to discuss."

Shindak pushed open a massive door that led through a main bulkhead and stood aside. Kheoghi hunched over to pass through the opening and then straightened up, relieved that the hold space afforded him the opportunity to stand up properly, which the main corridors of the ship did not.

Dappled squares of dim light illuminated the compartment from the deck grids separating the lower hold from the two immediately above it. The hold was the smallest of the three, yet even so the compartment was nearly twenty feet high. They had offloaded their latest treasures at Oombaroom Haven six days prior to encountering Flynn and their latest prize. Yet this prize had no cargo of any value to speak of, so far as the crew was concerned, and the holds had remained empty.

An empty hold is an invitation to change, thought Kheoghi. After a quick glance around the compartment, change seemed exactly what Shindak had in mind.

Several of Kheoghi's fellow crewmembers lounged about the sparse room. There were Lulm, Meln and Ogrob, the Goromok gnomes who sat against the far bulkhead with their legs crossed, as was their custom. Their three knit caps were faded by constant wear but their family colors could still be distinguished. Seven Hishawei hung from the ceiling, each insectoid exoskeletal frame hanging from the grating overhead by three appendages. The Hishawei formed cultural radials that mimicked their physical structure, Kheoghi recalled. Their bodies were designed with three sets of three radial appendages organized around the thorax, topped with a head with three eye clusters. Six of the Hishawei surrounded a seventh, larger member of their clan. Kheoghi recognized at once their "queen" in the center of the formation, although he considered the term a bit too high for a collective that consisted of only twelve beings on the ship. Things were somewhat worse, he realized, for the Uruh aboard—snake-women who usually enslaved a single male member of their kind for their own communities, but for whom none had been found on their travels thus far. Two of the Uruh were coiled in the far corner of the hold, engaged in an animated discussion, with all twelve of their arms gesturing in their excitement.

All motion ended, however, as Shindak entered the compartment.

"Where be the grog, Shindak?" Kheoghi turned to the elf with a scowl.

"Hear me first, Kheoghi," Shindak murmured, "then you'll get both your share and mine."

Kheoghi snorted his disbelief as the elf turned to address the assembled crew.

"We have labored long under the flag of Marren-kan." Shindak spoke without preamble. He felt the need to justify neither himself nor his position to those assembled. None present looked prepared to question him. "We have banded together for our mutual protection and, need I say, profit. What else could we do, being outcast brothers of the stars? The marshlands of the Uruh have long ago been laid waste . . ."

The snake-women hissed ominously their accord.

". . . The hives of the Hishawei were eons long lost mutated into hideous, weakened forms . . ."

Kheoghi heard the metallic sound of the gigantic insectoids' mandibles sliding against each other overhead.

". . . And the Goromok Caverns of Destiny are lost to their kin for all time."

The gnomes' heads dropped in silent loss.

"Even the great temple world of OomRamn-Ishka was transformed until the world was no longer recognizable to the OomRamn, who fled in the depths of their loss into the stars, bereft of their gods!"

Kheoghi's mane bristled at the words, the flat muzzle of his face lifting in his pride and his pain. He knew Shindak well enough to recognize that he was being manipulated by the crafty elf, but the ancestral wound ran too deep for him not to react.

"And what is the cause? Humanity! That most hated word among the outcasts! Humans—who came into the stars with an arrogance beyond comprehension. Humans—whose ego and selfishness declared their own form to be the standard by which good would be set and judged! Humans—who in time past brought us Lokan the Reviled, Lokan the Destroyer, Lokan the Enforcer. Their fleets crossed the stars from the rim to the core and everywhere they went that which was human survived, that which was nearly human was changed forever, and that which was not human was destroyed, obliterated, and scattered to the stellar winds. The greatness that was my people—the greatness that was each of our peoples— vanished under the cursed Nightsword of Lokan."

Elami, one of the Uruh in the corner, folded all three sets of her arms across her leather-vested chest and spoke up at last. "What be that to usss, Ssshindak? What care we for battlesss lossst so long afore our time?"

Shindak's dynamic oratory had been interrupted, yet when he turned to the snake-woman, he was smiling.

"Why, nothing at all, Elami."

Kheoghi turned toward the elf, squinting his black eyes as he tried to understand.

"The point is not whether we care or not," Shindak continued smoothly. "The point is whether the exile governments of our respective outcast races still care—and by your own reactions to my little speech, I think you all know that they will care very deeply indeed."

Ogrob cocked his head to one side. "What's the play, elf? What be you thinkin'?"

"I think that our captain—our human captain—has stumbled upon the passage beyond the Maelstrom Wall."

The hold echoed with a ripple of oddly timbered laughter through its expanse.

"Now that there's a fantasy," Lulm chortled to his fellow gnomes.

"We help Shindak find Shindak's mind," clicked the queen Hishawei merrily. "Him lose it somewhere nearby."

"I be thinkin' he's already drunk that Sartagon grog he offered me to get me here," bellowed Kheoghi, joining in the general revelry.

"Have your fun," Shindak said through an ice-cold smile. "I know differently."

The look on the elven face quickly silenced the crowd.

"I have seen the map, incomplete as it is." Shindak spoke quietly. "We sail for the core, mates. We sail to plunder the Lokan Fleet."

The silence of thought descended on the group. At last Kheoghi spoke up. "What be the end if we find this here Lost Fleet, Shindak?"

"If we find it, friend Kheoghi," Shindak replied, "then we shall most likely also find one of the most terrible tools ever devised by that cursed race of humanity. We shall most likely recover the Nightsword."

The elf paused, gazing into the faces of each entity in the room.

"Mates, I do not relish the thought of putting such a dangerous power in the hands of humanity once again. More importantly, in all the nonhuman governments that remain in the galactic disk, there is no price too high to pay to keep the Nightsword out of human hands once more. You could squander a decade's shipment of yardow and never come close to equaling the ransom such a prize would exact. There's never been a greater treasure just waiting to be taken."

"There be a catch then?" Elami said, hissing.

"Yes," Shindak said, looking casually toward the deck. "It would seem that only the humans can actually get us there. The map is incomplete. From what I gather, only one of the humans knows the full route."

"So, what would you have us do?" Kheoghi asked slyly.

"For the time being, you could join me in the galley

for that Sartagon grog that I promised you. Beyond that, everyone here should be watchful and wait for word from me." Shindak smiled enigmatically once more. "It has been a profitable endeavor but, quite soon, when the Nightsword is safely aboard, I believe the time will come for us to call into question the captaincy of our fine ship."

29

Buccaneer

THE SHIP WAS HIDEOUSLY BEAUTIFUL—OR BEAUTIFULLY HIDeous, depending upon one's point of view. The original Aendorian designs had been considerably embellished, as well as contorted, over the years by the spacers who tended her decks. Spacers of the core are renowned throughout the galactic disk as having an encyclopedic knowledge of diverse magic and crafts never to be trifled with. Individually they may be limited, but a collective crew of spacers is a formidable group. When properly selected and organized, there is rarely a situation in open space, regardless of the quantum region encountered in those wild regions, that one of their number cannot address.

So it was with the Aendorian ship. The original totems had been embellished, added to, and restructured in such a way that their figures now addressed the needs of the various magical zones they encountered during their wild and unpredictable flight. This greatly reduced the strain on the spacers themselves, as they were able to store up different quantum zone structures in the totems themselves.

Griffiths, of course, knew nothing of this. He simply shuddered at the sight of the tubelike corridor spiraling upward from the depths of the ship. The curved walls raged at him from a thousand silent, twisted mouths. Some were skulls of obscene creatures, angrily contorted. Others held the mere hint of unspeakable horror. Despite the images from which his mind recoiled, there was something powerful and fascinating about them.

A shove from behind nearly knocked Griffiths to the floor.

"Belay that lubberly gait," rumbled the behemoth from behind. "Haul yer carcass topside and be quick about it lest I draw and quarter ye here and now!"

Griffiths heard more than saw the steel slide from the scabbard of the beast. The image in his mind was far too graphic. He quickly climbed the spiral ramp past two additional deck openings until he emerged on the main deck of the ship.

Griffiths once more stopped short, sucking in his breath as the scene hit him like a solid wall.

He stood near the center of the vessel. Behind him was a large superstructure with elegant railings attached to what he assumed was the main mast of the ship: a massive wooden trunk rising up into a succession of yardarms, platforms, and rigging overhead. The deck under his feet was formed of carefully coopered wooden planks, each fitted tightly into a pattern. Upon this open expanse of decking was mounted a number of stiles and winches, as well as several additional hatches leading belowdecks. All the deck was held within the fingers of the ship's five prows, each of which arched high overhead until they nearly touched the rigging of the ship.

Yet it was the crew crowding the deck that made him stop short. It was an insane mixture of the sublime and the horrific. A small group of multiple-breasted snake-women wearing light leather tunics were in the rigging, their tails curled around the line as they hauled themselves aloft with their strong, broad hands and arms. Below them a mixed group of what he was sure were gnomes, dwarves, and willowy elves was fussing over a series of what looked for all the world like cannons mounted through gunports below the side rail. Several more brutish beasts like the one that had brought him up from belowdecks—minotaurs, he decided to label them—were putting their backs to a windlass that was hauling a large platform higher up on the mast. Now and then a fairy or two would dart among the crowd, each pursuing a special purpose of their own. Several more elves, tall and regal in their features with delicately pointed ears, were working the lines of a boom that needed to be shifted. All was proceeding on deck with purpose and organization, yet Griffiths remained stunned at the bizarre and eclectic collection before him.

Another painful jab to his lower back shook Griffiths painfully from his stupor. He glanced back sharply at the minotaur, whose brutish face only scowled in response. It looked for all the world as though the beast would just as soon be given an excuse for eating Griffiths on the spot. Instead, he gestured toward an ornate doorway accessing one of the five bow forecastles. Griffiths turned and began picking his way across the deck toward the opening.

It was true, he thought, he really had not seen much of the galaxy. Still, everywhere he had gone there had been a predominance of humanity. Sure, there were the occasional oddities wherever you went but truly alien life had been a rare thing. In all his travels, he had never yet seen such a massed collection of xenoforms. He had even wondered from time to time if nonhuman creatures could get along at all. Yet here they were, going through their tasks as though they were of one mind. Why hadn't he encountered more such wonder and diversity? Why did it frighten him?

He soon made his way to the door, his minotaur handler

behind him at every step. Griffiths reached for the door latch, but the hulking brute immediately slapped his hand away. To Griffiths's utter shock, the beast knocked quietly at the door and spoke in most respectful tones. "Cap'n! Beggin' yer pardon, but the gentleman you requested be here to see you."

"Enter," came the terse, muffled reply.

The beast moved forward, gave Griffiths one last warning eye, and then opened the door wide. The cool darkness of the portal beckoned him onward. He wondered what new horror awaited him next. Whatever it was, he knew that the lark he thought he had started on Avadon had somehow gone terribly wrong. Adventure had called him but had failed to tell him the price. Now he knew that such dreams are never bargains, and it looked to him as though it were time to pay the devil his due.

THE CABIN WAS ILLUMINATED BY THE THOUSANDS OF STARS streaming light through the twin bay windows that were fitted into either side of the hull. Everything smelled of old wood and sweat. The ceiling was oppressively low, much of its original meager height further reduced by the massive beams that crossed the overhead of the compartment. Ornate brass lanterns hung down, their crystal globes adding their light to the room as they swung slightly from side to side. Below these squatted a massive desk, the surface showing signs of a fine polish now long since dulled by time and use. Its carved features were grotesque in the extreme— foul, obscene, and repulsive. A series of small windowpanes formed a great curve along the back wall. The stars were grouped unnaturally close to Griffiths's eye as they shined brightly beyond.

Between the ancient, foul repugnance of the desk and the glorious vista of creation beyond . . . stood Evon Flynn. His back was to the magnificence, its grandeur lost on him. Instead, he was hunched intently over the evil desktop, his hands set wide on its surface. Before him was spread the same chart they had made at the cartographer's not so long and a lifetime ago.

"Captain Griffiths," Flynn purred smoothly, never looking up from his study of the map. "How good of you to accept my invitation."

"How gracious of you to have offered it—you two-faced bastard," Griffiths replied as smoothly as his host.

Flynn looked up and smiled one of his fabulous smiles. "Not at all! Only trying to help as best I can."

"If this is help"—Griffiths's voice suddenly reflected a cold edge—"then we'd just as soon do without it. Let Merinda go."

"Oh, I will, I assure you," Flynn said, his eyes dropping back to the map on the desk before him. "I've known Merinda a long time. She's both powerful and impulsive—a dangerous combination actually. She hates to lose and she's angry, but she'll get over that in time. She just needs to cool her temper and get her wits about her. I need her wits, actually. There are subtleties here that she just cannot appreciate right now."

"Right!" Griffiths snorted. "Leading us into this trap; that was subtle! Boarding the *Brishan* and abducting us? Ooh, more subtlety still! Locking us in the brig for three days? Very subtle indeed, Flynn."

"Hey," the tall man looked up and shrugged, annoyance growing in his features. "I didn't have a choice in this!"

"Choice?" Griffiths laughed. "You're the bloody captain of these pirates!"

"Yeah"—Flynn nodded back at the astronaut—"I'm the captain—fat lot of good it does me! I never wanted this job! I never asked for it!"

Griffiths opened his mouth but wasn't sure what to

say. He quite suddenly realized how much alike were their positions. He had often considered himself the butt of some great cosmic joke played on him by the universe. Now here he was, staring at himself in the form of this pirate captain.

Flynn looked away once more, gathering his own thoughts, and then rounded the desk to Griffiths's side. "Please sit down," he said, indicating a massive armchair standing before the desk.

"I think I'd rather . . ."

"Please?"

Griffiths slowly sat down in the chair. Leaning back against the massive table, the tall man crossed his arms over his exposed chest and continued.

"Some years ago, something happened that drove me out of the Omnet. I just couldn't live with some of the memories."

"Tentris?" Griffiths asked quietly.

Flynn's eyes widened. "Yes! How do you know about . . ."

"It's a long story," Griffiths said. "I'll tell you all about it later. What's your point?"

"The point is that I ran," Flynn said. "I ran as far as my wealth allowed. The core was the frontier then, just as it remains now. I figured that a wilderness—untamed and untamable—was just the place I needed to get lost in. The money ran out quickly enough and I found myself signing on to one of those bulk yardow schooners that operated out of Tsultak. The work was hard, the pay was lousy, but no one knew who I was, or who I had been, or who I had failed to be. I figured my past couldn't catch me there against the chaos of the Maelstrom Wall. At the time I hoped somehow that adventure would drown out the thunderous boredom and hatred of my own existence."

"What's that got to do with . . ."

"I'm getting to that," Flynn said, the cocky buccaneer appearing awkward for the first time. He stood up, working his hands nervously as he began pacing the room. "I was aboard the *Rhindan Pah*, a freight schooner captained by an idiot named Guppin. He was barely more than an animal. The crew was a minimum complement for that size craft because Guppin didn't want to have to pay out any more wages than necessary, bad as they were. That would have been bad enough under normal quantum conditions but to sail against the Maelstrom Wall with a minimum comple- ment was just short of suicide. He regularly ordered the bosun to administer discipline to the crew at his whim. Often as not there was no truth to the charges that were read: I believe he did so just for the pleasure of inflicting the pain. Not that we were short of pain. Working the ratlines of the rig through quantum wave after quantum wave left us all ragged. We were each doing the work of four men and had Guppin thrown into the bargain as well."

"Bad career move," Griffiths said without commitment.

Flynn laughed. "Bad enough. So, there we were just rimward of the Beltrix Shoals. We're easing between the eddies trying to keep our headway so as not to drift into one of the null-pockets about us. It's a dangerous trick, that passage, but can cut three days off the run time for those who can manage it. We were nearly out the other side when . . ."

"No." Griffiths's voice conveyed a boredom that he didn't feel. "Let me guess: pirates?"

"Exactly! Fact is that we ignored Guppin's orders to defend the schooner. We figured that anything was better than Captain Guppin—even Marren-kan himself. The pirates ransacked the *Rhindan Pah* and were going to set her adrift. Guppin remained aboard but couldn't possibly sail the ship without the assistance of a crew. I would have remained with him but it would have been suicidal to do so. Instead, I crossed over with most of the remaining crew to the pirate ship. Better to take my chances with them than with Guppin again!"

"So," Griffiths said slowly, "basically, you ran again?"

"Of course I ran, I had no choice!" Flynn spread his hands helplessly before him. "If I had stayed, I'd have been adrift with a madman captain on an unnavigable ship."

"So, that's why you became a pirate captain?"

"You're not making this easy, Griffiths," Flynn complained. "It's not as though any of this were my fault!"

"Really?" Griffiths raised his eyebrows in mock astonishment. "This I've got to hear."

"So there I was, a prisoner aboard a buccaneer ship. They forced each of the prisoners to sign their Ship's Articles and become a member of the Marren-kan. It was that or die, and I wasn't ready to die yet. It turned out that life aboard the Marren-kan buccaneer wasn't so bad. There were far more hands aboard the pirate ship than any other ship I had served on—that meant that the work was much easier, since it was spread around rather thinly. Most ships that we plundered simply dumped their cargo for us rather than risk the wrath of the Marren-kan. All we had to do is hove up alongside, wave our banner, rattle our sabers, and they would hand over their possessions. There's a lot less bloodshed in this profession than people are generally led to believe."

"Wait!" Griffiths held up his hand. "You guys use sabers and cutlasses?"

"Sure!" Flynn said cheerfully. "With all the various quantum zones around the Wall, they are about the only weapons that work all the time. A simple sharp edge works in nearly every quantum zone. Complex weapons will die on you nearly every time."

"Can we get back to this 'captain' thing?" Griffiths said impatiently.

"Right! So I was working the decks of the ship. The captain then was an honest-to-the-Nine Gorgon, old as the stars themselves, I swear."

"Gorgons?" Griffiths piped in. "I thought their race was extinct!"

"No. Not yet, anyway. Their home world is near the Wall itself and well hidden. Their history is a tragic one. They were once a great and proud nation, brought to ruin with the coming of humanity. It seems that in the ancient days of the Third Gorgon Dynasty . . ."

"Er," Griffiths interrupted. "One tale at a time: how you became captain?"

"Well, I was working the main deck, coiling some of the optic transfer lines from the upper rigging. This Gorgon captain—Neuden-kan was his name—came walking by to inspect the work. All of a sudden, near as I can figure, the old space turtle starts choking. I figure he has something caught in his throat, so I throw my arms around him and start squeezing as hard as I can. We both fall to the deck. I roll on top of him and start pressing his chest trying to dislodge whatever is choking him. It turns out that the Gorgon had an embolism or something and just died of old age! Before I know it, the entire crew is staring at me, sitting on the chest of this massive Gorgon captain who is lying under me deader than last week's rust."

"So they proclaimed you captain?" Griffiths shook his head.

"On the spot—something about the right of succession in the Articles. I can't run from these cutthroats—they have spies everywhere and they are basically ruthless. They are friendly enough on the surface but that doesn't mean that they won't eat your brains for breakfast if you cross them.

Every now and then I talk them into letting me go for a few months. I'm supposed to be 'searching for fresh prey' I tell them. I get to work in the Tsultak yards for a while and be nearly human until I arrange to bring another prize their way."

"Like us?" Griffiths said flatly.

Flynn stopped his pacing and turned to face Griffiths. In a sweeping motion, the buccaneer grabbed the map from the table and held it out toward the astronaut. "Yes—just like you! But you've got to see that I'm on your side! Don't you understand? The *Brishan* is a fine ship out on the perimeter but she's poorly equipped to run the core! She'll never make it through the Maelstrom Wall! But a ship of the Marren-kan—this ship—would stand a chance!"

Flynn dropped the map back on the desk and moved suddenly forward, grasping both arms of the chair. "You wouldn't have taken this chance, Griffiths, and neither would Merinda. I know what is at stake. Targ is coming for you, make no mistake about that. He will employ every means at his disposal to shake you loose. He will do it, too. He'll break you and Merinda both without a second thought. Then he'll have the Nightsword, and may the Nine have mercy on the galaxy then! With me, however, you've got a chance at beating him to his own prize! This crew will follow me so long as they know there's a treasure at the end of the chart!"

Griffiths looked suddenly up at the buccaneer.

"Look, Griffiths, we haven't gotten off to a good start, you and I. I'm offering you a chance to stop Targ and save Merinda from both that madman running the Omnet and herself. It's my one chance at escaping these cutthroats—and yours as well. Trust me, Griffiths! With your help, you and I can keep control of this crew, capture the greatest treasure in the universe—and we may even get out of this alive. What do you say to a little adventure?"

The astronaut sighed through a weary smile. "Did you ever sell used cars?"

"Used cars?" Flynn said quizzically. "What does that mean?"

"I think it means we had better both take another look at that map," Griffiths replied.

GAMMA:

INHUMAN

CREED

30

Shoals

MERINDA EXITED THE HATCH. THE BIZARRE CREATURES WORK-ing the deck commanded little interest from her. Their names and kind were familiar. It was the even more bizarre creature that swaggered toward her that caught her up short.

"Merinda! Are you all right?" Griffiths asked as he approached.

"I was about to ask the same of you," she replied with astonished disapproval.

Griffiths's great black cape billowed behind him as he moved. The astronaut wore a doublet of deep crimson fastened with a broad belt and brilliant buckle. The matching crimson pantaloons bloused out of the top of knee-high boots, both fitted with thick collars. It all fit him perfectly, right to the top of his twin-billed hat—an outrageous monstrosity overstuffed with massive plumage.

Merinda folded her arms across her chest. "And just who are you supposed to be?"

"Oh, you mean the uniform? Rather dashing, don't you think?"

"Is that what that is?"

"Well, of course!" Griffiths said with some pride. "Flynn has made me first mate on the voyage. He says that the uniform is part of the job."

"Indeed?" Merinda said through a quizzical smile. "And just what might that job entail, Captain Griffiths?"

"Nothing much, so far," Griffiths admitted, adjusting his hat to a more appropriately rakish angle. "Still, I think it's a good sign."

Griffiths moved closer to Merinda's side and took her by the arm, walking her slowly across the deck, his head leaning conspiratorially close to hers as he spoke in whispers. "Merinda, there's a lot more going on here than appears on the surface. Flynn is as much a victim of this piracy as we are—but we came up with a plan to use this ship of alien bandits to beat Targ to the Nightsword."

" 'We' came up with a plan?" Merinda's eyebrow arched skeptically.

"Yes, both Flynn and I worked it out last night." Griffiths stopped at the look on Merinda's face. "Now what's the matter?"

"Griffiths, what's wrong with you?" Merinda's voice turned suddenly edgy. "I've seen you in action before. You were skeptical enough of Targ to keep us all alive. You were commanding. You got us all the way to Tsultak with only the help of the synths. You acted and survived. Now here you are in that ridiculous outfit eating every word Flynn speaks as though it were the food of life! At least Flynn is acting on his own and not trailing along like some fawning pet!"

"Hey!" Griffiths stepped forward, leaning over Merinda as he spoke. "I wasn't the one who chose Flynn in the first place. I wasn't the one who got us boarded and I certainly wasn't the one who got blindsided by that same wonderful 'old friend' Flynn! I think I'm doing pretty damn well keeping us alive, high-and-holy Merinda Neskat. So, if there's anyone here that's lost their edge it isn't me!"

Merinda's eyes had transfixed his own. She could tell that her own face filled his vision. The cold blue depths of his eyes suddenly softened and warmed.

Her hand reached with lightning speed forward toward the hilt of his cutlass. She stepped back, planting her left foot solidly on the deck as both her knees flexed slightly for strength. The blade slid with a quiet ring from the scabbard as she stepped back once more, the edged steel already arcing through the air. It circled over her head once as she stepped back in toward Griffiths.

Plumage was scythed from the hat in a clean stroke, its newly freed white fluff exploding into the air.

The blade continued again, this time down the side and around as Merinda's left hand joined the hilt. Both hands swung down over her head as the blade split the air—and was suddenly arrested in its course to hover half a hands-breadth from the centerline of Griffiths's face.

Griffiths sucked in a breath.

Merinda's steel-gray eyes gazed at him from a face uncomfortably close and just behind the blade.

Somewhere, further out, feathers drifted down around them both.

"Some men know how to use their blade." Merinda's words were iron with a frosted edge. "But those who don't should know enough to keep it put away until they do!"

The blade dropped slowly out of view but Merinda's face and eyes never moved.

With a sudden ring, Merinda shoved the cutlass back into Griffiths's scabbard and turned contemptuously away from him.

THE *VENTURE REVENGE* SAILED THROUGH THREE SEPARATE quantum zones as it passed along the great expanse of the Maelstrom Wall. Each was duly plotted but it wasn't until they had reached the third that they were sure of their course. The length of each was off by a full two hours in each case, two of them longer than expected, and the third, considerably shorter. Flynn commented to Griffiths that it wasn't to be unexpected. The map that they had was many millennia old, and this close to the core there were bound to be many shifts in the actual quantum regions involved over such a long time.

Griffiths wondered if such shifts couldn't have just closed off the very corridor that they were looking for to enter the galactic core. He had attempted to ask Merinda about it, but the Vestis seemingly ignored the question and anything else Griffiths had to say, for that matter.

It was with some despondency then that Griffiths took to paying more and more attention to the drawn map on the chart table. There were areas of the map that he could see clearly in his head that did not appear on the map itself. The words were clear to him as he looked at the map but were unreadable to others.

Such a curious map, he thought.

He wondered where it had come from.

Griffiths suddenly pushed himself up from the map table as though struck by a bolt. "Of course! Why didn't I see that before!"

He quickly skirted the massive table and dashed out onto the deck. He looked about him in a frenzy, sighted Merinda standing on the quarterdeck surrounding the main mast, and in several quick strides, reached the ladder. He pulled himself quickly up to the elevated platform in the center of the ship.

The helmsman lay on his back between the ship's wheels, gazing up the length of the mast in the direction of the ship's travel. Flynn stood at the opposite rail, his eyes examining the rigging as the crew aloft reset the ship for yet another quantum configuration. Griffiths quickly moved to where Merinda was leaning against the rail, deep in her own thoughts.

"Merinda! I know where we're going!"

"Not now," Merinda said, turning away from him and staring across the rail. "You've managed to help me enough for the time being."

"No, Merinda," Griffiths said firmly. His instinct was to grab her by the arm and turn her forcibly around toward him, but the more sensible part of him had learned that such an act with Merinda—or any Vestis for that matter—could easily get him killed. "Not this time. You can't just sit around on this pirate barge. There's work to be done—your work—and you're the only one who can do it. Ready or not. Doubting or not. You're here and you're it. Are you coming, Vestis, or do I have to get violent!"

Merinda turned suddenly, her eyes ablaze, but one look at Griffiths and she suddenly laughed, warmth returning for a moment to her eyes.

"I . . . I'm sorry, Griffiths," she said haltingly, trying to regain control of herself. "It's . . . it's the uniform."

Griffiths felt humiliated, but Flynn had insisted that he wear the thing—and now Griffiths was beginning to wonder just why.

"Of course, I'll come with you," she said. "What about Flynn?"

"I think we can leave him out of this for the time being," Griffiths said, glancing at the buccaneer. "He's preoccupied for now. Let's leave it that way."

They both quickly moved off of the quarterdeck and crossed to the captain's quarters—mistakenly believing that their movements had gone unnoticed.

"THIS IS OUR CURRENT POSITION, IF I UNDERSTAND THE CHART right," Griffiths said, pointing to the lined location on the gigantic map sheet spread over the table.

"Yes," Merinda agreed, "that looks to be about right."

"OK," Griffiths said, straightening up from the table. "I was in here earlier, just looking at the map. There's this big blank space in the middle—something that the cartographer couldn't suck out of my head, I think. It is in my head, however. I can see it plain as day in my mind. Another thing—the symbols on the map. You'd think that the biolinks would eventually get around to translating for anyone looking at them. They don't. I can read them just fine."

"That doesn't make sense," Merinda said, squinting her eyes slightly at Griffiths as she spoke. "Biolinks are not only linked to the individual but they are linked to each other. That's how universal language is made so easy. When a biolink meets another species with a biolink, the two links transmit the coding for their own language to the nearby links."

"Right," Griffiths said. "My biolink is translating the ancient Lost Empire symbols for me just fine. So, why hasn't my biolink broadcast the translation information to your biolink—or Flynn's, for that matter, either?"

Merinda's face was puzzled. "I don't know. It's the first time I've ever encountered a biolink that selectively transmitted translations."

"Just follow me for a moment," Griffiths said, the excitement in his voice obvious to the trained Vestis. "I was pondering this as I was looking at the chart. It suddenly occurred to me that we really didn't know where this chart had come from. Who had created it? Who had put it together?"

"I think we all just assumed that the chart came from the Mantle of Kendis-dai," Merinda said. "You asked where the Lokan Fleet had gone and the Mantle gave you the answer."

"Yes, but don't you see," Griffiths said, his eyes afire. "Where did the Mantle get the answer?"

"What do you mean? The Mantle of Wisdom knows everything . . .

"No," Griffiths interrupted. "That's wrong. The Mantle of Kendis-dai only knows that which it has experience with. It doesn't look into the future. It isn't omniscient. It's true that there were other TFPs that were in communication with it—most notably the Nine Oracles, as you well know—but while it may have had a map of where Lokan intended to go—it didn't actually know where Lokan had gone."

"I'm not sure I'm following you." Merinda looked skeptically at the cape-bedecked astronaut.

"Look," Griffiths said, leaning over the chart once more and indicating the course line on the map. "This is the course that Lokan's fleet took. Its course lines are clear, using standard map references, right up through this point here."

Merinda moved up to Griffiths's side, her eyes following the line of his pointing finger. "You're pointing at the blank space, Griffiths."

"Oh, sorry," he said, pulling back his hand. "I see it in my mind. Notice how the last place the line crosses into is Bonefield Narrows. Well, just inside that is the last reference for the final course of the Lokan Fleet—at least as I look at it."

"So, what's your point?"

"The point is that this reference isn't like all the others. It's a vector."

"What?" Merinda said. "You mean it just points direction?"

"Exactly," Griffiths said, turning back to the map. "All the other coordinates reference external points: map grids, quasars, navigation beacons, you know. This last reference is just a direction pointing the way. Not only that, it's a very specific direction. The figures themselves factor down to nearly a thousand decimal places in both heading and elevation."

"Heading and elevation—of what?" Merinda said.

Griffiths turned to her and smiled. "In the last heading

and elevation from the source of this map. Don't you see it? The priests of Kendis-dai traveled with the Lokan Fleet. They had left the Mantle of Kendis-dai for the crusade. Only they could have given this map to the Mantle—who passed it down to us. At least one of the priests or priestesses must have survived long enough to transmit this information to the Mantle."

Merinda shook her head. "Survived what?"

"Remember the story of Targ's crashed Settlement Ship? It was the last known position of the Lokan Fleet. Someone, long ago, must have gotten a message from that ship back to the Mantle. That Settlement Ship and its dutiful, millennia-dead servant is the source of this map."

"Then the current attitude and heading of that ruin . . ."

". . . Coupled with the figures I can see in my head . . ."

Merinda smiled. "Point directly to the passage through the Maelstrom Wall!"

31

Ruins Vinculum

"CAPTAIN GRIFFITHS, IS THIS WHAT YOU HAD IN MIND?" Flynn said grandly, standing easily on the forward spar, his right arm gripping one of the forward stays with seemingly casual ease.

Griffiths stepped carefully up on the foredeck grids, gripping the low rail. There were numerous possibilities for handholds here, rigging lines and stays extending upward from the forehull spar and various cleats to either side. Still, Griffiths also observed that there was plenty of space between the complex rigging lines to tumble over the railing and fall clear of the side of the ship. Normally this would have left him sucking vacuum in space behind the ship's wake as she sped upward toward distant stars in the general direction her mast was pointing. Not now, however, as the ship's direction of travel had shifted for landing. Now it seemed as though she were hanging from her main mast, a Christmas ornament dangling from a spindly top. A lake drifted far below their hull, the gentle waves of its surface forming a corrugation that gave away the measure of its distance. The curve of the shoreline closed on them as they continued their descent.

The beauty of it all was lost on Griffiths at the moment as he fought off panic. Interstellar distances were so meaningless to the human mind. For that matter, even altitudes in airplanes never bothered the man—he always just thought the world had somehow shrunk in scale rather than admit to his own distance from the ground. However, standing here on the exposed forecastle of the *Venture Revenge*, Griffiths suddenly had all too clear a perspective on the distance he could fall. He could look down the side of the prow and see the twin draglines dangling from the ship as too perfect an exercise in visual perspective.

The whole thing was making Griffiths decidedly dizzy and disoriented, despite his rakish hat and billowing cape. The ample breakfast that he had enjoyed earlier with Flynn in his cabin was threatening to make an encore appearance.

Flynn, on the other hand, seemed to revel in the obvious danger of the ship's bow. He cut a dashing figure standing as he did so confidently in the native wind now that the ship's atmospheric dome was not needed. His dark hair was blown back from his chiseled face. He wore an open shirt with bloused sleeves that rustled in the wind.

Merinda stood there with him, her black Vestis uniform and cape a perfect contrast to Flynn's outfit. Her costume quickly suggested the strong beauty of her figure. Her honey-colored hair drifted back with the wind. The billowing clouds of the Bonefield Narrows formed a perfect backdrop for their pose, the island-worlds floating behind them in the perpetual opal twilight of the Narrows. With Merinda at his side, Flynn looked every bit the confident conqueror.

Griffiths hated the man all over again.

"I still don't understand why you insist that we land here, Merinda," Flynn said.

"Griffiths believes it essential," Merinda replied smoothly. "He says we need to get something from the ruins here before we can go on."

"Well, don't go running off without me." Flynn smiled

at her. "Just remember that you are still my prisoner, Merinda—technically speaking, of course."

"Thanks, Evon, you're all heart."

"Of course, that doesn't apply to our shipmate Griffiths!" Flynn's smile broadened noticeably. "He steers our course. Well, Griffiths? Is this not the place?"

Griffiths turned his face toward Flynn, unsure as to what color it was at the moment. "I think so."

Merinda pointed with her free left hand. "Yes, this is it. The Bonefield Narrows may have thousands of island worlds but it is in the nature of this quantum zone that they all stay relatively in the same position. That bay below us there—that almost certainly is the same cove where the *Knight Fortune* dropped anchor. Those crags on either side of the cove's entrance—they are the same as the yarnspinner described. Those yar trees . . . the white sand beach . . . it all fits. This is the place, Flynn. That's the cove. Here is where the hunt begins."

"You know," Flynn said, turning his smiling face toward hers, "You still haven't told me why we have to land on this miniature paradise."

"Because I said so," Griffiths piped in with an annoyance that Flynn promptly ignored.

Merinda glanced quizzically at Griffiths before answering. "I've already told you. We are here because we need something from the ruins—the first and last piece of the puzzle. This is the place where everything connects. This is the place that leads us to what we seek."

Flynn smiled again radiantly into Merinda's eyes.

"Then," he said, "I suppose we had better get ourselves ashore."

Merinda smiled back mildly.

Griffiths suddenly hated them all. Hated Flynn for taking Merinda away from him. Hated Merinda for never seeing

Griffiths at all. Most of all he hated himself for not being able to do anything about it, and especially for the vertigo he was feeling at the moment that prevented him from doing much at all.

"Master Shindak!" Flynn cried out to the main deck behind him.

"Aye, Captain, and what is your pleasure?"

"Set her down in the bay, Master Shindak. Have Kheoghi form up a landing party. We make to go ashore."

"By your word, Captain," the elf called back at once.

Flynn swung suddenly around the stay line and dropped down to the forecastle deck. He turned and offered Merinda his hand in assistance. She took it as he helped her down to the deck as well.

"Come, Captain Griffiths," Flynn said heartily. "We've a prize to win. You've got the key! What say we go find the lock, eh?"

Flynn slammed his broad hand against Griffiths's back.

Griffiths suddenly had a new perspective on distance as he watched his breakfast tumble away from the ship toward the water far below.

FLYNN FLOATED ABOUT A FOOT ABOVE THE WHITE SANDS EN-circling the bay, but then so did everyone in the shore party, Griffiths noted. Even the minotaurs hovered like lightly tethered balloons, though occasionally their hooves scraped against the ground due either to their height or their great weight. Broad, golden belts had been broken out shortly af-ter landing and distributed to those who were going ashore. Griffiths had been given his without comment by one of the gnomes. He had watched the others on deck put theirs on first before he finally committed himself to mounting the device around his own waist. Each had a massive orange stone mounted in a huge buckle. Two smaller gray stones were set to either side of the larger, central stone. These, Griffiths discovered through discrete observations, could be pulled out of the belt and fit easily in each of his hands. By moving the smaller stones relative to the larger one, he found he could drift upward, downward, spin, and move about. The control was quite intuitive. For Griffiths, whose position had been the remote piloted vehicle pilot on the Archilus expedition, the feel of controlling his own flight was quite natural and exhilarating. The belts had allowed them all to float over the side rails and leave the *Venture Revenge* anchored over the bay under command of a somewhat reduced crew.

Griffiths and Merinda had followed Flynn over the waters and to the shore. The Vestis hadn't said a word to him during the entire process, somehow lost in her own thoughts. Griffiths desperately wanted to break the silence but couldn't think of anything clever enough or germane enough to sound like casual conversation. Now that they were over dry land, he would have to wait longer: Flynn felt the need to give them all further instructions.

"The treeline extends, as you see, almost up to the shore itself. Beyond that is anyone's guess. We know that this is the correct bay. According to the legend, our objective lies just above a waterfall, but I wouldn't hold much store in that. The river feeding the fall may have changed its course several times since then. You won't see it from the air; it's cloaked, so stay as close to the ground as you can while searching."

"Well, Cap'n," the minotaur Kheoghi snorted, "now that you've got us clear on what we ain't supposed to look for . . . just what is it that we is looking for?"

"Ruins, Kheoghi," Flynn said through his smile. "The ruins of a Lokan Settlement Ship."

A ripple of laughter passed through the assembled pirates as one of the gnomes chuckled through his words. "A Lokan ship? Three thousand years of rust and rot in this jungle? What are we supposed to use to find it? A magnifying glass?"

Griffiths watched Flynn for his reaction but the pirate captain had obviously dealt with such insolence before. He only smiled back at the group.

"You won't need a magnifying glass, Ogrob," Flynn said easily. "As of about thirty years ago it was very much intact. It's about four miles across and about five to six thousand feet high. I don't think you'll have much trouble recognizing it once you come across it."

Kheoghi scratched his left horn as if to stimulate some thought. "If this here Lokan ship be as big as you be telling it, Captain—then why ain't we seen it from the *Venture Revenge*?"

Flynn shrugged. "The legends say it's hidden—some sort of invisibility magic."

Ogrob cocked his capped head to one side. "Magic? Still working after three millennia? You been eating the wild root again, Captain?"

Flynn turned toward the gnome. He was smiling, but now the smile was stiff and cold. There was a brightness in Flynn's eyes. "No, Ogrob," he said in a voice that was both quiet and carried to the listening ears of everyone assembled. "I have not been eating the wild root again. What you do need to understand is that I know what it is we're looking for here. Follow my orders and I'll bring you to treasure and power beyond your wildest dreams. Ignore me, and you'll cut yourself out of more than a share because I'll gully you here and now."

The gnome didn't flinch. "Aye, Captain."

Flynn turned back to the group. "Elami! You take your sisters and fan out towards the left. The Hishawei will move off to the right with the gnomes. Kheoghi! You and your brothers will follow me. I want everyone to stay within hearing of the beings next to you in the line. I don't think it will be possible to keep a line of sight and cover enough area . . ."

Griffiths turned to Merinda, who was drifting next to him, and spoke quietly to her. "Merinda, I don't understand. You're the Vestis here. This guy was a Librae at best. Doesn't that mean you outrank him or something?"

"Yes, Griffiths," Merinda said, her eyes still focused on some distant thought. Her answers were coming automatically, as though she wasn't really hearing his words. "Technically, I suppose you're right."

Flynn continued speaking but his words were lost under their conversation. Griffiths twisted the control globes in his hands and drifted slightly closer to the Vestis. "Then why are we following him? You're more capable than he is and a damn sight more reliable. I wouldn't trust him any further than this so-called crew of his!"

Merinda turned suddenly toward Griffiths as though she had heard him for the first time. "You, of all people, should know better than to try and tell me how to do my job."

"I'm not telling you how to do your job!" Griffiths shot back through his teeth. "I just think that it's about time that you *did* your job, that's all!"

"I *am* doing my job," Merinda said, turning away from him and watching Flynn as he spoke. "Sometimes it isn't a question of action, Griffiths, so much as knowing when it is the right time to act. The situation is fairly under control at the moment."

" 'Fairly under control?' " Griffiths gawked. "If it hasn't escaped your notice, we're light-years from any inhabited worlds and we have fallen in with alien pirates who, I am sure, would just as soon eat our livers raw as smile at us. I'm not sure what kind of control you're referring to but . . ."

"Griffiths!"

The prophet–astronaut turned suddenly at the sharp mention of his name.

"You and Merinda will come with Kheoghi and me. We don't have a lot of time. I'd like to have you find what you need and get this little expedition over with before the Tsultak decide to join our little party and spoil everyone's day. Let's go!"

"HALLOO, LEFT," CAME THE DISTANT CRY, FILTERING through the massive wall of the jungle drifting all about him.

"Halloo, right," Merinda called, her own voice sounding and feeling rather hoarse. They had been drifting forward and calling out in this same manner for what seemed like hours. The thick growth of the jungle had slowed their progress despite the levitation belts they were using. The ground itself was extremely rugged, filled with unexpected cliff faces rising precipitously from the jungle in some places or dropping into deep crevasses without warning. This was further complicated by the jungle growth, which made the ground nearly impassable. It was difficult enough flying through the thick foliage. Merinda would occasionally lower herself to avoid a solid block of the jungle canopy above, or shift left or right when the growth proved too thick to allow her to pass. It was like a three-dimensional maze through which she was drifting, unsure of her direction.

"Halloo, right!" Griffiths's voice was far away and tired.

"Halloo, left!" Merinda called back wearily.

If they didn't have to be so close to the ground, she thought, they could float quickly above the jungle canopy and get their bearings. She could be back to the *Venture Revenge* in just a few breezy minutes. Yet she couldn't do that yet, her mission requiring her to keep close to the ground.

It's just like my life, she thought. I feel like I'm drifting through my own jungle, too close to really see what's going on. I'd like to break loose and soar. Perhaps I could get my own bearing then. Perhaps I could even find my way back home, she thought.

"Halloo, right!" she called out absently.

"Halloo, left!" echoed the distant reply.

Of course, that was ridiculous, she realized. There would never again be a place she could think of as home. She realized that her home would no longer be a place that she returned to but would have to be a place that she forged for herself. Griffiths had found that out, quickly enough, when he'd become prophet of an entire planet—only to discover that he didn't much care for the job.

Merinda smiled at the thought of Griffiths. She wasn't entirely sure as to how such a naïve man had been chosen for what appeared to be a major exploration event by his backward and barbaric people. Still, while he might not appear as dynamic as Flynn, there was something rather endearing about the man. He seemed to her like a young, lost pet: cuddly and cute, yet yapping at all the unknown things around him regardless of how harmful or harmless they were. Merinda smiled at the analogy for a moment then shook her head. No, she didn't need a pet right now, no matter how cute it might be. It just looked like another bad choice in relationships, and she knew her track record along those lines.

On the other hand, there was Flynn. He was more dynamic and confident than Griffiths, she thought, but there was something about him that reminded her too much of Queekat. Something hidden, dark and dangerous. Perhaps she was wrong.

"Halloo, left," she called out automatically.

Silence.

"Halloo left!" she called once more, this time with loud annoyance.

There was no response from the thick fronds around her.

"Griffiths?" Merinda shouted suddenly, then reined in her drift and held as still as she could.

The leaves shifted about her but there was no response.

Merinda cried out, "Come, right! Come, right!" She rotated forward quickly and, not waiting for the reply from Kheoghi, flew into the jungle at her right. The fronds, leaves, branches, and vines rushed past her as she soared. She avoided the larger branches and smashed painfully through the smaller ones in her haste.

"Griffiths!" she cried out as she flew with a rush of wind. "Griffiths!"

Suddenly the jungle wall vanished. Her skin tingled with recognition as she passed through the mystical wall that divided the jungle from the clearing. There was magic working here. She arrested her flight as she emerged, more out of reflex caution than thought.

Rising before her were the broad steps of an enormous landing claw. So mammoth was the structure that she nearly mistook it for a temple ruin.

She could hear others of their landing party emerging from the jungle behind her, each of them stopping as they were confronted by the enormous structure rising before them. Merinda looked upward. The beautiful curved lines of the structure could still be seen, despite the encroaching growth which only recently had found its way around the magical barrier surrounding the craft. Higher and higher she looked, up to the curving arms embracing the vast dome glittering in the perpetual twilight of the Bonefield Narrows.

The Lokan Settlement Ship.

"Excellent work, Merinda!" Flynn said, suddenly at her side. "You've found it!"

"Griffiths!" Merinda shouted, her eyes searching the structure frantically. "Griffiths, where are you?"

Her eyes came to rest on two figures struggling at the top of the stairs. She rotated the control globes at once, her levitation belt propelling her upward above the sharply rising staircase. Her eyes remained locked on Griffiths. The astronaut was suddenly twisted around, his arm bent behind his back by a black-cloaked figure beyond. Merinda was barely halfway up the staircase when she caught the glint of a weapon pressed swiftly under Griffiths's right jaw.

"Stop now, Neskat, or the barbarian dies!" The husky voice of the dark figure drifted down to them.

Merinda arrested her ascent at once.

"Targ!" she growled.

32

Shades and Shadows

"I WAS WONDERING WHEN YOU MIGHT GET AROUND TO coming here," said Targ of Gandri. His tone was quiet and affable on the surface, but Merinda detected the high quiver of tension that ran through his words. "It was inevitable, of course, that you would come here. The only question was whether I could arrive before you, Merinda."

Griffiths continued to struggle but Targ's hold couldn't be broken. In a few moments a panting, sweating Griffiths stood passive, his right arm twisted upward into his own back, and Targ's weapon directed to fire through his skull with all too graphic effect.

"Don't be a fool, Targ," Merinda said with a calm that she did not yet feel. "You don't want to kill Griffiths."

"I've already tried to kill him once," Targ said, pressing the crystalline emitter of his force-projector weapon deeper into Griffiths's flesh just below his jaw. "Thought that I had succeeded rather spectacularly, too. Having believed I killed him once before, what makes you think I would have any compunction against killing him a second time?"

Merinda said nothing but drifted downward to stand midway up the stairs. There she stopped a moment and looked up again at Griffiths and the tall figure behind him, Targ's white hair shining under the twilight sky above.

"What? Merinda Neskat short of words?" Targ observed with an arch of his eyebrow. "I am astonished indeed. I would have thought that there were a thousand questions you might ask. As head of the Vestis order I am concerned. Why don't you ask me, say, how it is that I escaped that dungeon you placed me in on Avadon? You might ask me how it is that I came to this place so quickly or how I knew that you would come here so quickly. Indeed, Merinda, I am worried that you are slipping in your skills as a Vestis. Curiosity is supposed to be one of your primary motivations."

Merinda looked up. She squinted as though to better see the man who stood above her. "You once told me never to ask a question that I already knew the answer to."

Targ replied, "Actually, I said to never ask a question that you didn't want the answer to. Nevertheless, I have what I have chased you halfway across the galaxy to obtain—the mind of your barbaric friend, here. So, unless you have something more to say to me, I'm afraid we must all be going."

Merinda looked into Targ's eyes and spoke with a quiet, sure voice. "Vestis Prime Targ of Gandri, I hereby arrest you for crimes against the Omnet as specified in the Charter of the Dictorae. Specifically, the attempted assassination of the Prophet of Avadon, the attempted assassination of a fellow Vestis, and exercising your authority outside the bounds of the Charter and to the detriment of the better interests of the Omnet. Further charges are pending a complete investigation of your actions, but these charges are sufficient to detain and try you. How do you plead to the charges brought against you thus far?"

Targ laughed and shook his head. "I do not recognize your authority to try me, Vestis Neskat. In any event, just who would you get to enforce your sentence? Griffiths?"

Griffiths grimaced as Targ pressed the astronaut's twisted arm painfully upward. "Perhaps you're thinking of your old friend Flynn and his merry pirate band?"

Merinda lowered her head.

"Of course," Targ said. "You already know that Flynn has been working for me for some time now."

"That's not true, Targ," Flynn shouted from somewhere down behind Merinda. "I serve my pirate brothers here on the Maelstrom Wall. My allegiance is to them!"

"Nobly put," Targ said in response. "That allegiance, I suppose, included your little response to the Omnet concerning the whereabouts of a certain renegade Vestis of your acquaintance, did it?"

Merinda turned slowly to look at Flynn and gauge his response.

Flynn continued to look up at the Vestis Prime high overhead at the top of the stairs. "As a matter of fact, it did, Targ of Gandri. It brought you out of Central didn't it? You're here now, and unless I missed my guess, you didn't exactly bring the entire Centirion battle fleet with you. This entire thing stank from the beginning—and nothing stinks quite the way a man who is suddenly out for himself does."

Targ's lips curled. "Ethics from you? What a sense of humor! I'd love to stay and debate this with you but I've got an appointment with my own fate."

Merinda saw Targ's lips begin to move in quiet conjuration. "No!" she yelled, twisting the control globes in her fists full forward.

It was too late. Both Targ and Griffiths were shrouded in a deep violet aura. Both encased men rose swiftly above her and turned. In a moment the two figures rushed into the black open maw of the Lokan Settlement Ship.

Merinda didn't hesitate. "Flynn," she cried out. "Get moving! If we lose Griffiths, it's over!"

The pirate captain and his crew were already soaring toward the steps, but she was far closer. As the levitation belt gathered momentum, she quickly cleared the edge of the platform, spun the globes hard down, and vanished into the well of darkness before her.

Merinda blinked quickly, trying vainly to get her eyes adjusted to the darkness that surrounded her. The great curving walls of the ship were only menacing shadows whose distance it was impossible to judge as she flew on. She murmured a cantrip that enhanced her vision somewhat but transformed the shadows into eerie green glows still barely above her sight threshold. More importantly, however, the cantrip allowed her to clearly see the residual ether trail left by Targ's own flight spell. It was fading quickly to her sight. She realized that Targ was moving quickly through the interior of the ruin with a confidence and knowledge that she herself lacked.

She pressed on, pushing the levitation belt to its limits, twisting and turning in the increasingly complex labyrinth that was the interior of the ship. The walls were closer now; the turns more difficult to navigate. Still the trail before her continued to fade.

She cursed Targ once more. The man had been the director of the most important organization in the known universe and now he was running with a hostage on some crazed artifact hunt? Targ may have been a capable Vestis and a formidable enemy but right now none of it was making much sense.

Suddenly a wall appeared out of the darkness directly ahead of her. Merinda cursed again, jerked at the control globes, but only managed to soften the blow. She slammed into the wall with enough force to knock the wind from her lungs.

Merinda slid painfully down the curving wall and came to

rest, gasping for air, at the bottom of the crossing hall. Dust billowed around her, choking her as she struggled to regain her breath. Her vision had blurred momentarily from the impact. The cantrip was still in effect; the walls were still glowing a ghostly green.

She had lost the trail.

Frantically, she leaped to her feet in a billowing cloud of dust. The wall was curved from top to bottom. The hallway itself was also curved, its ends gently wrapping around into the distance. A quick glance about her discovered where the directional globes had come to rest after falling from her hands. She quickly picked them up and oriented them. Shakily, she rose into the air again and quickly glided down the corridor to her left.

She traveled that direction for some time but no evidence of the ether trail came to her. Cursing, she doubled back, soaring past the point where she had hit the wall . . .

. . . And very nearly running directly into Kheoghi in the process. She reined in her momentum just before she collided with the coarse-haired brute.

"Merinda?" Flynn asked, drifting slowly over to where she now floated. "Where in the Ninth Darkness are you going?"

Merinda was still slightly out of breath from her collision with the wall. "I lost . . . I lost them, Flynn! There was a tentative ether trail but it's gone."

Flynn just shook his head. "Wizards and technicians," he said with a laugh. "Life is so complicated for wizards and technicians. They always wonder how we got along without them for so long. Kheoghi?"

"Aye, Captain?" said the minotaur, whose massive bulk floated just a few feet away.

"Do you think you could find our friend Griffiths in this place?"

"Aye, Captain, if that be yer pleasure," Kheoghi rumbled. "Humans are a stinking race, beggin' yer pardon, sire! However, I don't mind tellin' ye that it gives me no pleasure!"

"You've got the best olfactory sense of anyone aboard, Kheoghi," Flynn said. "You've tracked no fewer than a dozen men for us in the last month. I thought you took great sport in it!"

"Oh, aye, sire, trackin' a man, that I do enjoy something fierce," the minotaur said, his head lolling from side to side as he spoke. "It's not that, sire!"

"Well, then, what's the problem?"

"Ye see, sire—I just don't much care for mazes, that's all."

With that, Kheoghi lifted his head slightly, gave a long sniff through his broad snout, and led them all off down the second right-hand corridor.

THE LAST CORRIDOR ENDED IN MASSIVE DOORS, EACH OF which stood slightly ajar. They had made their way far into the ship, farther than Merinda would have thought possible considering its size. They had broken out chemical torches early in their descent. Now their dim green light was unneeded, for the compartment beyond was obviously lit somehow, its beams spilling through the partially open doorway into the access hall in which they crept.

Merinda approached the doorway with great caution, keeping her back against the smooth wall and one of the doors between her and the room beyond. She motioned for Flynn, who was next to her, to slide closer to her so that she could whisper to him and be understood. "Targ is mine. You see to the others, but if I don't take Targ down first, then you'll have to get Griffiths and your crew as far from here as you can. A person is only given one chance at Targ; after that, it will mostly be a matter of how long I can keep him occupied before he kills me."

"Neskat, this is crazy!" Flynn argued under his breath. "We've got the cursed map! Let's just get out of here!"

"No, Flynn! The map's no good without either Griffiths or what he's looking for in these ruins. Get him and the map out of here and you may have a chance to come back later and find the control room. Lose Griffiths now and you'll never find the core passage in a dozen millennia. Targ will, however, and I just don't want to know what kind of galaxy his mind would shape. Now wait here until I make my move, then rush the chamber, grab Griffiths, and get the hell out of here!"

Flynn opened his mouth as though to protest, but then simply sighed quietly and nodded.

Merinda turned back toward the doorway. With silent, considered steps she made her way across the dust-covered floor. After several eternities passed, she crouched down near the floor and ventured to look into the room beyond.

The chamber was far more vast than she had imagined it would be. It was at least a hundred feet in diameter, its curved walls ornately decorated. There was a platform at the center of the chamber, lit by a single column of light.

By the Nine, Merinda thought to herself. This is the command chamber! This is where it all happened to L'Zari Targ all those years ago!

She took the scene in quickly, her mind analyzing it primarily from a strategic standpoint. Targ stood about twenty-five feet from her, his weapon apparently still dimpling Griffiths's skin at his neck. Beyond them was the platform of raised panels, lit by the dim column of light from above. Targ and Griffiths both stood in the way of the platform, keeping her from seeing its details.

It was Targ that kept her attention; that was the focus of every fiber of her being. The Prime was speaking to Griffiths as they stood with their backs to the doorway.

". . . Right here that I stood when it happened. Can you

possibly imagine it, barbarian? I was only a boy, really. I stood right here as that Gorgon bastard lifted my father up on his multiple blades and took him from me. All because that old spacer wouldn't give the Gorgon a stupid map! A piece of paper and ink!"

Merinda could see that Targ was working himself up toward something. There was an unbalanced, hysterical edge to Targ's voice that she had never heard before. Targ seemed to be pushing himself towards the edge of some mental abyss that she could barely fathom. It was obvious to her that there wouldn't be much time left for her to act.

"Can't you see it? Can't you picture it in your little brain, barbarian? Now it's I that want the map and you are going to give it to me or, so help me, I will do to you what those Gorgons did to my father right on this very spot! I've come too far and sacrificed too much to let a backwater, unedu-cated barbarian from some unknown world stop me now! Show me! Show me the chart!"

Time slowed down as she moved, her mind focusing on the task at hand, drawing up her resources from within her-self and preparing for the battle to come. She had her wits, her considerable Vestis skills, and a simple cutlass. She knew it was all she had. She knew it would not be enough.

Her first steps into the hall prepared her stance. The cut-lass came up, a focal point for the energies of her mystical powers. The edge of the blade had no chance of penetrating Targ's flesh for the Prime was far too well protected for such weapons. As a conduit for her own powers, however, the metal shaft of the blade would work quite well. She directed the point forward, summoning all her reserves. Her legs bent down as she prepared to accept the recoil of the blow she was about to deliver and prepared herself for the battle which would certainly follow her first strike.

Only then did she notice the dusts forming about her feet. Hands, legs, bodies, mouths . . .

Destiny! whispered the voices of the dead.

Merinda looked up.

Targ had heard them!

The Prime released Griffiths, pushing him with such strength that the astronaut was lifted into the air and fell several feet away. Targ turned, his projection weapon in hand, its crystal emitter swinging quickly toward Merinda.

Merinda's sword discharged, but the brilliant eruption of electric brilliance missed its mark, cutting raggedly across Targ's chest as he turned rather than through his spine as Merinda had intended.

Targ's weapon discharged, the force of Merinda's assault causing the Prime to trigger the device prematurely. Three red bolts of plasma force slammed in quick succession into the massive door behind Merinda, blowing the door backward off its mountings. The howling force of the explosions threw Merinda off her feet, and she sprawled through the dust billowing from the floor about her. She quickly pushed herself up from the chamber floor, crossing her wrists in front of her reflexively.

Her action came not a moment too soon. Targ had abandoned the spent projector weapon, forming his own arm into a dual-pronged javelin in less time than it took for the discarded weapon to fall to the floor. The prongs thrust forward toward Merinda but glanced off a white-flared shielding that sprang from her wrists.

Merinda glanced into Targ's eyes. They were locked on her but she suddenly knew that they no longer actually saw Merinda Neskat, a former companion and colleague. Now they only saw an enemy to be destroyed utterly. The coldness of his eyes was more frightening than anything she had experienced before.

"Now, Flynn!" she screamed. "Now!"

Flynn burst through the still smoldering doorway, with Kheoghi and Elami behind him. Merinda wondered for a moment how the pirates had even survived the sundering of that doorway by Targ's errant projector blasts. They are survivors, she thought, but perhaps not for long.

Targ turned toward the movement. The pronged weapon vanished with the distraction.

Merinda saw her chance. She lunged forward, blade still in hand, channeling everything she had left to enchant the weapon.

Targ was too quick. He turned, his cupped hand suddenly ablaze, and thrust the rigid fingers toward her neck. The flaming hand collided with the ice-blue shielding, shattering her protection into a thousand shards of glowing force. The force of the blow completely stopped her forward momentum and reversed it, throwing her bodily against the wall behind her.

Dazed and spent, she slumped against the wall. She was vaguely aware of the blood oozing from the back of her head.

Targ was moving toward her.

Beyond him, Griffiths was standing up.

It was all so much like a dream, she thought. Everything seemed to be happening slowly once more. Griffiths yelling at Targ, starting to run toward him. Targ turning around. She knew she had to stop it but there was nothing left in her to give.

Then, she saw Flynn. His leg swung across Griffiths's path. Griffiths tripped. His fall, headlong into the bones of the dead, seemed to take forever. He choked on their dust. In his place as the dust cleared stood Flynn, holding a rolled parchment up toward Targ. His words came to Merinda as though from a distant place, just as her consciousness failed.

"I have the map, Targ! We can make a deal!"

33

Deal with the Devil

GRIFFITHS LAY CHOKING AMID THE ASH-GRAY DUST OF THE damned. Their long-dead cells filled his nostrils and his gasping mouth. He coughed violently, pushing himself painfully up from the floor of the chamber, coated with the siltlike remains.

"NO!"

Griffiths craned his head around toward the unspeakable sound. Targ's cry was subhuman, a gusher of emotions without restraint that echoed from the depths of his being. The Prime looked as though he had been dealt a mortal blow. Indeed, Griffiths was suddenly hopeful that Merinda had succeeded and brought down the great wizard. Yet he could see Merinda where she lay slumped against the wall beyond where Targ stood, his eyes wide in horror and rage.

Griffiths rolled painfully onto his side with as much speed as his ribs would allow him. He had to see what evil could so frighten the most powerful man in the known universe.

Flynn! Griffiths gazed at the pirate in wonder, then sudden rage. You bastard! You tripped me up! I was going to save her, not you! You tripped me and now you stand there looking all powerful and noble. Damn you!

"That's right, Targ," Flynn said, his eyes ablaze as he held up the parchment. "I know where your precious Nightsword is and I've the means to salvage it!"

The lower half of Targ seemed to become suddenly molten. Griffiths felt the waves of heat radiating out from him through the floor. He quickly pushed himself unsteadily to his feet.

"Give it to me, Flynn," Targ said, his eyes turning a brilliant, glowing red. "It is mine by right! Give me the map!"

"We had a deal, Targ!"

"I no longer need you or your ship," the wizard intoned. He stepped closer to Flynn, the heat more intense than ever. "Give me the map or die, here and now."

Flynn glanced down at the metal floor plates beneath him. Several around Targ had taken on a dull orange tint from the heat, which was increasing by the moment. "Well, I'll be happy to, but you have to do me a favor first."

"The only bargain is the one for what's left of your life, Flynn," Targ said, stepping closer again.

Flynn ignored the comment. "Here's the deal, Targ: if you can read the map, you can have it."

Targ blinked quickly over his flaming red eyes.

Griffiths stepped back once, then twice, as he shielded his eyes from the intense heat.

"What?" Targ said.

"It's simple," Flynn replied, his eyes steady even as sweat broke out on his forehead. "Tell me what this map says—truthfully—and I'll give it to you and surrender my crew unconditionally."

The heat suddenly withdrew. Targ's molten half reformed into its natural form. About him, the floor plates faded, retreating the entire area back to its former darkness.

"Here," Flynn smiled. "If you can read it, it's yours."

Targ snatched the parchment with unexpected swiftness

from Flynn's outstretched hand. In a moment he had un-
rolled the map, found that he couldn't read in the darkness,
and hastily spun his left finger in the air next to his head. Instantly, a globe of soft, white light appeared in the air. Targ
grasped both sides of the large parchment, his eyes squinting
at the page.

"By the Nine," Targ muttered through clenched teeth,
his anger rising once more.

"By the Nine, indeed," Flynn said, casually hooking his
thumbs on his broad levitation belt. "You can't read it and I
can't read it. In fact, there's only one person here that I
know of who can read it."

"This is Lost Empire script," Targ said, his eyes scanning
the map. "*I* may not be able to read it, but I do know
someone who can!"

"Perhaps so," Flynn continued, seeming in Griffiths's
mind to be walking through the logic of his argument like a
man leaping precariously from stone to stone across a stream.
"However, you will notice that the final piece of the map,
the critical route that passes the Maelstrom Wall, is missing. That piece remains locked in the mind of my good
shipmate Griffiths."

As Flynn gestured with his open hand, Targ turned to
look squarely at Griffiths.

"Now wait just a moment," Griffiths said, holding his
hands up.

"One moment indeed," Flynn interrupted with a casual
manner. "You see, Griffiths has signed the Articles of my
crew. He is one of us, as every member of my crew knows.
He wouldn't be interested in betraying his old shipmates.
Indeed, he wouldn't tell you what you want to know unless he wanted to do so. Of course, once you learned what
you needed from him, you would no doubt be tempted to
kill him as I recall you did once before. He could use a little

protection, and my guess is that his shipmates are just the sort of family he's looking for right now. He knows he's safer with us than he is with you, don't you, Griffiths, old mate?"

Griffiths was catching the drift of Flynn's speech. It was intended as much for his ears as for Targ's. He would not put it past the vaunted Prime to kill him in some private corner of the galaxy just to keep him quiet about what he knew. As Flynn had pointed out, the man had already killed him once, or thought he had. Flynn was saying that Griffiths needed protection. Flynn and his mercenary cutthroats may not have been a good offer, but they were the best one he had at the moment.

"Yes," Griffiths replied to Flynn's comment, though his eyes remained locked on Targ. "I believe you are right, old mate."

"There," Flynn said through his easy smile. "So you see! I think we can make a deal after all! We'll take you through the Maelstrom Wall personally, Vestis Prime, and give you assistance on your quest. You shall compensate us for our time and effort once we return with wealth commensurate to the prize that we shall recover for you. Of course, my gallant crew shall require that we hold your little secret safe for you until such time as you deliver our fee. It's a simple enough arrangement. We give you the galaxy—all you have to do is pay us for it. Do we have a bargain?"

Targ turned his now-cold eyes back toward Flynn. "I shall eat your heart while it is still warm."

Flynn's smile didn't diminish at all. "You are assuming that it is warm to begin with. However, know this, Targ! If you harm me, or any of my crew, I'll see to it that Griffiths is murdered long before you ever find your prize. You may need him alive, but I do not. No offense, Griffiths."

"None taken," Griffiths replied through thin lips.

"So, Targ, once more: do we have a deal?"

Targ stood still for a moment, his shocking white hair aglow in the illuminated ball that tenaciously remained near his head. At last, he seemed to relax.

"The crew of the ship that brought me here: they did so on the condition that they are allowed to speak with the 'Prophet of Avadon'—this barbarian, in fact. Have you any objection?"

Flynn looked momentarily puzzled, then shrugged. "I don't care."

"Then, indeed, Flynn. We are agreed."

Flynn bowed slightly and extended his right hand.

Targ looked at it for a moment, then reached his own right hand out. Each firmly grasped the other's forearm up by the elbow.

Griffiths felt as though he had just been sold. He shook his head in disgust and turned from the two men, striding through the sighing dust to where Merinda lay. He quickly knelt next to her. She had a pulse and was breathing. The flood of relief that came over him was unexpected and surprising. He suddenly felt very alone.

A hand came to rest on his shoulder. Flynn's hand. "Well, shipmate, how's our friend doing?"

Griffiths grabbed the pirate's hand and pushed it violently away from him. "Stay away from me, Flynn. Just stay the hell away."

"You've got it all wrong," Flynn said behind him, his voice quiet and low. "I had no choice in this! What would you have had me do—stand around while that psychopath killed Merinda? Or maybe you would rather I let you go through with your attack on the most powerful wizard in charted space? Where would you be right now if I had let you finish that? There wouldn't be enough atoms of you stuck together to form a complete molecule. As it is right now, Targ knows he cannot kill you or any of the rest of us, for that matter, and we've still got the crew following me. So you tell me, Captain Jeremy Griffiths of Earth, just what would you have had me do differently?"

Griffiths turned to answer but there was no answer to give. "I . . . I don't know."

"Well, when you do, feel free to get back to me," Flynn said, looking around the chamber. "I don't know why we had to come to this rock in the first place."

"Perhaps not," Griffiths said as he stood up, "but I do. Keep an eye on her, will you? We need to get her back to the ship. She seems more weak than damaged. You may have stopped Targ's attack just in time.

"Excuse me, Targ of Gandri." Griffiths spoke, and couldn't keep the bitterness out of his voice. "If I'm going to be of any help, I need to find a bridge or command center or someplace like that in this pile of junk. You were here for quite a while. Would you happen to know . . ."

Targ was barely listening to him but it was enough. There was heavy sarcasm in his voice as he replied. "Congratulations, prophet, your powers have served you well. This is the command chamber."

THE COMMAND PLATFORM IS JUST THE WAY THE STORIES DE-scribed it, thought Griffiths as he sat in one of the ancient relic chairs surrounding the map table. It was all still there. Dark display panels under the single light shining from the optics emitter overhead. The central table, bereft of the coveted map, which Targ had found there so long ago. Even the dead priest was there, his remains scattered in a jumble with his pressure suit where Targ had pushed them decades ago.

Griffiths normally might have been moved to some

pity for the fate of this fallen leader and his hundreds of followers—all of whom had died in this hall. Unfortunately, his present troubles seemed to overshadow the tragedy of the past. It was difficult to muster tears for the dead when his own wake seemed imminent.

"Let's see." Griffiths spoke out loud, his words echoing through the chamber. Kheoghi had left him here alone at Flynn's insistence. No doubt there were other guardians posted around the room, but everyone wanted him to think his deep thoughts and find the one true path. So he was left alone to talk to himself with the realization that he had little hope of better conversation than his own. "If I don't find the heading coordinates of this ancient bucket of scrap, then I can't lead this collection of murderers and psychos to what is supposed to be the most powerful weapon in all the heavens. If I can't do that then I'll probably be killed in my sleep—or awake for that matter—either by this administrator-turned-fruitcake Targ, or by Flynn if he wants to, or by Flynn's crew if he doesn't. On the other hand, if I do find the coordinates and I do find the treasure, then any combination of the above will probably kill me anyway and destroy life as we know it. As it stands, either way Merinda probably won't give a damn."

Griffiths leaned forward in the chair and gazed down at the parchment map laid out on the table. He had insisted that he needed the map for reference and so Flynn had left it with him. Where, after all, could he go with it? Griffiths gazed at the map and weighed his options.

"I'm screwed," he said, and put his head down on the table.

"Hey, Captain," echoed a distant voice. "What does a girl have to do around here to get a drink?"

Griffiths raised his head from the table, astonishment and hope registering on his face for the first time in days. Part of

GAMMA:

INHUMAN

CREED

his mind couldn't accept it. Perhaps it was the ghosts of the room come back to torment him.

"Lewis?" he said, squinting into the darkness. "Lieutenant Elizabeth Lewis?"

"Hey-ho, flyboy!" Lewis said, waving from one of the entrances to the central chamber. Tobler and Ellerby were standing behind her. All of them were grinning stupidly. "Small galaxy, isn't it."

"Oh my God," Griffiths said, his voice filled with growing belief as he stood up. "You . . . you . . . you have got to be the most beautiful thing I've ever seen! No! Wait! Stay on that cleared path across the floor! The minotaur couldn't stand the whining ghosts and swept a passage."

Lewis appeared unsure as to what Griffiths was talking about but had at least learned to follow his directions. In moments she was stepping up to the raised platform. "Permission to come aboard?" she said with a smile.

Griffiths reached down, took her hand and pulled her, laughing, up onto the platform and threw his arms around her. In moments both Ellerby and Tobler had scrambled up as well and had joined in the general celebration.

"I still don't believe it," Griffiths said at last, tears in his eyes. "How in the hell did you ever get *here*? I thought you were looking for Earth."

"We were," Tobler said. "We bounced from one star to another in that saucer. We were just getting the hang of piloting it—it's a really sweet little spacecraft, Griffiths. You wouldn't believe how well it handles regardless of the quantum zone you're in . . ."

"Tobler," said Ellerby, his eyes rolling up in exasperation. "Get on with it!"

"Oh, right! Well, it suddenly occurred to us that we needed to stop and ask directions."

Griffiths looked at the faces of his colleagues. "Ask directions?"

"Captain!" Lewis said, nudging him. "We were in such a hurry to find our way home. Remember how we rushed our departure? We couldn't wait to park that saucer on the White House lawn?"

"Yeah, I remember."

"Since the big, scary, galactic Omnet didn't know where Earth was, we simply assumed that no one did." Lewis's smile took on a nervous edge. She was coming to the point and it was obviously an important one for her. "What we didn't think of until after we'd bumped around for a few weeks was that Kendis-dai must have had some knowledge of Earth—otherwise, how would the constellations have been the same on the access device?"

Griffiths nodded. "Sure, that follows."

"So," Ellerby prodded, "we thought that the Mantle would also know something of Earth."

Griffiths was still so giddy from the unexpected reunion that he hadn't come to the conclusion yet. "Sure, I suppose that follows."

"So," Lewis said carefully and more seriously, "we've come to ask you, oh, Big-Cheese Prophet of Avadon, if you know where Earth is located."

They had asked a question of the prophet.

"Hey, come on, guys!" Griffiths said, shrugging. "You've got to be kidding me! How could I possibly know . . ."

He stopped midsentence.

They had asked a question of the prophet.

"My God, Lewis! I DO know!"

34

Resurrections

"YOU ACTUALLY KNOW THE WAY HOME?" LEWIS SAID, HER face split with a huge grin.

"Yes, I do," Griffiths replied, blinking as though he were surprised by the knowledge in his own head. "It's amazing but when you asked the question, I just knew it. Hey, why do you seem so surprised? I mean, I never would have known if you hadn't asked and you guys didn't come this far just to talk about old times or anything."

Tobler giggled. "I knew you had the answer! It's just that—well, you know, you can hope for something to be true and believe it to be true but it isn't until it actually is true that . . . well . . ."

Ellerby spoke up. "It's just such a relief, Grif! I've got a family and kids out there that think I'm dead. They've probably already had the funeral."

"Well, as they say, reports of my death have been premature." Griffiths looked around at the command chamber buried deep within the ruins of the ancient ship. "On the other hand, we aren't out of the woods yet. We've got to find a way to get out of here. What about the ship you came in?"

"Well," Lewis said, leaning back against the map table in

the center of the raised platform, "it certainly could get us home. It's a remarkable technology—well ahead of anything I've seen in all the different zones we've passed through. It appears to be some variation of the TFP base technology everyone uses in their synthetic minds. I guess you could call it a morphing techno-mystic approach to everything. The point is that it adjusts itself to whatever conditions are locally encountered. It works better in some zones than others. It's slow in this particular zone, for example. It's also somewhat unpredictable, but we haven't had a complete failure in our travels thus far." Lewis looked around the command platform and stepped over to a blank console. "In fact, the controls look a lot like these panels. You just place your hands on either side where these indentations are, like this, and . . ."

A patch of light sprang into being on the console surface. A chime sounded. Lewis sucked in her breath as six lines of light traced themselves from the center of the panel, illuminating six additional patches of color in turn. Each appearance signaled another sound. Instantly more lines began tracing themselves from the six patches, some of them exiting the panel itself and running down the sides of the console toward additional consoles situated around the platform.

"Lewis!" Griffiths lunged forward, pushing her hands away from the panel. "Stop!"

Lewis stood still, shaking slightly next to Griffiths. Both of them stared at the panel as Ellerby and Tobler crowded around them.

"It's still functional!" Tobler breathed.

"Avast!" came the deep, echoing voice across the hall. Kheoghi had no doubt been guarding the exit in case any of them should try to wander off on their own. He held a massive and rather dangerous-looking weapon aimed in their general direction. "What trickery be ye up to?"

"Nothing at all, Master Kheoghi," Griffiths called back at the brute, with a smile plastered across his face. "Just getting reacquainted!"

"That noise be no mere acquaintance, mate!" Kheoghi scowled suspiciously.

"Oh, that! That noise?" Griffiths nodded. "That's just . . . that's just singing. We make these little singing noises when we meet after a long time. It's a culture requirement among our people that . . . that whenever we get together after being apart for a long time we sing . . . and dance our ritual greeting. If we don't then . . . well, then the gods get very angry with us and . . . and . . ."

"Curse?" Tobler offered helpfully.

"Exactly," Griffiths continued. "They curse any journey that we are on after that—er, immediately after that. So, we don't want the curse—so we did the song."

Kheoghi's red eyes narrowed suspiciously.

"Look," Griffiths said. He lowered his hands, bending forward slightly, then looked up. "Chung!" he croaked in as close an approximation as he could to the first sound that had come from the panel. He raised his arms slowly and waved them in front of himself as he turned slowly around. "Ding! Whazzah! Thum, pong, dong, KRONG!"

Griffiths gestured with his hands, encouraging his companions. Lewis rolled her eyes but complied, joining Ellerby and Tobler in the ragged and ridiculous chorus mimicking Griffiths's moves and sounds. "Chung! Ding! Whazzah! Thum, pong, dong, KRONG!"

Griffiths shrugged at Kheoghi. "It's a cultural thing . . ."

The minotaur stalked back beyond the chamber door.

"What a moron!" Griffiths shook his head, then turned back toward Lewis. "What do you think, Lewis? Is this old bucket still operational?"

"I don't know," Lewis responded, her eyes narrowed as

she thought through what had just happened. "How old is this ship?"

"If I understand correctly, about three thousand years."

Lewis arched her eyebrows. "I suspect it's out of warranty, Griffiths."

"Yeah, but will it fly?"

"It's hard to say without activating all the panels. Some of those sounds we heard were alarms, and there's bound to be some deterioration in the subsystems. Just because the lights come on doesn't mean it will launch." Lewis cocked her head to one side. "Why, Griffiths? Are you joining up again?"

Griffiths thought about Merinda. Things just had not gone according to plan. Not that there even had been a plan. Still, he thought, what chance did he have with the likes of Vestis Neskat? Perhaps it was, indeed, time to go home.

"Yeah," he said, looking away from Lewis as he spoke. "I guess I'm finished playing space ranger for now. The problem is going to be how to get out of here. The Marrenkan ship is out—it requires too many people to sail it effectively. We don't know if this monster is spaceworthy. If we take the ship you came in, then old Flynn and his crowd will just hunt us down. In this zone, you said yourself, the ship is a bit sluggish. The *Venture Revenge* would be on us before we ever got close to the quantum front."

"So where does that leave us?" Ellerby asked.

"Maybe the same place we were before," Griffiths said. "Which of these panels would give us navigational information—headings and craft attitude and such?"

"That one on the left, I think." Lewis pointed.

"Lewis, see if you can activate it. Tobler. Ellerby. Cover us with a little dancing for our ugly friend outside the door."

"What are you planning, Griffiths?" Lewis asked skeptically.

Griffiths turned back to the large parchment map on

the table. "I think we may be in a position to bargain after all."

"What are you doing?" Tobler asked.

Griffiths ignored the question, searching about the table for a few moments before discovering a brass ruler with a smooth, straight edge. "Ellerby, do you still have a pen with you?"

Ellerby chuckled as he reached for his breast pocket. "Am I ever without a pen? Here."

He made a small mark on the parchment. "Lewis, give me those coordinates. A few finishing lines on this map and we'll have something worth bargaining for!"

Griffiths laid the straight edge on the parchment, orienting it as Lewis called out the final navigation numbers of the Settlement Ship. As he set the pen tip down to the paper, he happened to glance down past the ancient map table to the skeletal remains of the last human to plot a course here.

The great miter that had once sat upon the skeleton's head lay next to the broken remains.

The ancient corpse was that of the Prophet of the Mantle. In the mythic time of Lokan, these bones had been bonded to the Mantle of Kendis-dai—just as Griffiths was now.

"So, it was *your* map that the Mantle knows," Griffiths murmured toward the dead. A sudden chill ran up his spine. Three thousand years ago, these bones had stood where Griffiths was standing, struggling to finish the same map to which Griffiths was pressing his pen.

"I hope this works out better for me than it did for you, old comrade," Griffiths said, sighing.

Quickly, he drew the first line and began noting the course next to it in small, tight figures.

———

"NICE FRIENDS YOU'VE GOT HERE," LEWIS SAID CASUALLY AS she gazed up at Kheoghi's massive bulk lumbering at her side. "Remind me to talk to your mother about the crowd you're hanging out with."

The group walked under minotaur guard down yet another magnificent, darkened corridor in the bowels of the gigantic ship. Flynn's crew had placed symbols at various points to aid in finding their way to and from the command center. It prevented them from getting lost in the vastness of the ancient relic. Armed with chemical torches, the minotaurs, Griffiths, and the other Earthers were emerging at last from the depths with a renewed hope.

Kheoghi seemed suspicious, as did his four brothers that accompanied them. They each had recognized a discernable change in attitude among these barbarian humans, and the minotaurs were certain that all change boded ill for them.

"They really aren't that bad," Griffiths said casually as he walked. The map, now rolled tightly in his fist, swung at his side. "They have a very interesting culture. They have seventeen different terms for friendship, each of which has a different degree of responsibility for both parties involved. Relationships progress through these seventeen degrees, with each one being very hard-won. It's really quite fascinating."

Tobler was trailing Griffiths slightly as they walked but was paying careful attention. "How do you come to know these things?"

"It's that Mantle of Kendis-dai," Ellerby offered. "He's a walking Encyclopaedia Galactica!"

Griffiths smiled. "Actually, there is such a thing, though it is more properly called the Galactipaedia. However, you're wrong about my knowledge of the OomRamn, as the minotaurs call themselves. It didn't come from the Mantle. I just learned it on my own. Say, I've been meaning to ask. Just how did you come to be in this unbelievably forsaken part of the galaxy in the first place? I mean, I've heard of coincidence but the chances of your being here at the same time as . . ."

"It's no coincidence," Lewis said. "It just seems like our fates are bound together for a while. Remember we told you that we decided to come back and ask you for directions?"

"Yeah," Griffiths said, grinning. "And apparently you were right to do so."

"Well, we turned around and made our way back to Avadon. Our timing could have been a bit better. The Order had returned, this time with reinforcements—heaven only knows where they scrounged them up. There was a pitched battle going on when we popped back into normal space. It was a mess. The Order was attacking the planet, the city-ships were attacking the Order with whatever they had left, and there was even a third fleet mixing it up with the other two."

"That would have been the Centirion Fleet." Griffiths nodded grimly. "They're the military arm of the Omnet. They must have dispatched ships to Avadon supposedly to protect it—no doubt under Targ's orders."

"Well, Avadon didn't need any help," Ellerby chuckled. "As soon as the wraith fleet attacked, the planet itself responded. It seems that Avadon was perfectly capable of defending itself."

"So," Lewis continued, slightly annoyed that she had to wrestle control of the tale back from her companions, "there we were, surrounded by ships of three separate interstellar empires, all firing at each other . . ."

"Technically," Griffiths interrupted, "the Omnet isn't an empire."

"Hey, do I get to finish this or not?" Lewis demanded.

"Sorry, go on." Griffiths smiled.

"There we were, surrounded by ships of the three fleets, all of them firing on each other and the planet erupts with its own magical, glorious defense system. You should have seen it, Griffiths! What a show! Anyway, it turns out that our ship is the only one that the planet will allow to land—we assumed it was because our craft originally came from that world. We put down on the tarmac exactly where you watched us take off only to be met by that Targ of Gandri."

"He was waiting for you?" Griffiths asked skeptically.

"Not exactly," Tobler answered. "He seemed to have come to the starport looking for any kind of transportation he could find to get off the planet. Of course, none of the Irindris shuttles would lift off—the planetary defense system had put some sort of force field around the entire world and wouldn't let anyone out."

"Anyone but us and our nifty ancient saucer that is," Ellerby added.

"Wait a minute." Griffiths stopped in his tracks, nearly causing the entire group to stumble over each other in their haste to stop as well. "You guys landed on the planet, just happened to meet this Gandri fellow, and decided to follow him across the galaxy?"

"No," Ellerby replied, "it wasn't that simple. A troop of Thought-Knight goons tried to arrest us when we landed. They said someone had tried to murder you and that we were suspected of being involved. Targ used some of his whammy on them and froze them solid—temporal stasis I think he called it."

"How nice of him, considering *he's* the one who tried to kill me."

"Well, how were we supposed to know?" Lewis griped. "Anyway, he recognized us or maybe it was the flight suits—I don't know which—but he offered to show us where to find you."

"Find me?" Griffiths echoed.

"Yeah, you," Ellerby continued. "He said something about your pulling a fast one on him and zipping off on

GAMMA:
INHUMAN
CREED

some crazed mission across the galaxy with this Neskat woman. He also said that if we wanted to ask the great Mantle anything, that we'd have to ask you, and that he was the only one who knew where you would be."

"You bought that?" Griffiths smiled.

"Hell, no," Tobler said. "We just thought he was another space-happy alien. Still, his story jibed with what the Thought-Knights had said, although it turned out he left out a few details."

"Like the fact that he tried to kill me?"

"Yeah, something like that."

Lewis put her hand on Griffiths's shoulder. "We figured he was our only chance of finding you and asking our question. Now that we have found you, all we need to do is figure our way out of here."

Griffiths nodded and began walking again. They could all see the bright twilight of the Bonefield Narrows in the gigantic opening ahead of them. "That's the entrance. It opens out onto a platform, then a set of stairs down to the ground. You guys stay with me. If we can get to Neskat, she can bargain for us. If we can just convince these cutthroats not to kill us, and maroon us here instead, I think we've got a chance of surviving right here."

Lewis shook her head. "What good does that do us? Targ can't fly the saucer, but he isn't so stupid as to leave us here without disabling it permanently first."

"True enough." Griffiths nodded, then grinned. "I guess it's too bad that this old Settlement Ship is inoperative." He glanced meaningfully toward Kheoghi.

Lewis returned his grin. "Yes, it's too bad. Still, I suppose living marooned here is better than dead."

"Exactly," Griffiths said smoothly. "We'll just stay here. Then Flynn and Targ can fight it out for their precious Nightsword. I don't think we'll have any problems after that."

They were just stepping onto the platform when they noticed something wrong with the sky.

For as far as they could see above the jungle canopy, colossal ships of unbelievable size filled their view. Griffiths had seen their kind before, although he had originally thought that they were building complexes rather than ships of the stars. Their hulls were spiny and horned. Leathery wings protruded from their decks. Griffiths couldn't begin to guess the number of craft he was looking at. Even as he watched, a cascade of dragons tumbled over the side of the lead ship, each one righting itself and gliding down toward the bay far below.

They all turned to run back into the opening but it was too late. Massive dragon heads curled around the sides of the entrance, blocking the way back into the ancient ruin. Griffiths turned to run down the wide staircase and descended several steps before noticing that the clearing itself was rimmed with dragons, each wearing battle armor displaying their individual battle flags and pennants.

He stopped on the stairs, aware that his friends and the minotaurs were standing just behind him on the platform.

Griffiths searched frantically for an avenue of escape

There was none.

His eyes came to rest, however, on a gray-robed figure standing at the base of the stairs. There was a darkness about the figure as it moved up the staircase, its face obscured within the folds of its massive hood.

"A Sentinel!" Lewis murmured.

The darkness fell away from the figure as it moved closer, drifting up the stairs with ghostlike smoothness.

Griffiths took a step back.

The cloaked figure reached up with both hands, grasping either side of the hood. In a single motion, the hood fell back to reveal the face of the Sentinel. His gray, flowing beard fell onto his chest—an ancient man, tall and thin, with a prominent nose and soft gray eyes.

The old man smiled at them.

The Earthers all gasped as one.

"You!" Griffiths said, his eyes wide with wonder.

"Yes, my boy! How awfully good of you to remember me—both you and your friends!" The old man's smile was genuine and friendly. "Sorry I'm so late for the party but I've brought you a gift!"

"Zanfib?" Griffiths whispered in awe.

"Why, yes, of course I'm Zanfib, you doorknob!" The old man seemed somewhat confused. "Or rather I'm pretty sure I am. If you say so then it must be."

The old man smiled and put his left hand on Griffiths's shoulder.

"I've been meaning to give you something." The old man cackled.

"What's that, sir?" Griffiths asked.

Still smiling, the elderly Zanfib drew back his right fist and swung it with surprising vigor across Griffiths's jaw. The strength of the impact lifted Griffiths off his feet to fall on the steps behind. Dazed, the astronaut bounced once and began to tumble down the steps, coming to rest in the clearing at the bottom of the stairs.

Lewis, Ellerby, and Tobler all hurried past the gray wizard to where Griffiths lay akimbo at the bottom of the stairs. Tobler gathered Griffiths's lolling head in her lap as she knelt next to him.

"Never leave a wizard for dead, barbarian!" The old man shook a thin, ancient fist back at where Griffiths lay. "Haven't you ever read any creative books! I'm not dead until I say I'm dead!"

"I think we may have a few problems after all," Griffiths said before he conveniently passed out.

35

Zanfib

TIME WENT BY, OF THAT GRIFFITHS WAS SURE, BUT HE couldn't say just how much time. There was discontinuity in his mind, which told him his consciousness had fled him for a while. It was probably just as well, he realized.

"Griffiths." Lewis's voice floated down to his ears as though through gauze. "Griffiths, come around."

"Jeremy," he murmured. "My name is Jeremy."

"Jeremy, then," Lewis said from some distant place. "Wake up."

"No."

"Jeremy, wake up." Lewis was insistent.

Griffiths opened his eyes. "Why, hello, Elizabeth! Has the situation improved while I've been away?"

"Not at all," Lewis said.

"Would you wake me up when it does?"

Lewis insisted on shaking Griffiths at that moment, although Griffiths could see neither need nor provocation for her to do so. "Snap out of it!" she said.

Griffiths sat up at the base of the stairs, his head pounding. There were massive dragons everywhere, each wearing massive spiked armor, ornamental and fierce, over their own scaly hides. Most of the dragons had rows of staffs which supported banners, pennants, and flags of various design. Their polished silver helmets—broad, with cut holes tailored to the individual dragon's crown of horns—gleamed under the opalescent sky. Each Tsultak dragon wore his clan's battle-kilt, into which was woven a chronicle of his clan's battles, both triumphs and defeats. The triumphs, Griffiths had learned while on Tsultaki, were a matter of family pride. The defeats were woven into the cloth to remind each dragon of who his enemies were when he met them again. Though armor on a dragon seemed redundant at best and was obviously created more for show than for any practical application, it was nevertheless terrifying.

They stood in the clearing at the bottom of the stairs, only a few feet from where Griffiths had come to rest. He couldn't have been out very long, he decided. He turned his head quickly to look up the stairs.

Yes, Zanfib was still standing there.

Griffiths stood up, somewhat shakily. He called out to the gray wizard, shaking his fist at him. "You crazy old coot! What the hell did you do that for?"

"That'll learn you, you little barbarian!" Zanfib called back. "I stuck my keester in the fire for you Earthers trying to get you free of that Gnuktikut demon and what kind of thanks do I get? You go running off and leave me behind the very first time I die! What kind of gratitude is that, I ask you!"

"But . . . but you were dead!"

"That's no excuse!" Zanfib shouted back.

Griffiths was at a loss for words. "Sorry, I'm not sure I understand . . ."

"Of course you don't," Zanfib replied, his hands shaking above his head with rage. "You're an idiot! If you had any idea what an all-powerful sorcerer I am, you wouldn't be standing there arguing with me! You would be quivering in terror, incapable of speech! I have simply got to get myself a better press agent! When you can't go out in the galaxy and inspire a little terror at the mere mention of your name, then what's the point?"

"Look," Lewis said, trying to take another tack, "all we want to know is why you're alive now."

Zanfib slowly began to descend the stairs as he spoke. "It's those space-happy religious fanatics—the Irindris. They found me dead where you left me and decided that it would be polite to resurrect me. Of course, I didn't get any say in it! That was bad enough, but then they waited around and waited around—trying to clear up the red tape or something—and it took them forever to get around to doing it. By the time they'd managed the incantations and brouhaha I was pretty well ripe, I can tell you! The point is that . . . the point is that . . . oh, now I've forgotten the point!"

"The point is that you're loony," Griffiths said with exasperation.

"Exactly!" Zanfib replied.

"What?"

"The point is that I'm loony," Zanfib replied with a sudden calmness in his voice.

Griffiths was suddenly distracted by a loud commotion behind him. The ranks of dragons had opened a path down which the crew of the *Venture Revenge* was being herded. Targ walked in front of them, quiet and thoughtful, it seemed. Behind him came Flynn, supporting Merinda, who seemed barely able to walk on her own. Watching them filled Griffiths with an inexplicable feeling of loss.

Targ reached them first. "Vestis Zanfib! What a surprise!"

"That's Sentinel Zanfib to you, Targ," Zanfib said, with his prominent nose thrust high, "for I am a member of an Order so secret that no one knows our names—not even myself!"

Merinda loosed herself from Flynn's supporting arm and

straightened slightly as she peered into the old wizard's face. "Zanfib?"

"Who?" Zanfib said, with a wink in Targ's direction. "Where?"

"Zanfib! It's me! Merinda!"

"Of course you are, my dear, and how wonderful to see you again," Zanfib said, taking Merinda's hand gently and patting it. "So sorry to have come to kill you and your friends but, as they say, all the galaxy's a stage and sometimes the main characters bow out in the second act!"

"Excuse me," Griffiths interjected, his head throbbing worse than before, "but just how long did you say you were dead?"

"Too long," Zanfib said, once again turning his smoldering indignation on the astronaut. "Much too long, and it's your fault. If I hadn't transferred the mission logs to your little brain, then I wouldn't have had the feedback to deal with. Memories and ideas from your own mind backwashed into mine in its weakened state. As it is, I was dead so long that your old thoughts and my own have become inseparably fused. Now I can't tell where I end and you begin!"

"Since when did you become a Sentinel?" Targ sniffed.

"Shush!" Zanfib said, putting a finger to his lips. "We're a secret organization and not to be recognized!"

"Right." Targ nodded, even as his eyes rolled upward. "So, when were you first not part of this organization?"

"I've not been part of this organization since its very inception," Zanfib offered with pride. "I was not a highly placed operative among the Vestis and I was not a supreme leader of the Order of the Future Faith until this barbarian clod left me for dead. We waste time, however. I have come for the map, if you please, for my destiny will wait no longer."

"You want the map, too?" Griffiths nearly choked.

"Hey," Flynn said, stepping into the group, "that map is mine. I paid for it!"

"As did I," Zanfib said, pulling out a second parchment map and unrolling it before them all to see. It was perfect in every detail; an exact duplicate of the map that Griffiths and Flynn had made on Tsultaki.

"By the Nine!" Merinda whispered.

"Actually, I didn't pay for it," Zanfib said matter-of-factly. "It would be more correct to say that Scrimshaw paid for it with his own life. It wouldn't do to have multiple copies of the real map floating around the Tsultak starport. Sadly, the artistry of his work will be missed."

"You've got the map," Flynn said gravely. "What is it you want with us?"

"Why what everyone here wants," Zanfib said with a sweet smile on his ancient lips. "To find the passage through the Maelstrom Wall. There I'll put right what this Earth-fool has made wrong—and my fellow Sentinels will once again offer me a place among their number."

"No one knows the way," Merinda said.

"That's not true, Merinda!" Zanfib replied in a voice that was almost tolerant and kind. "Griffiths knows—as he has always known. Once I have delivered him to my brothers and sisters of the Sentinel council, he should be more than willing to tell them everything that he knows—including the passage to the Nightsword's final resting-place. The council wanted the Mantle to protect itself—but the Nightsword is a device of supreme conquest. A far more proactive stance for the Order, would you not say?"

Zanfib smiled again from behind his great, gray beard. He walked with a confident gait past Merinda, Targ, and the other humans. He passed the Hishawei, the Goromok gnomes, the Uruh, the minotaurs and all the other assembled crew of the *Venture Revenge* with a smug confidence. At last he came to stand before the towering bulk of a dragon, its huge head dropping closer to the wizard that it might better hear.

"Dedrak Kurbin-Flamishar, Minister of Peace for all of Tsultak and the Majesty and Greater Glory of the Council," Zanfib said with great solemnity, "I hereby charge you to arrest these individuals for crimes against . . ."

"Wait!"

Everyone, including the dragon minister Kurbin-Flamishar, turned toward the sound.

It was Flynn. The pirate captain was running through the assembled crew directly toward the towering dragon minister. The ornate chain mail that draped down around Kurbin-Flamishar's head and neck rang loudly as the dragon craned his massive head in the direction of the charging human. Flynn didn't miss a step as he ran, reaching down and scooping up a fist-sized rock. Flynn skidded to a halt short of the dragon's jaws, which hovered just ten feet above the ground.

Everything seemed to slow as Griffiths watched.

Flynn drew back his arm to throw.

The massive dragon's eyes narrowed.

Zanfib was turning, puzzled by Flynn's initial shout.

"Flynn! No!" Merinda cried out.

Flynn let loose the stone. It sailed through the air, tumbling awkwardly as it made a straight line for the dragon's nose. It wasn't a particularly well thrown rock and didn't connect squarely with the center of the dragon's nose, as one might expect. Instead it grazed the beast's left nostril, bounced off, and clattered among the scales on the dragon's snout before falling at last harmlessly to the dirt below.

The dragon bellowed in rage. In the following instant the assembled dragons that encircled them all trumpeted their own chorus of anger and contempt. The sound seemed to fill all space with a horrible cacophony of their thunderous chorus.

"Tall Man," Kurbin-Flamishar raged, lowering his head to within a handsbreadth of Flynn's face, "you shall die for that insult!"

Flynn promptly reached up and slapped the dragon across his broad snout.

Griffiths's jaw dropped. "My God, we're dead!" he said, sputtering loudly.

"Been there; done that," Zanfib snarled.

The dragon, however, did not move.

"I am Captain Evon Flynn of the *Venture Revenge*," he shouted at the dragon, his fist raised in defiance. "Your race has grieved us much! We demand satisfaction on the field of honor and glory which your fathers have forgotten and your mothers lament and weep for to be once again."

Griffiths turned to Merinda. "What the hell is he doing?"

Merinda shook her head, unsure.

"My clan of shipmates declares war upon the Tsultak and all their Empire clan!" Flynn said.

Then he spit upon the dragon's gleaming black foreclaw.

36

Formal Declarations

"KILL HIM, FLAMISHAR," ZANFIB YELLED. THE ANCIENT WIZard pointed directly at Evon Flynn, even as he was hastily backing away. "Kill him now!"

The massive dragon's eyes blazed fiercely, yet he did not move. Instead, Kurbin-Flamishar reared up on his hind legs, his polished armor sparkling under the opal nebula above as he spoke. His voice shook the ground. "Tall Man—One Who is Unworthy of a Name—your people are small and weak. Your bones break pleasantly between our jaws. Your flesh is sweet to our taste. Your ship could not carry a single one of our young on its flimsy deck. What are you that we would make worthy warfare upon you?"

"That we are a weak and small race compared to the mighty Tsultak is true," Flynn asserted with his fists planted defiantly on both hips, his neck craned upward to see the face of the towering dragon. "But our cause is just, as your ancestors long passed into the Nine Heavens will avow when our fates are revealed. We have endured your insults and those of your people until they were no longer to be tolerated. This day we draw a line across the Tsultak path and declare no more! We claim the right of honorable warfare that the spirits of our ancestors may decide our fates through our own blood and prowess."

Zanfib was livid, a deep red flush washing over his balding forehead. "Just kill him! Don't stand there like an oversized doorknob! Don't talk—just eat!"

The dragon remained erect, his only motion for a moment being his thumb claw grating against his foreclaw in contemplation. "Will you accept the usual conditions of honorable warfare?"

Flynn nearly smiled. "We do—and expect no less from the honorable Tsultak."

"Very well," the dragon intoned. "There is no single sun by which the coming of night may be judged on this world. Will you accept our ship's chronometer as the arbiter of all timings for our declarations?"

"That depends upon the current time of your chronometer," Flynn said judiciously.

Kurbin-Flamishar turned to the smaller dragon—his aide—who stood next to him. After a discussion of some length, Kurbin-Flamishar turned back toward the waiting Flynn. "I am informed we are in the tenth hour of the day."

"Very well, dragon," Flynn said with mock concern, "in this we have agreement. We accept your timing for our declarations and shall meet you on the twentieth hour at this selfsame spot."

"It is agreed," Kurbin-Flamishar said, then suddenly dropped down on all four legs and folded his wings tightly against his armor. "A formal declaration of war has commenced. We shall return in the twentieth hour to this spot. Prepare yourself. Until that time, farewell."

"Farewell," Flynn replied with a smug grin.

"Wait just one gal-darn minute!" Zanfib huffed. "Where do you think you're going, Flamishar?"

Kurbin-Flamishar turned and began walking into the jungle. In every direction around him, the assembled army of dragons wheeled in unison to follow the dragon Minister of Peace into the dense canopy.

"Damn it, Flamishar!" Zanfib bellowed. The old wizard moved with amazing spryness back across the clearing after the dragon. He managed to grab the dragon's tail, which was dragging along the ground under the weight of the armor plating that Kurbin-Flamishar so seldom wore these days. Zanfib dug in his heels but it was a hopeless task. The dragon didn't even notice the additional weight. Zanfib began making a small furrow in the topsoil as he continued to yell. "Just stop, you oversized Gila monster! We're not finished here yet! I want my mind back, damn it! I want my life back!"

Kurbin-Flamishar plunged into the dark jungle, his tail dragging the old wizard with him. Zanfib's voice could still be heard for a time, becoming more and more distant—the wizard never giving up and, apparently, never letting go either. "Stupid dragons! Thick as posts, high maintenance, impossible to steer . . ."

In a most orderly manner, the dragons continued to file out of the clearing.

"Evon," Merinda said, amazement in her voice, "what was that all about?"

Flynn turned back to the group, letting out a long breath that he had forgotten he was holding. "The Tsultak dragons are massively powerful and ferocious enemies, but they have one flaw—they think of themselves as civilized. They wouldn't have hesitated a moment to arrest us as criminals— something of which that old geezer has apparently already convinced them. That process had already been completed."

"So," Targ said, stepping forward, "you declared war on them—an act which they were honor bound to address at once?"

"Yes," Flynn said, walking toward his assembled crew. "A declaration of war takes precedence over all other considerations. They will have to conduct a complete formal declaration of war now. Master Shindak?"

"Yes, Captain," the tall elf said smoothly.

"I am at something of a loss as to why you and the rest of the crew are here," Flynn said casually. "Is the *Venture Revenge* still secure?"

"Yes, Captain," the elf replied evenly. "The ship remains in good repair down in the bay as you left it."

"Forgive my question," Flynn said quietly, "but how is it that the entire crew and the ship itself escaped any harm during the ferocious boarding action that surely must have ensued?"

"I felt that surrender at the time was a more prudent option considering the force that opposed us," the cool elf said in response. "Would the captain have preferred a burned ship and a dead crew?"

Flynn chuckled. "Of course not, Master Shindak. However, I wouldn't make it a habit of abandoning my ship every time my back is turned. I might take offense."

"Why, Captain." Shindak barely moved, his drawn, pale features a smug mask. "Who would possibly want to offend you?"

"Very well, Shindak. Take the crew into the ruins here and settle everyone down. I'll be there directly to fill them in and give them their instructions." Flynn turned and began walking toward Merinda and the others.

"Indeed," Shindak murmured through a slight curl in his lips. "I suppose it's time that the humans-only club meets to find another way to botch this job!"

Flynn turned at once, drawing his cutlass. The sound of the metal leaving the scabbard rang through the clearing with electrifying effect. The anticipation from the various races of the *Venture Revenge* crew was instantly palpable.

"Do you have a problem with my orders, Master Shindak?" Flynn said in a voice that carried to the various types of ears throughout his crew. He held his cutlass firmly in his right hand, pointed directly at the chest of the elf. "Are you questioning my authority?"

"Captain." Shindak smiled without warmth as he spoke, his words chosen carefully. "We've all been through some difficult times of late, none more so than you . . ."

"Get this creature a sword!" Flynn cried out.

From somewhere among the crew, a cutlass tumbled through the air, landing flatly in the sands near the elf's feet.

"Pick it up, Shindak!" Flynn said, his eyes locked on the elf's gaze.

Shindak licked his lips. "Captain—you go too far . . ."

"Pick it up, NOW!" Flynn yelled.

All eyes were on the elf. No one breathed.

Shindak slowly drew his hands and arms open, away from his sides, palms facing Flynn. "No, Captain. I apologize for my remark. It was ill considered. I plead only for your mercy and forgiveness, for it was meant only in jest. I remain your servant. Do with me as you will."

"Then," Flynn said, carefully pronouncing each word, "my will is that you take the crew up into the ruins of the Settlement Ship and await my further pleasure. Are you clear on this?"

"Perfectly clear, Captain," the elf replied, bowing slowly, his eyes never leaving Flynn for a moment. "I remain your servant."

Flynn held his pose for a moment, the weapon's sharp tip fixed on its target. Then, as swiftly as it had appeared, Flynn's sword returned to its scabbard. The captain straightened. "Very well, Master Shindak. See that that sword on the ground is returned to its owner—blunt end first. I wouldn't want such a dangerous thing lying about. Someone might get hurt."

"Yes, Captain," the elf replied, then turned to the crew. "You heard the captain. All hands aloft to the ruins. We await the captain's pleasure."

A gentle breeze passed through the small clearing as the various crewmembers walked, scuttled, thumped, clawed, and slithered their way up the magnificent stairs of the ancient ship. The humans remained in the clearing, silently watching the bizarre and horrific procession. The last to enter the dark maw of the Settlement Ship was the hulking form of Kheoghi. He stopped for a moment atop the stairs on the landing, and looked back thoughtfully on the humans below him before turning and walking into the darkness.

When the minotaur had disappeared, Flynn turned to the group. "I think we're safe enough now."

"Safe enough?" Lewis scoffed. "You just declared war on a warrior fleet of dragons so large that their ships block out the sky!"

"Not to mention," Merinda said, leaning now on Ellerby for support, "the fact that you seem to have something of a discipline problem with your own crew."

"The crew will follow me," Flynn said, more it seemed for his own benefit than for theirs.

"Perhaps," Merinda countered, "but for how long? Zanfib isn't going to wait forever and neither are those dragons. If he has negotiated a deal with the Sentinels, then it's only a matter of time."

"Well, I bought us time," Flynn offered. "We've got a negotiation in a few hours but the Formal Declarations take three months before the Tsultak actually are allowed to attack. Both sides are supposed to use that time to ceremonially prepare for death and leave some sort of legacy for those who follow them. We've got time to figure a way out of this."

"I don't agree," Merinda said.

"Excuse me, Merinda, but what the hell would you know about it?" Flynn's temper finally flared. "I lived with these creatures. I know their customs and their weaknesses. It's how I make my living out here on the frontier and no stuck-up, brass-brained Vestis with a titanium rod up her . . ."

"No, Flynn, listen to me!" Merinda's voice cut across Flynn's anger. "You may know the dragons but I know Zanfib. We worked together on several assignments. Admittedly he's lost his grip on a lot of things. I could believe that he's crazy but I assure you he isn't stupid. The man is devious and cunning beyond anyone I've ever worked with. He rarely does anything without a secondary or tertiary plan backing him up. He wants Griffiths and he'll have him one way or another."

"Excuse me," Griffiths interjected, without success.

"He's made his play," Flynn said to Merinda, ignoring the astronaut. "He got the entire Tsultak fleet to come and get us and I stopped that cold."

"Yes," Merinda countered, "but now we're held here. What happens if we try to sail out of here before the three months are up?"

Flynn thought for a moment. "The Tsultak would take that to be a cowardly and dishonorable act—it would break the Formal Declarations."

Merinda nodded. "It would break the Formal Declarations and the Tsultak would be honor bound to attack us at once, correct?"

Flynn looked away and nodded his agreement.

"That Zanfib is a crafty one," Merinda continued. "Griffiths dashed the *Brishan* across half the galaxy as fast as the ship could travel. A fleet of ships couldn't catch us but one man in a small, powerful ship might. Zanfib did. He nearly had us on Tsultaki. He finally bagged us here. If he could capture Griffiths and learn what he needed to find the Nightsword, then that would be just fine. If not, then he's positioned himself to keep us here until his reinforcement arrives."

"Reinforcement?" Tobler asked. "What reinforcement?"

"If Zanfib truly is a Sentinel for the Order then . . ."

"My God," Ellerby blurted out. "The wraith fleet!"

"Exactly," Merinda said huskily. "He can afford to wait. Within a few days—a week on the outside—the wraith fleet of the Order will arrive to question Griffiths at their pleasure. Zanfib won't have to take Griffiths to the Order—the Order will come to Griffiths. And, I might add, when they get here, they'll be a lot closer to their objective than they would otherwise be."

"Damn!" Flynn ran his fingers back through his hair.

"I have one solution," Merinda said evenly. "The Order wants the Nightsword. The last time that weapon was loose in the galaxy it caused the fall of civilization and a thousand years of chaos. That was in the hands of someone whom legend describes as well meaning. In the hands of the Order it would mean a level of destruction unprecedented in all known history. I think my mind has been changed. I came on this journey to find the Nightsword. Now I think I may have come to prevent it from being found."

"So," Ellerby asked, "what's your solution?"

"We could kill Griffiths here and now."

"What!" Griffiths yelled.

"No," Targ said with ultimate finality.

They turned to look at Targ of Gandri. In the press of their immediate concerns, they had nearly forgotten the powerful and dangerous nemesis they had so recently fought nearly to their own deaths.

"Targ, listen to me," Merinda said, walking up to face him directly. "I am most fond of this strange barbarian. He has many wonderful qualities. I have fought to preserve our lives for this alone. You, on the other hand, have come for him to obtain this ultimate, terrible power. I beg you not to do so. It destroyed Lokan long ago. It will destroy you. In ancient times, it doomed knowledge and life from one end of the stars to the other. We have only now, three thousand years later, managed to pull ourselves from the rubble this Nightsword caused and begun to live as a galaxy once more. What is this man's life on the scales to that of a million, billion others? The Nightsword was safe—buried with Lokan in the core. Its terror died with him. Should it not die with this man, too?"

"Merinda," Targ said, his eyes softening as he looked at her. "He must not die because we need the Nightsword. There's a terrible darkness coming. The Dictorae has known it for several years now. The Sentinels are only the minor manifestation of the horror the lurks behind it. You must not kill him, or the Omnet and all that is good in it will fall. It is not enough that we keep the weapon from the enemy. We need the weapon to fight for our very existence."

"Then prove yourself by working with us," Merinda said. "I remain unconvinced, Targ. I don't know what you are up to, and your actions thus far have hardly inspired my trust. I'm willing to suspend judgment for the time being. However, know this, Targ. If you cross us once more I will kill him—and no one will ever find the Nightsword."

"Excuse me," Griffiths yelled, "but I've got something to say!"

Both Targ and Merinda turned.

"Look, all I want now is to get myself and my people home," Griffiths said. "You people can save the galaxy or not for all I care. The high-and-holy Omnet! Bullshit! The only friend I thought I had in this universe—your fine Omnet Vestis representative—just promised to kill me at the drop of a hat, so let's just cut through the crap!"

"An interesting expression," Targ replied. "What crap do you have in mind to cut through?"

"We all want to get off this rock before the wraith fleet gets here—no one more than I. The *Venture Revenge* wouldn't stand up against the Tsultak dragon ships for more than five minutes and from what I understand neither would Lewis's *Phoenix*. One of those ships might make it to the Maelstrom Passage—which I will tell you now is a lot closer than the exit from this quantum zone—but only if you had a diversion to keep the fleet busy while you ran."

"Diversion?" Flynn asked. "What kind of diversion?"

"Well," Griffiths said, turning to look at the still gleaming ruins of the Settlement Ship, "I was thinking of something rather large."

37

Friend or Foe

THE CURVED DOORS SWUNG RAPIDLY OPEN, CAUSING THE DEEP dust of the floor to swirl and eddy with sighs and moans. The doors slammed against the walls with a resounding boom, rebounding from the impact with such force as nearly to close. They were too late, however, to catch Griffiths as he strode into the central chamber of the Settlement Ship. Vague cries and lamentations could be heard as Griffiths passed toward the command platform.

"You cannot be serious?" Flynn asked incredulously, catching one of the doors a moment before it rebounded into his face. "This ship is over three thousand years old, Griffiths!"

"You see any rust, Flynn?" Griffiths called back as he mounted the platform.

"No, but after three thousand years . . ."

"Then I'd say it's in a helluva lot better shape than the *Venture Revenge*," Griffiths countered as he pulled himself up the access ladder and onto the platform. "Look, we can't wait and we can't surrender—either way the Sentinels win. All that's left is to fight our way out."

"Against the entire Tsultak dragon fleet?" Flynn gestured up at the ship-filled sky overhead. "That's suicide!"

"Look, why should you care?" Griffiths snapped, leaning over the control console. The anger spilled out all over again. He was tired and felt used by nearly everyone surrounding him. "You want to find your precious treasure, well that's just fine with me. I'm fed up with all of it. All you have to do is to take Merinda, get your crew, haul, crawl, slither, or slide your cutthroat asses back down to your ship in the bay and wait for my crew and me to take this behemoth the hell out of here."

"You don't even know this thing will fly!" Flynn yelled.

"She'll fly," Lewis said confidently, stepping around Flynn. Ellerby and Tobler were right behind her as she climbed onto the platform. Each of them quickly took positions, examining the inscriptions on the panels as they moved. Lewis turned her attentions momentarily back to the pirate captain. "We've activated these before. There's been zero deterioration of the systems—they've just been shut down for a long time."

"No."

Everyone turned toward the voice echoing from the side of the room.

Targ stepped through the open doorway. The billowing dust clouds seemed to part as the wizard entered, a whisper of fear drifting quietly through the room. Behind him, Merinda stood leaning casually against the doorframe, her arms folded across her chest.

"I don't think you appreciate your position, Captain Griffiths," Targ said as he moved forward. "Your plan may be the best offered thus far—indeed, I'm inclined to agree with you up to a point: that point being that you are mine, Griffiths. Your barbarian friends here can, no doubt, make this relic dance on a grain of sand. I've seen them operate that ship they call *Phoenix* and they've mastered the technology surprisingly well. You, however, are not going anywhere."

"Look, Targ," Griffiths said through clenched teeth. It was obvious he was working hard to rein in his emotions. "You tried to kill me once—and succeeded admirably, I might add—but we can make a deal. I don't give a damn anymore about your quest or your motives. I had my reasons when I started this thing"—he glanced at Merinda still motionless in the doorway—"but they're gone now. They probably weren't even really there in the first place. All I want now is to get out of this mess, this Omnet, this lousy universe and go home!"

Targ stopped. The color had suddenly drained from his face. "What are you saying?" he whispered.

"I'm saying, let us go and I'll give you what you want," Griffiths replied.

"No! Griffiths!" Flynn said urgently. "You don't know what you're saying!"

Targ stood stiffly, his jaw working in barely perceptible motions as he spoke. "Let you go and you'll give me what I want?"

"Yes," Griffiths said, his conviction faltering slightly. The sight of Targ's sudden change had shaken his resolve. "All you have to do is let us go."

"He's lying, Targ."

Griffiths looked up with sudden hatred. "Merinda!"

Merinda lazily straightened from where she was leaning, walking slowly forward as she spoke. Her voice was smooth and condescending. "All this barbarian has to do is lie to you and he's not only free but has led you off on some fool's errand. You go chasing off after his phantoms and, in the meanwhile, his crew cuts a deal with the Tsultak for the Nightsword. How do you know the course he gives you is the right one? He'll lie to you, Targ. He'll have the Nightsword and make you look like a fool all at the same time."

"Merinda!" Griffiths said desperately. "Stay out of this!"

"Oh, he seems like some kind of backwater fool on first blush," Merinda continued addressing Targ as she stepped up to the central platform, "but remember, he has the entire wisdom of the Mantle at his disposal. I can't explain it any more than you can, Targ, but no matter where he goes in the galaxy, the bond his mind has to the Mantle remains in force. Their communication is instantaneous no matter how far he is from Avadon. Couple that vast knowledge with a little cunning and you've got quite a dangerous combination. How far can you trust such a man?"

Targ's face suddenly went flush as he spoke. "You know this barbarian. Just how far would that be, Vestis Neskat?"

"This far!" Merinda grabbed Griffiths with both hands by the front of his tunic and swung him around. Behind her she sensed Lewis and Ellerby tense, ready to strike. She hoped the fear of her she had instilled in them on their first meeting would hold: a general combat was not her intention. Fortunately, they waited a moment too late. Merinda stopped suddenly and shoved Griffiths backward off the platform. Her timing was still good, she noted to herself. Griffiths fell backward directly toward Targ of Gandri. The Vestis Prime caught Griffiths before he fell completely to the floor and hauled him to his feet.

"Flynn," Merinda called from the platform. "Take the prophet here and Targ back to your crew, then get everyone moving toward the bay. Quietly, you understand. The Tsultak may have posted guards to keep an eye on your ship. We've got to get everyone aboard without the dragons knowing about it or the game is up."

"Damn you, Merinda," Griffiths yelled, his collar firmly in Targ's grip.

"Why are you doing this, Neskat?" Targ said, his eyes narrowing.

"Let's just say that I'm not ready to make my decision yet, Targ. If you are correct and the Omnet is indeed endangered without the Nightsword, then I am sworn to back you. If, however, this is some personal bid for power, to the detriment and destruction of the Omnet, then I am sworn to oppose you. I don't yet know what game you are playing at, Targ, but until I find out, I'm not willing to concede."

Targ chuckled. "Question everything—the unofficial motto of the Vestis. Very well, Neskat. We'll continue playing the game—so long as you realize just how very high the stakes are."

Merinda nodded, then turned to the pirate. "Get them out of here, Flynn. I'll set up the diversion with Lewis and her crew and join you shortly."

Flynn eyed Merinda for a moment as though trying to fathom her motivations, then shrugged and turned to Targ. "This way, if you please."

Griffiths looked up at Lewis. "I'm sorry, Lewis. I'll get you home when I can."

Targ pushed Griffiths toward the exit. Flynn closed the doors behind him with a resounding boom, as Merinda turned to face what remained of Griffiths's crew.

Lewis returned her gaze with contempt. Anger, pain, and rage registered on the faces of Ellerby and Tobler. Merinda watched them all carefully for a time but there was no sign that any of them would soften to her words.

"Lewis," Merinda said at last, "I need your help."

The lieutenant folded her arms across her chest and said nothing.

"We are in very real danger and unless we learn to trust each other, right now, there may be little hope for any of us."

"*We* are in danger?" Ellerby scoffed. "Just what 'we' are you talking about?"

"Look, as far as I see it," Tobler said, her voice emotionally detached from her words, "you just took our world away from us. He could have gotten us home, lady. All we wanted was to get home." Tobler's words were suddenly shaky. Tears coursed down her cheeks.

"We're not interested in your wars, Neskat," Lewis said, her voice thick with emotion. "We don't understand this universe that we suddenly find ourselves a part of. We come from a backwater world, as you so cruelly put it, and we know it. Why is your heart so cold? Why can't you feel the pain we feel?"

Merinda gazed at Tobler. The woman had collapsed into one of the command chairs and was openly sobbing into the map table now. Merinda moved silently around the table. Lewis and Ellerby watched her every move.

Slowly, Merinda stopped behind Tobler and reached down with her gloved hand. Then she stopped, withdrew her hand hastily and removed the glove, before reaching out once more with her long, delicate bare hand. With a deliberate, careful motion she touched Tobler's hair. The woman turned at once to face the Vestis, her face a tear-streaked mess. Merinda knelt down slowly, her eyes round and watery, locked with Tobler's own. Again Merinda reached out, delicately touching the astronaut's cheek.

"I am sorry, Marilyn," Merinda whispered, her own tears falling like brilliant jewels down her cheek. "Truly sorry— and I promise you that I will get you home. I had . . . forgotten . . . how important this was to you. And how desperate you must be feeling. I'll save Griffiths for us both. And he will take us all home."

Ellerby was suddenly embarrased by the raw emotion being displayed. He looked away to the floor.

Lewis narrowed her eyes skeptically.

Merinda took in a long, shuddering breath. "I'm fighting

for us all now," she said, looking up at Lewis. "I've been concentrating on the enormous implications of what is happening here. I've been thinking of it in terms of cosmic significance and politics and supremacy. Tobler's just reminded me that it comes down to uncounted billions of individual lives. Each of their pains. Each of their losses. Each of their vanished dreams."

Merinda reached up with her bare hand and touched a tear with wonder. She smiled suddenly with the warmth of true feeling. "You know, I think I had forgotten how to feel much of anything."

"I don't trust you," Lewis said without commitment.

"I know."

"Then why should we listen to you?"

"Perhaps," Merinda said with more conviction, "because I believe the people of your world are in danger as well."

Merinda looked about the consoles of the control chamber. She quickly located what she was looking for and pointed down at a set of raised symbols around the outside perimeter of the console. "Can you read that?"

Lewis glanced over at the symbols. "Of course. It says Force Distribution. There's an almost identical one over on the *Phoenix* . . ."

"I can't."

"You can't what?"

"I can't read it," Merinda said. "I recognize it as symbols but I can't read it."

"But it's clearly legible," Lewis said, unfolding her arms and crossing the platform to the indicated panel. "Ellerby, you can read this, can't you?"

"Sure," the big man replied, "It's Force Distribution. That one over there is Motive Force; that one's Defensive Barriers. They're all clear. What's the point?"

"The point is," Merinda said quietly, "that I can't read

them. Neither can Flynn nor Targ nor Zanfib nor any-one else that didn't come from your world, so far as I can tell."

"But Targ was with us all this time," Lewis argued. "He never mentioned anything about not reading the signs in the *Phoenix*."

"Perhaps," Merinda responded. "But did he ever once touch any of the controls? He's an expert pilot, you know, and should easily have been able to fly your saucer here all on his own. Why did he need you to pilot for him . . . unless he simply couldn't read which system was which?"

Lewis shook her head. "But that doesn't make sense. Those translation devices you stuck in our heads when we first met are supposed to translate anything for anyone."

"That's right." Merinda nodded. "The only thing they haven't been able to translate—or won't translate—is the language of the Lost Empire. At least, until you Earth-people came along."

"Why would the translation device care where we came from?" Ellerby asked.

"The biolinks are based on temporal fold processor tech-nology," Merinda thought aloud. "That means that they were originally reverse engineered from the discovery of the Nine on Mnemen IV. We aren't all that sure how they actu-ally work—they're based on Lost Empire technologies."

"You're saying," Tobler said, sniffing, "that the biolinks recognize us as having come specifically from Earth?"

"Yes," Merinda replied. "Not just as having come from Earth, but also the fact that since you come from Earth, you are allowed special access to information that the rest of the universe is not suppose to know."

"Well, what's so special about Earth?" Lewis asked.

"That's what we've got to find out," Merinda said. "But to do that we have to keep Griffiths alive."

"I thought you just suggested killing him?" Lewis said with sudden suspicion.

"Well, it was a logical solution—though not one I'd carry out. I needed Targ to protect him from Flynn's crew. My threat helped Targ to realize that Griffiths needed his protection." Merinda flashed a suddenly embarrassed smile. "I really do like him, actually. Keeping him alive can be something of a full-time job, however."

"So, what do you have in mind, Neskat?" Lewis said, chuckling. She had the horrible feeling that she was beginning to like this Vestis.

"First, we've got to get this ship to fly."

"Fine," Ellerby replied, "and second?"

"Second," Merinda smiled, "I've borrowed a little something that I want you to read for me."

38

Oblivion

THE WATER WAS COLD BENEATH HIM. HIS LEVITATION BELT was set to keep him just above the surface of the bay, but now and then even the gentle waves reached up and slapped him with a bracing chill. His impulse each time had been to shout, to gasp, or to curse with the sudden shock, but he knew the price if he did. Dragons were located all along the shore and any cry would have brought their attentions at once. If they were caught trying to reboard the *Venture Revenge*, then their own honorable status would vanish, the formal declarations would be null and void, and they all would be imprisoned at once. For him, that meant a quick trip to Tsultak, where he would be turned over to Zanfib and the rest of the Sentinels. Zanfib may have had his brains rearranged with a mix-master, but the other Sentinels certainly had not. Their efficiency and mercilessness he had already seen all too closely. They would take him apart and never bother with putting him back together again.

So, Griffiths thought as he drifted as quietly as he could across the frigid waters of the bay, I can either be used and abused by the Sentinels or I can be used and abused by Flynn and the pirates. He wondered if they would be sufficient to save his skin. Three of the Uruh snake-women slid smoothly through the water under him. They enjoyed swimming as a more natural way for them to move and were making excellent time toward the Aendorian pirate ship floating at the surface of the water before them. Behind him, Kheoghi drifted in his own belt, struggling to keep his clawed hooves out of the water—clearly not his favorite element. They were an amazing crew, but Griffiths felt that Flynn's hold on them was tenuous at best. Besides, when they looked at him, Griffiths always felt less like a shipmate than like their lunch.

That left him with the Omnet, in the person of Targ of Gandri, as his third option for salvation. He had seen Targ far too closely to have any illusions about the man helping him. Once Griffiths gave him what he wanted, he'd either toss Griffiths aside or—and he considered this far more likely—kill him on the spot. For all the vaunted goals of the Omnet, his experience had taught him that they were generally a ruthless bunch, barely above the cutthroat pirates he had fallen in with of late. Merinda had taught him that if nothing else.

Merinda, he thought.

Then he didn't know what to think. The woman was an exasperation, a thorn in his side and a danger to himself and everyone around her. She had saved his life nearly at the cost of her own only to drag him halfway across creation just to threaten to kill him herself. She was undoubtedly the most cold-hearted woman he had ever met, yet there was something wickedly playful about her, with a sense of dark humor a mile deep.

The distance to the *Venture Revenge* had closed quickly during his reveries. Griffiths suddenly realized he was in the shadow of the ship's hull. Gazing upward he noticed Targ and Flynn crouching behind the gunwales. He wondered at the sight for a moment, pondering what deal they must have struck, what price Flynn was being paid. Griffiths had longed for an adventure and now he certainly was in the thick of one. He had forgotten that adventures are built upon someone else's death and someone else's blood. Far more die than live to revel in the telling of the tale. At that moment he had few illusions as to which category he would shortly fit.

The lower hatch was open before him. Kheoghi had followed him closely—to make sure that Griffiths didn't "lose his way" to the ship. Griffiths grabbed the rope railings of the hatch and looked back toward the shore one last time.

Merinda, he thought. We started this together. The least you could do is be here when it ends.

LEWIS SAT IN THE COMMAND CHAIR, HER FEET COMFORTABLY— if irreverently—propped up on the map table. The vast command chamber lay all about her. Tobler and Ellerby leaned back against the command consoles. Both were far less relaxed than their commander.

"How much longer?" Tobler said nervously.

Lewis looked at her Pulsar watch. She was suddenly struck by it and flipped the release on the band. Holding it close to her face, she examined it carefully. It was an overly complex example of a chronograph that her father had given her prior to the launch. "Something," he had said, "to check up on that Einstein fellow." Then he showed her a duplicate of the watch that she wore, perfectly synchronized with hers. They had both laughed. Lewis smiled at the thought again. What a story I have to tell you, Daddy, she thought. You'll never have guessed where this watch has been.

"Lewis? How much longer."

"Oh, sorry, Tobler. Three minutes."

"This place gives me the creeps," Ellerby said, shivering slightly. "The ventilation in this place sounds like it's haunted."

Lewis flipped the watch back onto her wrist and fastened the latch. "Actually, according to Neskat, it isn't the ventilation."

Ellerby blinked. "Well, then, what is it?"

"She says the place really is haunted," Lewis said, leaning back in her chair and stretching.

"That's not funny, Elizabeth!" Tobler grumbled.

"Hey, it's what I heard," Lewis shrugged with a wicked little smile. "But I wouldn't put too much effort into worrying about it, Tobler. We've got plenty of other concerns to occupy our time."

"Such as?" Ellerby asked absently.

"Such as whether that Neskat woman is telling us the truth or not. Such as whether her plan is going to work at all. Such as whether this three-thousand-year-old ship is actually going to get off the ground or not," Lewis said. Her feet suddenly came down from the table. The lieutenant stood up and stretched, then tugged her flight suit back into its proper position. "Well, at least we can answer that last worry now. To your stations, one and all; it's time to make this heap of metal fly."

Tobler and Ellerby glanced at each other for a moment, then turned back toward the consoles all about them.

"Tobler." Lewis had adopted her command voice. "Activate the central power initiators."

Tobler pressed her hands against the panel. The central icon suddenly appeared with spidery light filaments darting from it across the smooth surface. Additional icons sprang into view.

"Initiators on-line, Lieutenant," Tobler responded. "One unit is not responding, however—its load has been transferred to the remaining seven units. Total output by this board appears nominal."

Ellerby's voice followed at once. "Systems overview

shows the current mode as Passive/Defensive Landing. Shield strength reads approximately twenty-eight percent. That's only two percent below the indicated nominal level."

"Very well, Mister Ellerby." Lewis was suddenly struck with how ingrained their military training had become. Here they were, so far from their own home world that the light around them wouldn't even reach their planet for several millennia and they were still clinging to tradition. Well, she thought suddenly, whatever works. "Mister Ellerby, is there something like an active launch mode accessible from that panel?"

"One moment, Commander." Both Ellerby and Tobler had taken to calling her commander when they were in flight. It seemed more appropriate than captain—which was more a function of rank than position—and the term suited her better anyway. "I have a cascade of general command options. Let me just sort through . . . got it! Cycle to Command Standby mode then branch to Launch Prep mode."

"Proceed, Mister Ellerby. Let me know when I have release of system command functions from the landing mode."

"They are available now, Commander."

"Thank you. Tobler, I'm bringing the main power distribution grid on-line . . . now."

A fountain of light sprang up from the central map table, flowing like an impossible, inverted waterfall against the curved ceiling overhead. The light radiated outward along the ornate petals that were carved into the curved ceiling of the room. Each of them glowed when touched by the liquid light. In moments the room was alive with light.

The air began to stir.

Must be the ventilation system coming up, Lewis thought, as her eyes searched the panel in front of her. From somewhere in the distance, she could hear massive equipment spooling up, awakening from its long slumber. She had to speak louder with each passing moment to be heard. "Launch preparation sequence enabled! Five inertial suppressors have failed . . . field strength within tolerable limits. Landing claw retract mechanism number two reads a malfunction. I've by-passed the alarm. Claw is retracting. Sequence is complete!"

"Spatial motive drives transferred from off-line to stand-by modes," Tobler shouted. "All motivators are go for power up, Commander."

"Initiating launch sequence . . . now! Guidance to my station! Ellerby, as soon as we've lifted off, get us into a defensive/active mode and shunt the weapons systems over to Tobler on her . . ."

"Oh my God!" Ellerby cried out.

The light spread from the fountain in the center of the command console, bringing the ceiling, the room, and the ship into glorious brilliance, and illuminating the bones and dust of the dead.

The awakened dead.

Dusts covering the mammoth floor began to shift with the vibrations of the lifting motors. Even as Ellerby watched in horror, they took form in the eddies and currents of the air, taking shapes of gray clouds coalescing in twisting, writhing forms. One, two, then a dozen of the shifting, ghostly whirlwinds formed in the air, each one crying, singing, wailing as it blew into being and then collapsed out of existence once more.

"Destiny!"

Tobler yelped. "What is THAT supposed to be?"

The engines of the ancient ship thundered through the room, mixed with the groans of metal too long at rest and suddenly awakened to move once more.

"Stay at your posts!" Lewis shouted. "This monster needs a living crew, not a dead one!"

The dust clouds in the room suddenly formed into thousands of charcoal shapes, each different from the next, each reaching up with ephemeral pleading arms, their hollow mouths agape and singing, keening . . .

"Forgiveness! Despair! Salvation!"

The shrieking of the dead pierced Lewis's ears over the roaring of the engines, the horrible noise causing her pain. "What do you want!" she shouted.

"Home! Take us home!"

Tobler began weeping once more, whether out of pain or sympathy, Lewis could not tell.

"Ellerby!" Lewis shouted, hoping she was heard above the din. "Launch us . . . now!"

The scene playing out around them had transfixed the huge man.

"Ellerby!" Lewis shouted once more. "Now, Lieutenant! Fly! Damn it!" Lewis suddenly pushed her way past the big man and slammed her palm on the sequence release. "You want to go home, eh? Well, so do I! Hang onto your souls, you miserable ghosts! I'm taking us all home!"

Suddenly, the deck lurched under her. The dome above them went suddenly clear and she could see the milky thick stars of the Bonefield Narrows shift across her view.

A chorus of joy and despair roared through the hall.

"The dead shall rise again, boys," Lewis shouted into the overwhelming sound. "This relic is gonna fly!"

"BY THE NINE!" TARG SHOUTED, HIS VOICE BURIED IN THE sudden avalanche of sound. He gripped the railing of the pirate starship, bracing for the worst. Behind him, chaos erupted as each of Flynn's crew scrambled for any brace or handhold that might provide them some measure of security. Targ was only dimly aware of their movement, however. His eyes were fixed on the horizon above the shore.

A mountain of shining metal, blue and hazy with distance,

rose slowly above the whipping trees. The sound was unbelievable, a deep resonance that sounded from inside one's own bones. The very air quivered with its power, the shaking it inspired threatening to separate plank by plank, splinter by splinter, the very wood of the Aendorean pirate ship. Forests of trees on shore were being leveled under the sound. The four-mile-wide ship rose majestically into the perpetual twilight of the Bonefield Narrows, the gentle curve of its upper hull becoming apparent, its towers reaching into the sky once more.

"Neskat," he said to himself through clenched teeth.

Targ turned. Griffiths was standing near him, gripping the rail just as he was doing. The Earth barbarian's face was filled with wonder at the sight of the ancient ruin wrenching itself free of the ground where it had lain for over three thousand years. Wonder and something else, Targ realized.

The Vestis Prime reached over suddenly, grabbing Griffiths by the front of his blousy tunic and dragging his face within a handsbreadth of his own. "What has she planned, barbarian?" he screamed. "What is she going to do?"

Griffiths stared back at him, a look of incomprehension mixed with resignation.

"You won't get away with this," he raged, shaking Griffiths with both hands. "I've waited too long—suffered too long to be stopped by the likes of . . ."

The *Venture Revenge* suddenly heeled over in the waters of the bay. The concussion launched by the Settlement Ship had reached them, pushing the hull and rigging over into a thirty-degree list. Every object that was not secure— lines, tools, cannon, and crew—slid suddenly across the slanting deck toward the waters now lapping at the gunwales. Griffiths's feet slid out from under him.

Targ locked his left arm around the railing and wrapped his free arm around Griffiths's chest. The strength of his hold nearly pressed the air out of the Earth-man's lungs.

"No, Earther," Targ bellowed. "You are the key—and you are mine. I'll not have you damaged before I gain my due."

The *Venture Revenge* began righting herself slowly as the sound abated. Targ looked back again to see the Settlement Ship rising on a brilliant blue column of power.

Suddenly a new sight presented itself. The ships of the Tsultak fleet, enraged at their truce having been so flagrantly shattered, began rising into the air in pursuit. A dozen. A hundred. A thousand ships rose as one toward the accelerating form of the gigantic ancient ruin.

"You wanted a diversion," Griffiths croaked.

Targ glanced once at the human and then released him. The roar of the Settlement Ship and its pursuers was rapidly diminishing.

"Indeed I did," Targ snarled. "Captain Flynn! Get this ship aloft now!"

39

Deadly Pursuits

EVEN BEFORE THE GYRATING SHIP SETTLED BACK IN THE waters of the bay, the spacers of the pirate crew scurried about the deck, rushing in a frantic panic to reach their stations. Cries, curses, and commands spat across the deck, colored by the accents of a dozen different worlds. The ancient wooden hull of the Aendorian ship shuddered under the uneven power of the rudely awakened ship's drives. Above the ominously creaking deck, the spacers cast their spells, weaving the drive sails into an existence that would function in the lost worlds of the Bonefield Narrows.

The chaos raged about Jeremy Griffiths, breaking against his tranquility. Targ had dragged him to the drive-tree mast of the ship, released him, and with a single gesture indicated that under no circumstances was Jeremy to move from that spot. That was fine with Griffiths. He leaned back against the mast and folded his arms. What difference does it make, he thought to himself sourly. What difference does any of this make?

He glanced behind him around the mast. There stood Evon Flynn, looking as dashing as ever as he tried to bring some order to his crew. "Well," Griffiths said, sighing to himself. "If she abandoned me, she abandoned you as well,

Flynn. Welcome to the club. I wonder how big a club it is?"

He looked up into the star-filled opal sky overhead. The massive Settlement Ship was now a blue flame streaking across the brilliant background. Hundreds of dark specks darted behind it in pursuit.

"Goodbye, Merinda," he said to himself amid the din around him. "Goodbye Lewis, Tobler, and Ellerby. You've abandoned me once again. It's working well, friends. The entire Tsultak fleet is on your trail. You've drawn them away from me—just as you said you would. Now it's up to me to be the savior of uncounted worlds across the galaxy."

He looked down suddenly, tears welling up in his eyes. "Only I don't want to be the savior of uncounted worlds. I can't do this alone. Damn it, Merinda, why didn't you come?"

The rumbling under his feet smoothed out suddenly. The deck lurched once and the ship vaulted skyward. Griffiths was forced to grab one of the lanyards to keep on his feet in the sudden acceleration. He grimaced. Once more he was racing into the teeth of adventure, and he knew their bite was getting too close for comfort. He was in the hands of more than one cutthroat and was pretty sure that any of them would kill him to spite the others.

A massive hand gathered his tunic at the back of his neck and shook him from his reverie. Griffiths struggled to keep his feet under him as he was dragged backward across the deck. His captor, however, had other plans. With a sudden tug from behind, Griffiths fell backward painfully to the deck.

"Where is it, damn you!" croaked the hoarse voice, choked with emotion.

Griffiths moved slowly. "Where is what, Targ of Gandri?"

"The map," Flynn chimed in. Griffiths noticed that his face was fixed with a look that seemed to be both outraged and fearful at the same time. His mouth twisted into a frightful rendition of a friendly smile. "Where's the map, Jeremy, old shipmate?"

"Is that all?" Griffiths rolled his eyes. He reached inside the breast of his long coat. "I even finished it for you. You know, you people really do need to lighten up a little. You could have just asked me and . . ."

Griffiths's eyes went wide.

"Avast below," came a cry from the rigging far above. "There's a Tsultak task force closing on us!"

"Where away?" Flynn called upward through cupped hands.

"Five points off the trailing beam starboard and closing, sir!" the distant voice returned.

"Well?" Targ said, his fists balled on his hips as he glared at the Earth-man.

Griffiths reached frantically about his long coat, jamming his hands into its various pockets. "Well, I . . . I had it right . . . I had it right here . . . somewhere!"

"You lost the map?" Flynn's words were pressed out through clenched teeth.

"No! I'm sure I've got it here!" Griffiths replied with an edge of panic in his voice.

"We've no time for this." Flynn reached down to his wide belt and pulled loose a massive blaster. In a single smooth move, he pressed the weapon to Griffiths's forehead. "Those Tsultak are going to bring us within range of their guns in about three minutes, Griffiths. When they do, we'll all be blown to the Seven Hells of Mingasel, but I am perfectly willing to send you ahead of us right now!"

"Tsultak closing fast, Captain." Shindak spoke smoothly from his post next to the helm. Griffiths imagined there was some satisfaction in the elf's voice at his master's apparent dilemma.

"Understood! Gun crews to their stations. Run them up,

Mr. Shindak," Flynn called out, his eyes never leaving Griffiths's for a moment. Sweat had broken out on the pirate captain's brow. His next words were quiet. "Where is the map, Griffiths?"

Griffiths stared back at him.

Flynn cocked the mechanism with his thumb.

"One last time, old shipmate," Flynn said, his words as cold as space. "Where is the map?"

Slowly, Griffiths reached up, curling the fingers of his hand until they pointed directly at his own head.

"You idiot," Griffiths sneered. "I *am* the map."

Flynn looked as though someone had just slapped him.

"Gonna shoot me now, you son-of-a-bitch?"

Flynn jerked the weapon back away from Griffiths's face.

Griffiths stood up slowly, facing the two men before him as though for the first time on even terms. "I'm going to use small words so you two can understand this. You want to find this precious Nightsword—well, that's fine with me. I'm the only one who knows how to get there. It's not just finding where to enter the Maelstrom Wall either. The passage beyond is a treacherous one. You'll never make it without me—in or out. Understand?"

Targ shook with rage. "I will not be dictated to by . . ."

"You will be dictated to and you'll take it, Targ," Griffiths cut off Targ's words. "I'll take you to your precious treasure and you'll keep me alive—both of you. Do we have a deal?"

Flynn spoke at once. "Deal done! Give me a course, Griffiths—we haven't much time!"

Griffiths turned to the tall, white-haired mage. "E'toris Prime?"

Targ hesitated.

A distant shout fell from the rigging. "Cannon fire aft, Captain."

Flynn turned to Targ. "We haven't any more time!"

Targ looked away from Griffiths's eyes. "Yes, we have a deal."

Griffiths turned to the elf standing by the helm, ignoring Flynn entirely. "Master Shindak, mark that point twelve degrees to starboard and down twenty-three. Come about sharply!"

"Aye-aye, sir," Shindak returned with a sly smile, then turned to address the helmsman. "Master Korgan, come about starboard twelve, twenty-three down. Stand by the rigging! Sharply now!"

Griffiths turned back to the captain. "Flynn, we're going to need a lot more speed out of this ship or we'll never penetrate the first quantum front."

"We could set the royals," Flynn replied. As he saw the blank look on Griffiths's face, he continued to explain. "They're yardarm extensions. It's an incredible strain on the mast, but if we can generate a good following force . . ."

"We'll never make it otherwise," Griffiths replied. "Shindak! Set the royals."

"Captain," Shindak said quickly. Griffiths was suddenly not sure whom the elf was addressing. "There shall be no time for the royals. Our pursuers are upon us."

"Stand by the guns," Flynn yelled. He ran at once to the gunwale and peered over the side of the ship. Griffiths dashed after him, gripped the wooden railing, and stuck his head over the side.

"There must be a dozen ships back there," Griffiths muttered more to himself than to Flynn.

"Yes," the pirate answered. "They're gaining quickly. You'll undoubtedly be happy to note that the secret course you just gave us will most likely die with us right here and now."

The massive Tsultak dragon ships danced their bobbing and weaving course far below them. The hulls were thorny and horned, black and menacing even from this distance. Shindak and the helmsman continued to thread the *Venture Revenge* through the myriad miniature planets that filled the region, but each of their moves was matched smoothly by the pursuing Tsultak. As they watched, their own hull thundered past a minor planet, seeming to graze the very tops of its mountains. The ship twisted and dove again between two small worlds. Griffiths held his breath and wondered if any ship could navigate such a thin passage at these speeds. Suddenly five of the Tsultak pursuers emerged from the gap, the shine of their black hulls evident. Griffiths could see the dragons moving about on the exterior decking, their claws digging into the wooden planking as they prepared themselves to breathe death as they passed the pirate ship.

Flynn pulled himself from the railing. "Shindak! We need those royals!"

"Captain," Shindak rejoined, "if we deploy those now we shall smash her against a planet. We'll never turn her at those speeds!"

"Hard to port!" Flynn yelled, as he gazed up the mast. "Steer for the nebula. When we're fully in, come smartly to starboard."

"Aye-aye, Captain," Shindak replied, then turned his pinched face upward as he called. "Aloft! Set the deep weather shunts! Move lively now!"

Griffiths continued to stare down the hull. The massive black ships drifted behind them, so close now that he could see their closing motion. He turned quickly back to call across the deck. "They're gaining on us, Flynn! It's too late for . . ."

Griffiths glanced up and was stopped short in his speech. There wasn't even time for him to swear.

A wall of cloud was rushing down on them with incredible speed. Griffiths had the fleeting impression of being

Chicken Little and actually watching the sky falling. It looked as though the clouds were dropping toward them like a mountain from above. Griffiths instinctively brought his hands up to protect himself.

The terrible crash did not follow. When he dared look again, the ship sailed blindly in the center of a glowing sphere of light. It's like sailing in the center of a Ping-Pong ball, Griffiths thought. It would have been peaceful and serene if Flynn and his crew were not rushing madly about the deck and rigging.

"Hold your course for three minutes, Shindak," Flynn said urgently, "then push this old girl over sixty degrees down by the mast. Hold that course for three minutes and then come to port ninety. See to it that those royals get set at once. We'll be coming out of this drift in about six minutes. If we've shaken them, we'll have a straight run on Griffiths's course into the Wall. If we haven't shaken them . . ."

"If we haven't shaken them," Targ intoned grimly, "then all of this has been for nothing."

"We'll shake them," Flynn affirmed with perhaps a bit too much certainty, as though he were convincing himself. "In any event, the gun crews are ready in case there's any additional problem between this drift and the Wall itself. However," he said, turning back toward Griffiths, "I seem to recall there being more to running the Wall than simply finding the right spot in the quantum front, eh, old mate?"

Griffiths walked across the deck and casually climbed the ladder to the command platform in the center. "That's right, Flynn. On the other side of the wall there is a vortex—a confluence of realities known on the map as Shauna-kir's Well. It's a whirlpool of space, time, and probability that drains down into the galactic core. The passage through it was marked—and trapped, I might add—eons ago during the Lost Empire."

"Let me guess," Flynn said, drolly. "You're the only one who can read the signs."

"You're learning." Griffiths smiled easily back. "I'm the only one who can read the signs."

Flynn snorted.

"Hey, it's up to you," came Griffiths's tired reply. "Once you fall into the vortex there's no stopping. If you miss one of those markers, however, the ship will drift into the Wall of the Maelstrom, near the core itself, and you can be sure that the differences between the tides of one reality and the next will tear this ship apart in very short order."

"Captain." Shindak spoke quietly to Flynn. "The nebula is thinning forward."

"Are the royals ready?" he grumbled back.

"Aye-aye, Captain."

"Well, Griffiths," Flynn rumbled. "It looks as though we're going to need you a little longer after all."

"We've cleared the nebula, Captain," Shindak called from his post next to the helm. "The royals are holding. Helm is sluggish but we're making smart time."

"Very well, Master Shindak. Set your course for . . ."

"Avast, below!" cried the watch from the masts above. "Dragon ship fleet closing hard! Five points to starboard off the mast! I make twelve ships!"

"NO!" Flynn shouted. "Not now! Not so close!"

Another voice from above called out. "Dragon ship fleet, fifteen degrees to port! Closing! Making twenty ships, sir!"

Suddenly multiple shouts erupted from the crew both aloft and on the deck. Cries of other fleets, other ships, for all quarters and points.

"Captain," Shindak said calmly amid the confused shouting, which grew more and more in its tenor and tempo by the moment. "The Tsultak fleet is upon us. If we surrender the ship at once . . ."

"No, Captain," Targ said at once, stepping forward. "You will not surrender the ship . . . not this close. Not when we have come so far and risked so much."

"It's over, Targ," Flynn said under his breath. "I cannot fight these odds."

"You can if the stakes are high enough," Targ said, taking a step closer to the man.

"No price is worth my life." Flynn held his ground.

"You value your life too much, Evon. I'll double your price . . . I'll triple it . . . whatever we agreed to," Targ said, stepping closer again until he was so close to the captain that his breath broke against the man's face. "I'll pay whatever you want . . . grant you whatever you desire."

Flynn looked as though he was about to object once more.

"I can even bring you peace," Targ said smoothly. "That peace that you have run in search of all your life. You run and run, Evon, and it never brings you rest—never brings you comfort to your wounded soul. I can end your torment, Flynn. I can give you a place where you don't have to run any longer."

Flynn blinked. "Run . . . I've been running . . . so long . . ."

"Prime the guns!" Shindak shouted. He voice sounded far away to Griffiths, caught up in the intensity of the drama between the two men standing before him.

Flynn shook once and his face hardened with his resolve. "And running is something I know well! Master Shindak! Deploy the royals! NOW!"

"Deploy the royals!" Shindak shouted aloft. Griffiths could feel the deck press up against his feet and the ship took on new speed.

"We run, boys!" Flynn shouted. "Run for the treasure! Run for the glory! Griffiths, quickly! Where is your precious passage?"

Griffiths looked up the mast. It was as though he had seen

these formations before, so clear were the recollections and memories planted in his mind by the Mantle of Kendis-dai. "Five points to port . . . fifteen degrees down by the mast!"

The ship lurched to the new course. The deck swayed beneath their feet, their speed dangerously high. The mast and rigging creaked ominously under the load.

"Hold her steady!" Flynn shouted. "Shindak! How long to the Wall?"

"Three minutes by my reckoning, Captain," the elf said impartially.

"How long until the dragon ships overtake us?" Griffiths asked quietly.

"Too soon," the elf returned, as he pointed across the deck.

They all turned as one to see what he was pointing at. A squadron of black ships was arcing around the hull.

"Stand by the guns!" Flynn shouted. "Prepare for battle."

"No," Shindak said quietly.

"What?" Flynn said incredulously.

"We cannot possibly win this battle. We shall not fight it for your pleasure, Captain Flynn," Shindak said evenly, then turned to the crew. "I stand for captaincy of this vessel. I say we stand down and give these Tsultak what they want. The Maelstrom Passage is not going anywhere! Flynn has promised us everything and delivered us nothing! He lies . . . and thus proves himself a human! I say we save our lives for battles we can win and live through! I say we divest ourselves of this human trash and win the prize for ourselves!"

Griffiths's eyes were on Shindak as he spoke, the crew not moving at their posts, weighing . . . waiting. He heard the sound of sliding steel to his left. Realization dawned on him.

Griffiths turned toward the sound.

Flynn lunged forward, his sword directed toward Shindak. Deadly accurate and backed by Flynn's full weight, the blade slid into the elf's flesh. Flynn's aim was perfect.

The blade missed the spine by inches, slicing upward and emerging through the elf's rib cage.

Shindak turned suddenly with such force that Flynn's cutlass broke off just above the hilt. Enraged, the elf leaped toward the pirate captain, the blade protruding from his chest. Flynn quickly dove under his own oncoming blade, knocking the legs out from under the elf.

The elf dropped to the deck, the blade still buried in him pressing sideways as he fell against the planks.

The pirate scrambled to his feet, the remains of his shattered blade protruding from the hilt still in his hand. "You damned traitorous filth!" Flynn screamed, his quick stride across the deck bringing him to stand over the struggling elf. "I'm the captain here!"

He kicked savagely at the blade in the elf's chest.

"I am the captain, damn you!" he shrieked. "It's my ship! It's my life!"

Red-faced with rage, tears streaming down his face, Flynn reached down with his left hand and pulled up Shindak's head by the hair. His right arm was raised up, the hilt of the broken sword poised to strike.

Griffiths was transfixed. The brutality of Flynn's attack was horrific.

A massive arm arrested Flynn's blow.

"Kheoghi! Let me go!" Flynn bellowed.

"I'm thinking not for the moment, captain sire," the minotaur rumbled menacingly. Kheoghi's eyes narrowed to bright red slits. "I'm thinking that humanity's manners may need a little adjustment. This fine crew followed yer orders here to the brink of the seven hells and now . . ."

The minotaur suddenly looked up, his brutish snout drooping in wonder.

"By all the gods!" he growled.

Griffiths turned back toward the railing, to see just what it was that had caught Kheoghi's attention. A chill suddenly fell over him.

The massive form of the Lost Empire Settlement Ship emerged from the clouds like a resurrected leviathan. The towers of the ancient craft suddenly erupted in multiple bolts of deadly force. The brilliant javelins lanced several of the dragon ships at once, each collapsing in a flash of dazzling finality.

"Merinda," Targ murmured behind Griffiths, his voice filled with satisfaction.

Griffiths heart sank. His one consolation had been that they, at least, may have gotten away. Merinda had said she would come back and now he wished so fervently that she hadn't.

"The Tsultak are turning to attack the Settlement Ship," Targ said, pointing to the various dragon ship elements wheeling away from the *Venture Revenge*. "Merinda's clearing our way for us."

"She's not alone," Griffiths said hopelessly. "My crew is with her."

"Aye . . . and mine will be with me," Flynn sneered as he turned back toward the xenoforms of his awestruck crew.

The dragon ships formed into coordinated formations, wheeling as though commanded by a single mind to attack the gigantic relic ship as one.

"There's your chance, mates!" Flynn shouted to the crew on deck and in the rigging. "You might have followed this spineless elven traitor to an uncertain future, or you can have it all right now! Opportunity's in the sky! This is the moment! Do you want the prize?"

"Aye," answered a few voices in ragged chorus.

The *Venture Revenge* continued to dash upward toward the Maelstrom Wall, the helmsman having been given no alternate course.

"Do you want your reward now?" Flynn bellowed.

"Aye!" the answer came more firmly.

The Settlement Ship's weapons flared again, knocking a handful of dragon ships from the sky. Not enough, however, Griffiths determined ruefully. The dragon ships opened fire, their weapons exploding against the defensive armament of the huge craft. Griffiths noted grimly that the dragon fleet weapons effectively breached the defenses in many places. The surface of the ancient ship burst apart at a dozen points as the dragon fleet concentrated its fire.

"Will you follow me there, mates?" Flynn screamed.

"Aye!" came the shouted chorus.

The dragon fleet ships, almost indefinable swarms of black dust at their present range, passed across the surface of the enormous disk. The bolts from the weapons towers were far fewer now than before.

"Turn . . . evade . . . run away . . . DO SOMETHING!" Griffiths urged the Settlement Ship. Still the ship held its course, never deviating from its protective following position behind the *Venture Revenge*.

"Look lively, lads!" Flynn shouted up the mast. "We're sailing to hell!"

"Damn you, Merinda!" Griffiths raged. "Get the hell out of here!"

The swarming black dust of the dragon fleet wheeled again toward the Settlement Ship, now falling far behind them.

Griffiths caught his breath.

The ancient ship exploded suddenly, a force wave of compressed energy released catastrophically from the ship's collapsing engines radiating in a sphere, slamming into the dragon fleet.

In that instant of despair, the *Venture Revenge* hurtled at full speed against the Maelstrom Wall.

OMEGA:

EYE

OF THE

MAELSTROM

40

The Gate

GRIFFITHS PITCHED TO THE DECK UNDER THE IMPACT. DARKness engulfed him. The ship was reeling through the Maelstrom Wall, buffeted by forces that howled through the rigging. He had passed through numerous quantum fronts these last few weeks—especially during the mad dash he had piloted across the disk toward the galactic core—but none of them compared to the fury of the storm they had collided with under full sail.

Griffiths began pushing himself up against the acceleration of the deck. He heard a sharp crack overhead and had the dim impression of something whipping past him at high speed. The ship lurched suddenly to one side. Griffiths felt himself sliding across the decking, images of tumbling over the gunwale passing through his mind. Panicked, he flailed in the darkness for some hold. Pain shot through his arm as it hit against a ventilator cover, but he held tight just as the deck pitched once more in the opposite direction.

The sound was overpowering. The atmosphere of the deck seemed alive with it: a constant bombardment of a moaning, shrill rage. Through it, Griffiths thought he could hear the distant cries of the crew all about him. They seemed to call to him from the rigging, from the deck, from everywhere. Their words were drowning in the cascade of sound, swallowed until their meaning was lost and only their desperate tone remained.

He managed to pull himself onto his side. The contrast between the opal brightness of the Bonefield Narrows and the pitch-darkness of the passage was startling but not complete. Beyond the clear mystical dome that encompassed the deck and most of the drive-tree, Griffiths glimpsed a million suns rushing past them, their light frozen with the quantum flux and dust clouds spiraling down around their wake. Though densely packed this close to the galactic core, their light was only a dim shadow of their glory, diffused and dampened by the chaos variance that surrounded the ship. Griffiths's sight was slowly returning to him as his eyes became accustomed to the new gloom through which the ship now hurtled.

He was still on the captain's walk, he realized gratefully. The ventilation grating had stopped him just short of the railing which, he noticed with a start, was now completely missing, shattered by a yardarm that had broken loose. The cables that had once held it in place writhed snakelike through the air. Beyond that he could dimly perceive movement on the deck below and something beyond the gunwale along the outside edge of the hull.

His eyes widened and he suddenly looked up. "Oh, my God!" was all he could say.

The Maelstrom Passage was a tortured funnel of gray stars and shifting dust, twisting forever toward the center of the galaxy. In a sudden reversal of perspective, Griffiths suddenly knew that he was not flying up into the center of the tornado so much as he was falling down it.

He realized it would be a fall that would last for all eternity.

He quickly glanced around the captain's walk. Cable and debris littered the deck but the drive-tree remained intact. Shindak was trying to pull himself back onto his feet next to the mast. Targ clung to one of the backstays, his face turned upward defiantly toward the storm that fell savagely around them.

Suddenly, the *Venture Revenge* hurtled past a massive nearby star, its passage flashing the star's illumination across the deck. In that flash Griffiths caught sight of Flynn. The pirate captain stood with his feet set wide apart. Both hands gripped the helm wheel. He was shouting into the gale, his voice barely carrying over the horrendous sound.

"Damn you," he shouted. "Hold your course in the center of the vortex! We're going to stay in the channel until we come out the other side!"

"No!" screamed Griffiths. With supreme effort, he pulled himself up from the deck, trying desperately to get his feet under him. The deck failed to cooperate. The ship pitched suddenly away from him. Griffiths once more reached out and wrapped his hands in a death grip around a backstay cable.

Griffiths could see more clearly now. The walls of the twisting vortex were closing in on them the further they sailed. Now he could see that the tempest's wall was studded with debris that was taking on regular shapes.

The signs, he realized. The signs are here.

Griffiths gritted his teeth, swung about on the line, and planted his feet back on the deck with renewed determination. Taking aim, he lunged toward the helm. The deck pitched yet again as he moved, but his momentum carried him through to the wheel housing. At the last moment, he managed to grip the lateral wheel and keep his feet under him.

"Griffiths!" Flynn shouted angrily. "Don't touch that! We've got to hold our course until we break through!"

"No, Flynn," Griffiths yelled back. "We've got to turn the ship!"

The pirate captain glanced at him with unquestionable

horror. "Are you mad? Turning in the midst of a wave front passage is suicide! We've got to get to the other side!"

"We'll never get to the other side," Griffiths screamed into the thunderous roar about them. "There *is* no other side!"

"What?"

"There's no other side," he repeated. "The map calls this a temporal vortex. It leads to the gate, but the gate is in the wall of the vortex, not the end—there is no end!"

"This is madness," Flynn replied. "You'll kill us all."

"Will I?" Griffiths spat back. "Look at the walls of the vortex, Flynn. Tell me what you see there!"

Flynn glanced past Griffiths. Suddenly, the pirate's eyes went wide. "By the Nine!"

"Those are ships, Flynn!" Griffiths went on, still gripping the helm wheel as he pressed his face closer to the pirate. "Ships who tried this passage once before without the map. Ships who just wanted to get to the other side. The vortex got narrower and narrower and the time distortion became greater and greater until now they're all stuck in a temporal event horizon. They still think they're sailing, Flynn! They still dream of glory and riches on the other side—only they don't know that they will never get there, Flynn . . . never!"

"You led us here, you bastard!" Flynn cried, reaching out across the helm and grabbing Griffiths by the collar.

"That's right," Griffiths replied. "And I'm the one who is going to lead you out of it so get your hands off my shirt!"

Flynn clenched his teeth but released the astronaut.

"There's a gate in the vortex wall," Griffiths went on. "We've got to turn this thing into it right now!"

Flynn looked at Griffiths suspiciously. "Why are you so anxious to help me now?"

"Let's just say I've got a reason to live," Griffiths replied.

"What reason is that?"

"I need to be around long enough to see if they still hang people like you."

Flynn smiled. "Fair enough! Give me a course, Captain Griffiths!"

Griffiths looked up into the constricting vortex overhead. Even with his untrained eye he could see that there was extensive damage already done to the drive-tree and its yardarms. "There!" he pointed. "That dark spot in the wall. Make for that!"

"Aye-aye, Captain," Flynn said with a sneer, spinning the wheel under his experienced hands.

The ship groaned loudly under the load. At first, the gallant pinnacle of the drive-tree did not shift against the spiral toward which they were plunging. Slowly, however, the ship's course altered. The buffeting of the hull became far more pronounced as she turned. The vortex seemed to sense its prey moving to escape and its furies increased. Griffiths saw the main mast bending back and forth under the new loads. Several of the backstays snapped with the crack of a whip, lashing up dangerously from the deck behind him.

"We are losing the main yard," Shindak shouted, on his feet at last behind them.

"Have it braced!" Flynn yelled back.

The dark spot was quickly resolving itself into a great ring set impossibly into the wall of the tempest.

"Too late," Shindak called out.

Griffiths looked up. The massive wooden beam was rushing downward from above. He leaped out of the way. Too late. The yardarm smashed the decking next to him, dragging him down into the shattered bowels of the ship. He felt himself falling, tumbling into the blackness, into death. He almost welcomed it, he thought at last. Then his head struck something terribly hard.

"GRIFFITHS-MATE?"

Go away, he thought. I'm dead.

"Griffiths-mate?" the rough voice intruded. "Come about, thar be sights to be seen and thar be no doubt about that."

Everyone I know is dead, Griffiths pondered. Why can't I be dead, too? He considered Zanfib's words for a moment and wondered if perhaps he, too, were not some sort of wizard-prophet after all. A fleeting image of himself in robes of midnight-blue velvet flashed through his mind as he commanded scores of bucket-wielding brooms. He shook his head to clear that image from his mind and then, reluctantly, opened his eyes.

He started visibly. Kheoghi's bull-like face was pressed near his own. He should have recognized the voice and matched the face to it but the sight still came as something of a shock.

"Sights to be seen is right," Griffiths mumbled to himself. For a moment he was not sure where he was lying. Suddenly he remembered the falling yardarm, the splintering wood. Indeed, there were smashed timbers all about where he had finally come to rest with this monster standing over him. He suddenly realized that Kheoghi seemed to be surrounded by a bright nimbus of light streaming down from beyond him.

Perhaps I *am* dead, Griffiths thought.

"Come, Griffiths-mate. Cap'n Flynn ask that I see to you and bring you up on deck. A stout one, you are, for a human that is. Still, I'm thinking you might have been dead altogether if it weren't for that Targ of Gandri. Saw you fallin' he did. Worked his magic but it weren't enough to keep you out of the hold."

"Great," Griffiths shook his head. "You mean that I now owe my life to that bastard?"

"Well, Griffiths, he may not be one of the Brethren of the Wall but he didn't give you the soft farewell either. He also wants you topside. Thought you might be a bit interested in seeing where you've led us, so to speak." Kheoghi extended his massive left arm.

Griffiths accepted the offered help to his feet and looked around them. The remains of the yardarm jutted with jagged edges from the various shattered bulkheads and debris of the broken hold. A soft white light streaming down from the broken hatch overhead seemed to beckon him upward. The ladder mounted to the wall of the compartment remained intact. Kheoghi had already hauled himself up its rungs by the time Griffiths began climbing his way back to the main deck.

There was a surreal quality to the surroundings as he emerged. He couldn't place his finger on it for a moment. Then he realized what had made him uncomfortable. Though the xenomorphic crew of the *Venture Revenge* was still present, they all were standing motionless and silent in their awe. More than that was disquieting, however: there were no shadows anywhere to be seen.

"By the Nine, Griffiths." Flynn spoke softly as the astronaut approached him. "Look where you've brought us!"

Griffiths looked.

The expanse of space itself was glowing with a soft whiteness as though someone had taken a photograph of the night sky and somehow, impossibly, printed a negative instead. He had to remind himself, however, that this was no mere picture. The great glowing whiteness was studded with black stars that drifted over the deck in a slow procession. All this was veiled in a procession of nebulae glowing in hues of salmon and deep turquoise. It was an image of heaven, Griffiths thought to himself as the ship drifted slowly through the milky expanse. Its beauty had robbed the pirate crew of their speech. Its wonder brought tears unbidden to Griffiths's eyes.

"What are those?" Flynn asked quietly, his outstretched hand pointing to yet another of the huge rings drifting past them in the procession of the sky. There were hundreds that studded the sky from place to place.

"I don't know," Griffiths said, looking suddenly away. His sight stopped on Targ.

The Vestis Prime alone seemed unmoved by the spectacle. He stood near the shattered captain's walk, his feet wide apart and his arms folded across his chest. "We have not come as tourists here, Captain Flynn," he said with impatience. "We are near the prize. May I suggest that we finish what we have started?"

"What's he talking about?" Griffiths asked.

"He's talking about that," Flynn said, smiling hungrily as he pointed once more.

Griffiths looked again. A new sight drifted into view overhead.

"My God," Griffiths whispered.

There, hanging above them, was a dazzling blue light. Arrayed all about the light were thousands of drifting ships. Their elegant hulls were ornate and gleaming, untouched by the centuries that had slipped past them. Here they drifted about the light as they had no doubt done for over three thousand years—undisturbed in their rest.

"Lost Empire ships," Griffiths said in a voice filled with wonder.

"Aye, Griffiths," Flynn said with boundless satisfaction. "It's Lokan's bloody, treasure-laden fleet."

41

Ghost Fleet

"ENOUGH," TARG SAID WITH FINALITY. "GET THIS SHIP UNDER way, Flynn."

"Excuse me, Vestis Prime," Flynn said testily as he turned toward the austere shape of the tall, white-haired man, "but just how do you expect me to get under way? We've got extensive damage to the drive-tree. The stay lines are a mess, let alone the rigging itself. There may even be damage to the hull, for all I know. We'll get about the repairs and make way when I say we're good and . . ."

Targ was upon the pirate captain in three quick strides, the obvious impatience and anger building in his face with each step. With his right hand, Targ reached out and gripped Flynn by the throat. The Vestis gave every appearance of being in his mid-fifties or early sixties, so far as the stunned Griffiths could tell, yet Targ possessed enough raw strength to press a suddenly choking Flynn to his knees.

"Your rig is not so damaged as you profess, Captain Flynn," Targ said with chilling disdain, "and I'll brook no further delay. You're an insolent, churlish speck who whines too much and does too little." Targ raised his left hand to strike.

"No, Targ," Griffiths said simply.

The Director of the Omnet froze at the unexpected words.

"You need him."

"I need no one!" Targ pressed the words out between his clenched teeth.

"You're wrong," Griffiths continued. "You need me because of what I might know that you do not. You need Flynn, his ship, and his crew to get back through the vortex gate."

Targ smiled suddenly at Griffiths. "You're only partly right, you know. I do need you." In a flash, Targ turned his burning eyes back to Flynn, whose face was decidedly taking on a purple tint. "I've warned you before and this is certainly the last time. Stand between me and my destiny and I shall tear your lungs out with my bare hands. You will get this ship under way, understand?"

Flynn managed to nod above the constricting hand.

Targ released Flynn with a slight push, sending the pirate captain sprawling onto the deck. "You will steer a course through the wrecks. I will direct you."

"Direct us toward what?" Flynn said sullenly, rubbing the raw skin of his neck.

"Toward my destiny, as I have said," Targ said.

"That may work for you," Flynn replied, picking himself painfully up from the deck, "but we'll need to see a little more than just your destiny."

"Your conditions for selling out a friend were quite clear when you contacted me," Targ replied stiffly. "You will be most welcome to collect on that—but only after you have fulfilled it to me in the utmost measure. Now, will you get this ship back on an even keel, or shall I be forced to promote someone from among your crew to the rank of captain?"

Flynn drew a sharp breath but thought better of giving voice to the reply that had so quickly come to his mind. Instead he turned to his crew. "Master Kheoghi, bring the crew to their stations! I want the weavers into the rigging, and get the second watch rousted to clear this deck. Gather a few of your own choice and see to the helm yourself."

"Aye-aye, sir," Kheoghi snorted in reply.

"I want this drifting hulk moving like a ship of the line and I want it to happen yesterday!"

"By your will, Captain!" Kheoghi responded, before he began bellowing at the crew. The visage of the minotaur wearing an enraged expression was more than sufficient to shake the crew from their stupor. "Put your backs into it, mates! We're within sight of the glory, now!"

Flynn turned back to face Targ. "Is there anything further I can do for you, Prime?" Flynn spoke the words evenly though they were laced with contempt and hatred. "Anything at all?"

Targ didn't give any recognition to the pirate's tone although Griffiths was certain that it had not escaped the Prime in the least. Instead, he cocked his face upward and to one side, as though trying somehow to see a great distance overhead. "Bring us to even keel and then enter the derelict fleet there," he said, pointing to a spot above him and slightly to the left, "between those two massive Settlement Ships. That is where we will begin."

"Begin what?" Griffiths asked.

"The hunt, of course," Targ replied.

GRANDEUR DRIFTED COLDLY PAST GRIFFITHS. THE SHIPS OF the Lokan Fleet were gargantuan monuments of metal and glass. They were indeed beautiful, he thought, shining as they were under the blue light from the center of the formation. However, the more he watched them passing, ship after massive ship, the more there came upon him a chilling realization.

The ships were beautiful—but they were dead.

The sheer scale of what he was coming to think of as a graveyard was mind-numbing. They had passed uncounted Settlement Ships as the *Venture Revenge* wove its course between the stationary vessels. Each of those must have carried several thousand people in the ancient past. Men and women, families and children were their purpose and their cargo. What fate had brought them to such a horrible, silent end? The frigates, the escort tenders and massive command ships— or so he had fancied them as each type came past him— where were their crews?

He glanced about him and knew he was not alone in his reveries. The spacers of the core are a superstitious lot. Their beliefs were not without merit and existed primarily to preserve their lives in the various places that dealt out death quickly and without warning, or so Kheoghi had told him. Sailing among the dead ships of the Lokan Fleet was not apparently cause for joy. The crew had once again fallen silent and communicated with each other in the quiet voices one reserves for visiting a tomb.

Only Targ seemed oblivious to it all, so intent was he on his objective. He stood with his back to the gunwale as he gazed up the mast toward their direction of travel. His voice seemed too loud when he spoke and he occasionally drew sharp looks from the crew who seemed to hold more reverence for the place than did the Prime. "There," he called out to Flynn. "Bring us between those two large packet ships just to the left."

"Helmsman, come to port twelve degrees," Flynn said in a bored voice. "Steady as she goes."

They were apparently making their way toward the center of the formation where the mysterious blue light illuminated everything. Frankly, Griffiths didn't give a damn. For that matter, the only person who seemed to care at all was Targ, who grew more and more animated the deeper among the dead ships they sailed.

Griffiths still wondered about the man. He was the leader of the Omnet—unquestionably the most powerful single person in the entire galaxy so far as he could tell—and yet he seemed to have thrown all of that away on this hell-or-high-water obsession with the Nightsword. Power? If Merinda was right, there was no more powerful man in the entire galaxy. Wealth? Griffiths shook his head. Vestis Prime of the Omnet was practically the ultimate definition of the term. His father had died years ago on this same quest, apparently killed right in front of him. Griffiths supposed that such a thing could be a powerful motivator, but if the stories were true, then it wasn't really his fault that his dad had died. There was something missing from the picture, Griffiths knew, that would bring all the parts of the man into focus. Something had driven Targ to jeopardize everything he had stood for over the last forty years. Until he knew what that was, the man would remain a mystery.

Mysteries were dangerous, Griffiths thought.

"There!" Targ cried out.

The dual mammoth ships drifted across their vision, unveiling a scene of incredible grandeur. Filling their vision was a massive sphere of blue fire and glass; the glowing center of the formation. The crystalline sphere was impossibly huge, larger than a planet—perhaps larger than a planetary orbit—the scale was impossible to tell. The fires that raged within the sphere created tumbling patterns that seemed at once alive and beautiful. "Bolok!" Kheoghi cried out, his huge bull-like frame falling to the deck in fear. "It is Bolok—palace of the gods! Forgive us! Forgive us this trespass!" The others of the OomRamn also fell to the deck, their bellowing becoming a chorus chant.

It's the heart of the galaxy, Griffiths thought with a sweet sadness.

The crystal sphere seemed flawed, however, by a dark mark across its face. Griffiths realized at once that the black imperfection was growing as they approached. Soon it outlined the hull of an enormous angular construction.

"The Treasure Ship of Lokan," Flynn murmured hungrily. "By the Nine, Targ, the wealth of the entire ancient empire is on that ship!"

"Yes," Targ replied somewhat distractedly, "I suppose it is."

"You suppose it is?" Flynn was incredulous.

"Closer, Captain Flynn, if you please." Targ was intent now, concentrating so fiercely that a sweat was breaking out on his brow. He pushed himself up from the gunwale and turned to grip it intently. "Follow along the side of the hull over there. I think it may be just beyond that superstructure jutting out about half a mile ahead of us. Slow as you approach it."

The bulk of the treasure ship filled their vision, cutting off the blue light from the sphere. The hull plates were tooled with ornate inscriptions and designs of all kinds and sizes. Griffiths was jolted suddenly with the realization that he could read them.

"What is it, Griffiths?" Flynn asked, watching the astronaut curiously.

"Histories," Griffiths replied. "They've carved their histories onto the hull plates of the treasure ship. My God, world after world after world is up there! Histories for civilizations from before the Shattering of Suns—from before the fall of the empire. The history of all these people is there, above us!"

Flynn gazed up for a few moments. "Well, if it is, Griffiths, then it's for you alone. You're the only one that can read it." He turned his attention back to his crew. "Ahoy the rigging! Weave sail for three marks! Slow her down!"

The structure formation that Targ had indicated was coming quickly past the ship. Above Griffiths the spacers were releasing the weave on several of their mystical fields. He could feel the ship slow perceptibly.

"There!" screamed Targ, pointing excitedly overhead. "As I had foreseen! As it had been prophesied! It is there!"

Griffiths and Flynn both hurried to the gunwale. "What?" Griffiths asked. "What is it?"

"Thank the Nine," Targ said, his voice choked with emotion. Griffiths was worried for a moment that the man was going to come completely apart.

"Will these wonders ever cease?" Flynn placed his fists on both hips in disbelief.

Griffiths looked up. There, moored to the side of the Lokan Fleet derelict and dwarfed by its incredible size, was a black, waspish ship from which still trailed a long, red banner.

"She's a Gorgon ship if ever there was one," Flynn said with a mixture of fear and admiration. "That ensign trailing her is the stuff of legends to every spacer on the Maelstrom Wall. It's Marren-kan's old ship!"

As the *Venture Revenge* continued to slow, it drifted under the hull of the Gorgon ship.

Suddenly, Targ's cheer collapsed.

Griffiths looked up once again. There, moored on the other side of the Gorgon's ship was a saucer covered with the ornate markings of the old empire. He had seen its like before.

"It would seem someone has preceded us." Griffiths smiled as hope began to dawn in his soul.

Both Targ and Flynn spat the name with venom at the same time.

"Merinda!"

42

Excursion

"DAMN THAT WOMAN," TARG THUNDERED. "DAMN HER TO the Fourteen Hells! The Earther's saucer brought me into the Narrows and now she's beaten us here in that same ship!"

The *Venture Revenge* drifted sideways slightly under the gargantuan hull that now stretched over them until it filled their entire vision. Several large clamshell doors were closed above them. Only the upturned lanterns mounted on the pirate ship's hull gave any illumination to the scene, casting harsh shadows across the surface of the ancient spacecraft.

Griffiths was still looking upward, hardly daring to believe that Merinda had actually made it this far. Suddenly he thought of the Settlement Ship. Merinda must have convinced Lewis, Tobler, and Ellerby to fly the larger ship as cover for her coming here and beating everyone to the prize. If so, he suddenly realized, then Merinda had convinced them to fly to their deaths. The coldness of the woman was evidenced to him again and a cold chill ran down his spine. Why did he care about such an obviously unfeeling and apparently megalomaniacal female.

"It's a dead ship," murmured Elami just to Griffiths's right, her snakelike tail curling tightly as she visibly shrank from the sight. "Dead ship with a dead crew."

"The dead don't pinch!" Flynn snapped savagely at the Uruh snake-woman. "Dead is dead. Their riches didn't save them, nor their great power, nor their glory."

"What if this here treasure be cursed?" Kheoghi grumbled. "What then, Captain?"

"There . . . is . . . no . . . curse!" Flynn emphasized each word as though trying to hammer a thought into a child's mind. "The only curse in this ship is the one we make in our own minds. You start thinking up curses for us, OomRamn, and we'll doom ourselves before we begin. We're boarding this ship! We're going to strip her of her value until our ship's hold refuses to carry a single bauble more and then we're going to strip her again!"

"No," Targ barked.

"What?" Flynn spat in anger and surprise.

"You are going to do nothing of the kind," Targ said roughly. "You are going to maneuver this ship next to one of those bay doors and then you and your fine crew are going to wait."

"Wait?" Flynn was red-faced and astonished. "Wait for what?"

"Wait for us," Targ said as he strained against his own outrage with monumental control. "I've not the time nor the inclination to explain this to you, so listen carefully this one final time. You will dock this ship as best you can near these closed bay doors. You will wait patiently until we have returned with the Nightsword. Then we will set sail once more back through the vortex gate and return to normal space, where you and your miserable crew will be rewarded beyond all reason for your lackluster and begrudging assistance in this matter. Your reward there will be far more than your hold here could possibly carry. So, for the last time, demonstrate more intelligence than you have exhibited thus far, and sit here with your crew until we get back."

"Until we get back?" Flynn countered. "Who else is going?"

"Just a minor expedition," Targ said at last. "Just two of us."

"You and who else?" Flynn asked suspiciously.

"Why, our great prophet, of course," Targ smiled.

"Hey," Griffiths chirped. He had been following the dialogue with detached amusement but the flow of the conversation had unexpectedly included him. "Count me out!"

"My translation seems to be in error," Targ said, turning his cold gaze on Griffiths. "What did you say?"

"I said forget it! Deal me out! I'm not going!"

Griffiths felt his feet suddenly leave the deck. Smoothly, and with a single gesture, Targ drew the levitated astronaut across the deck toward him.

"Quite the contrary, Captain." Targ's words were arsenic with a patina of honey. "I am in great need of your assistance. I suspect you shall come in handy when I find your good friend Merinda Neskat. She seems to have gone to a great deal of trouble to keep you alive—even to the point of convincing me to be your protector. I believe it would be in our best interests to oblige her a little while longer."

With a flick of his wrist, Targ sent Griffiths sailing into Kheoghi, nearly knocking the giant OomRamn to the ground. Griffiths himself bounded off the minotaur's chest and collapsed on the deck.

"Find vacuum suits for myself and my prophet friend here," Targ said to the crew in general. "You are all about to be very wealthy sentients. Cross me and you'll never see the stars of home again."

THE VACUUM SUIT STANK. GRIFFITHS WOULD HAVE MANIfested his displeasure in more graphic ways but as an experi-

enced astronaut knew that was out of the question. It is hard
to hold your nose while your head is in a bubble.

He and Kheoghi were in what the minotaur had called
the "Ready Room." From what Griffiths could gather, it
was where the crew prepared for boarding party assaults.
There were a number of vacuum suits that were either hung
in wall niches or simply dropped unceremoniously on the
floor. Kheoghi had wasted no time in finding one that
looked appropriate for Griffiths and stuffing him into it.

The suit selected was an odd patchwork used by the
pirates on those occasions where they needed to board a
vessel by leaping across cold, raw space. To Griffiths, the suit
was far too light and too flexible. The rubberized suits of
NASA may have been bulky and inconvenient but there was
a certain level of confidence that all those layers gave when
one was setting one's life a few small inches from sudden and
rather ugly death. The vacuum suit that Kheoghi had stuffed
him into reminded him more of his old flight jumpsuit than
a pressure suit. Worse, it had obviously been assembled out
of a number of different and mismatched components. The
main body of the suit was a mottled brownish color. The
boots were a bright neon-orange color that seemed to seal
themselves at the top to the legs of this suit. The arms and
chest were encased in an overlayer of what appeared to be
curved plates of articulated plastic in a dull forest-green
color. They might have been very stylish if several of the
plates were not obviously missing.

Perhaps the most distressing part was the enclosure for his
head: he could not bring himself to call it a helmet. He was
used to the hard, high-impact protection of a solid bubble
for a brain bucket. This suit, however, only featured a clear
hood, which Kheoghi had pulled forward over his head and
sealed to his collar. It reminded Griffiths strongly of putting
his head in a plastic bag—and a thin one, at that. He even

began to panic for a moment before Kheoghi smashed his open palm against the chest plate of the outer armor and a sudden inrush of air inflated the bag over his head.

The smell suddenly worsened.

"IT STINKS!" Griffiths yelled at the top of his lungs, hoping his words would penetrate the plastic.

The minotaur drew suddenly back, then Griffiths heard him speaking in normal tones. "Pipe down, ya ground-lubber. I can hear ya just fine. That thar suit lets you be heard clear and true—even in a vacuum. Thar be other things that you'll be needing to know. That thar strip on both yer forearms be a wind tester."

"Wind tester?"

"Aye, it tells ye when thar be wind about you rather than empty space."

"Got it; an atmospheric pressure device."

"Aye, but it be more than that. If the wind about you be bad for yer breath, it remains green. If it be yellow, then ye'll be breathing fine without the suit about you."

"Right. Green is breathable and yellow is not."

"Nay, fool." Kheoghi clubbed him in the arm with a blow that the minotaur might have thought of as playful but which nearly toppled Griffiths off his feet. "Yellow is good and green is bad."

"Sorry—but it still stinks in here," Griffiths said.

"Aye. This be Flurn's old suit," Kheoghi replied as he fussed for a time around the fittings. "He were a good shipmate—may the night rest his soul."

"He's dead?" Griffiths choked. "He didn't die in this suit, did he?"

"Oh, aye, that he did," the minotaur rumbled. "Do you see that thar patch between your legs?"

Griffiths instinctively bent forward, then nodded.

"Took a bad hit, he did, while we were boarding a transport off the Mikli passage," Kheoghi said casually as he fussed. "Cannon shot right there. Ol' Flurn liked to keep the pressure in his suit too high, and I warned him time and time again. That thar cannon shot took a chunk of his suit and the pressure just sort of shot him out of the hole. All that were left of him were a wee bit of mess and this here suit for salvage. Good bit of luck that were . . . a suit is a hard thing to be replacing."

"I think I want to throw up," Griffiths said weakly.

"Now, none of that," the minotaur cautioned. "This here be the best suit of the lot. You wouldn't want to be embarrassing old Kheoghi now, would you?"

Griffiths took a deep breath. "No, I suppose not."

"That's a good lad." The minotaur smiled, which Griffiths found unnerving. "You be ready to walk now."

"Walk?" Griffiths asked.

"Aye, walk the plank, lad!"

Griffiths suddenly hoped that there was something wrong with the translation again.

"OH, LORD, IT IS A PLANK!"

Griffiths stood on the deck in his vacuum suit. Targ stood in a similar suit not far from him. Between them, the crew had extended a large plank beyond the gunwales of the ship, the end of which now hovered apparently about a hundred feet from the sides of the treasure ship itself.

Targ turned to Griffiths. The Prime attached a thin cable between their suits. "It's time to fly, Captain, to our destinies. You to yours, and me to mine."

Targ stepped over the gunwale onto the plank. Anxiously, Griffiths looked over the edge. In his mind, the hull of the ancient spacecraft now next to them turned into a vertical wall of almost infinite depth. He closed his eyes for a moment, dizzy with the acrophobia and then, when the universe resettled in his mind, stepped over the rail as well.

Slowly, Targ preceding Griffiths, they made their way to the end of the extended plank. When they reached the end, Targ turned back toward the ship and called out.

"Stay here until I return," Targ instructed Flynn. "If I am not back within twelve hours, then come after me, but not a moment before."

"I understand you perfectly clearly, Targ," Flynn said casually.

Targ then turned to Griffiths.

"You will jump first, Captain," he said, "then I will follow. Just look at the wall and jump toward it."

Griffiths turned. He jumped as hard as he could. His boots released from the plank and he was weightless, drifting toward the wall. Glancing back, he saw Targ leap after him, the tether still between them.

It was only then that he realized the import of Targ's words. He had said when "I" come back—not "we."

KHEOGHI WATCHED THE HUMAN FIGURES DWINDLE IN SIZE AS they drifted toward the hulking relic. At last he turned and spoke.

"Captain Flynn, why do you allow this braggart fop to breathe? We've found the treasure ship. She's ours by right of our blood and sweat. Why do we sit here like nursery children at his behest?"

"Master Kheoghi, there are, by my count, two Vestis on that treasure ship, or will be very shortly. Taking Merinda alone would be trouble enough, but to take Targ as well, that would be a task worthy of Marren-kan himself."

"So, then," Kheoghi's nostrils flared, "we just sit here on our claws?"

"No, my friend," Flynn said with a smile, his eyes never leaving the drifting figures of Targ and Griffiths as they softly made contact with the distant hull. "We simply have to find out what Neskat and Targ are really up to and pick the right time to play our hand. This requires some finesse."

"What's the play?" Kheoghi asked, with sudden interest.

"As soon as Targ and his bizarre companion have found a way into the treasure ship, take a party over to Merinda's saucer and find a way to cut it loose. Have the spacers propel it well into the night. Use explosives if you have to, but disable that ship and set it to drifting far from here. While you're at it, do the same for that relic ship of Marren-kan as well. I wouldn't want anyone leaving me behind. More than that, I want to be their only ticket home."

"By your word, Captain, it shall be done," Kheoghi enthusiastically replied.

"One more thing," Flynn said, smiling to himself. "Break out a few additional vac suits. I think, perhaps, that twelve hours is far too long for us to wait. Indeed, I suspect that you and I should keep a closer eye on Targ. You never know when the opportunity to strike will come."

43

Tomb

THE GRAY WALL OF THE ANCIENT SPACECRAFT EXPANDED before Griffiths as he drifted toward it. It was a mountain of technology covered with intricate hieroglyphics, each skillfully carved into the plates of the craft itself. Much to Griffiths's astonishment, the picture forms of the ancient language resolved themselves into frames for smaller carvings as well . . . words within words . . . bringing those dead millennia suddenly to life under his reading eye. The smaller carvings had lost the raw edge that he had supposed they possessed. Dust particles had gravitated over the intervening centuries, softening the finer details of the surface.

Griffiths spun with a slow grace until, moments later, he gently bumped against the hull. The dust particles, suddenly loosened from the plates, erupted into an expanding cloud around him, quickly dissipating into the immensity of the milky white space. Griffiths rebounded from the gentle impact and began to drift slowly away from the hull. A moment of panic passed before he remembered to twist around and plant the boots of his vac suit against the hull. Their mystical technology engaged at once. Quite suddenly his inner orientation changed and he felt as if he were standing on a vast plane of metal.

He glanced above him. The *Venture Revenge* hung stationary above him about a hundred feet away. He could easily watch the crew as they moved about the deck and the rigging performing their various tasks. Behind him was a great tower which extended away from the hull and to which both the pirate ship artifact of Marren-kan and what he fervently hoped was Merinda's saucer were both moored. Many other towering structures of various shapes and purpose jutted from the hull into the distance. Each was beautifully formed, an expression of the soul of an artist who melded function and purpose with life and vision. To Griffiths, however, the hope expressed by the artist took on a sudden melancholy feeling. The future toward which those structures hoped was never attained. The vision they expressed had been a doomed one and had become a monument to their failure.

Griffiths suddenly felt the futility of the ancient tragedy that lay broken all around him. This was a tomb that had remained sacrosanct for thousands of years. A tomb which he was about to desecrate and rob.

The bile suddenly rose in his stomach at the thought.

Targ landed feet-first against the hull several feet from him. It was obvious that such a maneuver was not new to him. The dust again erupted around the new arrival and dissipated quickly. The tall man with the flowing white hair turned at once toward him.

"The dome shapes over there appear to be bay door hatches." Targ's voice was clear across the void. "We should be able to find ingress there. Let's go."

With cautious steps, they began traversing the uncertain terrain of the ornate hull. Each of their steps loosened small puffs of dust which spun away quickly into the vacuum about them.

"This is a graveyard, Targ," Griffiths said as he walked. "I don't much like the thought of disturbing the dead."

"You're assuming that the dead are resting," Targ replied.

He walked ahead of Griffiths, the expression on the taller man's face therefore unseen. "Sometimes the dead are restless and need some satisfaction. I see our mission as not so much waking the resting dead as bringing peace to ghosts whose past still haunts them."

"Just who is being haunted, Targ?"

The Prime did not answer as he had come to the edge of an immense, low dome protruding up from the hull and spanning at least fifty feet in its diameter. Targ spoke as he pointed down toward the edge of the dome. "This is one of the bay hatches. There must be some way of activating this hatch. Look at the writing—what do you see?"

"So that's why you brought me along," Griffiths shook his head.

"We all have our little problems," Targ answered coolly. "Mine is that I cannot read the ancient language of the Lost Empire. Yours is that your own mortality could be so easily extinguished by my very whim."

"Subtlety was never your strong point," Griffiths sighed.

"Only when necessary," Targ replied.

With a shrug, Griffiths began searching the edges of the dome. There were genealogies, family stories, testaments to Kendis-dai and the great crusade, all of which were scattered amid more mundane labels for conduits and warnings about the locations of pressure relief valves. It took him several minutes before anything caught his eye.

"Here's one that says it's a maintenance release for the hatch locks," Griffiths said, pointing at a small hatch next to the dome. "There's a warning not to activate it unless the pressure warning light has changed from blue to yellow."

Targ stepped quickly to where Griffiths stood. "What color is the light?"

Griffiths straightened. "No color at all. Geez, Targ, the ship's several thousand years old. It might not work."

Targ kneeled down next to the access panel and opened it. "The Settlement Ship in the Narrows had rested in a dense jungle the same length of time. It was subject to a great deal more wear than this ship and it seemed to fly quite well, I recall."

Targ reached down and grasped the handle.

"Wait!" Griffiths called out.

Too late. Targ pulled sharply up on the handle. Griffiths felt an impact through his feet as the clamps disengaged. The dome next to them began to shift. Dust erupted all around them, completely obscuring Griffiths's vision. He stood in the center of an undefined grayness. He held perfectly still, waiting for it all to pass. Hoping that it all would pass.

The gray fog began to thin. The dome still remained, only partially retracted. At Griffiths's feet had appeared a long arc of an opening, a space that was only about three feet wide at its widest point.

"It is enough," Targ declared. "After you."

"You can't be serious!" Griffiths squawked. "After me—to where?"

Targ looked up at Griffiths. "You want to find Merinda . . . I want to find Merinda. She is inside. I know it. I see it. I feel it. She is inside. If you want her . . . this is the way."

Griffiths glared at the Prime for a moment, then turned. Grabbing both sides of the opening, he pulled himself downward through the black maw of the partially open hatchway.

The whiteness of the space outside was instantly eclipsed by the dark interior of a huge spherical bay. Only the crescent of light coming through the opening dimly lit the space. It was now obvious to Griffiths why the hatch had only partially retracted. A spacecraft of some sort nearly filled the compartment. It was wedged between the retracting hatch and the inner bay wall. The ship had elegant, forward-swept wings and appeared to be carved out of gold, although it was difficult to tell in this light. The access umbilical was still attached to the side of the craft despite its having shifted loose of the overhead mounting bolts. Griffiths could see a set of windows next to where the access umbilical entered the ship itself. The portals were dark and the scant light entering the compartment did not illuminate anything beyond the sheen of the window's surface.

"The only exit appears to be through the umbilical," Griffiths said, more to himself than to Targ.

"Let's check the spacecraft then," Targ replied as he drifted into the dim compartment beside him. "If there's another way into the smaller ship, then we can pass through to the main ship."

Griffiths reached down and pulled the two spheres from either side of his belt. He had used them before to hover over the water in the Narrows but here they worked for him like a small propulsion unit. It took a little getting use to and he had to remind himself to move slowly. After a minor test or two, he managed to orient himself and began to slowly float across the cavernous bay.

There were dust particles drifting in the confined space of the sphere, brilliantly illuminated by the crescent of light cast by the partially open door. It added an eerie quality to the docking bay, as if the light accentuated the cold and desolate feeling of the gigantic artifact. The ship was dead so far as he could tell. No lights of any kind. No movement. His suit felt suddenly colder.

Griffiths drifted over the leading edge of the wing. The fuselage of the ship extended backward from where he now floated. A row of dark windows stared back at him. There was too much dust floating in the bay for him to see anything clearly through them. Then something caught his eye.

"There's a starboard-side hatch here," he called back to Targ. "It looks to be about even with where the umbilical connects."

"I'll be there in a moment."

"The mechanism is clearly labeled." Griffiths looked closer at the markings outlined on the smooth surface of the golden ship. "I think the release is right here. There's a small window in the door."

"Wait there and do nothing!"

Griffiths pressed his helmet closer to the window. "Hey! I can see the door on the other side! It looks shut but I think that's the way in. Targ?"

Silence.

"Targ? Where are you?"

No response.

"Targ! Come in, Targ! Targ are you there?"

Suddenly the Vestis Prime appeared next to Griffiths. "Will you shut up! I'm working on something here!"

"Sorry."

"Just open the door now, will you!"

"Fine!" Griffiths twisted back and planted his boots on the casing of the spacecraft. Bending over, he pressed his gloved fingers against a depression next to the hatch outline. A long handle sprang loose from the side of hull where it had previously lain flush. Griffiths pulled up on the handle as far as it would go, pressed it back down, and then pulled up again. He repeated the process several times until he felt a satisfying thunk under his feet. The hatch, once smooth with the hull, suddenly popped open by a few inches.

Targ grabbed the edges of the door and rotated it open on its hinges. Placing his feet against the floor, the Prime quickly walked across the width of the cabin to the opposite hatch.

"After you," Griffiths murmured with disdain. He pulled

himself through the hatchway, placed his feet against the floor so that they would have something to hang onto, and looked around.

It reminded him strongly of commercial airliners back home, he thought. There was a short, transverse compartment between the access hatches. He could see Targ working on the opposite door, which apparently had a different mechanism to get from the inside out than the one they had used on the outside to get in. There was a closed door to his right. The main cabin appeared to be through the open archway on his left.

Griffiths slowly moved into the compartment and turned to look into the cabin on his left. The interior of the cabin was very dark. Pillars of dim light were drawn by the windows, which marched down between the ranks of forward-facing seats. Seats which were filled with . . .

Griffiths's eyes went wide.

"Oh, my God! Oh, my God! Oh, my God!" he screamed, his feet pushing him violently back against the forward bulkhead.

Targ turned from his contemplation of the hatch mechanism. "Griffiths! What is it?"

"Oh, my God!" was all that Griffiths could say. His feet were still flailing against the carpeted flooring of the golden ship even though his back was against the wall.

Targ grabbed the man by the front of his vac suit. He was having a hard time holding onto him though Griffiths was barely aware of it. "Damn it, Griffiths! What is it!"

"They're still here!"

"What are you talking about?"

"They're . . . still . . . here!" Griffiths repeated, his wild eyes glancing back at the compartment. The adrenaline rush was still pounding through him, he was having a hard time getting control of himself. He had to look again, if only to confirm that he had not made a mistake . . . that he had not imagined it.

Targ turned as well. "By the Nine!" he murmured.

People stared back at them.

Row after row of seats, lit only dimly from the filtered light through the starboard–side windows, were filled with passengers over three thousand years dead. They sat perfectly preserved in the darkness. Men sat with their hands patiently folded in their laps. Women sat smiling with their hands clasped around their children's hands. Each stared back at them in perfect stillness.

They were smiling.

Griffiths and Targ held perfectly still for what seemed like an eternity. Targ glanced down at the arm of his vac suit. The indicator was black. Pure vacuum. Yet here these people sat, color still in their cheeks as though they should simply stand up and walk out of the cabin.

At last, Targ released Griffiths, and, straightening up, took a step toward the aft cabin. Griffiths held his breath.

Targ leaned forward toward one of the nearest seats where a young woman with bright eyes and exquisite features sat calmly facing forward. A hint of a smile played on her full lips. She looked as though she were about to speak. She wore a white tunic with a short skirt—an outfit which seemed to be common between both the men and the women, so far as Griffiths could see in the dimness of the compartment. Her shapely legs were cocked casually under her seat.

"Are they alive?" Griffiths asked in a whisper, as though the sound of his words might break some mystic sleep.

"In a vacuum?" Targ turned his head toward the Earther and scoffed. "You must be mad."

Griffiths shuddered. "Just give me a minute and we'll see."

Targ turned back to examine the woman more closely. "She's perfect. I wonder why . . ."

Targ shifted his footing slightly, the knee of his vac suit brushing slightly against the woman's own knee.

Griffiths wanted to look away but somehow could not force himself to do so.

The flesh over the woman's patella crumbled away as dust from the impact, drifting away in the weightlessness of the cabin. The insignificant force of Targ's brush cascaded as the knee bones separated. Her tibia pressed downward, the supple flesh of her calf scattering over her slippered feet. The woman's femur drifted backward, scattering the flesh of the thigh across her skirt.

"By the Nine!" Targ exclaimed in horror as he stepped back.

The flesh scattered from her leg like dried leaves in a gentle, unseen wind. The femur rebounded against the pelvis bones, flipping upward, end over end, until it brushed her beautiful face. Her left cheek vanished into powder as the large leg bone continued upward. Her hair parted with the scalp, drifting like seaweed suddenly freed as the skull beneath it separated into its component pieces. The flesh of the right side of her face drifted away from the collapsing skull in a single piece, a horrible mask floating directly toward Griffiths.

Griffiths couldn't stop watching.

Suddenly Targ's fist smashed through the ghastly face, shattering it into dust.

Griffiths suddenly realized he was holding his breath. "We've got to get out of here!"

Targ quickly moved closer to Griffiths until the clear bubble of his vac suit was pressed against Griffiths's own, filling his vision and blocking out the grizzly scene beyond. "Think, Griffiths! Merinda's in there! Are you going to leave her in the middle of this?"

"We . . . we don't know she's in there," Griffiths stammered. "She might not be in here at all! She might still be in her ship! That might not even be her ship!"

"It's hers, all right." Targ spoke in clear, even tones. "She beat us here and now she's inside, here among the dead. We've got to find her, don't we, Griffiths?"

Griffiths stopped and thought for a moment, gathering his composure. "Yes," he said, nodding. "We've got to find her."

"You've got to open this door," Targ said to him, an oiled edge of menace in his tone.

Griffiths looked into Targ's eyes. He knew that the vaunted Prime didn't at this point give a damn whether he found Merinda or not.

Jeremy pushed off from Targ and, spinning in the weightlessness, examined the still-closed port-side door. "What is it that you are looking for among the dead, Targ," he said, as he began working the release handle. "What drives a man who has all the power of the galaxy at his command to throw it all away on a cursed artifact?"

"My reasons are my own," Targ said simply. "Is there pressure on the other side of that door?"

"Now how the hell am I supposed to know that?" Griffiths was sweating now both out of fear and his exertions with the door. "It's dark through the porthole. I can't see a thing, let alone tell you what the weather is like!"

The door shifted suddenly away from the outer frame.

"Well, since I wasn't blown out the other door, I guess there's no atmosphere in the lock either," Griffiths said, shaking his head to clear the sweat from his eyes. "What are you doing now?"

Targ had closed his eyes, presenting the palms of both hands in front of his face. He then raised both arms high above his head and made a sweeping motion, first clockwise, then counter-clockwise, across this body. Both hands suddenly clapped together and, when they parted, a point of dazzling light hovered just in front of Targ's chest, illuminating the area. Griffiths studiously avoided looking into the compartment beyond Targ.

"Open the door," Targ said quietly.

Griffiths pulled back on the door. It easily rotated backward and swung out of the way, exposing the access umbilical.

"Damn!" Griffiths shouted.

The dead blocked the entire corridor leading to the interior of the ship. They stood as though waiting to board, sometimes singly and sometimes in pairs. Their ranks stretched back into the darkness of the walkway.

Targ raised his hand. The point of light he had created rose in response, casting shifting shadows across the faces that stood before them. Targ pointed and the light flew past the silent men and women, who quickly became grotesque silhouettes as the light receded down the access corridor. Griffiths was shaking uncontrollably at the sight.

"The far door appears to be open," Targ said with satisfaction. "We can enter here."

"You are insane," Griffiths said through chattering teeth. "Enter here? How?"

Targ pressed Griffiths back against the bulkhead. The first man standing in line appeared to be holding a large luggage bag in his hand. Targ reached forward and, grasping both sides of the case, pulled it toward him. The man's arm disintegrated. Targ braced his feet on either side of the doorway. He raised the case over his head, the bones of the dead man's hand still entangled in the handle, and threw it squarely down the corridor.

The first man was hit squarely in the chest by his own heavy luggage, exploding into dried leaves, shattered bones, and strands of hair and cloth. The careening baggage continued to spin down the umbilical, barely slowed in its path of terrible destruction by the bodies interposed in its path. A couple locked in earnest conversation disintegrated, their hands still clasped together, suddenly free and drifting. An overweight woman broke in two, her massive arms flailing in the air. A noble-looking man vanished into dust. One by one, the force of Targ's throw shattered their tranquil deaths.

"That is how," Targ said. Then he grabbed Griffiths and shoved him into the bone-strewn access umbilical.

IT WAS A DESCENT INTO HELL THAT GRIFFITHS WAS SURE WAS never going to end. The corridor had indeed opened onto a departure or staging area of some kind. Just as before, there were the ancient dead standing or, depending upon your viewpoint, floating in the darkness. The stark illumination from Targ's floating light brought the figures out of the blackness for the first time in three millennia, if Griffiths understood the dating correctly. The shifting light caused the shadows falling across the figures to move, playing tricks with his eyes and causing him to glance nervously at the dead forms from time to time. There was no getting past the haunting visages of these ancient dead frozen in these tableaux.

"Griffiths," Targ had said, "what do you make of this?"

Griffiths turned in his vac suit. Just when you think things can't get worse, he thought to himself, they always do.

There, on the floor under the harsh point of light, lay a man facing the ceiling. There was a huge stain in the carpet beneath him. His lips were pulled back in a terrible grimace of pain. Standing astride him was a man in some sort of uniform, a crimson version of the tunic-and-skirt style that seemed to be prevalent among the dead. In his hand he held an ornate, gleaming object of curved metal that appeared to be a weapon. The uniformed man's head was drawn back in frozen, hideous laughter.

"My God," Griffiths exclaimed. "That's terrible!"

"Yes," Targ said distractedly. "But notice the people situated all around them."

"What about them?"

"Don't you see," Targ said. "They are taking no notice of the scene. It's as though this terrible violence has taken place right at their feet and they didn't even stop in their conversations to take a casual look at what has happened. Intriguing."

Then Targ turned and moved out of the room. As his light receded with him, Griffiths hurried to keep up. It was all he could do to avoid touching the dead around him and maintain the determined pace that Targ was setting—a pace that led deeper and deeper into the bowels of the ancient interstellar coffin.

Hideous as the scene in the waiting room had been, the sights they saw as they descended became increasingly strange and grotesque. Time lost its meaning, and Griffiths soon could not seem to recall a blessed time when he was not walking carefully among the shockingly revolting and insane. The naked woman seeming to sleep on a dining platter in the center of a crowded mess hall as officers lined up with plates and long knives. The children who formed a circle holding hands in a play area, laughing around the figures of two smiling adults who were hanging by their necks from a cable.

"Where are we going," Griffiths asked at last.

"We follow the vision," Targ replied.

"The vision? Is that some sort of spell or whammy that you've cast?"

"Yes," Targ replied. "I have called on the mystic forces to give me the Sight. It guides me towards the form that I seek. It gives me direction and distance. I see it before me even now—as I have always seen it, even without the magic and the spells. Its form has haunted me for these many decades.

Now I shall look upon it once more . . . and I shall have peace at last."

The point of light drifted before them as they moved across a bridge through a black space of unknown and unknowable dimension. On the other side they came to a set of doors.

Targ reached forward with his gloved hand. His fingers spread as he gently touched the door.

"It is on the other side," he said, murmuring to himself. "This is the place of which I have dreamed and loathed since my youth. This is where I shall find the end of the tale. This is where I discharge my final duty."

Griffiths watched him carefully. "Why are you here, Targ of Gandri?"

The tall man turned his white-haired head to look at Griffiths. It was as though he did not recognize the Earther. "I was the last one," he said simply, though he seemed to be talking to someone beyond Griffiths. "It was up to me to bury the dead. But the dead wouldn't stay buried, the tale was unfinished, and the song had no end. The songs of the dead, they drifted through my mind each night and each day, like a siren to my soul. It tempts me . . . it torments me. It drives me and gives me strength but, oh, how I long for peace. How I long for the song to end and the book of the tale to be closed!"

He turned again to the door, rage building in his voice. "It ends here. At last, it ends here!"

With an animal yell, Targ pushed on the great doors. They separated before him.

The circular hall was filled with dancers, all permanently affixed in their positions, their finest and most ornate costumes draped about them. Pillars had been placed around the outer promenade, guards in ornate armor standing with their long sabers held to the ready across their chests. Great cloaks were affixed to their armor plates, their faces hidden by massive hoods that cast deep shadows across their helmets. On the far side of the rotunda, a massive throne sat between the pillars, a lone figure slumped among its cushions.

Targ was animated. "Look there, Griffiths!"

Griffiths saw a scaled vac suit of greenish-brown lying on the floor. It was a mammoth suit, however, and appeared to have four arms and a massive, horned helmet.

"A Gorgon!" Targ said, nearly giddy. "Look there's another . . . and another!" Targ moved quickly across the floor, his hasty motions disturbing several of the dancers in their poses, shattering their arms and destroying the illusion of the tranquil scene. "We are there, Griffiths! We have come to the place where . . ."

Suddenly Targ stopped.

Griffiths couldn't see what the Prime was looking at and moved slightly to one side to try to get a clearer view. It was no use with the various dead couples between them. He watched as Targ bent over and then stood, holding a small crystal globe in his hand. Targ's light shined down on him from above.

"Oh, Father," Targ said softly.

Griffiths blinked, unsure for a moment of what he had seen. Suddenly he knew that it had not been an illusion.

"Targ!" he called out.

Targ looked up.

Next to the throne, one of the guards was moving. In a single motion, the guard reached down to the figure on the throne and picked up a large, ornate sword.

"The Nightsword," Targ breathed, as he turned to face their foe.

The hood fell away from the clear helmet of the ancient vac suit.

It was Merinda.

44

The Edge

"IT'S GOOD TO SEE YOU AGAIN, GRIFFITHS," MERINDA SAID, though her steel gaze never left Targ for a moment.

"Nice to see you, too," Griffiths replied with relief, "though I'm getting a little weary of grieving over your death."

"The day is yet young," Merinda replied.

"I, for one, agree with you," Targ said casually, a scowl on his face. "I will not insult you by saying that this is a pleasant surprise, inasmuch as your presence is neither pleasant nor surprising. Just what do you intend to do with that thing?"

"I intend to borrow it just long enough to see that you stay, Targ," Merinda said through the globe of her vac suit. The sword was set menacingly before her. Though the blade was wide and appeared heavy, she held it with a single hand, balanced and deft. Her left hand was raised behind her for balance. "We three—pardon me, four, if we count our host there on the throne—are the only ones who know the exact location of the Nightsword and I intend to keep it that way."

"You've . . . borrowed it?" Targ's eyebrows arched in disbelief.

"With the owner's permission," Merinda replied, nodding her head back toward the throne.

"Lokan!" Targ scoffed. He began to move toward Merinda with deliberate footsteps. "You asked that old corpse if you could borrow the Nightsword and he just let you have it? 'Pardon me, Lokan the Terrible, but would that happen to be the most powerful device in the known universe in your hand? Would you mind if I just destroyed a few worlds with it since you're dead and won't be needing it for any time soon?' "

"He's not dead, Targ," Griffiths said from the side of the hall.

The Prime stopped walking toward Merinda. "That corpse is over three millennia old, Captain."

"No, Targ," Merinda countered, taking two quick steps back and settling in her stance between the Prime and the throne. "Lokan lives, here on the throne before you."

"Impossible!"

"No, not impossible," Griffiths said, trying to move carefully into the room so as not to disturb the dancing dead around his vac suit. "Anything is possible with the Nightsword. He who wields it changes the nature of reality around them. That's what the Nightsword is—a selective causality device. Any reality desired by the possessor of that device simply happens. That's how Kendis-dai established the first empire. For a vast interstellar empire to function efficiently, it needs a cohesive, single reality. Interstellar shipping, trade, communication—all of these things become vastly easier when you don't have to worry about multiple quantum zones of reality. Kendis-dai used the Nightsword to force his empire into one, massive quantum zone. Only something went wrong in the courts of Kendis-dai. The great emperor was gone and Lokan gained control of the Nightsword in his blind quest to rescue Shauna-kir and rule in the Emperor's stead." Griffiths looked over at the shriveled form on the throne. "He wanted to live forever."

"Lokan's body is but a shell—that is true," Merinda said clearly through the vacuum. "His mind is mad beyond all comprehension from the loneliness he has suffered from here. Still, he lives, nevertheless. For thousands of years he has been trapped by his own desire for immortality. It was his driving desire, his obsession. To achieve it he stripped himself of every moral foundation that gave his life meaning in the first place. Now he lives on, but without purpose or a mind to even comprehend more than his own survival."

"A sad tale, indeed, from both of you," Targ replied. "But what is such a tale to me?"

"Targ, leave this place," Merinda replied with passion. "It's your tale, too. The obsession; the abandonment of values; the wake of destruction. This is your story as surely as it was Lokan's. You've found your father's fate . . ."

"No!" Targ said through clenched teeth.

". . . Let the dead rest with our memories . . ."

"No!" Targ said louder, shaking his head back and forth as though the act would keep the truth from falling on his ears.

". . . Let go of your past, Targ, and leave us here!"

"NO!" Targ screamed. He reached out for the saber of an officer standing nearby, pulling the sword from the corpse's shattering hand. He cut downward quickly toward Merinda, with a powerful stroke. Merinda barely had time to counter with her block, the power and ferocity of his attack pressing her back in her stance. Several quick, instinctive blows followed in a blur of motion: arcing swings toward her head and torso. Merinda blocked and deflected each blow with difficulty, backing up the platform steps before the throne.

Griffiths turned about him, frantically looking for something he could use as a weapon. His eye fell upon one of the guards lining the perimeter of the room. He turned toward it, desperately trying to keep the soles of his vac suit boots connecting with the floor on each step. He knew that if they both left the floor at the same time he would be weightless and no good to either Merinda or himself. It made his progress toward the guard agonizingly slow. He moved with nightmare slowness in a nightmare world. At last he reached the corpse, grabbed the hilt of the sword and shook it loose from the disintegrating grip of the ancient guardian. A sword fight in vacuum suits? he thought as he turned back to face Merinda and Targ. Am I crazy?

Suddenly, Merinda countered Targ's attack with a series of her own. Targ stepped back from the onslaught. Merinda pressed her advantage and thrust the Nightsword toward Targ's chest. Targ's own blade spun in a clearing move that deflected the blow, but the point of the sword sliced into the left arm of Targ's vac suit.

Atmosphere gushed into a crystal cloud from the tear for a moment before the suit sealed itself. Targ staggered backward, his sword hand instinctively reaching for the wound which, Griffiths did not doubt, was bleeding within the suit. Targ looked up in astonishment.

Griffiths began circling the hall, moving from pillar to pillar. He knew he would only have one chance at this. He had no hope of defeating Targ in a stand-up fight. It was murder him or be murdered and he didn't much like the sound of it either way.

"It must end here, Targ," Merinda panted. "It must end with us."

"In my hands the Nightsword would work miracles," Targ growled.

"In your hands it would destroy you just as it destroyed Lokan," she replied.

Targ looked suddenly at her, realization dawning in his eyes. "But not in yours?"

"What do you mean?" she asked, taking a step back, preparing, wary.

"You hold the Nightsword, Merinda," Targ said, his own sword coming to the ready once more. "The greatest and most powerful weapon known in all time, yet you mark my shoulder with it as though you were a beginning fencer!"

Targ swung his own sword in a quick combination. Merinda parried each quickly, backing with each blow, trying to find some room.

"You can't use it can you?" Targ said, smiling.

"I am using it," Merinda cried out. "You'll die by it!" She cleared with a sweeping arc, then pressed her own withering attack. Targ gave no ground, however, meeting her blow for blow.

"Using it? Then why am I not dead already?" Targ sneered. "Why haven't you used its magnificent and omnipotent powers to rob me of my breath, or turn me into a bird or a fish, or simply vanish the very reality of my existence?"

Targ lunged suddenly. Merinda cleared as she stepped back but her foot caught on the level behind her. The distraction was enough. Targ recovered, advanced, and sliced his own blade into the thigh of her suit.

Griffiths gritted his teeth. Targ's back was between him and Merinda but he could still see clearly. I'm almost there, Merinda, he told himself. Just hang on for a few more seconds.

Merinda dropped in pain to her knee as the short explosion of gas crystallized before the suit sealed. She screamed savagely, blocking Targ's attack as she knelt, spun, and regained her footing, though now with less assurance.

"You haven't used the powers of the Nightsword because you can't," Targ taunted.

Merinda held the sword again at the ready. The throne was directly behind her. Her eye caught Griffiths's in a single glance. Targ noticed it at once and began to turn.

Now! Griffiths thought and began moving as quickly as he could, heedless of the dead couples disintegrating in his path. He raised his sword, beginning his swing. Merinda was raising her own sword when a sudden look of terror crossed her face as she looked beyond Targ and Griffiths both.

Incredible pain shot through both of Griffiths's calves and up through his thighs. He felt himself lose control of his legs as they collapsed under him. Both his feet lifted free of the deck plates. He careened weightless, bowling through the corpses in the hall and scattering them into dust. As he rotated around, he saw what had so startled Merinda.

Three of the dead guards had reached for their ornate sidearm weapons and drawn them. Others around the hall were attempting to do the same.

The dead were moving.

Griffiths slammed painfully against the far wall. He twisted around quickly as he rebounded, grasping one of the pillars, and desperately oriented himself to find Merinda.

Targ had taken the advantage. In a deft move he had disarmed Merinda. His previous weapon spun lazily through the space above them. Now he held the Nightsword in his own hand, its blade edge held threateningly across the bottom of Merinda's head bubble. He held her, pulling her backward up the steps.

"I've been blind!" Targ said as Merinda struggled in vain against his grip. His voice was hoarse and bordering on hysterical. "I couldn't use the Mantle of Kendis-dai because it was bonded to Griffiths. The other artifacts must be bonded to their owners as well. Interesting safety feature, wouldn't you agree? So long as the owner lives then his own weapon can never be used against him. All this time the voices were calling me! All this time I heard my father reaching out to me and begging me to come and discover his fate and it wasn't him at all, was it? Was it!"

"Your father is dead!" Merinda cried out.

"Yes, he is dead, isn't he!" Targ yelled at her. "He died right here with his precious stolen director globe and his Gorgon captors. They killed him right here because he couldn't give them what they wanted. But we're going to change all that, Merinda, you and I! We're going to change all that because we've been invited here!"

Targ began dragging Merinda backward toward the throne. The guards around the hall raised their hand weapons. Griffiths watched helplessly from his twisting perch, his legs still without feeling or strength.

"No, damn you, Lokan!" Targ screamed. "Some part of you wants release! You'll fight me if you can, but some part of you called me here!"

The guards fired, blue bolts ripping from their weapons. The shock of the recoil shattered each of their arms, driving the weapons through their shoulders even as their hands continued to fire bolts into the ceiling.

Two of the bolts blasted into Merinda. She cried out with the impact, her body suddenly going limp as Targ held her as a shield.

The dancers in the hall, some of them only fragments of their former selves, began wheeling across the floor.

Targ released the lifeless Merinda and turned to the throne as more bolts lanced around him. There sat Lokan, his face withered as driftwood, his eye sockets dry and glazed. His head was pulled back and his mouth was drawn open into a gaping maw.

"Let go!" Targ screamed as he drew the Nightsword around to strike. "I've got to atone! I've got to right what I've done! Let go, damn you!"

With that, Targ swung, severing the head of Lokan. Black ichor gushed from the wound, drifting in thick globules as the head drifted upward, its flow soon stopping.

The dancers lost all cohesion, their bones, flesh, hair, and cartilage spinning into dust. So, too, did the guards vanish into their elements.

Merinda drifted to the floor, as did Griffiths. Gravity was reestablishing itself in the hall. Griffiths happened to glance at his right arm. By the indicator, it would seem that atmosphere was returning as well.

All by the will of Targ of Gandri—bonded master of the Nightsword.

45

Betrayal

GRIFFITHS BEGAN PULLING HIMSELF ACROSS THE FLOOR. The feeling was beginning to return to his legs—a fact that he deeply regretted. The pain was excruciating although he sensed that there was not a great deal of actual damage. Rather, it occurred to him, it was as though the circulation had been cut off for some time and the blood was suddenly returning. Every nerve ending seemed to be firing at the same time—an itching, maddening pain that threatened to overwhelm him.

Still, lying on the floor as he now was, he reached again over his head, planted his hand, and dragged himself forward a few more feet across the ancient floor.

Merinda lay near the center of the rotunda, facedown and still. Her robe had nearly covered her where she came to rest. He couldn't see her face.

He had to reach her. He extended his other arm. He pulled. His vac suit scraped the stone tiles under him as it slid.

Griffiths glanced toward the throne. Lokan was dead at last. Targ was raising the Nightsword over his head in triumph, the blade smeared with black ichor. As Griffiths watched, the room about them began to change. The pillars remained but beyond them existed different shapes, places, vistas, and horizons. The place became an auditorium, then suddenly was a mountaintop looking across the tops of clouds at a three-mooned sky. The mountaintop vanished, replaced by a huge office suite. Everything shifted as Targ struggled to gain control of the device he had just won.

Griffiths reached above his head and pulled himself a few feet closer to Merinda.

The rapid pace of their shifting surroundings was beginning to slow. They were not just projections or images of the places. Somehow, Griffiths sensed, they were those places in every sense of the concept. Targ's control was nearly complete. There was little time left. As soon as Targ was sure of his power, the end would come, he was sure of it.

He touched Merinda and pulled himself up next to her. The feeling in his legs had returned with a vengeance. He could sit, he discovered, with considerable pain. He reached across the woman and turned her over carefully to cradle her in his arms.

Beyond the pressure bubble of her vac suit, Griffiths could see that Merinda's honey-colored hair had fallen across her eyes.

"Merinda." He spoke, shaking her slightly.

The dark eyes opened with a start.

Griffiths smiled down at her. "Good morning, this is your wake-up call."

Pain suddenly filled her eyes.

"Where are you hurt?" Griffiths's face filled with concern. "What's wrong?"

Her voice was a whisper through the vac suit bubbles. "Oh, Griffiths," she said, tears coming to her eyes. "I'm so sorry. I've failed."

"Failed? You? What a stupid thing to say!" Griffiths spoke

as comfortingly as he knew how. He still didn't know if she were badly injured.

"I had to stop him, you understand," she said earnestly. To Griffiths, it felt like a desperate confession. "Worlds, lives, civilizations . . . the Nightsword destroyed them all once and would destroy them again. You were the only one who knew the way . . . the only key who could unlock its location. Had to bury the key . . . bury the key . . ."

"You threatened to kill me once," Griffiths said softly to her. "It might have been a better solution."

Merinda smiled weakly.

"Why didn't you kill me, Merinda?"

Merinda looked to her right. Griffiths followed the line of her gaze.

Targ had turned to face them from the throne.

As they watched, the pillared room vanished. In its place appeared the central control chamber of the ancient Settlement Ship from the Narrows. They found themselves lying amid the dust of the dead once more as Targ stepped down from the command platform.

"How very touching," he said coldly. " 'Why didn't you kill me?' the young warrior cries. She didn't kill you for the same reason I didn't kill you: so long as you lived no other could sit upon the Mantle of Kendis-dai and discover what you discovered. Now, however, I have the Nightsword and your life has just become superfluous. Indeed, killing you now releases the Mantle from your control. My forces have the planet quarantined as it is."

"Your forces, Targ?" Griffiths replied. "I thought the Centirion were the Omnet's forces."

"A technicality which I shall, with the Nightsword's help, soon rectify," Targ replied as he gazed admiringly on the device. "The Omnet shall be truly mine. No more troublesome Dictorae requiring each policy to be discussed. No more politics. You are looking at a new dawn of enlightenment: an age of peace and unprecedented prosperity for the galaxy. No more Order of the Future Faith. No more rebellion. No more petty and bloody interstellar war. The galaxy has been tearing itself apart since the Shattering of Suns and things haven't been improving. I can fix all that. All of the broken past . . . I can fix it."

"That's what all of this is about, isn't it, Targ," Merinda said, her voice shuddering. "For all your words and all your high ideas, all this is really about is fixing your own past."

"Shut up, Merinda," Targ said menacingly. "You're wrong about me."

"Am I?" Merinda countered, struggling to sit up without success. "I am a Vestis Inquisitas, one of the best in the greater galaxy. As a member of the Inquisition it is my task to go beyond the facts and find the truth. Only those who know the truth may manipulate it—or at least so you told me. Truth is our weapon."

Griffiths looked suddenly about them. Shadows had passed across one of the chamber's walls. "Something is coming, Targ!"

"You know nothing of the truth, Neskat." Targ laughed nervously.

Merinda continued to speak directly at the Prime, "The truth is, Vestis Prime, that you don't give a damn about the galaxy or its people. This isn't a quest for noble dominion—it isn't even a quest for power. The only destiny you've come to change is your own."

Targ stood silent.

Merinda glanced around at their surroundings. "So, tell me, L'Zari Targ, just where are we? When are we? What reality have we come here to change?"

Targ's jaw muscles worked for a moment as he struggled for control of himself. "You can't spoil it! You can't! I won't let you!"

"It's my job to ask questions, Targ . . . You taught me that," Merinda said evenly, her voice gaining strength. "So just who is it that's approaching, Targ? Is it the Gorgons, coming once again as they did forty-three years ago? Will Marren-kan, somehow alive and breathing, step through those doors once more? You're not the brash youth you were back then, are you, L'Zari? Now you're a grown man—more than that, you are a great and powerful sorcerer."

"Shut up!" Targ raged, moving toward them threateningly.

"Your father's very real remains lay not ten feet from where you stand, Targ! He is dead!"

"NO!"

"Dead, Targ! Dead as the past! That's the end of your story, Targ! That's where your duty stopped! Your father cannot speak to you—you cannot gain the peace you seek!"

"No, damn you!" Targ screamed, grasping the hilt with both hands and raising the sword above them to strike. "You're wrong!"

Griffiths raised his arm protectively between the sword and Merinda, some part of his mind realizing that the gesture was foolishly inadequate.

Targ twisted slightly back to bring power behind his blow.

"L'Zari?" came a deep voice from behind Griffiths.

Targ froze, the sword cocked high behind his shoulders ready to strike.

"L'Zari? Is that you, lad?" the voice spoke once more.

Targ's head jerked up. He began shaking visibly.

Griffiths turned quickly to get a look at whoever was speaking. There, behind where Griffiths sat, standing amid the dust, was a strong man with a graying beard and long, iron hair. His open shirt was yellowed and ancient but there was a brightness in his eyes.

"Well, lad, I see you've grown right well, now!" The man

spoke robustly. "What's troubling you? Don't you recognize an old shipmate?"

"Sir?" Targ whispered in a quavering voice.

"Sir, is it? I asked you never to call me that, did I not?" the man said good-naturedly. "By the Nine Gods of Kel, can't you get that through your skull in all this time? And is there some point to raising that weapon on me, boy?"

"Yes, er, no . . . Kip." Targ smiled, lowering his sword. "I've come for you, to save you."

The man laughed heartily. "A long way, indeed, boy! Forty-three years is a long course! I'd say I've come a good deal further, however, seeing as I'm dead!"

Targ's smile fell slightly. "No! No . . . you don't understand! Here you are alive! Here I can change what happened. You don't have to die!"

"Now, lad, whoever put such a fool notion into your head," Kip said. "You were here, Boy-Out-of-Nowhere! They gullied me right before your eyes, they did! Right properly done, too, right after you gave them the map."

"No . . . no, you've got it wrong, Father," Targ said, water brimming in his eyes. "I never gave them the map! You said so long as we kept the map everything would be all right!"

"Son," Kip said, looking squarely up at the tall, white-haired man standing before him. "You've lied to yourself all these years. Think, lad. Think back."

Targ blinked through the tears spilling over his eyes. "You said, 'Give me the map.' I gave it to you. Then you bargained with the Marren-kan . . . He took you away . . ."

"No, lad," Kip said. "That's a lie. That's a lie you've been telling again and again since your mother's ships came and rescued you from that terrible place. Think, lad, think . . ."

Suddenly, off to Griffiths's left, a youth appeared in the chamber. He was speaking to a younger version of Kip-lei

Targ. Beyond them stood several hideous creatures that Griffiths took to be the dreaded Gorgons he had heard so much about. *"Father, no! There's got to be something we can do . . ."*

"The crew is dead already, son—dead if they're lucky. Gorgons are really amazing healers, lad. They know more about medicine than any human I've ever met does . . ."

Targ turned around, horror and pain in his face as the scene—all too real—played out around them. The young vision of Kip-lei continued. *". . . They took Old Phin's breath just before they found me. I was their last man until we discovered you about. I'd barter for our lives, boy, but there's nothing I can offer . . ."*

"Wait! Yes, there is! I found a map!"

"What, lad?"

"I found a map—a Lost Empire map. It shows the passage to the core."

"Give it to me, lad! Quick! I've the devil to deal with!" The boy quickly pulled the folded map from his case and showed it to his father. Kip winked at his son. *"Don't you be showing that to anyone, boy. It's our ticket home."* Kip pushed the map back into the case. Standing, he then turned toward the Gorgon. *"Captain, would you be interested in a proposition?"*

"The only proposition I'll have of you now is the squeal of your own blood in your throat!" Marren-kan spit the words, drawing his twin sabers from both scabbards and thundering toward the human, his tail flailing in anticipation. *"You've declared your last man. It's time to put an end to your thieving words!"*

The sabers crossed each other, advancing on Kip's neck.

"Not even for the treasure of Lokan?" the young L'Zari suddenly yelled, panicked. *"Not even for the passage to the Nightsword?"*

The Gorgon stopped. L'Zari waited. He could hear the faint cold sound of steel rubbing against steel.

"Your deal?" the towering pirate intoned, speaking to the lad.

The razor edges of both swords hovered only centimeters away from Kip's neck. *"No, lad! Don't do it!"*

"No!" the elder Targ cried out from across the chamber. "Don't do it!"

"This man's life for the passage to untold wealth and power," the young L'Zari said. *"His life for the secrets of the core."*

The steel slid backward slightly, away from the old spacer's throat. *"No! I want to taste his blood . . . And just where are these secrets kept?"*

"Here," the young L'Zari said, frantically searching for the pouch. *"Here . . . here's the map! You can have it! Now, please, let my father go!"*

The Gorgon laughed. It was a hideous sound: deep and rumbling yet spiced with the squeal of nails on slate. In moments the huge beast was nearly in hysterics, his weapons lowered casually to his side while his third arm reached out and grasped Kip's shoulder, seemingly for support.

"You'll give me the map to the greatest treasure of all time in exchange for this worthless human's life?" the Gorgon brayed. *"That is the full extend of your bargaining?"*

The young L'Zari smiled hopefully. *"Yes."*

"Fool!" laughed Marren-kan.

The Gorgon chief suddenly thrust upward with his swords, holding his target still with his third hand. Both blades passed straight through the old spacer's body under the rib cage. The strength of the blow carried the sabers cleanly through up to the hilts, the blades themselves undeterred by the bones and spine they passed through. The movement continued upward, the Gorgon's laugh turning suddenly into a horrendous battle cry of rage. Kip's body, his face frozen in a mixture of surprise, pain, and horror, was lifted clear of the ground, impaled on the blades.

The young L'Zari screamed and rushed forward but the second Gorgon was too quick. A single blow brought a merciful blackness crashing down on his conscious mind.

The scene suddenly vanished with a cry from Targ. Griffiths turned around to see the Prime on his knees, weeping uncontrollably.

Kip stepped forward, passing where Griffiths and Merinda lay, and resting his hand on Targ's shoulder. "Now, stop that, lad! It weren't your fault!"

"It was my fault," Targ said haltingly. "I shouldn't have tried to bargain with him. I should have trusted you."

"It were no good, boy. He was set on killing me anyway. It would have made no difference," Kip said. "It were good of you to try, lad. No one else ever tried to save my life the way you did."

Targ, his eyes bleary and red, stood up, nearly a head taller than the man before him. "Father?"

"Aye, lad?" The old man looked up into Targ's face.

"I've found it for you," Targ said through his tears, holding out the Nightsword. "I've found the treasure."

"Aye, that you did, lad," the old man said with a smile. "And right proud of you it is that I am of that. You're a good lad, L'Zari."

Kip opened his arms to his son.

Targ smiled, tears streaming down his cheeks. Reaching out, he folded his arms around his father. They embraced warmly.

There was a puff of suddenly crystallizing gas.

Griffiths pulled Merinda back instinctively.

The point of a blade rammed its way out through the old man's back. Targ, still embracing his father, arched backward in pain and surprise.

The Nightsword spun out of Targ's hand.

In that instant, the chamber reverted once more to

Lokan's throne room. The pillars rematerialized, Lokan's body returned. Gravity evaporated as Griffiths and Merinda, both still partially paralyzed, drifted up from the floor.

Kip's body collapsed into bones and dust under Targ's embrace. The Prime floated suddenly free of the floor, the soles of his vac suit lifted by the force of the blow from behind. As Targ's body drifted higher and higher, impaled on the sword, Griffiths could see at last the source of the attack.

There, behind Targ, floated Captain Evon Flynn with both hands still upon his cutlass's hilt.

The Nightsword turned slowly end over end away from Targ.

"Griffiths," Merinda yelled as she and Griffiths drifted way from the floor. "Get the Nightsword!"

"I can't reach it," Griffiths replied in frustration. "It's passing us!"

"Use the belt!"

"What?"

"Your levitation belt," Merinda said desperately.

Damn, he thought, why didn't I remember that earlier instead of crawling across the floor! He reached down and pulled the control globes from the buckle. He oriented himself quickly, thrust quickly toward the leisurely turning sword . . .

. . . and ran directly into the chest plate of Kheoghi the minotaur. The brutish pirate arrested Griffiths at once and held him above him.

Kheoghi held the Nightsword pointing directly at Griffiths's throat.

"You'll be releasing them thar control globes at once, mate," the minotaur growled, "else I'll be forced to pop your pretty bubble."

Griffiths let go of the levitation control globes. They drifted off into the chamber as the power in the belt stopped. Kheoghi pulled Griffiths around, holding him in front of him tightly with the Nightsword fixed across the throat of his vac suit bubble.

Flynn still held the hilt of his sword, now buried up to the guard in Targ's back. Targ struggled but Flynn held the sword firmly, adding his own twists to the hilt from time to time.

"Die, Targ, you bastard!" Flynn yelled. "Now it's my time! Here's the balance on the ledger, Targ!"

The vac suit suspended above Flynn struggled a few moments more and then stopped moving. At last, Flynn released the cutlass hilt, setting the body of Targ to drift with the blade still passing through him, the vac suit sealed to the metal of the blade. Griffiths could see brilliant red liquid beginning to stain the interior of the Targ's vac suit helmet.

Griffiths looked away.

"Oh, poor spacer," Flynn mocked. "A bit too squeamish for the work, are we now, Master Griffiths?"

"It's not in my line," Griffiths replied.

"No, I suppose not," Flynn sniffed. "But I've seen worse things done by this same man in the name of honor and justice. He's dead. I'm not. I have the prize and he does not. That's all that matters in the end."

Vac-suited snake-women drifted toward Flynn, holding Merinda between them.

"They'll hunt you," Merinda said. "They'll hunt you and they'll find you. There isn't a government among the stars that the Omnet won't either buy or coerce into giving you over."

"Only if they find out," Flynn smiled. "Which, unfortunately, means that there's only going to be one side of this story told—my side."

"So we die?" Griffiths said.

"No," Merinda said suddenly.

"Really?" Flynn said with feigned astonishment. "And what ever makes you think so?"

"Because Kheoghi wouldn't put up with it," Merinda said calmly. "Griffiths signed the Articles. He's a member of your own crew."

"A traitorous one," Flynn pointed out.

"Perhaps," Merinda agreed. "But a member nevertheless. What do your Articles say about that, Quartermaster Kheoghi?"

"They be clear indeed," Kheoghi intoned. "Traitors from our company be given access to a cutlass, sundry items for survival, and then marooned on a deserted place beyond the reach of aid."

"Marooned? Here?" Griffiths was incredulous.

"One could hardly think of a more deserted place than this," Flynn replied. "I may be a liar and a thief, Griffiths, but I'm not entirely devoid of feelings. Merinda's right: I couldn't possibly kill you—against the code of our Articles which you signed, oh fellow pirate. As to Merinda," Flynn turned to her and smiled warmly. "Well, let's just say that I owe her her life. We've been through much together. It's said that dead men don't pinch but I rather think that marooned ones don't either—especially when they're marooned in a place that no one has ever been able to reach before."

"What are you going to do, Flynn?" Merinda said in tones devoid of feeling.

"Why, it's already been done," Flynn grinned. "Quartermaster Kheoghi has already rendered the ship you came in useless and sent it drifting off into the void. I've taken the same precautions with old Marren-kan's ship, so I'm afraid she's lost to you as well. Of course, you might try using one of the local ships, but it seems there is some local phenomenon that drained the energy out of these hulks long ago. I'm afraid they're better used as tombs than as transports these days."

Flynn glanced upward at the slowly twisting form of Targ.

"It's too bad, really. The man just wouldn't listen to a deal."

"The wraith fleet will be waiting for you," Merinda said. "Do you really think you can cut a deal with them?"

"You don't get it, Merinda," Flynn smiled. "I already have. Kheoghi! Hand me the Nightsword. It's time to claim our reward."

The minotaur did not move.

"Kheoghi! The Nightsword . . . now!"

The great beast turned toward Flynn.

"Kheoghi?"

"No, Flynn. I claim the Nightsword."

Flynn looked confused and suddenly upset. "Kheoghi! I'm the captain! I speak for the crew!"

"No longer, Flynn," Kheoghi said in a deep, rumbling voice. "I stand for captain!"

"Traitorous idiot!" Flynn exploded. "I led you here! It was I that brought you this treasure and now you throw me aside!"

"Flynn-human." Kheoghi's eyes narrowed in slowly kindled anger. "We may be selling our souls to this life but we be not selling the souls of our clan! This here bauble brung us all to this ruin! I be claiming this here evil weapon in the name of the OomRamn and all them creatures that were wronged by the human Lokan. If thar be a clan that can set right the wrong what was done to us, then it be a clan other than human!"

"Aye!" came a ragged chorus from the Uruh and gnomes in the rotunda.

"So what say you?" Kheoghi scowled at Flynn through his enormous vac suit. "Will you acknowledge me captain and serve the cause . . . or will you be joining your friends here on this lovely barge?"

"As my nervous system appears to be returning to normal"—Merinda smiled wickedly as she tentatively flexed her legs—"I personally would be grateful if you stayed, Flynn. I would relish the opportunity of explaining the consequences of betrayal to my old friend over an extended period of time."

Flynn's face reddened. He knelt at once. "Fine! Kheoghi, I relinquish the captaincy. By your word!"

"Your allegiance is required by the Articles," Kheoghi commanded. "Fail me, Flynn, and we shall resolve our differences in personal combat . . . and I *never* turn my back on anyone. Escort Master Flynn back to the *Venture Revenge*. Uruh, make preparations for sail."

"Aye-aye, Captain," the Uruh chorused as they drifted out of the chamber behind a still-fuming Flynn.

The minotaur then turned to Merinda and Griffiths. "I'll be leaving air regenerators at the landing bay where you came in, Griffiths-mate. There'll be food and water as well, such as I can spare, and the weapons as provided for by the Articles."

"Then you intend to maroon us as well?" Griffiths sighed.

"Aye, mate, I do," Kheoghi grunted. "There be no other way of it by the Articles."

"That's a terrible thing you hold in your arms, Kheoghi," Merinda said, pointing to the ancient sword.

"Aye, ma'am, that it be," Kheoghi said. "Still I be thinking that it will be safer among us minotaurs than by most."

Kheoghi turned and walked to the doors leading out of the chamber. He stopped and spoke over his shoulder.

"Of course, you never know when I might be coming by this way again."

With that he stepped out and closed the doors behind him. The sound echoed throughout the tomb.

Epilogue

Marooned

THE ECHOES STILL WERE SOUNDING THROUGH THE THRONE room as Merinda began to act. "Griffiths! Quickly! Get those control globes for your levitation belt! We've got to get to Targ!"

"Targ?" Griffiths said, as he began looking about the room for the globes. "The man was run through with a sword, Merinda! What are you going to do? Give him first aid until the paramedics arrive?"

"The what?"

"Never mind! Here they are!" Griffiths walked carefully across the floor and grabbed one of the globes. The other was outside his reach. He leaped away from the floor, sailing up into the rotunda, and grabbed the other. "Fine; I've got them. Now what?"

"Bring Targ down here to me!"

"You've got to be . . ."

"Just do it! Now!"

Griffiths twisted the globes and approached the still rotating Targ. He avoided looking into the clear bubble of the helmet. Grasping the sorcerer's leg under the crook of his arm, he twisted the globes once more and pulled the body back toward the floor.

The moment he was within reach, Merinda turned him over. "Hold him here," she commanded. Griffiths obeyed.

Putting a foot against the small of Targ's back, she grasped the sword and pulled. The blade slid free with a flash of frozen air as the tear in the vac suit sealed once more.

Merinda twisted Targ's body back again to float in front of her level with the floor.

"I don't know how much I'll be able to do," she said more to herself than to Griffiths. "He's comatose and there's a lot of internal bleeding."

Griffiths was astonished. "You mean he's still alive?"

"Remember what Zanfib said?" Merinda spoke as she worked, first rubbing her hands together and then gesturing over the body. "Never underestimate a wizard. Targ was the greatest of our time but it wasn't enough. This place has a dampening field of some kind that seems to prevent mystic energies from being applied. It might be bound up in whatever drained the power from the ship systems here. I don't know. I do know that he's still alive."

"Why?"

"Because I don't think the Nightsword has been used yet. Those pirates are probably wondering what the big deal is with this sword right now because it's still bound to Targ."

"Can you heal him?" Griffiths asked.

Merinda seemed too busy to reply.

"GRIFFITHS?"

Griffiths awoke to their third day in the tomb.

"Yes, Merinda?"

"He's gone," was all she said.

"I'm sorry." It was all he could think of to say.

They sat on the steps in the throne room hall. Merinda

had not dared to move Targ for fear of compounding his injuries. Now Targ had finally given up his life despite Merinda's best efforts. Their watch was over.

The three days had passed somewhat slowly. Griffiths had busied himself with an occasional trip back to the landing bay for a few supplies. Kheoghi had been as good as his word—it looked like they would be able to live in their little vac suits for a long time, now that he had figured out how to get the food through the bubble helmets with a little help from Merinda. He was also far more comfortable now that he had figured out how to use the waste dump system in the suit with a little embarrassing help from Merinda.

When he wasn't busy shuttling supplies he kept Merinda company as best he could. When she was too busy tending to the fading Targ, he kept occupied by reading the inscriptions that covered the walls of the throne room. When the histories and glories of the Lost Empire no longer fascinated him, he simply sat and watched Merinda.

He had come on this jaunt for her—part of him hoping that he could find out why such a frustrating woman held his fascination so completely. There was someone beyond the training and the discipline and the cold efficiency that he longed to know. Now he wondered if he ever would.

The silence was long as they sat.

"Merinda?"

"Yes, Griffiths."

"I'm sorry about Targ. You did everything you could."

"It wasn't enough."

"No . . . but it was everything. How much more than everything is there to give?"

Merinda looked across to him.

Griffiths shrugged.

She smiled.

He looked away, embarrassed at his own embarrassment,

if that were possible. He felt like a schoolboy on his first date all over again.

"Look, back when I asked you about killing me . . . was all that that Targ said true?"

"You mean about my not killing you just so Targ couldn't get control of the Mantle?"

"Yeah."

"Mostly."

"Mostly?"

Merinda laughed again. It was a sound that Griffiths had not often heard. She had a musical laugh, warm and generous, when she allowed herself the comfort. "Well, partly, at any rate. The truth is that I've been rather selfish lately. It's been pretty hard keeping you alive these last few weeks but we've seemed to manage. The truth is that my luck with intimate relationships has never been very good."

Griffiths brightened. "Well, hey! I'm a pretty lucky guy!"

"Oh, really!" Merinda scoffed. "I've seen your luck, Griffiths. Your record on good fortune isn't your most endearing quality."

"Well, then," Griffiths suggested hopefully, "what is?"

"That you're funny."

"Funny!"

She laughed and the dark room seemed to brighten for him once more. "Yes. A part of me wishes we could just stay here forever, just the two of us with the entire galaxy spinning around us."

"Well," Griffiths said with a grudging sigh, "it seems as though your wish has come true."

"No, Griffiths, we've got to get back to the Mantle and discover the location of the Starshield."

"What?"

"I had hoped to keep the Nightsword safely hidden," Merinda explained earnestly. "I hoped to move it before

Targ could get to it, but there was no time. Now that it's out in the galaxy, it's only a matter of time before someone takes it and uses it."

"Kheoghi's got it and intends to take it to the minotaurs," Griffiths said as he considered the problem. "The device won't work for nonhumans—their genetics won't bond."

"Yes," Merinda agreed, "but they don't know that. They'll eventually decide that the Nightsword is a fake and sell it off to someone. The Order most likely. Someone will eventually use it. The Starshield is the only device that is known historically that could counter it."

"Well," Griffiths said, "it won't do to ask the Mantle. The Mantle doesn't know."

"You're sure?"

"Hey, you're talking to the prophet here!" Griffiths said. "However, I do have a little surprise for you."

"What surprise?"

"Well . . . all these walls," Griffiths gestured, "are covered with the history of the Lokan Crusade and the Lost Empire. Would you believe that I discovered the location of the Starshield two days ago?"

"Yes," she smiled, "I think I would. Where?"

Griffiths smiled and looked around casually.

"All right!" Merinda punched him in the arm. "Tell! Where?"

The punch was a bit harder than Griffiths thought necessary, but he took it for play. "Would you believe . . . my own planet?"

"Earth?"

"Yep."

"Your Earth?"

"The very same."

"By the Nine!"

"Too bad, I guess." Griffiths gestured around them.

"We're the only two people in the entire galaxy who know where the Starshield is and here we are stuck without so much as a tow."

"I could just kiss you, Griffiths!"

Griffiths smiled warmly. "Well, please do! I'm a little hard-pressed to understand just how you'd do that through a vac suit . . . Hey! Where are you going?"

"Come on! We've got to get to the landing bay!"

"Merinda? Why?"

"Because I've got a little surprise for you!"

Griffiths found himself standing once more on the hull of Lokan's massive ship. It was surprising, he thought, how short the distance was between the throne room and the landing bay when you did not have to deal with the dead in between.

"Great! So we're out in space," Griffiths said. "What is it you wanted to show me?"

"Watch," she said.

He watched. For a while nothing happened. Then he saw it. Something moving among the thousands of dead ships. It shifted, turned, moved again. Its course was somewhat sporadic, but it was definitely coming closer. Suddenly it moved directly toward them, growing larger by the moment. The shape was the familiar saucer form of a Lost Empire ship. It slowed, wheeled, and then came to hover directly over their heads.

A voice suddenly boomed through his vac suit helmet.

"Hey, Captain!"

Griffiths's eyes went wide. He glanced toward Merinda.

She nodded and smiled.

"Lewis?"

"Damn straight, flyboy," came the answer. "You know, my mother always warned me about picking up hitchhikers—especially in bad neighborhoods. I should just leave you here."

"How the hell did you get here?" Griffiths yelled.

"Your friend Neskat worked it all out. She figured you both might need a lift later on. After we took this bucket off that Settlement Ship, we just waited until the fireworks died down and followed you here. We've been waiting for two days for her signal . . . Say, what have you two been up to for the last two days?"

"Lewis!" Griffiths said with feigned shock. "In a vac suit? Just how much *could* we be doing?"

"For two days? Innovating," came Ellerby's voice. "I'm cycling the airlock now. We should have you aboard in about two minutes."

The great iris doors above them began to open.

Griffiths turned to Merinda. "Merinda, I . . ."

Merinda looked at him, her head cocked to one side. "Not now, Griffiths, we're in the middle of a rescue! What's more, I'm the one doing the rescuing. I believe that it is therefore up to me to dictate the terms of the reward."

"Indeed?" Griffiths asked. "You seem pretty sure of yourself."

"I've known success and failure, Griffiths," Merinda said. "I'm not perfect or invincible. That's sometimes a hard lesson to learn. But I do learn—and that's something."

"Very well, then, my rescuer, my life is yours. Name your reward."

Merinda smiled. "I don't think I want to own your life, Jeremy, but I might be interested in sharing it. I have a hunch that getting to know you could be a real adventure . . . and I know just where to start."

"Where?"

"By taking off these vac suits!" Merinda said, smiling at him, as she climbed through the airlock hatch.

About the Authors

Margaret Weis was born and raised in Independence, Missouri. She attended the University of Missouri, Columbia, graduating in 1970 with a BA in creative writing. In 1983, Weis was hired as a book editor at TSR, Inc., producers of the *Dungeons and Dragons* role-playing games. Here she met game designer Tracy Hickman, and the two teamed up to write the bestselling *Dragonlance®* novels. Weis has two children, David and Elizabeth Baldwin. Weis and her husband, Don Perrin, live in a converted barn in Wisconsin with two collie dogs, Laddie and Robbie; a sheltie, Jo-jo; and two cats, Nickolai Mouseslayer and Motley Tatters.

Tracy Hickman was born in Salt Lake City. He recently returned to the state of his birth, and currently resides in St. George, Utah, with his wife and four children. He has coauthored with Margaret Weis four *New York Times* bestselling series, including *Death Gate Cycle* and the *Dragonlance®* series—which have more than eleven million copies in print—and has published his own solo works as well.